A Single Spark

Book 1 of
Fae-Touched Exiles

Mandy Burkhead

A Single Spark
Fae-Touched Exiles, Book 1

Text copyright © 2023 Mandy Burkhead
All Rights Reserved

The characters and events in this book are fictitious. Any resemblance to persons living or dead is strictly coincidental and unintentional.

ISBN: 978-0-9989866-8-5 (print)
ISBN: 978-0-9989866-7-8 (ebook)

Cover designed by JV Arts

Title page font: "Berold"
Book font: "Book Antiqua"

Burkshelf

Acknowledgements

I would like to thank my parents for always supporting me emotionally and financially. I finished this book during the pandemic, during which time my husband and I had to move back in with my parents after losing our rental house. Thank you for always putting a roof over my head and for helping us to finally become homeowners (and to fix up our home).

Thanks go to my wonderful husband for letting me bounce ideas off you whenever I got stuck, for helping me create the map, and for reassuring me after each rejection letter. You are my best friend, and I love you so much.

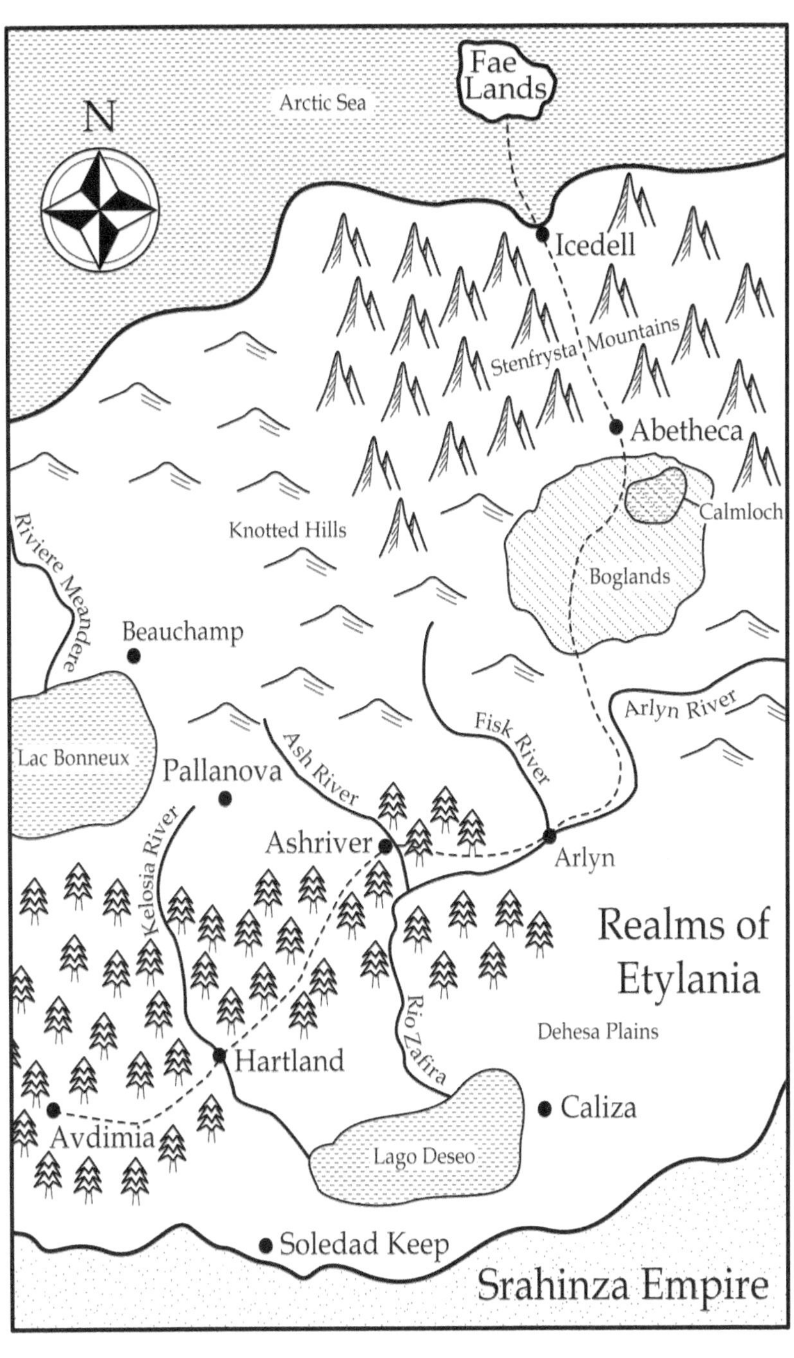

N
Fae Lands
Arctic Sea
Icedell
Stenfrysta Mountains
Abetheca
Calmloch
Knotted Hills
Boglands
Riviere Meandere
Beauchamp
Fisk River
Arlyn River
Lac Bonneux
Pallanova
Ash River
Kelosia River
Ashriver
Arlyn
Realms of Etylania
Rio Zafira
Dehesa Plains
Hartland
Caliza
Avdimia
Lago Deseo
Soledad Keep
Srahinza Empire

Mackenna

Mackenna's feet ached from walking. She and her father had spent another long day of delivering poultices to the sick and injured near their village. It seemed every day there were more refugees, often injured, who'd upended from their homes by the conflicts with the Srahinza Empire. She wanted nothing more than to get home, scrub the dust of travel from her skin, and curl up by the fire.

But as they ambled down the dirt road that led into town, she realized that something was not right. There were no sounds of children playing, villagers gossiping, or livestock being brought in for the night. As they approached their home, the only sound was that of a voice barking commands.

The villagers crowded around her father's cottage, nervously shifting back and forth. Soldiers stood before the crowd, burnt orange tabards adorning their gleaming armor. She recognized the dreaded symbol on the tabard: a silver, diagonal arrow with the cross guard of a sword where fletching should be. Witch hunters. The soldiers had broken the latch on the front door and were ransacking their home, throwing their belongings into the street.

"Mackenna, what is happening?" her father whispered, squinting his clouded eyes towards the commotion.

One of the soldiers addressed the crowd, answering for her: "There is no point in hiding him! We know that the hedgewitch lives here. We have found his plants and potions. Turn him over now, or we will tear this town apart looking for him!"

They were here for father? Mackenna's father Finn had a natural affinity for growing plants of every kind. These plants he made into potions, salves, and poultices, making him incredibly popular in their cluster of small villages. It was the only reason the townspeople tolerated them at all.

Rumor had been spreading that the witch hunts had begun again. Except instead of burning them at the stake, the witch hunters were arresting suspected witches and taking them away. Nobody was quite sure where the accused witches were being taken or what happened to them afterward. The witch hunts two hundred years ago had wiped out most witches in the Realms of Etylania. Some suspected that magic users were being rounded up for fear that they were spies for the enemy. Srahinza, unlike Etylania, was a haven for those with magical abilities.

A glance at her father revealed his face to be white with fear, his mouth set in a grim line. He gripped his walking stick tightly in one hand and Mackenna's arm in the other. She quickly turned them away from the crowd, hoping that they wouldn't be noticed.

"You there. Halt!" a voice commanded behind them. Mackenna walked faster, pretending not to hear. "I said halt!"

The thud of metal-clad feet sounded behind them, and suddenly Finn was yanked from her grasp. Mackenna spun to find a soldier looming over them. "Commander Riley, this one fits the description! An old blind man with red hair. Finn of Avdimia, you are under arrest for witchcraft."

Finn ignored the soldier, his focus instead on Mackenna. "Mackenna, get out of here. Go to the inn. Find Miss Henriette. Now!" His tone was hard, his order clear.

Two more soldiers emerged from her home, pushing their way through the nervous crowd to stand beside their comrade.

It was just like her father to be more worried about her than himself. "No father! These men can't arrest you." She turned to the soldier holding her father. "He's a healer. He's never hurt anyone! We've lived here all our lives, ask any of the townspeople. We aren't Srahinzan spies!"

The gathered crowd muttered their agreement. Even so, she didn't miss that many of them backed away as the tension escalated, throwing Mackenna wary glances.

"Get out of the way, little girl," said the commander. "Your daddy's coming with us." He gave her a shove. Mackenna fell to the hard-packed road, barely avoiding landing in a pile of horse droppings. Bread, cheese, goat's milk, and a mended shirt—payment they had received that day in exchange for Finn's potions—scattered across the ground as she lost her grip on the basket she carried.

"And because the rest of you did not give him up fast enough, each house in this village will be fined twenty-five duques," Commander Riley bellowed. Gasps of shock and anger echoed through the villagers. Most of them only made two hundred duques in a year. "Now disperse before I raise it! Erickson, see to controlling the crowd and collecting the fine. Those who don't have the coin can pay in food and other goods. Arrest any who refuse. Kosa, put the witch in chains."

Erickson nodded and pushed through the crowd. The townspeople scurried away, throwing glances at her over their shoulders. Mackenna knew that their fear was not directed entirely towards the soldiers.

"That was very rude of you," Finn told the commander. "Had you asked respectfully, I might have peacefully gone with you. But I will not tolerate you taking advantage of these people. And I especially won't allow you to become physical with my daughter."

"And what the hell are you going to do about it, old man?" the soldier Kosa taunted. "Going to cure my headcold?"

Without responding, Finn raised his walking stick, bringing it down across Kosa's arm. The soldier's armor protected his bones from breaking, but the force of the blow loosened his grip, and Finn quickly stepped out of his grasp. Her father swiped his staff under Kosa's knees, sweeping his legs out from under him.

"Stand down, or I will cut you down!" the commander yelled, drawing his sword.

Mackenna leapt to her feet and jumped on the commander's back. She clawed at his face, hoping to distract him and keep him from hurting Finn.

"Get this damn bitch off me!" Riley commanded. Kosa scrambled back to his feet and hastened to his commander's side. He ripped Mackenna off of the man and yanked her arms behind her back. She struggled against his iron grip, the metal of his gauntlets biting into her flesh.

Finn used the commander's distraction to his advantage. He raised his staff and swung it down towards Riley's head.

The blow never landed. Gasps filled the air. Finn stumbled forward and sank to his knees, his knuckles white around the staff. Erickson stood behind her father, metal glinting in his hand. Was that a dagger? Why was it dripping with blood?

Her heart stopped, her mind frozen in denial of what her eyes saw. Time slowed as a crimson flower bloomed from the center of her father's stomach. As he collapsed to the ground, he called out for her.

The hands holding her loosened. She struggled free, crawling to her father's side. Mackenna pulled Finn into her arms, babbling incoherently as she pressed at the wound in his gut, trying to remember all that he had taught her about healing. Was it in the spleen, or the stomach, or the liver? Depending on where the blade had landed, she could stop the flow of the blood, pack it with herbs and stitch it tightly. It was just a matter of mending it quickly before he bled out.

"Medicine," she croaked out. "I need medicine! And a needle and thread!" None of the townspeople moved. Some held hands to their mouths in shock. Others turned tail and fled. Why did nobody try to help? Father had nursed them through illnesses, set their bones, helped them deliver their babies.

There came a gargling sound from Finn. Blood trickled from his mouth. No. No that couldn't be good. He wheezed, gasping for air. His hand lifted toward her face, and she took it in her own, holding it tightly. His mouth opened and closed, as if he were trying to speak, but no sound came out. As his breathing slowed, his eyes drifted closed. The hand she clenched went limp. Mackenna felt at his neck, the way he had taught her to, but there was no beat from his heart.

"No. No please," she whispered, hugging him to her. "Please wake up, father. Please don't leave me."

Her heart thudded in her ears, muffling the sounds around her. Distantly, she heard the commander groan. "Bloody hell.

We needed him alive, you moron! Kosa, pull that girl off him. We'll at least take in his body as proof that we found him."

The pounding of her heart grew louder and more erratic with each passing moment. This couldn't be happening. Why were they even after father? There was no one kinder or gentler. It was *her* the townspeople feared, not him.

The noise was building to a deafening roar. Mackenna's whole body trembled. She needed to get away from here, away from these people. She needed to control herself. "Take deep breaths, Mackenna," father would say. But Finn didn't speak, didn't say a word. Without his voice to guide her, she felt her control slipping.

When the soldier's gauntleted hand grabbed her shoulder, the tether snapped, burned away by a familiar, frightening rage. Her father had taught her to resist it, to calm it whenever it rose to the surface. But he was not here now to help her quench the flames.

She turned with a feral scream, her hand igniting as she swiped it across the soldier's face. He wore no helmet to protect him, and she left a trail of fire where her nails made contact with his skin. The flames quickly leapt to his hair and clothing. He jerked away from her with a scream, clutching at his burning skin.

Mackenna gave in to the heat that burned from inside out, igniting her skin and hair with flames. All she knew was hatred. All she wanted was revenge. The fire turned her clothing to ashes, but she felt no pain.

The soldiers would feel pain, though. The very earth around them erupted in a ring of fire. It trapped Commander Riley, the wool tunic under his shiny metal armor quickly catching. He rolled on the ground wailing as the metal turned bright red.

She had lost track of the first man, the one named Kosa, but it mattered not, for she had eyes only for Erickson. The bloody dagger slowly slipped from his fingers, falling to the earth without a sound. He put up his hands in surrender, hands stained with her father's life. There would be no mercy for him. Mackenna lunged, her hand latching onto the man's throat. She brought her face close, reveling in the fear in his eyes.

His blood-curdling cries of agony were music to her ears. She only wished that they lasted longer. The bright reds and yellows of the conflagration consumed them both, and the smoke blocked out the world around them, so that in his last moments, she guaranteed that all he saw was her face, all he knew was her hatred. She inhaled the scent of burning skin and hair as his flesh blistered. His windpipe collapsed between her hands. There was nothing left of him to punish. She dropped his flaming husk to the earth and searched the smoke for the other two.

The commander was no longer making noise. He lay still on the ground, his armor glowing and smoking. The third soldier was nowhere to be found. She stepped out of the ring of fire, peering into the distance, and saw him slumped over on his horse as it galloped away. The townspeople had likewise fled, scattering in every direction to escape the flames. To escape her.

She moved to follow him, but something caught her eye, making her pause. On the ground lay a familiar figure. The flames that spread to the buildings around her had reached him, singing his clothes. She couldn't remember why, but she knew that it was imperative that the blaze not reach his corpse.

Mackenna knelt to the ground beside him, the flames on her own naked body extinguishing. She patted at his clothes, putting out the embers. Mackenna ran her hand through his red hair, which had begun to gray. He had a kind face, with a peppered beard and filmy eyes half open in death. "Papa?" she heard a voice gasp and realized after a moment that it had come from her.

The inferno continued to rage around her, but it was no longer under her control. Mackenna's eyes welled with tears that dried as soon as they fell onto her scalding cheeks. No matter how hot the fires burned, they would never hurt her. As she felt the inevitable dive towards unconsciousness that always followed a flare up, she laid her body across his to protect him as best she could.

Sensations returned slowly. First was the feeling of something shaking her. Then, the sound of someone calling "Wake up, child!" near her ear. The heat in the air was stifling, and her mouth was parched, tasting of ashes. The stench of smoke permeated everything.

Smoke meant fire. And fire meant… Her eyes shot open. Why was she outside on the ground? Something lay beneath her. No… someone. It took a moment for her mind to register the identity of the body. Memories came flooding back. Memories of blood, flames, and smoke.

Mackenna barely managed to turn her face towards the ground before she began retching. A hand rubbed her bare back, and she realized she was naked. Of course. Her clothes would have burned away. After she had rid her stomach of its contents, she lifted her eyes slowly.

The fires had died down, though homes around her still smoked and burned. Those in the immediately vicinity were hollowed out husks, their contents destroyed. Including the one she shared with her father. Besides the body of her father, there were two others on the ground, their husks shriveled and smoking in their melted armor.

"There you are child. Here, drink." Henriette shoved a wooden cup into her hand. The feel of the wood grain beneath her fingertips, the cool slide of water down her throat, helped to ground her somewhat.

"You shouldn't be here," Mackenna croaked. "You could have gotten hurt."

"I came back as soon as I saw the fires dying down. Now, you must hurry. There isn't much time before the others return, and they will be out for blood."

Her eyes drifted again to the two dead soldiers. "Was anyone else... did I kill any others?"

The woman shook her head. "I don't think so. Everyone fled when the fires started. But you've destroyed their homes, and now your father isn't here to protect you anymore. You need to leave — quickly."

Henriette was the tavern keeper in the town. In her thirties, married with one child and another on the way, she and Mackenna had little in common. But she was the only friend Mackenna had ever known besides father.

Father. "I have to... I must bury him," she whispered. The sun was setting. According to her people's customs, he must be buried before it rose again. Should a body be left out overnight, the spirit could become restless and turn into a ghost instead of passing on. It was best for the soul that the body be put to rest immediately.

Henriette was shaking her head. "Listen to me! The other townsfolk will either kill you themselves or turn you over to witch hunters. They may already be on their way here. You have to leave now. I will see that he is cared for, but you do not have time."

The woman's eyes drifted over to what was left of Mackenna's home. She hauled Mackenna up, pulling her towards it. "We must see if there is anything left that you can salvage. A dress, some food perhaps."

The thatched roof was gone, its ashy remains coating everything. The stone outer walls had survived but were blackened with soot. The inner walls had been made of wood and had burned up in the fire, so that as she stepped over the threshold, she could see from one end of her small home to the other. Most of the furniture was destroyed beyond repair. As Henriette rummaged through the cabinets, pulling out any provisions that had survived, Mackenna looked over what remained of her bedroom. She squatted down and dug through the rubble, finding a book of folktales, a clay toy horse, a few glass marbles. She left them in the ashes, turning instead to the charred remains of her bed; at its foot was the chest that held her clothes. Although the chest was scorched, it had thankfully protected the contents, so at least she still owned a few items of clothing. She pulled them on blindly, not caring what she wore as long as she was decent.

She had been wearing her only pair of good shoes to walk to the nearby villages. All she had left were some cloth slippers that she wore to tend the garden. They would do little to protect her feet, but she put them on anyway.

Henriette had started throwing any salvageable food into a leather backpack. Mackenna joined her in the remains of the kitchen, opening the medicine cabinet where her father stored his poultices. His journals, in which he had detailed the properties of every plant he had ever encountered, were destroyed, their pages barely legible. Years of his work gone in an instant.

But the glass medicine bottles were mostly still intact, as were the leather pouches that held dried herbs. Her gaze lifted to the little garden behind the house. Some of the plants had managed to survive, but she hadn't the time to harvest them, nor could she dig them up and bring them with her. She would have to make do with what was left and rely on her foraging knowledge for the rest.

"That will have to do," Henriette said, packing the last of the medicines in the bag and helping it onto Mackenna's back. For holding what remained of her worldly possessions, it felt far too light. And yet unbearably heavy. "Have you any coin?" Henriette asked.

Mackenna nodded, opening the little box where her father kept their coin purse. It jingled pathetically. "Not much."

"Keep it out of sight while you travel. A woman alone..." Henriette bit her bottom lip. "I wish I could do more for you, child."

"You have already done more than enough. Won't the others blame you for helping me escape?" Mackenna asked.

"I don't plan on telling them. Let them think you left on your own." The woman suddenly pulled Mackenna into a tight hug. "For years we—they all feared that this might happen. I could not hate and fear you as they did, but I also cannot blame them for it." The woman led Mackenna out of her home. She took a moment to drink in the sight of her ruined home, the only one she had ever known, before turning away.

Henriette led her between the squat buildings. At the edge of the town, the woman stopped. There was a field of crops before the woods started. If the innkeeper went any farther, others might see her helping Mackenna, even with the dwindling light. "Stay off the road for now, mind you. Stick to the path in the woods that we take to the swimming hole. Then follow that upstream; it will lead you to the road going north. By then, you should be just past the last village for leagues, and hopefully it will be safe enough to travel."

The woman held Mackenna's shoulders tight, gazing into her eyes. "If you see a villager, don't stop. Just run. Most of them fear you too much to try anything themselves. It's the witch hunters you need to be wary of. Now that they know you exist…"

"They'll be after me," Mackenna finished.

The woman nodded, wiping at her eyes. "Go now. And the gods be with you." Henriette gave her a little shove, and Mackenna started walking, then jogging, towards the protection of the trees. She wasn't sure if she expected a mob to spring up from hiding in the late summer crops, charging at her. Or perhaps for rocks to come flying at her from the woods. Nothing happened. If any villagers watched from afar, they were no doubt all too happy to see her leave.

Once under the canopy of the trees, she slowed, treading carefully lest she sprain her ankle in her flimsy shoes. She found the familiar path that many of the townspeople took to the swimming hole. Mackenna never went there when any others were around—she had never been welcome—but she and Henriette had gone together many times, usually in the evenings after the other villagers had returned home. The light was dimmer in the woods, but she knew the path well enough that she didn't need it.

She reached the stream a half hour later. She examined the forest around her, ensuring that she was truly alone before taking off her backpack and hanging it from a tree. She stripped off her clothes next, soaking her dress and underthings briefly to help remove the smell of smoke before hanging them beside her bag. Then she sank into the chilly waters.

Mackenna grabbed some moss from a nearby rock and scrubbed furiously at the soot that coated her skin until her flesh was raw and pink. She dipped her head beneath the surface, scrubbing at her scalp.

As she cleaned herself, the numbness of her shock began to wash away as well, leaving her soul as raw as her skin. A scream rose from deep inside her, and she opened her mouth under water, letting it out where none could hear it save the fish. She should keep her mouth open, let the water rush in to fill her lungs, drown herself then and there. She was cursed. And now her father was dead, and it was her fault. If she didn't have this damned magic, her mother wouldn't have died giving birth to her. Her father wouldn't have died at the hands of those witch hunters. The only reason he'd put up a fight was to protect her, so that they didn't take her too.

A distant part of her knew that she needed to leave, that she needed to put as much distance between herself and the town. And yet a part of her couldn't bring herself to care. She had nowhere to go. She had nothing but a few worldly possessions and some knowledge on herbs. She would likely be dead within a month. She would do the world a favor by drowning herself in the stream. The water could carry her away, and then they wouldn't even have to worry about burying her. The fish could eat her skin and muscles and organs away until there was nothing left but bones.

Even as these dark thoughts weighed her down, her body, longing for air, pushed towards the surface. She broke it with a gasp, coughing up the water that had gotten into her mouth. Her coughing turned to sobs, her tears and snot mixing with the murky river water. She cried and screamed until her body ached, until there were no tears left in her.

A bone-deep exhaustion came over Mackenna as her sobs slowed and finally stopped. She floated on her back, staring into the canopy of the trees above. The daylight was almost gone. Birds flittered back towards their nests. Squirrels hopped from branch to branch, chasing one another. The water bubbled and flowed around her.

The world did not care that her life had ended. It had to move on. The sun would continue to rise and set, the animals to hunt and forage, the people to go about their lives.

Mackenna pulled herself out of the stream. She slowly donned her damp clothes. She pulled up her socks, laced her shoes, slipped her arms into the leather straps of her pack. Gazing upriver, she took a heavy step. Then another.

The world had to go on. And so did she.

The solitary, quiet road gave Mackenna little to do but walk and think. And no matter how hard she tried not to, her thoughts kept returning to the events of two days before. The image of her father's body lying on the ground was burned into her mind. As she ambled down the dirt road, Mackenna idly ran her fingers across the cooking knife she had slipped into her belt. Its weight felt foreign.

The only experience she had with a knife was for cooking and preparing poultices, and she wondered what good it would do her if she were attacked by bandits or highwaymen. After all, she was a lone woman traveling with all of her possessions—few though they were—on her back, and she didn't even know where she was going, only that she was heading north, away from the war at the border. She had never been outside the cluster of small villages near her home, and she didn't know which roads went where. While she had never had many friends, this was the first time in her life that she had ever been completely alone, and fear of the unknown gripped her tightly, almost paralyzing her.

But her exhaustion from the other day still hung heavy on her, despite her fear. She knew from experience that she would be tired for a few days at least. It had always been like that. She'd been cursed by the fire her entire life. She didn't doubt that her fire was the reason her mother died birthing her, though her father had always assured her that was not the case.

When she was a few years old, her father had begun to suspect that she had magic. Little things would happen. She would touch a hot pot and her fingers would not be burned. When she threw a tantrum, the fire in the hearth would grow suddenly stronger and hotter. Her bathwater always remained warm, no matter how long she sat in it.

But when she'd hit puberty, her father's suspicions were confirmed. Those little quirks soon became much more. Her magic would spring up at the slightest provocation, shifting as quickly as her moods. Her father spent years teaching her patience, discipline, and restraint. They would spend evenings meditating together, and if she ever found herself losing control of her anger, she was to recite in her head the properties of medicinal plants.

As she'd reached her late teens, the outbursts had become less frequent, smaller, more manageable. She was never able to control them, and she doubted she ever would, but at nineteen years of age, she had finally begun to feel as if she might have some freedom from her curse.

But not anymore. Never before had she lost control to this extent. It was as if the fire itself had taken control of her, burning away any trace of Mackenna, leaving only a mindless rage. She shuddered at the thought of what more she might have done had she not exhausted herself in the process. The exhaustion she knew. But this was the first time she had ever felt so empty afterwards, as if she were a log that had burned away until there was nothing left but ash.

A sensation tingled at the back of Mackenna's mind. Had she heard something, or had it merely been the wind rustling the branches? She paused, examining the road ahead and behind her, but she could see nothing. There it was again, the soft neigh of a horse, the slight creak of a leather saddle, the faint rhythmic clank of metal on metal. Someone was coming down the road from behind her.

Mackenna immediately darted into the trees, stepping as lightly as she could to avoid rustling the leaves on the ground. There was a mass of thick brush just ahead that would hopefully conceal her. As she sank into it, briars snagged at her hair and dress. She cursed silently, trying to detangle herself, when a flash of orange caught her eye.

The orange tabards of the witch hunters. Two of them riding side by side down the road, eyeing their surroundings wearily. Looking for her, no doubt. She grabbed at her dress, trying to work it free of the brambles, not caring that they jabbed into her fingers and made them bleed. She finally got the dress free, but her hair was another matter. Mackenna grabbed the knife from her belt, cutting the strands free, and managed to collapse to the ground out of sight.

Had they seen her? Mackenna held her breath, listening for them, but heard nothing. Did that mean they'd stopped or moved on? The brush still rustled from her struggle, but perhaps they would mistake it for the wind or a small creature scuttling around.

A sudden caw sounded above her, startling her. Mackenna looked up to see a crow perched on a branch above her hiding place. Its head shifted to and fro, its eye rolling towards her, then the road, then to the brush in front of her. A strand of her hair fluttered softly in the breeze, the bright red color catching in the sunlight. Of course. Crows loved brightly colored things.

She silently waved at it, trying to shoo it away. It eyed her, unimpressed, then returned to staring at the tangled strand of hair. It cawed again before seeming to make up its mind, launching itself towards the strand of hair and grasping it in its talons. The frantic rustling of the brush as it struggled to free her trapped hair, finally succeeding and proudly taking off with its new treasure, was loud enough to alert all the animals in the vicinity as to her location.

The question was whether or not the witch hunters were still around to notice. The only way for her to know would be to get an eye on the road, though that could mean revealing her location. Mackenna lifted herself up off the forest floor as gently as she could. Remaining crouched, she found a gap in the brush and peered through it. What she could see of the road was empty. Had she managed to elude them?

Another *Caw!* Came from above, startling her. She jumped, whirling to glare at the crow that had retaken its perch. It watched her now. Perhaps it wanted more hair? She glared at it, and it tilted its head, then swiveled its gaze behind her. Did its caw sound different this time? Almost like…a warning?

Mackenna whirled around, following the bird's gaze. A horse rounded the brush she hid behind, within a stone's throw. Her eyes lifted, meeting those of its rider. "I've got her!" he called out, wheeling his horse towards her.

Mackenna didn't give herself time to think. She sprinted deeper into the woods, her legs carrying her without her needing to command them. She heard a yell and glanced back briefly to see a flurry of black feathers launching itself at him and his horse, and then she turned away, her focus narrowing to the woods before her, her mind carving out the safest, quickest path only moments before her feet reached it. Though she knew they couldn't be far behind, she could barely hear their horses trampling through the forest over the sound of her own heart thundering in her ears.

The woods flew by in a blur, each tree blending into the next, the foliage so thick that it snagged on her clothing and cut into her skin. Her pursuers seemed to have it even worse, trying to wield their large beasts through the thick clump of trees and stones. But all the same, she knew she hadn't lost them.

Mackenna feared she wouldn't last much longer. Her breathing was hard and heavy. Though her legs kept pumping beneath her, she couldn't feel them, and feared that she would place a foot wrong on the rough terrain, twisting or breaking an ankle. But she didn't have time to slow. Sweat ran down her forehead and back, and her heart felt like it might burst from her chest. At least it would be a quicker death than what they would give her.

Mackenna's exhausted legs stumbled, and she found herself rolling down a hill into a ravine. She tucked into a ball to protect herself as best she could, finally coming to a stop at the bottom. Forcing herself to her knees, she crawled toward an ancient oak, clutching it desperately. The trees spun in her vision, and she knew the soldiers would be on her any moment now, their blades whipping low, slicing her head clean off her shoulders.

But that blow never came. The horses' labored breathing and the hiss of a sword being drawn were drowned out by another sound, much closer. A deep, low growling. Mackenna lifted her eyes slowly. A huge, hulking body, white and black fur all on end. It had wide blue eyes, huge paws, and long, sharp teeth. A wolf. It growled as it approached, though its eyes were focused past her, at the armored men on horseback.

Mackenna glanced back at the soldiers. They descended the hill but did not approach further. Their horses, sensing the predator, kept trying to back away from the beast despite their owners' commands. One man held a sword and the other a mace. The man with the mace dismounted and tied his horse's reins to a nearby tree before taking a few steps in her direction.

The growling grew louder, and Mackenna flattened herself to the ground just in time, feeling a breeze against her back as the wolf leapt over her. She looked up from the dirt and leaves to see the wolf pacing between her and the soldiers, baring its canines. "Call off your beast, witch," The mace man spat, glaring at the wolf.

"What?" Mackenna asked, crawling backwards from both the wolf and the men.

"We know you are a witch," answered the other man from his position atop his horse. "Call of the familiar you have summoned and surrender peacefully. You are to be brought back to the commander to see justice done."

"Justice?" Mackenna spat. "Justice has already been done. My father is dead! And now so is the man who killed him." She did not believe for a second that these men meant her no harm. Her father had taught her to always be wary of strange men, especially when she was alone.

"Enough of this!" The first man yelled as he raised his mace. The wolf reared up to meet him, clamping its powerful jaws down upon his right arm, the force causing him to drop his weapon to the forest floor. He howled in pain and flailed, trying to shake off the beast, but it was unmoved.

The other soldier reared his horse to action, raising his sword to bring it down upon the wolf. Mackenna screamed in terror, feeling an affinity for this savage creature that unintentionally protected her. But before his blow could land, there was a whoosh of air followed by a thud, and his sword dropped to the ground uselessly. An arrow was stuck through his hand and emerged out the other side. As he screamed in pain, Mackenna's eyes darted around the forest, but she saw no one else. Wherever the arrow had come from, it had moved too fast for her to even see it.

The man who'd been shot hissed, "Do you call upon the Folk, witch?" His eyes too searched the forest for the hidden assailant. "Are you in league with them?"

Mackenna did not have time to answer.

"You will drop your weapons and leave now, or the next arrow will land between your eyes." The voice came from above, or behind, or perhaps everywhere, seeming to echo through the forest.

"Who speaks?! Show yourself!" the soldier on horseback commanded.

"You dare to command the Forest Folk?" the voice called. "If you wish to leave my home alive, you will walk away from this fight now."

"Just get this damn beast off of me!" the first man yelled, still struggling beneath the weight of the unmovable wolf.

"Do you surrender?" the voice asked.

"Yes! Yes, I surrender!" the man appeared to be crying.

The other one also nodded, lifting his arrow-pierced hand in the air in surrender.

"If you wish to live, leave your weapons and horses and walk away," the voice commanded. Then came a faint whistle, and the wolf immediately lifted its head, releasing the man beneath it and stepping back, though it never took its eyes off of them.

The man with the arrow gingerly helped his comrade off of the ground. The second man's arm was a bloody, mangled mess that he held close to his body. Together, the two helped each other scramble up the hill, glancing back only once before retreating out of sight.

Mackenna slumped against the large tree, trying to catch her breath, which she felt as if she'd been holding for the entire exchange between the soldier and the bodiless voice. But she couldn't calm herself completely. The giant, wild wolf was still there, and though it no longer growled, it had now turned its attention to her. It stepped closer, slowly, and she shrank against the tree, eyeing it warily. It was a beautiful animal, in a feral sort of way, with a long, sleek coat of silver that blended into black at its spine. It had a dark gray mask of fur framing its face, and it gazed at her with blue eyes like pools of ice.

Soon it was within arm's length, and she timidly reached out a hand towards it, hoping it wouldn't suddenly decide to bite off her fingers. It tentatively reached its bloody nose forward, sniffing her. Were you supposed to look canines in the eyes or not? It was too late now to change her decision, and after they had stared at each other for a few seconds, it opened its mouth and licked her fingers before pushing its head under her hand gently. She scratched the animal behind the ears, exhaling in relief.

"You really must be a witch. She doesn't let just any stranger pet her." There was that voice again, though it seemed now to come from directly behind her. Mackenna jumped up, whirling around to find a young man standing there.

"Wha-where did you come from?" she sputtered. He glanced up into the canopy of the enormous tree she leaned against, and she followed his gaze. The branches above were high, very high, the lowest one at least twenty feet in the air. But they were also shaking, as if someone or something large had just been swinging on them. "You saved me. Are you…human?" Mackenna asked tentatively.

The man shrugged his shoulders. "As human as you. And I didn't do it to save you. I did it to protect Myst." He nodded at the wolf, which trotted over to him, seeming no more threatening than a pet dog.

"Even so, you drove those men off," Mackenna said. "Thank you. I am indebted to you."

"Yeah, I guess you are, aren't you?" the stranger replied with a smirk.

Foulan

Foulan leaned back against the tree, intertwining his fingers behind his head as he sized up the girl before him. Worn cloth shoes peeked out from under a woolen brown country dress that was too short for her long legs but hung loose on her. If her torn and soiled clothing was anything to go by, she was poor, so expecting payment in the form of money or barter was likely out of the question.

"I don't suppose you have any money on you?" he asked, though he expected her answer.

"I have but enough for travel, and even that won't last me very long," the girl replied.

"So that would be a no, then?" He sighed, looking her up and down. "Skinny as you are, I doubt you can provide me with what I need."

Her eyes widened as she took a step back from him. The girl's hand flew to her belt, from which she drew a small knife, holding it out in front of her in a way that suggested she hadn't the slightest idea of how to use it. "You will not make such lewd suggestions to me, sir! I will not hesitate to fight you!"

He scrunched his eyebrows in confusion. Lewd suggestions? Realization dawning, he couldn't contain his snort. Besides her flaming red hair, which was currently plastered to her face and neck with sweat, there was nothing particularly attractive about her.

She was on the tall side for a girl, and not at all curvy, at least as far as he could tell under her baggy dress. Her face was cute, he supposed, in a sort of childish way, with big green eyes and round, freckled cheeks. But gods she was pale, and she had dirt under her nails and smeared across her dress and face. The girl looked ridiculous brandishing that pathetic little knife in front of her like a great sword, the trembling of her hands revealing her fear despite the stubborn set of her jaw.

It seemed she didn't like being laughed at, or perhaps she found it even more threatening, for she suddenly lunged at him, brandishing her dagger carelessly. He automatically lifted an arm to block her attack, hissing at the sting of the blade.

His mirth disappeared. They both glanced at the small slash on his forearm, which had begun to bleed, and the girl's face went white. He glared at her and stepped forward until they were toe to toe, looming over her as he grabbed her wrist, holding it so she couldn't swipe at him again. "You should not let your imagination run wild and make assumptions," he hissed. "I was merely *suggesting*, as you put it, that you repay me with breakfast, for you have deprived me of my own."

"Breakfast?" she squeaked, her green eyes gone large and round like a doe's.

"Yes. I was hunting a wild boar and was about to make my shot when you frightened it away with all that ruckus you and your *friends* were making. Now I have to return to my clan empty handed. But by the looks of you, all skin and bones, you probably can't even cook worth a damn."

"Oh." Her fear and residual anger seemed to deflate. "I'm sorry. I shouldn't have assumed…"

"No, you shouldn't have." He looked down at her chest, which was currently pressed against his, though that didn't do much to add to her paltry cleavage. "Especially when you haven't anything to entice a man with anyway."

He smirked and stepped away just as her face fell into shock once more, and she glared at him. Foulan didn't let go of his tight grasp on her wrist, though, just in case. "You… you are foul!" she yelled. "I don't owe you anything! Unhand me!" He did so and quickly stepped out of reach, but she seemed more intent on escaping him than attacking. Returning her knife to her belt, she turned on her heel and stomped away into the woods.

Foulan shook his head and approached the horses, giving them time to sniff him. Myst whined, staring off after the girl. "It's not my problem if she gets herself lost," he muttered. He picked up the sword and mace, eyeing them. Someone in his clan would likely want them for protection. If not, they'd fetch a nice price. Strapping the weapons to the horses and taking their leads, he whistled to Myst, but she sat staring into the woods, ignoring him.

"You're really going to do this?" Foulan asked the wolf. She huffed, continuing to stare ahead. "Fine. But she attacks me again, and I'm leaving her behind." He swung up into one of the saddles, guiding the horse after the wolf, the other following behind.

On horseback, it didn't take him long to catch up to her. She stood gazing around the woods in confusion but whirled to glare at him when she caught sight of him. "Why are you trailing me?"

"Because, you still owe me my breakfast, and a mended shirt, I might add." He gestured to the sleeve she had ripped. Thankfully the cut had been shallow and had already ceased bleeding. "And besides, you're clearly lost."

"I… I am not. I just need to find my way back to the road," she answered, though she didn't sound very convinced.

"Which road?" Foulan asked.

She opened and closed her mouth, looking like a fish trying to drink air. "I… I dunno the name. It goes north out of my hometown."

"And the name of your town?" he asked. She bit her lip, eyeing him warily, and didn't answer. "How about which town you are going to? I can get you to the right path." Still, she kept her mouth shut. Stubborn.

Foulan sighed, rubbing the bridge of his nose. This girl was starting to give him a headache. "Look, I didn't save you from witch hunters just to turn you over to them. You don't want to tell me, fine. I can take you back to where my clan is camped, and then you can go on your way. Otherwise, you'll be wandering around these woods lost until you starve or are mauled to death by a wild animal." Her eyes darted to the wolf at Foulan's side. "There's no point in saving someone's life if they're just gonna go getting themselves killed. Especially since you still haven't repaid me."

"Fine," she muttered. "If you know how to get out of here, you lead the way."

He turned the horses in the right direction. "Would you care to ride?"

The girl shook her head. "I'd rather walk."

Foulan rolled his eyes and slid off of his horse, guiding it behind him. He certainly wasn't going to ride while a woman walked, no matter how insufferable she might be. He glanced back to make sure she followed and noticed Myst trotting at her side. The girl's hand absentmindedly stroked Myst's fur.

"How do you even know which way to go?" the girl asked, finally breaking the silence. "It all looks the same to me."

"I'm a hunter," Foulan replied. "I hunt in woods like these all the time. In my mind I mark certain landmarks. A strangely shaped tree, a large rock, an animal burrow. Then I follow them back to where I came from. Plus, if I do get turned around, Myst's nose never leads me astray."

They continued to walk in silence for another hour before they emerged onto the road. As they followed it towards camp, the girl's eyes kept darting around, like a rabbit sensing a predator. By the time they reached camp it was midmorning, and his clansmen were up and about, breaking down camp, loading the wagons for the day's travel, and chasing after children to sit them down to eat. At their approach, a few looked up and smiled at Foulan, some waving their hands in greeting. They eyed the girl curiously but did not stop them. Mercia, the Wanderers' leader, called out to him from where he sat beside a fire. "Foulan! I send you off to catch us some meat and instead you bring me back a wood sprite! Tell me, Fair Lady, how he managed to snare such a beautiful creature."

The girl blushed under the attention, bobbing in a shallow curtsy. "I got lost in the woods, and… and Foulan," she said, his name sounding foreign on her tongue, "offered to guide me."

"And you were traveling with two horses and… weapons?" Mercia asked.

The girl froze, her eyes darting to Foulan's, silently begging him to help her. Anyone who knew anything about horses could tell that these were bred and trained for battle, not some beasts of burden that a country girl might own. But the girl clearly didn't want the truth to be known, so he had to think of something quickly. "We actually just found the horses on the road not too far from here. They appear to have gotten free of their masters and wandered off. No doubt they belong to one of the forts around here. Perhaps we'll find their owner on the road and will be rewarded for returning them safely. And if not, we can keep them for ourselves."

Foulan could tell that Mercia was not convinced, but the man nodded. "Right, well then. You are welcome to travel with us to the next town. These roads can be unsafe for a young woman alone."

"I can make myself useful," the girl offered. "I can cook."

Aishah, Mercia's wife, looking up from the baby she was feeding, eyed the girl with a snort. "How good of a cook can she be?" she asked in their native tongue so the girl wouldn't understand. "She's too thin."

"I say that's a fair trade," Mercia replied in the common tongue. "You can use my fire, if you like. But first, Foulan, you must introduce us to this fair creature."

Foulan opened his mouth, then closed it, realizing with embarrassment that he had not actually asked the girl her name at any point, nor had he supplied his own. "My name is…" she paused, eyes darting around nervously, before saying, "Maple." The name was no doubt a fake. Still, Foulan kept his mouth shut.

Mackenna

"Mercia," the man replied, placing one hand over his heart and nodding at her. "Welcome. Well, we must get to work packing up camp. Bahira here can show you where some food supplies are if you would like to cook some breakfast." The man gestured to a girl about Mackenna's age. With that he and Foulan walked off, leaving Mackenna alone with the girl.

Mackenna grabbed half a dozen eggs and some mushrooms, peppers, spinach, and an onion from the food stores. As she cooked an omelet, Bahira sat beside her, a wide grin dimpling her cheeks. "That will need more spices for sure."

Hoping to impress the girl, she added parsley, basil, and chives. She noticed numerous other jars of spices, but in their powdered state she could not identify them and didn't wish to embarrass herself asking. As she cooked, Mackenna noticed that people went from fire to fire, visiting other families and exchanging food. To her surprise, they approached her as well, offering some of their own food for hers. Not one of them failed to comment that it needed more spice.

She understood why after taking a single bite of the food that was offered to her. It was some sort of pastry filled with meat, but the spice overwhelmed the savory flavor she had expected. After just a few bites her nose was running, and she had to drink a whole mug of water in order to finish it off. She could tell the people around her were laughing behind their hands.

"Don't be bothered by it," Bahira said with a smile. "They don't mean anything by it. Most locals can't handle our food."

"Are these spices from your homeland then?" Mackenna asked.

She nodded, though there was a hint of sadness. "With the war, though, all trade with Srahinza has been cut off. Some have tried growing these herbs here, but with our traveling lifestyle and the cold and humidity, they don't do well."

"Where did Foulan go?" Mackenna asked. "There's hardly anything left for him to eat."

Bahira simply shrugged. "He's an adult. He knows where the food is if he gets hungry."

Yes, but she'd come here and cooked this food because he'd asked her to in exchange for saving her life. And now he wasn't even going to eat it? How rude! Mackenna fumed silently as they cleaned up the dishes.

Thinking she was done after this, Mackenna was surprised to learn that the Wanderers would make quick use of any free hands. Because she knew nothing about preparing their large wooden caravans for travel, she was asked to keep an eye on the many children. They all clamored for her attention, pulling her in different directions to show her their toys, to play with her, and even to touch her hair, as apparently they had never seen red hair before. Their curiosity didn't bother her. After all, she had never met a Wanderer before in her life, and they were not quite what she had imagined.

Unlike most of the people in and around her hometown of Avdimia, who were light skinned and fair or red haired, the Wanderers had brown skin and thick, shiny hair as black as night. Most of them were tall compared to her, even the women, despite the fact that she had always been on the tall side in her village. The women were curvy and the men muscular, and they wore the most beautiful, vibrant clothing, in reds and blues and oranges and yellows, matching the bright paint on their wagon homes. Not one of them seemed to be half as modest as the people she had grown up with. Most of the men wore vests with no shirts beneath, revealing the dark curls on their chests and stomachs, and the women all had low-cut blouses, many with no sleeves, and some even wore trousers which revealed their shapely, toned legs. Observing them, she never would have guessed that Foulan was one of them had they not treated him like family.

He had the same features, certainly: brown skin, black eyes, and long dark hair that hung to his shoulders. But that was where the similarities ended. While most of the men sported thick, bushy black beards, he kept his own facial hair trimmed short. He did not wear the bright colors of his fellow Wanderers, but rather a subdued dark green tunic over a brown shirt and the same forest-colored trousers. While the other men and women adorned themselves with necklaces, bracelets, and rings, he wore only a pair of simple leather bracers. And while she could assume most of the Wanderers had weapons nearby or in their wagons, he was the only one who sported a magnificent wooden bow on his back and a quiver of arrows at his hip.

As midmorning came and went, the caravans were packed and the clan was ready to travel. Mackenna shifted awkwardly from foot to foot, wondering what she should do now. She hadn't a clue where she was anymore, nor where she was going. The Wanderers seemed nice and welcoming, but would it be rude to ask to tag along? Would they think her annoying and pathetic?

"No point in dawdling, Maple," Bahira's voice said from beside her, and she linked her arm in Mackenna's, pulling her along after the wagons. Mackenna breathed a sigh of relief, thankful for Bahira's friendliness.

In addition to the horses and mules used to pull the wagons, there were many other animals that travelled with the Wanderers. In the back of one wagon was a cage with chickens, beside which sat a couple of goats. No doubt kept for eggs and milk while on the road. Some of the Wanderers also rode horses, though most walked. In addition to the wolf Myst, there were a few other dogs that chased behind the wagons and played with the children, and she saw more than one cat napping on a wagon porch or roof, no doubt with more inside.

"Why don't people ride in the wagons?" Mackenna asked.

"Trust me, you wouldn't want to," Bahira replied. "Their terribly stuffy, and it's a bumpy, swaying ride. Most of us prefer to walk. Only the elderly, babies, and infirm travel inside."

Bahira was more than happy to answer Mackenna's questions as they walked. In fact, she seemed to quite enjoy it, as she chatted almost constantly. It was strange at first, though certainly not unwelcome. Mackenna hardly ever had anyone to talk to besides father and Henriette. Nobody in the village had liked her. They'd all been afraid of her, and that fear made them hateful. The extent of her interactions with them were usually glares, though the kids her age had occasionally thrown rocks at her or played other cruel pranks. Thankfully, though, their fear usually kept them at a distance.

People generally treated her better outside the village, but father and Mackenna only ever left to tend to the wounded and ill. While their patients were grateful for Finn's help, they usually had little time or energy to spend on pleasantries. Mackenna's childhood had thus always been fairly quiet and contemplative, father her constant and often only companion. She had long since grown used to the loneliness of not having anyone else her age as a friend.

The Wanderers were certainly friendly and welcoming, but no doubt that would change if they ever found out about her abilities. And gods, it was a breath of fresh air to have someone just be nice to her for once, without the air of suspicion that she was accustomed to. Were they always this nice, or did they just find her amusing because she was so different from them? Did it even matter? She soaked up their attention and kindness like a plant feeling rain for the first time after a long drought.

Then there was Foulan. He was the only exception. Whenever Mackenna caught sight of him watching her, he was frowning, his eyes dark. What was his problem? Hadn't he rescued her? Hadn't he followed her in the woods and told her she was lost and invited her to go with him? Yet now he glared at her and stalked alone behind the caravan.

Bahira must have noticed at some point. "Oh, don't worry about him." She rolled her eyes. "It's nothing against you; he always has that look on his face. Like he left his wagon windows open in the rain."

Mackenna chuckled. That was a relief, at least. Though it still felt like his angry looks were directed specifically at her.

They didn't stop to eat lunch. Instead, everyone ate rations of dried meat and fruit as they walked. In the afternoon, some of the younger children crawled into their wagons to nap. Occasionally the adults switched out who rode on the horses or steered the wagons, but clearly the younger people were expected to be on foot the entire day. As the sun set, they stopped for the night, the Wanderers creating a circle with the wagons in a clearing by the road. Everyone set to work immediately, unpacking food and pots and pans, setting loose the chickens and goats and cats to roam, building fires to cook, and going out to hunt and gather. At least this last one was something Mackenna was good at, and she wandered away from the camp to gather mushrooms, blackberries, and elderberries.

The sun grew low on the horizon, the greenery of the forest fading to gray with the twilight. She'd gotten caught up in the meditative repetition of foraging and lost track of time. She hadn't brought a torch, but thankfully she could see the Wanderer's campfires like a beacon in the distance. She made her way back to camp, but before entering the ring of wagons, she spotted two figures standing in the shadows talking. The first person's voice she recognized immediately as Foulan's, and it didn't take long to realize who he spoke with: the Wanderer leader, Mercia. She had no intention of spying until she heard the word "maple." Mackenna paused, peeking around the corner of the wagon to watch them.

"While this girl is certainly welcome company, I have to wonder what really happened this morning. You just found a girl wandering the woods alone while you were hunting? And then you came across two war horses on the road? It seems a little too coincidental," Mercia said from where he perched on the back of a caravan.

Foulan frowned, the light from a nearby campfire illuminating his face. "I was up a tree waiting for my prey when she came bursting through the woods like a rabbit being chased by a fox." His eyes narrowed. "I realized she *was* being chased… by knights on horseback. They wore the tabards of witch hunters. I didn't know if they really thought she was one, or if they were just hoping to take advantage of their station. It certainly wouldn't be the first time."

She realized after a moment what he meant. He'd thought those men were planning to rape her? Then again, who was to say they wouldn't have? "I wasn't sure what to do. She collapsed right under my tree, and Myst leapt to her defense." Mackenna's eyes strayed down to the wolf beside her master. Her head lifted and ears perked up at the sound of her name. "What else could I do? I couldn't just sit up there and watch them defile the girl, nor could I let Myst come to harm protecting her."

"You did the right thing, no doubt. But these men, these knights, did you kill them?" asked Mercia.

"No. I shot one of them. Myst mauled the other. They must have really believed she was a witch, though, 'cause they accused her of summoning Myst to defend her. I played along, hiding up in the tree and pitching my voice to scare them." Foulan smirked. "Anyway, as they hadn't seen my face, I allowed them to escape with their lives. I made them abandon their horses and weapons so they couldn't just circle back around and attack again later."

"And that's the full story?" Mercia asked. "You're sure they didn't see a Wanderer help her?"

"Positive. I stayed in the tree until they left."

Mercia nodded, resting his chin against his steepled fingers. "Good. From the pack she's carrying and the fact that she hasn't asked for directions home, I would guess she's a runaway. I'll welcome her to continue traveling with us."

Foulan had begun shaking his head before Mercia had even finished talking. "I don't think that's wise. As fond as you are of doting on strangers, she could bring us trouble. The locals are already suspicious of us with tensions escalating at the border. I saved her and helped her out of the forest, but I didn't think she'd tag along like a lost puppy."

"You propose we just abandon her then? That certainly isn't the chivalric thing to do, Foulan," Mercia scolded.

The boy snorted. "You should run her off quickly, before she gets too comfortable here."

Mercia stood to his full height and crossed his arms, glaring down at Foulan, who averted his eyes, looking sheepish. "Well, perhaps when *you* are clan leader, you can make such a decision. But as it is, I will welcome her as long as she wishes to stay." He grinned at the wolf, giving her a pat on the head. "Besides, your four-legged companion is quite astute when it comes to strangers. If she trusts Maple, then so do I."

"Fine. Just don't say I didn't warn you." Foulan straightened up and walked in her direction. Mackenna backed away, hoping to escape his notice, but she wasn't quick enough. Suddenly Foulan stood before her, those dark eyes staring down at her, inscrutable. Myst, however, trotted up to her and left a slobbery kiss on Mackenna's hand. The boy grunted and walked past her without a word, whistling to his wolf to follow. Mackenna silently rejoined the other Wanderers, her face hot with embarrassment and anger. Of course their kindness to her couldn't last. How long before he turned them all against her, and she was cast out once more?

Bahira braided her hair as they sat by the fire, adding the occasional bead or flower in the Wanderer style. She and many of the other Wanderers seemed to have a fascination with Mackenna's red hair, though she couldn't fathom why. As they chatted, thunder rolled in the distance.

"Where will Foulan sleep if a storm comes in?" Mackenna asked. She had noticed in the fortnight that she had traveled with the Wanderers that he always slept outside, usually away from camp. In fact, it seemed that he did everything alone. When they traveled, he followed separately, usually at the back of the train. When they set up camp, he disappeared into the woods with Myst in tow and reappeared hours later with game for the clan to share. Myst seemed to be his only constant companion.

"In Mercia's caravan," Bahira replied. Mackenna had gleaned that they were kin, but wasn't sure of their exact relationship.

"Did he… did he do something? To get the clan's ire?" She has been wanting to ask this for some time but didn't want to be rude sticking her nose in clan business.

"What do you mean?" Bahira asked.

Mackenna shrugged. "I mean, he seems like an outcast. He's always alone. He never talks to anybody."

Bahira laughed. "No, that's just the way he's always been. Mercia's usually the only one who can get more than a few words out of him. His mother, Nadya, she's the same way. Some people just prefer to be quiet, I suppose." Mackenna vaguely recognized the name Nadya. They had only exchanged a handful of words in the past two weeks, usually apologies if they got in each other's way. The woman always seemed busy caring for the Wise Woman.

"Wouldn't he sleep in his mother's caravan?" Mackenna asked. She had noticed that in most cases, each family had its own caravan. When the weather was nice, many people chose to sleep outside the caravan, often stringing hammocks between them to keep off the ground. Bahira was the only daughter of her parents, so there was plenty of room for Mackenna in their caravan.

"Mercia is Nadya's brother and Foulan's uncle. Nadya sleeps in the Wise Woman's caravan in case she needs anything in the night. But that is an honor only reserved for the Wise Woman's caretaker."

"What about Foulan's father?" Mackenna wondered if she was being too nosy, but Bahira always seemed happy to gossip.

"Foulan doesn't have a father. Well, he does somewhere I guess, but Nadya's never said who it is, just that he was a Wanderer from another clan. Anyway, Mercia has acted as a father to Foulan growing up. When Foulan reached his majority this year, the Wise Woman announced her decision to make him clan leader when Mercia decides to step down. Come to think of it, he has become especially reclusive ever since then. Even for him."

"How come?"

"I think he doesn't want to be leader, and so he started avoiding the clan, hoping that the Wise Woman would change her mind and choose someone else. To be honest, we were all surprised when she chose him."

"Wouldn't Mercia have to die for the leadership to pass on?" Mackenna asked.

"Of course not!" Bahira replied. "You're thinking of kings. Most of the leaders give up their position when they grow older and become tired of it, usually once their grandchildren are born. While the clan rulership can pass on to next of kin, it doesn't have to. The Wise Woman always chooses whoever she sees as most worthy. To be honest, I'm not really sure what she sees in him, besides that he can hunt."

Mackenna had heard of this Wise Woman, even glimpsed her on occasion, but had yet to actually meet her. "The Wise Woman sounds more powerful than the clan leader, if *she* chooses *him*." Mackenna had never heard of such a thing.

Bahira nodded. "I guess you could say most clans have two leaders. The Wise Woman guides the clan, gives advice to the leader, and chooses the leader. She often uses divination or has the gift of Sight to help guide the clan's future. But she doesn't bother herself with the everyday chores of leadership, like solving disputes and putting people to work. She's much too important for that."

"And these leaders she appoints can be men or women?" Mackenna asked curiously.

"Why not? It's whoever the Wise Woman chooses. The only rule is that whoever she chooses must have reached adulthood." Bahira said this all as if it were the most natural thing in the world. To Mackenna, the thought of a woman ruling was a completely new, and exhilarating, concept.

"So, Foulan, then, has been chosen, whether he likes it or not?" Mackenna asked, trying to get it all straightened out in her head. "He can't just refuse?"

"Nope, no one can refuse the position. Only a calling greater than clan leadership can allow one to," Bahira told her.

"Like what?" Mackenna asked.

"I don't know," Bahira said thoughtfully. "I'm not sure it's ever happened before."

Foulan

The last two weeks had been hell for Foulan. The girl, Maple, had proven to be quite a nuisance. She had insinuated herself into his Wanderer clan like one of their own, and they all adopted her without bothering to question how much trouble she might bring. Foulan didn't regret that she had overheard him warning Mercia about her. He didn't trust the girl. While he was sure she was harmless in herself, those soldiers had to have had good reason for why they were hunting her.

But it wasn't just the girl's presence that was making Foulan so miserable. Mercia kept hinting at withdrawing from his position soon and passing it onto Foulan, despite the fact that he knew Foulan hated the idea. If he were clan leader, he would be surrounded by his people at all times, listening to their complaints, settling domestic issues, and acting as political intermediary between his clan and the local residents of whatever land they called home for the moment. He would be responsible for the lives of all of the Wanderers in his clan, and should he ever feel too suffocated, there would be no escaping into the wilderness to be alone with his thoughts. He would never again have a moment's peace.

Foulan's misery increased when they reached the city of Hartland. Hartland was a trade stop along the Kelosia River. Around the city was sprawling farmland that profited from the rich soil created when the river flooded, and the city was large enough to be divided into three sectors: the business area where the shops and markets were located; the residential district with its townhomes and even small mansions that housed the rich landowners; and the slums comprised of rundown homes, seedy taverns, and low-class brothels.

Foulan hated cities. He hated the houses all crammed together, the people residing one on top of the other. He hated the large crowds and the awful smells of thousands of people living and dying in one small space. He hated the lack of trees and meadows and wild beasts. So it was to Foulan's chagrin that the clan veered off the road towards Hartland, needing to restock on supplies before continuing their journey northward. Most annoying of all, the girl, Maple, followed.

As they didn't reach the town until evening, the Wanderers decided to stay the night. The caravans were too large to all find a spot inside the city walls, so they set up camp outside in a communal pasture while some of the Wanderers gathered wares to sell in the merchant district the next morning. Just as Foulan was beginning to feel relieved that at least for tonight he wouldn't have to actually enter the city and be surrounded by all those people, Mercia took him aside with that sly grin of his that told Foulan he wasn't going to like whatever the clan leader suggested.

"Foulan! Maple tells me she's never been in a town this large before. My wife and I have decided to take her to a pub so she can enjoy the nightlife firsthand. You should join us." Mercia clapped him on the shoulder.

Without looking up from the fire he was building, he replied, "I'm busy. I need to set up camp and prepare some traps so we can catch fish from the river."

"Nonsense. Others can do that. You should enjoy yourself while you're young. Join us for some drink and dancing," Mercia said.

Foulan switched tactics. "I can't leave Myst all alone. You know they won't let a wolf into the city gates." Foulan glanced up at Myst, who was currently bounding through the open pasture, searching for a hare or groundhog to chase.

"Foulan, you worry too much," Mercia said. "Myst has been with us since she was a pup. She'll behave if you leave her in another's care for the evening. It wouldn't be the first time others have watched over her, and besides, it will only be for a few hours. Come."

"I'm not interested," he bit out.

Mercia shrugged. "Well, that's fine I suppose. I'll invite Bahira's parents instead, and you can stay here and be in charge of watching the children for the evening in their place."

Foulan groaned. The only thing more annoying than being in a tavern surrounded by drunks was being stuck with a hoard of children who chattered nonstop. "Fine. I'll join you." Mercia grinned, steering Foulan away from camp and towards the town. Myst, seeing he was leaving, chased after him, and he had to gently coax her into staying behind in the camp. She cocked her head in confusion, as she rarely left his side, but after he found her some food to eat, she finally settled down on his bedroll next to the fire.

In the end, seven of them went: Foulan, Mercia and his wife Aishah, Yasmine and Kamal (who were in the midst of courting one another), Bahira, and Maple. It seemed Maple, country girl that she was, had indeed never been in so large a city before, for she was practically bursting with wonder, staring in awe at the huge gates that they passed through; gazing at every stall and in every shop window that they saw; and smiling and laughing at the bards, jugglers, and other entertainers in the street who performed for her amusement and her money. Mercia gave them each a few bairnes, the smallest denomination, as a tip, so the girl wouldn't have to spend her own coin, and Foulan rolled his eyes. It seemed Mercia was intent on spoiling his new little pet.

Finally, they reached a pub that was to Mercia's liking. Inside was crowded and warm, despite the fact that the shutters were thrown open to let in the night air, and the scent of pipe smoke drifted through the room. The establishment was small, so they only had the one meal for purchase, fish and rice. After dinner, tankards of mead were passed around. Apparently the girl had never drunk mead before either, for she was quickly intoxicated, her cheeks bright red as she joked and laughed with Mercia and the others. Yasmine and Kamal went off to dance to the lute player's music, and Mercia and Bahira taught Maple the steps to a group dance, trying to coax Foulan to join. No one seemed surprised or pressed him further when he refused.

In all the revelry, only Foulan noticed that there was something amiss in the tavern. The barkeep whispered with his wife, and they grabbed one of their servant boys, who'd been filling up the mead cups, and pulled him aside. They kept their gestures minimal, but Foulan could tell they were talking about the Wanderers, shooting glances in their direction between pauses in conversation. The barkeep's wife had a piece of parchment in her hand that she kept pointing at, and finally they seemed to come to a conclusion, sending away the boy, who slipped out the back door silently.

Foulan gritted his teeth. No doubt they were about to throw the Wanderers out with some vague excuse. Hopefully the owners wouldn't also try to make some false accusation about them stealing or some other nonsense. He was used to being treated like a criminal just because he was a Wanderer. He stood and gestured at Mercia, trying to get his attention. Hopefully they could all duck out quietly.

Suddenly, the front door slammed open and in walked three thugs. A quick glance out the windows revealed that there were also two at the back door, blocking them in. One of them, clad in mismatched leather armor, appeared to be the leader of the gang. She was a giant of a woman, with thick muscles, a half-shaved head, and scars crisscrossing her face and arms.

"You there, girl," she bellowed, pointing at Maple. "I'll be asking you to join me and my friends out back for a bit."

They were looking for Maple? He glanced over at her. The girl's eyes grew wide as she stared at the woman, then at the other thugs outside the door. She looked like a hare trapped by a fox as she eyed her surroundings, searching for an escape. Though the woman didn't yet reach for the wicked-looking dagger on her belt, Maple's eyes passed over it warily as she backed away.

"What is the meaning of this?" Mercia asked, eyebrows drawn together as he glared at the woman. "Who are you, and what right do you have to come barging in here ruining our evening?"

"Who am I? I'm the leader of the Blackbriars," the woman answered. "Me and my boys see to it that this city runs smoothly, and being an upstanding citizen of the law, I am obliged to turn in any criminals when I hear of them."

"Blackbriars?" Mercia asked, crossing his arms over his chest. "You sound like nothing more than a gang to me. Just whose law do you uphold?"

The leader spread her arms in an all-encompassing gesture. "Whoever's law best suits my needs at the time. And right now, what I need is the bounty on that pretty redhead." She nodded at Maple. "After all, running a city can get mighty costly."

"And what could this young woman have possibly done to warrant a bounty?" Mercia asked. "She couldn't hurt a fly."

The woman shrugged, reaching into her jerkin and pulling out a crumpled piece of parchment. She unfolded it and held it up, revealing a sketch of Maple. It wasn't perfect, but it was clearly her—though there weren't nearly enough freckles on the image. Most eye catching of all was the price—four hundred duques—followed by the words "Wanted alive. Mackenna of Avdimia." There was a wax seal on the parchment to prove its validity.

"Says hear she's wanted for arson, witchcraft, and murder. And it must be mighty bad considering what they're offering." The woman tucked the bounty between her breasts and shrugged. "Now, the bounty is only good if the girl is alive. So, while I would normally let my boys have their fun with a lowly criminal, I'll make sure to keep you with me at all times." The wink she gave Maple—or was it Mackenna?—made Foulan's skin crawl.

Mercia's wife, Aishah, stepped around her husband. Though she had to look up into the thug's eyes, she had a presence that made her appear to tower over everyone. Foulan had always known her to be a gentle woman, but when she spoke her mind, people listened. If they knew what was good for them, anyway. "A piece of paper gives you no right to take this girl for your own filthy uses. She is under our protection, and we won't be handing her over to criminal scum like you."

"I admire your tenacity, little lady," said the Blackbriar leader, "but right now you are aiding and abetting a criminal, and such things can get you thrown in jail. And trust me when I tell you that you wouldn't like the jails we have in our city." The woman pulled out her dagger, revealing the serrated edge and curved tip. "They are overflowing with criminal scum, as you so put it, and we simply don't have the space to separate the men and women." She cleaned under her nails with her dagger. "Now, you'd all best step aside, lest this turn violent."

"I see," was Mercia's only reply. He gazed between the wicked dagger in the woman's hand and Maple's frightened face before stepping out of the way with a shrug, pulling Aishah aside with him. "Well, the Wanderers are nothing if not law-abiding citizens."

The gang leader grinned, clearly believing Mercia to be genuine. Foulan knew better. He tensed, his hand aching to reach for his bow, but he did not wish to move without Mercia's cue. Mercia turned his head ever so slightly in Foulan's direction, giving him a small wink and glancing at the back door. Foulan was the only one near the back door and the men standing guard there. There were too many obstacles between him and the others. He would have to fight two men on his own.

Foulan would have cursed aloud if he'd had the time. But Mercia's intentions were clear, and he had no choice but to join in. As soon as the thug's hand wrapped around Maple's wrist to pull her away, Mercia's own hand struck out, slipping a dagger from under his shirt sleeve and plunging it into the woman's wrist. The woman screamed and released Maple before lunging at Mercia with her own dagger.

Foulan didn't have time to worry about the others. They were a family — a cohesive unit. They had gotten into more than one scrap over the years. He didn't bother with his bow; the room was much too tightly pack for him to load and fire it quickly, and besides, he would risk hitting an innocent bystander. Instead, he grabbed an empty tankard, glad they were made out of heavy pewter, and lunged for the thug beside him, bringing the tankard across his temples. The man collapsed, but Foulan knew he wouldn't stay down for long, and these didn't look like the sort of men who had any qualms about killing. Foulan drew his own dagger and plunged it into the fallen man's calf, ripping it open as he yanked the blade out. That ought to keep him down.

The first one, sadly, was the easy one. The element of surprise was no longer on his side, and much worse, the second guard at the back door was a huge hulking brute of a man, two heads taller than Foulan and at least twice his weight. And most of it looked to be muscle. The man had drawn his weapon, a flail. One swipe would spell Foulan's death; his only hope was to get inside the man's swing.

Large as he was, the brute managed to move surprisingly quickly. Each swing of his flail broke something in the tavern: a chair, a bottle of wine, a cask of ale. Foulan ignored the barkeep screaming in the corner, all of his focus on the spiked ball swinging dangerously close to his head. What he needed was a moment of distraction.

Almost as soon as he thought it, he got his wish. There came another scream, and Foulan felt a sudden surge of heat at his back. While the brute was momentarily distracted by the fire behind him, Foulan took his chance. He moved forward inside the man's swing and dug his dagger into the brute's armpit where a gap in his leather armor left him unprotected. The man would have a damn hard time swinging that flail now.

Thankfully, Foulan didn't have to worry about following up with another blow. The chaos of the fire that had broken out had people scrambling for both exits from the building. Foulan found himself buffeted by fleeing patrons and struggled to keep from being trampled. The flail-wielding brute grabbed his barely conscious companion with his good arm and hauled him from the building. With the immediate danger gone, Foulan was able to search for Mercia and the others. He caught sight of them leaving out the front door. The fire raged in the middle of the room, separating them. Maple was on his side, and he realized in horror that her clothes were burning. Foulan grabbed her without thinking, turning and dashing from the burning building out the back door.

Once they were safely outside, he grabbed her dress, ripping it from her shoulders and down her body. She struggled to put out the flames that had caught her hair while he stamped out her dress.

"My clothes! What are you doing?!" Maple yelled.

"Saving your damn life!" Foulan yelled back. Shouldn't it have been obvious? Now was not the time to worry about decency. Foulan looked up from her smoking dress, trying to assess Maple's skin in the dim light cast from the building. She clutched her arms around her midsection, embarrassed to be clad in only her shift.

Foulan spotted Mercia jogging towards them. "I sent the others ahead, back to camp," he said. "Are either of you hurt? Can you make it back okay?"

"Maple is burned," said Foulan. "She'll need a healer." He turned away to give her a moment of privacy as she pulled back on her ripped dress, which still smoldered in a few spots.

"I'm fine. I wasn't burned. Is everyone else alright?" she asked.

"But your clothes—"

"I said I'm fine," she repeated, glaring at him. "It was just a few embers. They didn't even reach my skin. You overreacted in the panic, is all."

There was something in her voice, a warning or a plea, he wasn't sure which. But glancing at her skin, she did appear perfectly unmarked. How, when he had seen her very clothes and hair being licked by flames mere moments ago? Her dress was black with scorch marks, his own hands stung from pulling it off of her, and yet she showed no signs of damage.

"Then we need to get back to camp and leave as quickly as possible, before those thugs come after us," Mercia said and turned to the lead the way. Now was not the time to question her.

Though Foulan was determined that he would, once this was over.

They stumbled through dark streets and side alleys instead of taking the main road out of town. Before the camp was even in site, Myst came bounding up to them, sniffing and licking at

Foulan's hands. "What happened to your hands?" Mercia asked.

Foulan glanced at Maple, who looked away. "Just burned them a bit," he said. "It's nothing serious."

"Good, 'cause we're leaving at once. Go to my caravan and wait there. You too," Mercia commanded Maple. "Those thugs are looking for you. I want you out of sight. Foulan, keep an eye on her until we're safely away from the city. Then we'll all have a chat with the Wise Woman."

Foulan nodded, trying to hide his annoyance. Why did he have to get stuck being the girl's guard? He grabbed her shoulder, steering her towards Mercia's caravan. Myst followed them inside, and he barred the door.

"Sit," he commanded. It seemed to take the girl a moment to realize that he was talking to her and not Myst. She sank onto the bed. Myst jumped up beside her and made herself comfortable.

Within a few minutes the caravan began to rock as the clan started moving. Foulan hated traveling inside them and avoided it all costs. It was safe enough; every piece of furniture was bolted to the wall or floor to keep it from sliding around. Even so, he bristled at being stuck inside the cramped, stuffy space, and the rocking made him nauseous. He sat by the door and laid his hands palm up on his knees, trying to ignore the stinging. He could already see red, angry blisters forming.

"You need to clean and treat those," Maple said.

"It's fine," he grumbled.

"My bag of remedies is with Bahira's caravan. Do you know if Aisha has any food ingredients in here?" He jerked his head to a cabinet hanging on the wall. The girl rummaged in the cabinet, examining bottles and jars of spices and other foodstuffs, occasionally opening them to smell the contents. "My... my father taught me how to treat wounds using all kinds of stuff. Sometimes you run out of something and have to improvise. Ahh, here we are."

She approached him with a cloth in one hand and a bottle in the other, looking expected. When Foulan didn't respond, she rolled her eyes. "It's the least I could do. Please." Foulan just shrugged, and she seemed to take that as acceptance, gently taking his hands and examining them. "They don't look too bad. You'll have blisters for a few days. After that, you should be fine. But we definitely need to clean and bandage them."

"Why?" Foulan asked.

She lifted an eyebrow and glanced at Myst, who was sound asleep already. "Burns are prone to infection. As I said, yours aren't bad, so the risk isn't as great, but you let your wolf lick all over them. Canines' mouths aren't the cleanest."

As if she heard them, Myst snorted in her sleep and rolled onto her side. Mackenna poured some of the liquid over his hands, and Foulan hissed. It stung like hell and stank. "Is that vinegar?"

She nodded, wiping gently at his hands with the rag. "It will clean out any infection." When that was finished, she put up the vinegar and returned with another small jar.

"Honey?" he asked.

"It helps with the blisters and pain and also keeps infection at bay."

"They'll be all sticky," he muttered.

"Hence the bandages. You should only need to keep it on overnight." She slathered his burns with honey, then wound gauze around his hands.

"So, is Maple even really your name?" Foulan asked as she finished tying the bandages.

"No," she whispered. "It's Mackenna. I... I'm sorry I lied."

"You're sorry?" he scoffed. "Do you have any idea the kind of precarious position the Wanderers live in everyday? How many people will look for any excuse to run us out of town or do us harm? And now we've aided a criminal!" She flinched at the word criminal. "You have a lot of explaining to do to Mercia and the Wise Woman."

"I'm sorry," she whispered again, sinking back down onto the bed and pulling her knees against her chest. She buried her head in her arms, her red hair coming down between them like a curtain. He didn't miss the telltale sniffles that gave away that she was crying. He felt a twinge of guilt at how pathetic she looked but steeled his resolve. He still had no idea what she had done, so he certainly wasn't going to take back what he'd said. The silence hung heavy in the room as they rode and waited.

Foulan jerked awake as the caravan came to a stop. He stood and glanced out the shutter to find they had settled in a forest clearing off a small path that must connect back to the main road. The dawn was just beginning to break. The door opened and Mercia stood in it, gesturing to them. "Come," he said, "it's time to speak with the Wise Woman. You too, Foulan. You need to see what it is to be a leader."

Normally Foulan hated when Mercia spoke of such things. He'd resisted for the past six months all of Mercia's attempts to mentor him on leadership. But this time, Foulan was more than willing to join him. He was surprised to realize that he was genuinely curious about this strange girl's story.

"She's ready for you," Nadya said when they approached the Wise Woman's caravan. "I will stay out here. It will be a bit too crowded with all of us. Come and find me when you're done," she directed the last part to Foulan, who nodded.

Inside was dark, the shutters closed for privacy, the only light coming from a few low-burning candles. As with Mercia's caravan, shelves were built into the walls, though these held an arrangement of strange trinkets and magical devices. Foulan could only guess what half of them were used for. At the back of the caravan was a single-person cot, and in the center of the room was a small round table with two chairs, where Drynka the Wise Woman was currently sitting, a large round orb resting on the table in front of her. It was a fascinating object, seeming to both absorb and reflect the light in the room at once, scattering strange colors over the old woman's lined face, which pulled up in a smile.

"Sit, child," she said to Mackenna, gesturing at the chair across from her.

Mackenna swallowed hard and stepped forward, then paused, as if a thought had occurred to her. Suddenly, she dipped into a low curtsy, bowing her head before Drynka. "Thank you for having me, Wise Woman. My name is Mackenna, daughter of Finn, and I hail from Avdimia."

"Yes, I know," Drynka replied. "Sit. Let me see your face."

Mackenna did as she was commanded, sliding into the seat before the Wise Woman, though she kept her face down, staring at the table. The girl's hands were clenched to the edges of the table, wrinkling the purple silk tablecloth. Drynka reached out an aged, spotted hand, tipping up the girl's face and gazing into her eyes. "You are here to tell me a story, hey." She did not state it as a question, but merely as fact, and without waiting for confirmation from either Mercia or Foulan, she continued. "Well, then, tell your story. And pray, make it an interesting one. I do love a good tale."

"It is not all that interesting, I fear," Mackenna began. "Those thugs were after me because... because I killed two soldiers. They murdered my father, and in my rage to get at them, I... I knocked over a floor lamp and set fire to our home. They died, but I escaped."

"Hmph." The Wise Woman looked unimpressed. She glanced at Foulan. "Tell me, boy, do you believe her?"

He shook his head. "I don't believe she tells the whole truth, Wise Woman. She's already lied to us before." He watched as Mackenna's shoulders tensed.

"How so?" Drynka asked.

"First, she gave a false name, Maple. And then at the tavern last night. There was a fire there, as well. And I saw the flames on her body. I went to put them out, but after I did, she was unharmed," Foulan replied.

Mackenna seemed to shrink into the chair, as if she could make herself smaller. "Your eyes simply misled you."

"I don't think the burns on my hands are all that misleading," he replied, and she flinched.

Mercia sighed in annoyance, kneeling down to look the girl in the eyes. "Mackenna, I like you," he said. "That's why I helped you out. But I can't continue to help you unless you are completely honest with us. That's why I brought you to the Wise Woman. She has a knack for knowing when people are lying. Do you remember what the wanted poster stated were your crimes?"

"Yes," she whispered, and Foulan thought she might begin crying at any moment. "Arson, murder, and… and witchcraft."

"I understand why you might be afraid," Mercia said gently. "But look around you. Do you really believe that we are the kind who fear witches?"

Mackenna looked up slowly, gazing around the room. Her eyes fell on the Wise Woman, whose lips were quirked up in a grin. "Then you are a…?" she trailed off.

"You'll have to speak up, girl. I'm old and hard of hearing," Drynka replied. "A what now?"

"A witch?" Mackenna breathed.

The Wise Woman chuckled. "I am many things, girl. An old woman. A leader. A crook. Much of this," she gestured around the small room at her various trinkets, "is just for show. But yes, I am also a witch. I was born with the gift to See the future. To an extent."

Mackenna swallowed, staring at her hands. "All my life, I have been hated and feared because of my curse. There is a rage in me, one that I often lose control of."

"And when you do?" Drynka prodded.

"When I do, things have a tendency to… to catch fire." Mackenna took a deep breath and launched into her story, and Foulan listened with rapt attention. He learned how her father had been killed, how she had lost control of her unusual talent and slain his murderers, and how she had been forced to flee her village. She told of the soldiers who found her and chased her into the woods, intent on capturing her. From there Foulan knew the rest of the story that she recounted for the Wise Woman. She ended with the previous night's events, confessing that she had caused the fire in the tavern in her fear.

After she had finished, the room was silent for a few moments. "Is this the whole truth?" Mercia asked, though his question was directed at Drynka.

"Aye, she speaks truth," the old woman replied.

"Now that we've aided a criminal, we'll have a mess of trouble on our hands," Mercia said with a frown. "What do you propose we do, Wise Woman?"

"Well, we could use the money from that bounty," the old woman said. Mackenna gasped, and even Mercia looked taken aback. Drynka cackled. "Only a joke. Lighten up, you three. Mercia, we have always walked a fine line with the law. How is this any different now? And besides, Etylanians can't tell one Wanderer clan from another."

"Then you propose we let her stay?" Mercia asked.

"Oh, I didn't say that." The old woman shook her head with a smile. "She is volatile, quick to anger, in little control of her powers, yes?"

Mackenna nodded shamefully. "It is a curse."

"Pah!" the old woman scoffed. "'Tis not a curse. 'Tis only a natural ability, one you were born with. It's more interesting than a nice singing voice or being able to paint a pretty picture, that's for sure." Drynka smiled, nodding. "But until you know how to harness what you have, you are a danger to yourself and everyone around you." The old woman leaned forward. "Do you see this crystal orb here?" Mackenna nodded. "What do you see when you look at it?"

"It looks… fuzzy. Like there are clouds drifting through it. Or smoke…" Foulan looked at the crystal in surprise, wondering if it had somehow changed. But it looked the same to him, casting those strange, flittering colors across the room.

"Well, when you learn to open your eyes, you can see so much more. When I look into it, I can see fleeting images. Some of the past. Some of the present. Some of the future. That is how I know you're not lying. Now, girl, you have told me an interesting tale indeed, and in return I will tell you something."

The Wise Woman did not spread out a packet of tarot cards on the table or wave her hands over the orb or read the lines on Mackenna's palm. Foulan knew that these were merely for show, to impress those who would pay money in the hopes of gleaning their future. When such a fortune was told, it was almost always false, the Wise Woman simply telling people what they wanted to hear. But what she did now was real magic. If she really had watched Mackenna's story in the orb earlier, Foulan hadn't noticed a change in the room or the woman herself at the time. But he noticed one now.

She took Mackenna's hand in her own and closed her eyes, humming lightly to herself. The air in the room grew gradually thicker and seemed to shimmer at the edges of Foulan's vision. Every time he tried to catch sight of whatever it was that was glittering there, it would disappear from his field of view. There were other noises interwoven with the humming of the old woman, at first indecipherable, but soon he realized what he heard was the whisper of many faraway voices overlaid. In all his life, Foulan had never once witnessed the Wise Woman perform her magic. It was something sacred and private, and he wondered why she let Foulan and Mercia stay for such a thing.

Then the old woman spoke, but it was no longer merely her speaking. The voice came from her but also from everywhere at once, her own voice just one among many. Her words echoed through the room. "First, of the past. You lost your mother when you were just a babe. But you must not blame yourself."

"Wha — what do you mean?" Mackenna whispered, as if she was afraid of breaking this strange spell.

"Your mother sacrificed herself to protect you," the Wise Woman answered. "But the guilt you carry at her absence is unfounded."

"I do not understand. What do you mean, sacrificed?" Mackenna asked. "I thought she died giving birth to me?"

The old woman hummed, then shook her head. "The spirits will not let me say more on that subject. Now, of the present. Know that you are never alone, for your father's spirit travels with you always. He sends his love from the Earth Mother's womb. Should you ever miss him, simply look to the trees around you, and there you will find his soul lingers.

"And finally, of the future. Your life is not the only thing in danger. There are those who seek you, who wish to use you as a weapon against their enemies. If you do not learn to control your magic, it will soon rule you, and you will be nothing but a pawn in their game. You *must not* let this happen. If you wish to prevent this, you must find the Fae and seek their guidance.

"But you will not be alone. Two companions will guide you on your journey and protect you from harm. Foulan and Myst will travel with you."

Foulan froze in shock. Had he heard right? Was he really going to be forced to escort this girl on a crazy mission to find the Fair Folk?

He wasn't even sure if they truly existed or were just children's stories. Some stories said that their home was the center of the earth, others claimed it was high in the clouds, and still others said that they existed all around but were invisible. But no matter where they resided, all of the stories of the Folk spoke of a capricious, often cruel race of strange creatures. And every story of them had the same warning: the Fae were dangerous and not to be trifled with.

He wanted to say something in protest, but his words died in his throat. It was as if the magic all around stopped him from making a sound.

And then the magic was suddenly gone, like a veil being lifted from around his eyes. Foulan gazed about, blinking in the darkness of the room, wondering if the shimmering lights and the ethereal voices had been nothing more than a trick. He glanced at Mercia and Mackenna, who appeared as dazed and astonished as he felt. And then suddenly the room was bursting with protests all spoken in unison.

"The Fae? But, but they are just children's stories!" Mackenna babbled.

"You can't send Foulan away now! Who will become the next leader?" Mercia objected.

"You don't seriously expect me to go with her," Foulan protested.

The Wise Woman raised a hand, silencing them all. She gazed at each of them, answering their protests in turn. "Mackenna, I know all of this is frightening to you. But the Fair Folk will not harm you as long as you are careful. As to where to find them, I know someone who may be able to help you."

Next, she addressed Mercia. "Foulan was chosen to be the next leader. But he is called to a greater purpose and thus must abdicate the position."

She turned her eyes to Foulan. "Boy, don't scoff at such an errand as a waste of your time. This girl's problems are not only her own but yours as well. The lives of thousands of people, Wanderers included, hang in the balance. Magic is not something to take lightly, especially magic as powerful as hers. Besides," and here the old woman smiled wryly, "think of this as your saving grace. This is your only opportunity to escape being the next leader, the thought of which you hate with such passion."

The Wise Woman eyed each of them in turn, those old, dark eyes gazing so deeply Foulan thought she could see into his soul. "I have spoken. Anyone else want to question my word?" They were silent. "Well then, you two should begin preparations. Your journey will be a long one, and you must leave at once. You are to seek out our sisters, the Halah clan. Their Wise Woman has had direct dealings with the Fae and may be able to help you."

"But… but how will we know where to find them?" Foulan asked. After all, the clans moved independently of one another, their only contact the Gathering that occurred every five years. And that was not set to happen until next spring.

The Wise Woman smiled. "That should be easy enough. They always winter at the same lake, called Calmloch. Mercia can give you a map to guide you. Two young people traveling light should be able to reach them in two months' time."

They each bowed before leaving the Wise Woman's caravan, then stood outside it for a few moments, absorbing what they had learned in silence. Finally, Mercia spoke up. "The Wise Woman's word overrides my own. Go and prepare to leave."

Mackenna spoke up. "But, they know my face now. Everywhere we go, there will be people trying to hunt me down." Foulan was surprised by the fear in her voice. He had not expected to hear it from such a headstrong, fiery-tempered girl.

"Perhaps there is something we can do about that," Foulan offered. "After all, they're looking for a *girl*, aren't they? We might not be able to do anything to change your face, but we can at least change your gender."

"Excellent thinking," Mercia said, catching on. "Come with me, Mackenna. We'll do something about that hair and those clothes while Foulan packs what you'll need for travel."

It didn't take long for Foulan to gather everything they needed. The lighter their load, the more quickly they could travel, and the faster he could be done with this fool's errand. He could simply leave the girl with the other clan, spend the winter in isolation, then rejoin his own clan in the spring. They usually worked in the fields in the western provinces of the Realm that time of year. Wanderers that they were, they traveled with the seasons, finding work in different towns depending on the season's needs, then moving on when that work was done. But over the years, they had established anchors in certain towns that they returned to each year. If nothing else, he would find them at the Gathering in late spring.

He went over the gear one last time, making sure he wasn't missing anything. Their supplies consisted of two bedrolls, a small tent that could snuggly fit two, his bow and arrows, a few hunting knives, a pot and spoon for cooking, food to last them three weeks if they rationed, and warm furs for when the weather started to turn cold.

It only seemed appropriate to take the two horses that Foulan had commandeered from the soldiers a couple of weeks ago. Such horses would stand out too much in the Wanderer camp, and they were built for strength and speed. After loading their gear on the horses, he went and found Myst, giving her a good scratch under the chin as he told her all that had transpired. Foulan had no clue if she understood his words, but she seemed to realize they were going on a journey, for soon she sat in the path facing back towards the main road, awaiting their departure. All that was left was to get the girl and a map.

He rapped on Mercia's caravan, entering when Aishah told him that Mackenna was decent. He lifted an eyebrow, examining the "boy" that stood before him. Mackenna's hair fanned out from the top of her head like feathers, not a single strand longer than his finger. She sported a pair of brown slacks that hugged her legs. Over top of a grey woolen shirt she wore a rough leather jerkin that had been dyed a dark green. Foulan realized it was one of his that he had outgrown years ago, though it hung a bit loose on the girl and ended at her thighs instead of at the hips like it was supposed to. A leather belt was wrapped around her waist, her rusty dagger hanging from it on one side and a belt pouch on the other. Someone had managed to find her a pair of old, knee-high leather boots and bracers that fit her, which would give her some level of protection if needed. From her shoulders hung a worn cloak. He couldn't tell the cloak's original color, it having turned a muddy brown with age and wear.

She definitely looked much less feminine and childish than she had before. It ought to at least work from a distance. Foulan smirked, crossing his arms over his chest as he looked her up and down. Mackenna blushed under his scrutiny. "Well, what do you think of my work? Does she look like a boy or not?" Aishah asked.

"You certainly outdid yourself this time, Aishah," he said. "Though it probably helps that she wasn't particularly feminine to begin with." Foulan almost laughed as Mackenna gasped, her hands flying up to her chest defensively.

"Now, now, don't complain. I have a friend in another clan who must bind his breasts. At least you'll be able to breathe comfortably," Aishah said. "I do wish I had black dye to change your hair, though. It would make it easier to claim you are brothers traveling together."

"Absolutely not!" Mackenna pouted. "You already made it too short. It's shorter than his!" She pointed at Foulan, whose hair hung past his shoulders.

"Yes, but dear, he looks more like a man than you," Aishah said. "You haven't any muscles on you and no facial hair. At least you're tall, though. Just try not to speak too much and hopefully you won't give yourself away."

Mercia ducked his head in. "Are you both ready?" They nodded.

Most of the clan, having traveled through the night, had turned inside to sleep once the camp was set up. Those who were awake gave Foulan and Mackenna hugs and wished them luck. Bahira, who had obviously taken a liking to the girl, seemed especially upset to see her leave, and warned Foulan to be nice to Mackenna. As they headed towards the horses, Foulan saw a familiar figure standing with the animals, her back to him.

She turned, hands on her hips, a stern expression on her face. Foulan lowered his head respectfully. "You're leaving then?" she asked.

"Yes, Mother—"

"You look at me when you talk to me, young man." Foulan looked up, meeting Nadya's gaze. Her hard features suddenly crumpled, and he saw tears in her eyes as she stepped forward, wrapping her arms around him and pulling him into a tight hug. "I always knew you would leave me someday," she said, her head pressed against his shoulder. Before Foulan could return the hug, Nadya stepped away, putting her hands on his shoulders and gazing up at him. Her face was once again calm and stoic. "Sons are meant to leave their mothers. They are meant to go off into the world. But you listen to me boy," she said, lifting a finger and wagging it at him. "This is your quest, nay, this is your life now, so you'd best do it right, you hear me? You take that girl to the center of the earth if you have to, and then you return to me safely."

"Yes, Mother," Foulan said, his lips pulling up into a smile at her words.

"Good." She stepped away from him, her arms dropping to her sides. "Now go."

He nodded, giving his mother a kiss on the forehead, and turned to find Mercia and Wise Woman Drynka waiting by the horses. "Are you sure it's a good idea to take them?" Mercia asked. "I know you are the one who captured them from the soldiers, but riding stolen horses when you are already on the run from the law…"

"We need to travel far and fast, which is what these horses were built for," Foulan explained. "Besides, the clan has already been put in enough risk. I would rather you didn't have any evidence of your association with a criminal."

Mercia nodded, unrolling a parchment and showing it to Foulan and Mackenna. Mercia tapped a spot on the map in the southern end of the Realms. "This is where we are now." His finger moved along a line—a major road—up and to the right, landing in an open mass of land. In the process, his hand traveling across a few borders between countries. "And this is where you're going."

"Why that route? Wouldn't this road be much faster?" Mackenna asked, indicating a more direct route.

"True," Mercia responded. "But that would take you through the country of Wachluana. They particularly hate Wanderers and will immediately turn you away. Also, their border security is extremely vigilant. They check everyone's rite of passage. If they were to recognize you from the bounty, they would arrest you on the spot."

"Rite of passage?" Mackenna asked.

"Do you have one?" Mercia asked. "It allows you to travel between the Realms of Etylania. Even the Wanderers have to have one, though it doesn't always stop them from turning us away."

She shook her head. "The furthest I've been from home is a few towns over to deliver medicine."

"Hmm. What did I tell you?" Drynka said, jabbing an elbow in his side. "I had a feeling I would need to dig these out." She opened a box she'd been holding, which housed the rites of passage of Wanderers in their clan who had died.

"We keep a few extra on hand," Mercia explained. "From Wanderers who've passed. By law, you're supposed to turn it in when the person dies, but well," he shrugged. "Wanderer deaths often go unreported. We hold onto the rites just in case."

"Yes, this one will do. It even sounds similar enough to your name that hopefully you won't forget it. You're to be Merik now, lad." Drynka handed a small carved stone that proclaimed a person's name and country of residence. Because the Wanderers had no country, their stones simply read "Foreigner," which was used to identify anyone from outside the Kingdoms of Etylania. Despite the fact that most of them had been born in Etylania and had never set foot in Srahinza, the Wanderers would be forever considered foreigners because they refused to swear allegiance to any one country in the Kingdoms.

Mercia turned once more to the map. "This route will take you through Ecrau. They're much looser with their borders, one of which is the Arlyn River. The river is a major trade and travel route, and with so many people traveling through, you can more easily be lost among the crowds there," Mercia explained. "After crossing the Fisk River at the city of Arlyn, you'll follow the Arlyn River northeast. That will lead you through the boglands to Calmloch."

"And when we get there? What then?" Mackenna asked.

Drynka grinned, her crooked yellow teeth showing. "When you do, seek out their Wise Woman. She has had dealings with the Fair Folk directly, and will be able to help you contact them. That is as far as I could See, and even if I knew more, I wouldn't be able to tell you. If you know too much of your future, you're likely to screw it up!" The woman cackled and rolled up the parchment, holding it out. Foulan reached for it, but Mackenna's hand beat him to it, taking the map. She ignored his glare. "Now, off you go!" the Wise Woman proclaimed.

Foulan mounted his horse and glanced back to see Mackenna eyeing the beast before her wearily. Mercia had to give her a boost after she awkwardly tried to pull herself up onto the horse and fell back off again. Once settled on the horse, she looked even more out of her element, seemingly unsure where to put her hands. He resisted the urge to roll his eyes and rode up beside her. "Here, you grab the reigns here," he took her hands, placing them on the ropes. "This is how you steer. Squeeze the horse's side to get it moving. Then pull back like this to get it to stop. Side to side to make it go in the direction you want. Got it?" Foulan asked.

The girl nodded slowly, though she didn't look certain. Why had he expected a girl who'd never been more than a day's walk from her village had ever ridden a horse? He was going to have to teach her, but there would be plenty of time for that while they travelled. With one last farewell to his clan, they left the camp, Myst trotting beside them with her tail wagging.

Mackenna

Mackenna had never known such pain. Even as a child when she had fallen out of a tree and broken her arm and father had to set it. Even when she was on her moonblood and the cramps were so harsh that the only relief was drinking an herbal tea before curling up in bed until it was over. Even then, she had never had this kind of bone-deep ache before.

It was the damn horse's fault. Dawn was what Foulan had named it. Foulan's horse, Dusk, seemed to be much better behaved for his master than Dawn was for her. The damned mare stopped to eat whenever it wanted and refused to budge no matter how much Mackenna squeezed her sides. Only when Foulan pulled her reins or Myst nipped at her heels did she start moving again.

Then she was ill-tempered at best. She would start to trot on long, open stretches of field without warning, Mackenna holding on for dear life. Or, as they made their way through the woods, she would buck forward at the slightest provocation, nearly throwing Mackenna off. And she seemed to shy away even from her own shadow.

To say the least, after a week of long, hard riding, Mackenna was sore. Everything from the waist down ached. Her legs were chafed. The accumulation of sweat and dirt between her thighs disgusted her to no end. Foulan kept up a grueling pace, but every time they stopped to rest, she could hardly walk around normally, and she feared her legs had become permanently bowed.

Mackenna was tired of riding hard day in and out. She was sick of waking up at dawn's light and making a fire so they could have breakfast, all before the sun had had a chance to warm the cool morning air. She hated sleeping on the hard earth with just her bedroll to protect her from the air and any little critters that crawled around on the ground. She was especially fed up with going to the bathroom in the woods, but at least with her vast knowledge of plants, she knew which ones to use to clean up, so she didn't have to broach *that* particular embarrassing topic with Foulan. Mackenna longed for her home, with its warm straw bed, outhouse, fireplace, and bathtub.

But most of all, Mackenna missed her father. She tried not to think of him because every time she did, she felt tears welling up and had to squeeze her eyes shut to press them back. But no matter how hard she tried not to, hours of riding behind Foulan in silence left her with nothing to do but think, and her thoughts always drifted back to her father. His smile, his warm laugh, his caring nature, his craving for knowledge. Whenever the memories of him crept up, she would push them away with any little distraction she could. She would recite the names and properties of every tree, grass, and flower she passed, to make sure she wasn't forgetting anything he had taught her.

Mackenna dared not complain to Foulan. The few times she had, he had made some snide comment or rolled his eyes. Her ego refused to let him see the pain she was in. In the morning she woke with the sun as he did, during the day they rode, and at night she helped him with camp and dinner. They spoke very little. Only Myst seemed comfortable around them both, often moving from one side of the campfire to the other during the evening to keep them both company.

"We'll stop here for the night," Foulan said presently, halting them and dismounting. The small clearing in the woods looked the same as every other one they'd slept in for the past week. In the distance was the sound of water trickling over rocks. Mackenna preferred the flat land and soft grass of fields to sleep in, but Foulan insisted the woods offered better protection from both the elements and possible predators. She wasn't sure if he meant the human or animal variety, and she hadn't asked.

Mackenna dismounted slowly, hiding her wince from Foulan. She didn't need to bother, though, as he was already headed off into the woods to collect firewood. "I'll just get us some water," she called after him, watching him raise a hand to show he'd heard. Myst glanced between the two of them, clearly wondering whether to stay with her master or Mackenna. "Well, go on then," Mackenna told the wolf. "Help him catch a pheasant for dinner." Myst's ears perked up, and she bound after her master.

With a sigh, Mackenna gathered their waterskins and cooking pot, heading towards the creek. It was larger than she had expected, with a fairly deep pool in the middle. It was only early fall, the leaves just beginning to turn, so the weather was still warm enough to swim. She could actually bathe! And even wash her clothes! Sure, all they had was a rough bar of lye soap, but this was still better than nothing.

Mackenna quickly stripped off her clothes and waded into the water, which was blissfully cool on her hot skin. While she had to admit that trousers were much more freeing than the long skirts she was used to, all of that leather right against her skin was uncomfortably hot, even more so with a wool tunic over it all. After washing her clothes and filling up the waterskins, she went for a swim, quickly forgetting the time. It wasn't until she heard Myst's bark that she realized it had grown late, the sun on the horizon.

"Well, what do you want?" Mackenna called to the canine, which stood at the edge of the river, whining and jumping from paw to paw. "C'mon, then. Get in here if you want!" The wolf gave a happy bark before jumping in, splashing Mackenna as she swam laps around her. "You were sent to retrieve me then, I guess? Foulan couldn't be bothered to do it himself, I see."

By the time she had dressed and returned to camp, Foulan had already tended to the horses, lit the fire, and started dinner. Mackenna felt in a fine enough mood to grace him with a smile, taking him by surprise. The look on his face changed, though, as soon as Myst shook off right next to him. "Ahh, gross! Myst, you're all wet! What did you do to my wolf, Spitfire?"

"We just went for a swim… wait, what did you call me?" Mackenna asked.

Foulan stilled, looking sheepish. "Oh, uh, Spitfire. 'Cause that's what you do, right? Spit fire?"

"I don't spit it, thank you. I'm not a dragon." Mackenna combed through her wet hair with her fingers. At least it was much easier to do now that it was short. "Can't you just call me Mackenna?"

"Yeah, but I like Spitfire better." Seeing her irritated face, he grinned. "It could be worse. I could call you Ginger like some of the other Wanderers had taken to."

She grimaced. "Ah, no. The other one's fine." Mackenna spread out her bedroll on the ground, sitting in her usual spot across the fire from Foulan, who handed her a bowl of stew. She ate it silently, staring into the flames.

"I know this pace is hard on you. You're probably not used to traveling long distances." Mackenna lifted an eyebrow, surprised at his sudden words. "But it's necessary. We've a two-month journey, and autumn has already begun. And we're moving north, which means the climate will grow cooler as we go. This is not an area I've been to before, and I don't know how early the snows start there."

She shrugged. "I'm fine. You don't have to slow down on my account."

He didn't have to admit that he was moving slowly just for her. She already knew it. More than once he had ridden ahead, tired of her pace and constant need for breaks, only to have to stop and wait for her to catch up.

"Yes, well… I just wanted to tell you that you're doing fine, Mackenna," he said.

She stared at him suspiciously, wondering why he was now suddenly acting so nicely. "Okay, what do you want?" Mackenna asked, setting down her now empty bowl.

"Whatever do you mean?" Foulan said, the look on his face too innocent.

"Why are you being so nice? You must want something."

His eyebrows knitted. "I'm sorry? Aren't I always nice?"

She glared at him, her hands on her hips. "No, you aren't. Ever since you rescued me from those soldiers, you've been nothing but rude. While I was traveling with the caravan, all you wanted was to be rid of me. Don't object; you know I heard your conversation with Mercia that first night. And this past week, all you've done is give me disgusted looks because I can't keep up with you. Don't think you can start flattering me now just because you want something."

A guilty look crossed his face at Mackenna's accusations, but by the time she was done it had turned to irritation. Foulan stood, arms crossed over his chest, glaring down at her, likely trying to intimidate her with his height. Well, she wouldn't be intimidated by him. She got to her feet, standing her ground. "Ever since you showed up you've been nothing but trouble," he grumbled. "I rescued you, and you only put my clan in danger. And now I have to give up everything to travel with you on some gods-forsaken adventure I never wanted just because you can't control your temper?!"

Couldn't control her temper indeed! She was having trouble keeping it down just then. All she wanted was to leap over the campfire and strangle him. "You are so arrogant, so self-absorbed!" she shouted. "You ignore everyone but your dog—" Myst flattened her ears with a whine, "—because everyone else is below you! You never even talk to anyone unless it's to make some snide remark! I can't stand you!"

He stepped forward, grabbing her wrist in his hand. "Listen, Spitfire, you don't have to like me, but you are my responsibility now, so we could at least try getting along. I just thought maybe with a little bit of encouragement you could pick up the pace some… And she's a wolf, not a dog."

She glared at him, her anger reaching a boiling point. How dare he?! How dare he touch her, and how dare he treat her like she was just cargo to be transported from one end of the map to the other! She was not weak! She was not a child to be coddled!

She may not be as muscular as him or skilled with a bow and arrow, but she was just as strong, if not stronger!

Before she could stop it, she felt her hair suddenly alight. Foulan jumped back in shock, pulling his hand towards himself. Mackenna clenched her fists, wanting to hit him, but knowing it would just burn his obnoxious pretty face. As angry as she was, it was nothing like when her father had been killed. She still had control over herself. And she had gotten what she'd wanted. The fear in his eyes was evident. He would think twice about underestimating her. Mackenna turned, walking away from him to find a place to cool off.

Cold water suddenly splashed the top of her head. She paused in shock, turning her head slowly. He stood behind her holding his now empty waterskin.

"Wow," he breathed. "You… your hair was *on fire*. I mean, I knew fire happened around you, but I didn't realize that you would actually catch fire."

She took a deep breath and spoke slowly in an attempt to reign in her temper. "I'm only going to tell you this once. That little bit of water won't save you if I actually lose control, so I wouldn't suggest pushing me in the future."

Mackenna spun on her heel to stalk away, but his words stopped her. "Yeah, I realize that now. Maybe I shouldn't have pushed you so far. I just kinda wanted to see for myself."

"What?" she hissed.

"I wanted to see what happens," he said. "When you go all… dragony. Didn't think it would be quite so scary though. You had me afraid for my life for a second." While he tried to sound nonchalant, she didn't miss the slight tremor in his voice. His fear had been real.

"You… you did that… just because you were curious?" she bit out.

"Well, yeah. I mean, I wanted to know what to expect." He actually grinned, the cocky bastard.

"You… you idiot!" she shouted. "I could have killed you! I could have burned you to a crisp and this whole forest with you! Did you even think of the consequences?! A skin of water?! That was your plan to stop me?!"

"Hey, now, don't go catching fire again," he held his hands up, laughing nervously. "I was just curious. It was… a jest, y'know?"

"It wasn't funny." She stomped past him to her bedroll, slumping to the ground and putting her head in her hands. "Even a small fire like that isn't without consequence. It leaves me feeling drained and achy. Not to mention that this is the only outfit I have."

"So?" Foulan asked.

"So, if I couldn't get control of the fire in time, my clothes would ignite and be quickly destroyed. I'm immune to fire, but my clothes aren't. I would have been walking around starkers for the rest of this trip."

Did she imagine it, or was that a blush on his cheeks? "Ahh, yes, well, we wouldn't want that." He grinned sheepishly. He seemed to decide that it was safe to sit down again, with the campfire between them, of course. "After all, you're so pale your bare arse would likely blind me." She gasped, shocked at his language, and grabbed her empty dinner bowl, throwing it at him. He managed to dodge just in time. "Not gonna light up again, Spitfire? Even at that?" he asked in amusement.

"You must have a serious death wish, Rover."

"Hey, what happened to Foulan?" he asked.

"If you insist on calling me that ridiculous nickname, then I'll do likewise," Mackenna huffed.

She laid down on her bedroll, her back to him and the fire, content to stew in her irritation.

The next morning was awkward as they tried to cook breakfast and prepare the horses without speaking to one another. They danced around each other, their conversation consisting of glares, grunts, and huffs as they avoided eye contact. Once on the road, it was easier to ignore each other as her horse fell behind his. Staring at his back, she let her annoyance with him warm her against the morning's chill.

After they had ridden for a few hours, he stopped and got off his horse. "I'm going into the woods for a bit," he announced without looking at her. It was the code they had adopted to indicate that they needed to relieve themselves, as they were both too embarrassed to admit such a thing out loud. She got off her horse and went into the woods on the opposite side the road to do the same.

When she emerged, she saw him sitting on a log nearby. "Are we ready to go then?" she asked. When he didn't answer, she glanced over at his face, surprised by the look on it. He was staring down at his hands, at the blisters now nearly healed. Did he seem almost… sad? After a few moments of silence, he finally spoke.

"I, um… I'm sorry. About last night. I shouldn't have riled you up like that just to satisfy my curiosity." He didn't look up from his hands as he spoke. "You *have* been nothing but trouble, but… it's not all bad. This journey has saved me from a fate I didn't want. I'm not cut out to be clan ruler."

He sighed, running a hand through his long hair, and stared off into the distance. "The truth is, I'm not good with people, as you may have noticed. I don't have the same sense that Mercia does. I don't know how to console people, how to calm them, how to solve problems. I don't even know how to talk to people. I've never been good at it. I just can't seem to find the right words to say. But since we're stuck together… ahh, that's not what I meant. I mean to say, since we're traveling together… perhaps it would be easier…" He sighed again in frustration and stopped talking, seeming to give up.

Mackenna was annoyed at the twinge of pity in her gut. Why should she feel sorry for him just because he didn't want to be a leader? That was none of her business. But it seemed like it ran deeper than that. Did he even have any friends besides Myst? Mackenna glanced over at the wolf, who sat in the road panting, gazing back at them in confusion.

And she didn't want to admit it, but she also felt a bit guilty. She could practically hear her father's voice chiding her; her passive aggressive attitude was unproductive. As he'd said, they were stuck together, so they needed to learn to work together. Mackenna took a deep breath, releasing her anger with her exhale, her body suddenly feeling lighter. She sank onto the log beside him. "I think I understand. I'm sorry too. Truce?" she asked, holding out her hand.

He shook her hand cautiously, and she used the opportunity to examine the healing blisters. "Oh yeah, I guess I have you to blame for the burns on my hands, huh?" Foulan asked.

"Well, it serves you right. Maybe from now on you'll be more careful when you're playing with fire." He let out a small chuckle. "They're healing well though."

"Hurt like the Serpent's bite those first few days," he said.

"Oh, don't be ridiculous," she said. "You can't even see the Serpent yet. Not until early winter." They both glanced toward the southern horizon, where the Serpent constellation would soon appear at night to slither its way across the sky while the earth lay frozen and desolate beneath it.

Mackenna sighed, figuring she would use this moment to dump the dirt and pebbles out of her boots. "You've holes in your socks," he said, surprising her. She hadn't realized he'd been watching.

Mackenna shrugged. "I don't have any needle or thread."

Foulan got up and rummaged around in one of his saddlebags. Returning to her side, he cut a piece of thread and threaded it through a needle, holding it out to her. She didn't even bother to take off her sock as she closed up the hole. The stitches were ugly and wide, but they would do for now. Mackenna hissed as the needle poked her, drawing blood.

"Here, let me," Foulan said with a snort. Without waiting for a response, he knelt down in front of her, placing her foot on his thigh. He undid the stitches she had made and started to resew them. Why was he touching her? He could have just asked her to take off the sock. The feeling of his fingers brushing her ankle was uncomfortably distracting. "There, all finished," he said, releasing her foot and standing to return the items to his bag. So quickly? She looked down at his stitches. They were neat and small and perfect.

"I've never had the patience for such things. It was always father who did the mending at home. Where'd you learn to do that, anyway?" Mackenna asked.

"Lots of practice," he answered. "Mercia taught me how to use his tanning rack and how to sew. I make all of my clothes, actually. Well, I had help with the cloak. I can't spin wool."

"You sewed all of this?" She looked his outfit over once more, appraising it.

"Is it so surprising that I might have some skills besides hunting?" he asked.

"It just seems so… domestic. You're very good," she complimented.

He shrugged. "The bright colors and silks that my people wear aren't suitable for blending in with the forest. I learned out of necessity. I was too embarrassed to ask the women in the clan to help me."

"Why?"

"Well, for one, I'd have to strip so they could take my measurements, which is awkward enough." Mackenna's cheeks flushed. She'd never actually had clothing made for her personally; growing up, her clothes had been purchased from other villagers' children who'd outgrown them. "And two, I don't care to ask for favors. It makes me… uncomfortable. Owing someone. Anyway, we should get back on the road."

Kazumi

Kazumi glanced in a window, checking their disguise in the reflection. The guard they'd knocked out and stolen the armor from had been much stockier than them, although shorter. The clothes didn't fit quite right, but nobody would notice the man had grown a few inches taller, and the bulkiness of the uniform hid their slender frame. The most important part was making sure the face looked right. They'd gotten through the courtyard and most of the halls without anyone noticing anything off about their comrade, but now they had to walk past a guard to get to the general's office, and the man would have to look right at them.

Satisfied that the disguise held, Kazumi rounded the corner, approaching the guard. The man glanced up in boredom, nodding. "About time you got here to relieve me. Nobody's seen you all afternoon. Thought you were in town again visiting the whores and forgot the time."

Kazumi just gave a noncommittal grunt. If they spoke, the other guard would no doubt recognize that his comrade's voice had suddenly changed and adopted an Isumijian accent.

"Anyway, general's at the mess hall getting dinner. Should be back within the hour. You need anything?" the guardsman asked.

Kazumi shook their head.

"Not very talkative tonight, eh?"

They simply shrugged noncommittally. The other man frowned but obviously didn't care enough to push it. No doubt tired from guarding the general's office for the past six hours, he left without another word.

Waiting until his footsteps had receded down the hall, Kazumi let out the breath they'd been holding. That was always the hardest part of the job, but they refused to just let all those years of training go to waste. They may be doing solo jobs now in a faraway land, but they would at least do their damned best at them.

Kazumi opened the door slowly, peeking into the room. The small office was empty, just as the guard had said. Kazumi slipped inside, closing the door behind them. The room was spartan. A large desk took up most of the space, the paperwork on it neatly stacked. A shelf in the corner held rolls of parchment, messages from other keeps, no doubt. Against the other wall was a small cot, the bed perfectly made. Surprising, considering the army didn't employ maids at the keep. Instead, the greenest soldiers were given the tasks of cooking and cleaning. The only other piece of furniture was a table with a basin for water and a shaving kit, a small mirror hanging above it.

It was clean and tidy. Kazumi immediately warmed to the general. They appreciated anyone who shared their sense of cleanliness. Going to the desk, Kazumi rummaged through the papers, then began opening the drawers.

Ahh, there it was. The general's logbook. They opened it to the bookmarked page, flipping backwards to the previous week.

Soldiers Marcus Kosa and Theodore Erickson and Commander Dunstan Riley were dispatched from Soledad Keep to the village of

Avdimia to apprehend a man suspected of witchcraft and bring him in for questioning. Only Kosa returned to post and was badly injured, much of his body covered in burns. He remained unconscious for a full day. Upon regaining consciousness, he was questioned regarding the status of his comrades.

Kosa explained that when the soldiers attempted to apprehend the suspected witch, the man resisted arrest. In the scuffle, soldier Erickson accidentally killed the man.

The man's daughter, who was also present and interfering in the arrest, then apparently caught on fire. According to Kosa's claim, she had gone insane with rage, killing both Erickson and Riley. Kosa managed to escape, but not without being badly burned.

It would seem that witchcraft runs in this family. We were not aware of another family member with magical abilities. More soldiers have been sent to scour the countryside to find her.

Kazumi flipped forward to see if there were any more recent reports regarding this witch. There was one from a few days later.

Soldiers Demetrius Darnell and Gideon Fletcher were among those sent to look for this witch. They investigated the village first, questioning the villagers about the girl and learning her name: Mackenna. It would seem the girl's ability to wield fire is not a secret in the village, nor were any of the villagers particularly saddened to learn that she had run away. Many of them spoke of their distrust of her, which was only tempered by their need for her father's knowledge of healing herbs and remedies.

The team then split up, taking different roads from the village. Darnell and Fletcher apparently encountered the witch a half day's ride away. She attempted to escape into the woods, and they gave chase, following her for quite some time. When they believed they had cornered her, the men reported that she summoned a wolf seemingly from thin air. The wild beast attacked them, injuring Fletcher.

When Darnell attempted to strike down the wolf, he was shot by an arrow. Neither soldier knows from where the arrow came, and they have indicated their belief that the witch called upon the Fae, which some locals still seemingly believe in, to defend her. They also claim that a voice, which seemed to come from the trees, commanded them to leave their weapons and horses if they wished to survive.

The soldiers returned two days later on horses commandeered from a nearby village. They have been summarily punished for their failure, the cost of their stolen weapons and horses have been taken from their pay, and they have been assigned to a month of latrine duty. The identity of the archer remains unknown. The witch Mackenna is still at large, and a bounty has been placed on her head and issued to the nearby cities.

It was that same bounty that had caught Kazumi's attention and convinced them to break into the keep to gather more intel. The price on it was especially intriguing. Four hundred duques for a single girl? That kind of money would take a tradesman a year to make. Why so much for one girl?

Kazumi heard the sound of approaching footsteps. Fuck. They were three stories up, so there was no escaping out the window. They rushed to the mirror on the wall, glancing at it, taking deep breaths in an attempt to remain calm.

They failed. The face of the soldier whose identity they'd stolen was melting away. The bulbous nose and double chin shrank. The cheeks became sharp. The skin paled. The eyes slanted. Lips became soft and pouty, brows thin. The short head of hair grew longer, reaching midway down the back, and turned black and perfectly straight.

Kazumi stared at their familiar reflection, cursing mentally. Once they'd lost their concentration, the magic always fell apart. It was the reason they'd failed to find proper employment in the Isumijia Dynasty and had fled to the Realms of Etylania in frustration and embarrassment, becoming a self-employed bounty hunter and general mercenary for hire.

Well, there was nothing for it. Kazumi would be caught momentarily, so they needed to make the best of it. They slid into the general's chair, kicking their feet up on the desk and linking their hands behind their head in feigned nonchalance.

The door opened and in stepped a man whose crisp uniform, perfect posture, deep scowl, and air of authority left no doubt in Kazumi's mind that this was the general of the keep. The man's eyes widened upon seeing Kazumi in his chair, and he drew his sword without hesitation. "Who are you and how did you get in here? Where is the soldier who should be guarding the door?"

"Now, now, general, I mean you no harm," Kazumi said, lifting their hands placatingly. "I go by Kazu, and I am a mercenary for hire. I've come to ask you a few questions about the bounty on the witch Mackenna." They retrieved said bounty from their pocket, unfurling it with a flourish. "Wanted for witchcraft and murder. And that price. I simply had to know more."

"And you didn't think to just send a letter? Or present yourself to my guards to ask for an audience?" The man ground out.

Kazumi shrugged. "Let's just say I like to do things a little bit... different."

"I will ask you again, where is my guard?"

"Easy. He's fine. Just sleeping off a hangover and a bit of a sore head at the whorehouse," Kazumi replied.

"You have one minute to convince me not to throw you in the dungeon," the general warned.

"Certainly. Judging from the price on the girl's head and what you've written in your logbook," the general's scowl deepened even further, if possible, "it's clear that you need a professional. You're already operating with a skeleton crew here in the keep. No doubt most of your soldiers are on the frontlines fighting against the Srahinza Empire, yes?"

"Forty-five seconds."

"Your monetary resources must be tight at the moment. So why offer such a high price? Certainly not just to see justice done. Which got me thinking. Why has the military of Etylania suddenly revived the order of witch hunters? Why direct valuable resources to such an effort when you are at war with Srahinza? Unless it is specifically because of the war with Srahinza."

The general's eyes narrowed in contemplation. Kazumi had his attention now. "While no official announcement to the effect has been made, rumor has it that the witch hunts from centuries ago have begun again. But they are different this time. The witch hunters come and take the supposed witches away. Those found to be falsely suspected of magic are returned home. The others, however, disappear. People fear the worst, but I wonder, why no public trials and executions? No burnings at the stake that the witch hunters of old were famous for? Is it because they aren't being killed at all? Then why are they being taken? And then I realized. They are being conscripted—no doubt against their will. Because Etylania is losing the war."

The general lowered his sword, sheathing it smoothly. "Very perceptive. What was your name again?"

"Kazu."

They noticed the general eyeing them up and down, clearly uncertain about something. "Forgive me asking, but is that mister or misses?" Forward and to the point. Kazumi had to give him credit for that. Their appearance was completely androgynous. Some assumed them to be female due to the pretty face and long hair. Others assumed male from their height and alto voice. Rarely did anyone actually bother to ask.

"Just Kazu is fine," they answered, wondering how the general would respond.

The man seemed unphased. "I am General Dagrun Olwenyo, though I can only assume you already knew my name. Your revelation is, unfortunately, correct. We are losing to Srahinza. Unlike the Realms of Etylania, Srahinza has always embraced magic. We simply cannot beat the power of their wizards."

Kazumi dropped their feet from the table and leaned forward, their elbows on the desk, their hands steepled. "Why not simply tell the people that and ask for any magic users to volunteer?"

"And cause mass panic? Right now, the countries of Etylania are united. How long will that last once they learn that Srahinza will likely defeat our forces within the next year?" Dagrun asked.

"Perhaps it would unite them even more?" Kazumi said with a shrug.

"Not likely. People are naturally cowardly. Once they learned the truth, the northern countries would withdraw their support from the southern countries. They would instead amass their resources in an attempt to protect themselves once the southern kingdoms were invaded, which would cause us to fall even sooner.

"Besides, with Etylania's history of witch hunts, how many people do you think would willingly step forward and admit to having magical ability? It would only drive them into hiding."

"Yes, but you may not end up with dead witches and soldiers every time," Kazumi retorted.

"This is the first time such a thing has happened. Some have resisted, certainly, but ultimately they were apprehended. But the truth is, this is the first time we have come across a witch with such power. The fact that we did not even know of her existence prior to the encounter with her father goes to show just how poorly a job our witch hunters are doing at singling them out."

"And now she's escaped a second time, and you've placed a bounty in the hopes that someone will bring her in. Well then, you're just in luck, because that someone happens to be me."

The general still seemed uncertain. "Why go to all this trouble? Just for the money?"

Kazumi grinned. "The money got my attention. But you are right to assume that I want more than that."

Dagrun narrowed his eyes. "And what would that be, exactly?"

"Let's just say... I would like to be recognized for the contribution I have made to the war efforts by bringing this witch to you. I want more than to just be paid."

"And how do you want to be recognized?" the general asked.

"A position. I no longer wish to be a lone mercenary. I want to be employed by someone powerful. With status."

"In other words, you want to be hired as a personal spy and assassin for a noble?" the general surmised.

"My, you are blunt. I prefer the term 'professional espionage'. As a general for the military of the Realms of Etylania, there is no doubt that you have connections to very powerful people. What I am asking is not particularly difficult. Simply put in a good word for me with a few royals here and there, and I'll do the rest on my own."

"Hmm," the commander snorted but said nothing more on that topic. "And how exactly do you propose to subdue her and bring her back when my own soldiers have failed?" he asked. "Last I heard of her, she'd been spotted in the city of Hartland, where a gang had unsuccessfully attempted to capture her. She's a slippery one, apparently."

"Excellent. Then I know where to begin my search. As for the how, you just leave that up to me."

"We need her alive," Dagrun reminded them. "And preferably unharmed."

"General, I am a professional. I always fulfil a contract as requested." Kazumi stood from the chair, moving around the desk. The general did not flinch away, but he did keep his hand near his sword. "Now, I would appreciate it if you didn't send out any more bounty notices. I don't really like competition."

"That won't be happening. I have no guarantee of your ability besides your bluster and that you managed to sneak into my office. That money will go to whoever brings her to me first."

Kazumi shrugged. "So be it. But I won't hesitate to kill any other bounty hunters who get in my way."

"As long as the job gets done, that is all that matters to me," the general replied.

Kazumi smiled. "Ruthless. I like it. I look forward to doing business with you again in the future, general." With that, they departed the keep. Their first stop would be Hartland.

Mackenna

Mackenna grunted as she fell from the horse's back once more, noticing that the sound had startled Foulan awake. He sat up with his knife already drawn, ready for a fight. When he saw that it was simply Mackenna struggling with her mare, he relaxed back onto the bed roll, sheathing his dagger.

"Damned worthless horse! You are way more stubborn than any mule I've ever met. Why won't you behave?!" Mackenna glared up at Dawn.

"Morning. Lover's spat?" Foulan yawned. He sat up slowly and stretched, then glanced at the sky, where the rising sun was turning it a light blue in the distance. "I'm surprised you're up this early. Planning on running off without me?"

"No," Mackenna muttered as she stood, brushing the dirt off her bum. "I thought I would wake before you and try to talk some sense into this mindless beast. I know I'm slowing us down, but it's the damned horse's fault!" She pointed at it with a glare. The mare blew at her and rolled its eyes.

"Perhaps she just doesn't like taking orders from irate redheads?" Foulan rolled himself out of bed, pulling on his boots. Mackenna blushed and looked away while he tugged his shirt and hauberk on. While he always wore his pants to bed—he claimed it was so that he could be prepared for an attack in the night—he slept shirtless. "You just need to establish a connection with her. Thankfully, that's easy to do, seeing as she's ruled by her stomach." He grabbed an apple out of their supplies, handing it to Mackenna. "Now feed this to her. With an open hand, mind you. You don't want her to mistake one of your fingers for a bit of food."

Mackenna frowned but took the apple, holding it out tentatively to Dawn. The horse sniffed at it cautiously before eating it whole. "Now, give her a good pat on the neck," Foulan advised. Mackenna did so. Dawn's ears flattened briefly, but other than that she showed no signs of ill will.

"So, that's it? She'll behave now?" Mackenna asked skeptically.

"If you keep rewarding her, sure." Foulan shrugged. "Horses don't take kindly to yelling and stomping. You have to learn to be gentle but firm. When you get worked up, she recognizes that *she's* controlling *you*. They're actually very intelligent creatures."

"But she never listens to my commands," Mackenna complained. "Disobedient is what she is."

"Nah. She's just free-spirited. Like her mistress." Mackenna blushed at Foulan's comment.

"I can't tell if that's a compliment or not," she replied.

Foulan laughed, though it sounded uncomfortable. After a moment of awkward silence, he changed the subject. "Well, let's eat and get moving."

It was midday when their small path widened and split off, soon followed by the appearance of farms and homesteads. The weather was warm and sunny, and both the horses and Myst seemed eager to stretch their legs. "Care to pick up the pace?" Foulan suddenly asked Mackenna.

"You're kidding, right?" she answered. "I can barely stay on this beast as it is."

"You have to learn sometime. We'll start out slow, with a trot. Just give her a light squeeze around the midsection like this." He demonstrated, clicking his tongue at the same time. Dusk perked up his ears and began to walk faster, then to trot. Before Mackenna could even issue the command, Dawn was following suit.

Mackenna hadn't thought riding a horse could be any more uncomfortable. But now she found the steady swaying that she had grown accustomed to had become an unsteady jostling. The saddle slapped her backside and made her teeth clack together. Within moments she and Dawn were passing him up. "Let go of the pommel," came Foulan's voice from behind her. "You need to hold onto her reins. That's the only way you'll have any control over her."

"If I let go of the saddle, I'll fall off!" Mackenna objected.

"You have to learn to trust your body," he called. "And to trust her. Take the reins in both hands. Pull back gently if she starts to go too fast. But don't pull back too hard, or she may buck."

Mackenna did as he commanded, easing the mare back to a trot so that Dusk could catch up.

"Good. That's not so bad now, is it?" Foulan asked.

"Except that my arse will be black and blue by the end of tonight," Mackenna grumbled back.

Foulan laughed. "That's because you're sitting wrong. When we're just walking, it's fine to keep your seat on the horse.

But when we get up to a gallop, you actually want to stand up in the saddle, like so." He straightened his own legs in demonstration, so that his rear hovered over the horse's back. "That way, you'll lean forward in the saddle, which will give you more control, and you'll still be able to walk tomorrow."

Mackenna nodded. They continued at a brisk canter for a few minutes, before Foulan turned to her with a wicked grin. They had emerged from the canopy of trees to a field full of wheat, likely belonging to the farmhouse they could see off in the distance. Not too far away, the woods started once more, but the open stretch seemed to make the horses antsy. "I'll race you to the end of this field," Foulan challenged.

"No," she said. "No way. I'm still just learning how to—" Before Mackenna could finish protesting, Foulan had squeezed his horse's flanks, taking off at a gallop. Mackenna barely had time to adjust her seat in the saddle the way he'd showed her before Dawn followed suit, and Myst ran ahead of them both, barking in excitement.

There was no controlling the beast beneath Mackenna. Dawn's gallop soon became a sprint, and it was all Mackenna could do to hold on for dear life. Soon she found herself side by side with Foulan, and he laughed in surprise as Dawn overtook Dusk. Within minutes they were back under the cool canopy of the trees, and Foulan caught up to Mackenna, grabbing at her reins and slowing both of their horses to a trot.

"That was pretty impressive," he said with a chuckle.

"I hate you," Mackenna hissed between gasping breaths. She was winded, as if she had just been the one running that distance.

A hand went to his heart dramatically, and he gasped as if in pain. "You hurt me, Spitfire. Truly."

She glared at his backside as he took the lead once more, imagining ways to get back at him.

Not two days later, Mackenna had to put her new riding skills to the test. They were riding through a patch of forest when a scream pierced the air. Foulan and Mackenna both froze, listening to the woods ahead of them. The scream was followed by shouting. Before Mackenna could speak, Foulan held a finger to his lips, indicating that they should be silent. His bow was already drawn, an arrow notched. Mackenna nodded grimly as he led the way, slowing the horses so that they would not make as much noise. The voices grew louder as they reached a bend in the road, and soon they caught sight of the commotion.

A wagon was stopped in the middle of the road, its contents spilled across the ground. There was a man lying beside the wagon with a bruised and bleeding face, and a woman and her three children—an older daughter in her young teens, a little girl of perhaps five, and a toddler—all huddled on the ground together crying. A man towered over them with an axe while another rummaged through their cart, pulling out any valuables and tossing them into his saddlebag. Both men wore long leather coats, hats pulled low, and scarves across their faces.

"Highwaymen," Foulan whispered.

"What should we do?" Mackenna asked. Beside her, Myst was silent, though her hackles were raised and teeth bared, ready to attack at Foulan's command.

"If we attack them, they may hurt those people," Foulan replied. "It may be best to simply let them take what they want and go on their way."

"But that's robbery! It's wrong!" At his warning glare, Mackenna lowered her voice. "Can't we do something?"

"Is it worth risking their lives and ours?" Foulan asked.

She opened her mouth to retort but was cut off by another scream. The man who'd been holding the woman and her children at axepoint was now grabbing the woman, lifting her to her feet. He pulled the toddler away from her and threw it to the ground. There was a ripping sound as he tore her dress from her shoulders. The elder daughter launched herself at the man, beating him with her fists, while her little sister picked up the toddler and ran towards the woods. "James, you take that one. We'll switch when we're done," the man said with a laugh to his friend, who yanked the teenage girl off his comrade. She screamed and bit him.

"Foulan, they're going to rape those women! We have to stop them!" Mackenna hissed.

"Okay, here's the plan—" This was not the time for plans but for action. Before he could finish speaking, she'd grabbed her horse's reins and was urging Dawn forward at a gallop, screaming a war cry as she closed in on the first man. The man pushed his captive away and raised his sword at Dawn, slicing towards her flank and causing the horse to rear up. Dawn kicked him in the face, sending him flying back into the ground. Mackenna imagined it must have looked very majestic right up until she was thrown off of the horse, landing beside the mother in the dirt.

The other highwayman, James, quickly assessed the situation, tossing aside the younger girl and launching himself towards Mackenna. Mackenna looked around for Foulan in a panic, finding him racing towards them on horseback with his bow drawn, Myst running beside him. In one smooth motion he pulled back and fired, his arrow hitting the highwayman in the chest.

Mackenna's brief distraction resulted in her being taken by surprise by the first highwayman. He jumped on her, his face a bloody mess from Dawn's kick. They tangled on the ground together, and she fumbled for her dagger. The highwayman knocked it out of her hand before punching her in the stomach. The force of it took her breath from her, leaving her gasping and defenseless. Suddenly, his grubby hands were around her throat, squeezing what little air remained out of her.

Then she felt an impact, and his weight was suddenly lifted from her. She sat up to see Myst biting down on the man's wrist, digging her teeth in until blood gushed and the bones snapped. Mackenna crawled on all fours to where her dagger lay in the dirt, snatching it up. Foulan dismounted, standing before the man with his arrow trained between the stranger's eyes.

"Mackenna, you okay?" Foulan asked, forgetting her pseudonym in the chaos.

"Yeah," she wheezed in reply, struggling to get her breath back. She looked around for the other robber. He lay unmoving on the ground. She watched to see if his chest rose with his breathing. It did not.

The woman ran to her children, checking to make sure they were safe, before collapsing at her husband's side. "Oh, my Henry!" she sobbed. "Please be alive!"

Mackenna took a moment to mentally assess herself and determine that the worst she had was a few bruises. Then, she pushed herself off of the ground and made her way toward the family. She knelt and felt at the father's neck for a pulse, sighing in relief to find it steady. "He's still alive," she said. "He just appears to be unconscious."

"Oh, thank the gods!" the woman cried, kissing the man's face.

"Now, what do we do about him?" Mackenna asked Foulan, glancing at the highwayman who still lived. Myst had released his arm and stepped back by her master's side, and the man lay on the ground moaning in pain.

"Madam, would you happen to have some rope we could use?" Foulan asked.

The woman nodded. "There should be a tether for our mule somewhere in the mess." The teenaged daughter rummaged around in the spilled goods, finding the rope and giving it to Mackenna.

"Merik, I want you to tie his hands together, tightly now, so he can't get away." Mackenna approached the man cautiously, while Foulan threatened him. "If you try to hurt him or escape, I'll put and arrow between your eyes."

The highwayman cursed at him, but between Foulan's arrow and Myst growling at him menacingly, her muzzle dripping red, he stayed put. Mackenna grabbed the man's wrists, tying his broken, bleeding right one to his left behind his back. She took a grim satisfaction in his cries of pain as the rope cut into the mangled mess that was his arm.

Foulan glanced over the knot before lowering his bow. He searched the man for any other weapons, then turned to the family. The husband had begun to wake, and the daughters had finished reloading the cart with their family's belongings.

"We will leave this vagabond with you to do with as you please. You can kill him or bring him to the next town to be dealt the Realms' justice. It's up to you," Foulan told the wife.

Her husband sat up slowly, one hand clutching his head while the other was extended towards them. "You saved my family from robbery and my daughter and wife from a fate far worse. How can we ever repay you?" he asked.

Foulan shook his head as he took the man's hand, helping him to his feet. "It was not done in expectation of reward. We only wish to know if you want us to deal with this highwayman now, or if you would like to have your own justice."

"No, leave him for me," the father replied, his gaze going cold as he looked upon the highwayman. "But please. You must take some form of payment. Let us cook you supper, if nothing else."

"It's not necessary," Foulan replied, and Mackenna knew him well enough now to see that he was growing uncomfortable from the attention. "We are trying to reach the city of Ashriver before nightfall."

"Ahh, it's much too far to reach today," the father said. "There is a small town before the city. We were traveling there for trading day tomorrow. If you accompany us, we will pay for your room and board for the night. A hot bath, even. What do you say?"

Foulan seemed ready to protest, but Mackenna kicked him in the shin as discreetly as she could. A free bed and a bath? How could he possibly pass it up?

"That sounds wonderful," he gritted out. "I'm Foulan, by the way." He placed his hand over his heart, bowing his head, as was the customary greeting for Wanderers meeting someone new. "And this is my brother."

"Ma—rik. Merik." She imitated the Wanderer greeting.

"You don't look like brothers," said the younger daughter, eyeing them suspiciously.

"We have the same mother but different fathers. So still brothers," Foulan explained smoothly.

If either of the adults found this explanation strange, they didn't show it. "Well, it is a pleasure to meet you, Foulan and Merik. I am Oliver, this is my wife Melanie, our two daughters, Blythe and Brynne, and the young one is our son Benjamin. Come, it is only a little way to the town, and I am sure you are hungry and tired."

They contemplated whether or not to bury the dead highwayman's body, but deciding that it would take too long, they wrapped it in a blanket and tossed it in the back of the wagon. Foulan strung a lead rope between the injured highwayman and the back of the wagon, forcing him to walk behind it as they rode.

Mackenna sat in the back of the wagon with Oliver while his wife drove. She felt at his head for lumps, trying to remember everything her father had taught her about concussions. Determining that he shouldn't have any lasting damage, she recommended rest and gave him some willow bark to chew on to ease his headache.

Within the hour they had reached the town, though it was far from small in Mackenna's eyes. It housed three inns, each with their own eatery, as well as a separate tavern, a guardhouse, numerous stables, shops and outfitters, and of course, homes. She guessed it to be only a little bit smaller than Hartland. Just how small was her hometown? Compared to Hartland and Knotted Hill, Avdimia seemed more of a hamlet now.

The family led them to an inn known as The Frolicking Mare, which sported a horse alongside the traditional image of a bed and moon on its sign. Oliver left them there to take the highwayman to the constabulary, who would see to it that he was punished and that the other man's body was disposed of. After their horses were properly brushed, fed, and stabled, Mackenna and Foulan, followed by Myst, joined the rest of the family in the inn.

Upon entering the inn, they were greeted by a cheer. Melanie sat at a table with her daughters, surrounded by a small crowd. "There they are! The ones who saved us." She smiled and beckoned them over. Foulan and Mackenna were seated and given steaming bowls of beef and potato soup, loaves of hot bread, and a tankard of ale each. Mackenna was too hungry to bother with greeting the gathered crowd. She shoveled the food into her mouth, too tired for manners. When she finished with the food, she tried to leave to find their room. However, Melanie and her husband Oliver kept ordering more drinks and food, intent on spoiling their saviors, and she didn't wish to seem ungrateful.

Thankfully, the crowd had moved on to telling other tales of heroes and villains and damsels in distress. Someone brought a lute and began to play, followed by a piper, and the patrons drummed on the tables and mugs. Finally, Melanie must have realized that Mackenna was nodding off despite the lively music, and the woman pulled her aside. "There's a hot bath upstairs waiting in your room."

She had said "room." Singular. Mackenna nearly protested the impropriety of the situation, but then she remembered that these people all thought she and Foulan were brothers. As family, it would be perfectly reasonable for them to share a room or even a bed while traveling.

Upon entering their room, she was relieved to find it at least had two beds, with a small metal tub between them. She ignored the strange twinge of… disappointment? No, of course not. She had merely been looking forward to arguing with Foulan over who would sleep on the bed and who on the floor. She shook the thought from her mind and slipped out of her clothes and into the steaming water.

She washed her clothes first, then sank into the tub with a sigh. It must have been a lot of work for them to bring up the bath. At home they'd had a pump attached to a spring underground. They would pump the water into a giant metal tub that was heated with coals underneath, and then Mackenna and her father would use the hot water to wash their clothes and dishes and to bathe in. This tub, however, had nothing beneath it to keep the water warm, so clearly it was heated elsewhere and then carried to the room, likely up the stairs from the kitchens below. How much must it have cost Oliver and Melanie for such lavish treatment?

Mackenna washed her hair and body, scrubbing off weeks of grime and dirt and turning the water cloudy. She sighed in contentment as she leaned back into the tub, enjoying her full belly and the warmth of the water easing her aches and pains. It was the most relaxed she had felt since… well, since father had died. Her eyelids grew heavy. It couldn't hurt to close them for just a bit.

Foulan

Foulan sighed into his mug of frothy ale, wishing Mackenna would hurry up and get finished with her bath so he too could bathe and go to sleep. As the bench he sat upon shifted under the weight of a new person, Foulan looked up to see Oliver staring at him with a thoughtful look on his face.

"I wanted you to know that this showed up at the constabulary's a few days ago," Oliver said, setting a rolled up parchment between them. Foulan didn't even have to look at it to know what it was. "The resemblance to your... brother is uncanny."

As slowly and gently as he could, Foulan reached down into his boot, where he kept a hidden knife. He unsheathed it, holding it at the ready under the table. "And what exactly do you plan to do about it? Reveal us and cash in the bounty? Likely it could feed your family for a full year."

"Now, now, young man, no need for any of that," Oliver replied. "I just wanted to know what she'd done to deserve this. 'Tis true it's a hefty bounty, as you say, and I fear for you." Oliver noticed Foulan tense at the feminine pronoun and chuckled. "It wasn't that hard to figure out."

If he was going to turn them in, he would have by now, so there was no point in keeping it a secret. If it did come to a fight, there was no doubt he could beat the man, seeing how poorly he'd defended his own family from highwaymen. Hopefully it wouldn't come to that. "If you wish to know, she killed two of the Realms' soldiers in an act of revenge," he replied. "For taking her father's life. Would you turn in a young woman who'd watched her father be murdered right in front of her and only wanted retribution?"

"I see. In that case, I can find no fault in you or her. Besides, if it weren't for the two of you, my family and I could be dead now." Oliver reached out, picking up the warrant, and Foulan tightened his grip on his dagger. But Oliver simply held it over the candle on their table, watching as it lit up. Once it was burned to just a scrap of paper, he dropped it, still smoldering, into an empty mug. "I can tell from the way you speak of her that you care for this girl. Take care of her," the man said.

Foulan started to object—she was just his charge, nothing more—but before he could form the words, Oliver stood and left him, returning to the group still gathered in front of the hearth playing music and telling stories. Foulan sheathed his dagger and stood, stretching out his sore muscles. Mackenna really ought to be done with her bath by now. He left Myst where she slept curled up by the fire and headed upstairs to their room.

"Mackenna?" Foulan called, knocking on the door. There was no answer. He knocked harder, calling her name once again, but again she didn't respond. Growing worried, Foulan tried the handle, finding the door unlocked. Stupid country girl! Just because she was at an inn, she thought she could leave the door unlocked so that anyone could walk in her room and attack her? Drawing his dagger once more, he burst into the room, weapon at the ready.

He realized three things simultaneously. Mackenna was alone. She had fallen asleep. And she was still in the tub.

Her face was flushed from the heat of the fire behind her, which cast a warm halo around her short hair. Her soft lips were parted. Foulan's eyes traveled downward, over the pale, creamy skin of her neck and collarbone, his eyes landing on her small breasts. He'd made fun of her before for having no curves. It was true that compared to the Wanderer women, she was quite thin. He could even see her ribs. Yet he found himself mesmerized by the way her breasts rose and fell with her breathing.

His foot stepped forward against his will, his eyes traveling further down, drinking in the sight of her soft, flat stomach, which held the slightest hint of muscles, and her small hips.

Foulan's dagger fell from his limp hand, clanging to the floor. It startled both him from his trance and Mackenna from her slumber. Foulan jumped away, averting his eyes as Mackenna yelled. A bucket flew by his head, bouncing off the wall with a clatter.

"I—I'm so sorry! I didn't see anything, I swear!" he lied.

"Haven't you ever heard of knocking?" the girl yelled, the sound of water sloshing behind him indicating that she had gotten out of the tub.

"I did knock!" Foulan responded, defensive now. "Loudly! I even called your name! When you didn't answer, I became worried!"

"Worried about what?" He heard her fumbling with her clothing. "You are always worrying. Whenever we go into town, you're worried someone will recognize me. Whenever we're out in the woods, you're afraid someone will attack us in the middle of the night."

"And for good reason," he muttered.

"What? Why? Because of those highwaymen today? We did fine, didn't we?" she asked.

"No, *we* didn't," Foulan corrected. "*I* did. If I hadn't been there, that man would have killed you along with that family."

"What?! How dare you!" She grabbed his arm, spinning him to face her. She was clothed once more. He tried to shake away the image of her naked body in the tub and his disappointment that she was once more covered. "I can fend for myself! Or have you forgotten how we got in this predicament in the first place?"

"Of course not! I was just reminded again a few minutes ago," Foulan hissed, stepping closer so that they were nearly nose to nose.

"What?" the anger fell from her voice, and she looked worried. As she should. "What do you mean?"

"I mean that word has spread quickly. You clearly pissed off those soldiers, they are intent on getting their revenge. Thankfully, our friend Oliver chose to look the other way in light of today's events and burned the warrant. Hopefully it was the only one in this town." Foulan grabbed her shoulders. "It is my job to protect you, and seeing how poorly you did today in hand-to-hand combat, I can see that it's going to be a lot of work. The least you could do is lock the door when you're bathing alone!"

She swallowed, unable to say anything, and Foulan realized just how close they were, their faces inches apart. He pulled away and turned his back, running his hand through his hair in agitation.

"Your magic is only useful if you can control it, and you can't. And besides, we don't need to draw any more unwanted attention to ourselves," Foulan said, his voice calmer now.

"Anyway, I need to bathe. The water's probably cold by now," he grumbled.

"Sorry," Mackenna said, then yawned widely, eyeing her bed. "I can leave if you want," she mumbled, though he could tell she didn't want to.

Foulan felt himself softening, the residual anger melting away. She was much too cute to stay mad at for long. "Don't worry about it. You can go to sleep. Just no peeking," he teased.

She blushed, looking offended, but didn't say anything. Instead, she crawled into her cot and pulled the covers up over her head. Within minutes her breathing had grown deep with sleep. After bathing and washing his clothes, Foulan followed suit, falling fast asleep in his own bed.

Kazumi

As soon as they'd left the fort, Kazumi had headed to the city of Hartland. It hadn't taken long to find the gang that ran the city and pay them for information about the girl. Apparently she'd been traveling with a group of Wanderers who had defended her against the bounty hunters. A brawl had erupted, and the girl had set fire to a tavern to escape.

The gang leader didn't know which way the Wanderers had gone when they'd fled that night, so Kazumi asked around with the farmers living outside the town. It became evident pretty quickly that none of them cared for the gang that ran the town and charged them protection money. While they'd been unwilling to tell the gang anything, for a few coins they were more than happy to point Kazumi in the right direction.

Kazumi asked around the towns and villages at each major crossroad which direction the caravan had gone. They also tore down and destroyed any wanted posters they saw as they went. No point in enticing any further competition.

Wanderer caravans travelled slowly, so it only took them a week of tracking to catch up to the caravan. Upon finding the Wanderers, however, it became quickly apparent that the witch was gone. Kazumi had considered waltzing right up to them and asking after her outright. After all, the Wanderers could have abandoned her upon learning she was a wanted criminal. But Wanderers weren't exactly known for being upstanding members of society, often branded as thieves and vagabonds themselves. Perhaps the Wanderers had turned her in already and collected the bounty themselves? Yet Kazumi had the feeling that the Wanderers were likely protecting her, especially considering the way they seemed guarded, often looking over their shoulders as they travelled.

For three days now, Kazumi had stalked the Wanderers' caravan, hoping to discover where the witch had disappeared to. Kazumi could try luring one of them away, stealing their identity, and infiltrating the camp. But with a small, tight-knit group like this, especially people from the same family who'd known one another since birth, it would be almost impossible to pull off. Not only would the different voice be an issue, but people tended to notice when their loved one's mannerisms suddenly changed or they seemed to forget important people and memories. It was one thing to briefly imitate a guard and quite another to try to fool a family member.

After watching them for a few days, Kazumi had begun to glean the Wanderers' social rankings. While there was one man that everyone seemed to turn to for advice and leadership, there was another figure who seemed to be above even him. The old lady lived in the largest and most elaborate caravan, despite it just being her and her caretaker. When she came out, the others treated with her a sort of reverence. She was frail, and if she couldn't be bribed into giving Kazumi the information that they needed, then she could easily be threatened. The only problem was her caretaker, who seemed to be with her constantly.

So Kazumi watched and waited for an opportunity, until finally one arrived. The caravan had stopped outside a town to trade. The leader announced in the square the wares they had for trade, including that their Wise Woman, as she was apparently called, could tell a person's future starting at just fifteen prinz. That kind of money could get a person three mugs of ale at a tavern, but it seemed at least some of the townsfolk were interested, even if they knew it was a scam. Living in a boring country town like this, with nothing to do but farm and raise livestock, they were no doubt starved for any kind of entertainment they could find.

Kazumi took out the hand mirror that they always carried with them. Gazing into it, they willed their facial features to change, making them look younger and feminine. They shortened their hair and made it a muddy brown instead of its usual jet black. Kazumi had no one in particular in mind, but they would still prefer not to show their true face. After all, the Wanderers could still have a way of contacting the witch to warn her should they so choose. And besides, Isumijians were a rare sight in the Realms of Etylania, especially in such a sparsely populated area as this. Kazumi's foreign and androgynous appearance would attract too much attention.

Once satisfied that an unremarkable girl of thirteen or so looked back at them, Kazumi emerged from the woods and joined the line of people waiting to get their fortunes read. The old woman's caretaker waited outside the wagon, collecting the entry fee and then ensuring no one else entered the wagon while the old woman read that person's fortune. So it seemed Kazumi would be alone with the fortune teller. Perfect.

Once it was their turn, Kazumi paid the woman and stepped inside, closing the door behind them. They blinked, trying to adjust their eyes to the dimness inside the caravan. The only light came from the slatted shutters and a lamp hanging from the ceiling. The old lady sat in the middle of the room at a small round table. Atop its brightly patterned table cloth was a crystal ball and a deck of cards. "Well, come sit now. Tell me, what is your name?"

Kazumi slouched in the chair across from her, eyeing the room as if it would reveal the secrets they needed to know. "Shouldn't you already know that?" they asked.

The old woman sneered. "Ahh, a smartass, I see. That's fine, your money's still good as any others', whether you believe in it or not." The old woman held out her wrinkled hand expectantly. "I can guess it if you want, but just know, the more of my skill you require, the more you'll have to pay."

Kazumi laid their hand in the old woman's, who grinned, turning it over and running her fingers across their palm. "Interesting. You've been on a long journey, and you've gone by many names in your travels. As for your true name… Hmm. Masumi? No. That's not it. Izumi? Not quite… Perhaps a prinz or two will help me to glean it better, eh?" The fortune teller held out her other hand, motioning for a coin.

Even with their disguise, Kazumi couldn't hide their accent. No doubt in her travels the old woman had come across other Isumijians and simply learned the sound and cadence of their accented speech. The names she guessed were common enough. Still, it was surprising how close she was or that she even knew any Isumijian given names.

Kazumi pulled out a reque piece, placing it in the woman's hand. Her eyes widened in surprise. A reque was worth 100 prinz pieces. With each larger denomination, the value of the metals used to make the coin increased, as did its size. The coin immediately disappeared up the woman's sleeve.

"Let's just cut to the chase. I came seeking some very specific information, and I hope that you will be obliging, madame fortune teller," Kazumi said.

"Most who pay me that much want to know who their true love is or the exact moment and nature of their death. What would you care to know?"

"Nothing so abstract. I am looking for someone in particular. A very talented young woman with an affinity for fire. Her name is Mackenna, though you may have met her under an alias, for she is in a bit of trouble with the law."

"Ahh, a bounty hunter." The old woman leaned back with a grin. "What makes you think Madame Drynka would know anything about this girl?" she asked.

"Don't play coy with me, fortune teller. I happen to know that she traveled with your caravan for a time. It would seem that after you learned of the bounty on her head, you parted ways. I simply would like to know which direction she's gone," Kazumi said.

"She's gone in search of the Fae," the woman grinned, showing crooked teeth.

Kazumi's patience was growing thin. They pulled a dagger from their boot, tapping the cool metal of it against the woman's arm, at the artery. "Perhaps I wasn't clear. I need to know exactly where she's gone, and you are going to tell me everything you know."

The woman didn't look the least bit intimated. If anything, her grin widened. "You're not making the best case for yourself now, dear. I know the nature of my end, and it's not at your hand."

Kazumi's grip tightened. "I know enough to turn over your entire clan to the authorities in this town. Members of your group aided and abetted a criminal, started a fight, and burned down a tavern in the process. While the people here seem friendly enough, I think we both know how quickly that can change. Suspicions are high with the war between your homeland and this country. They might even suspect you of being Srahinzan spies."

"Now you're starting to learn to play the game!" the old woman cackled. "Put your silly little blade away, dear. I'll tell you what you want to know… for a price."

"You've already been paid handsomely," Kazumi replied, lifting their dagger from the woman's arm but keeping it in their free hand.

"You misunderstand. This sort of information is more valuable than money. I will only trade it for its like." With her free hand, the fortune teller pulled the cloth off of the crystal ball that sat between them.

"You wish for information in exchange? What exactly do you want to know?" Kazumi asked.

"Look into the crystal," the woman commanded. "Tell me what you See."

Kazumi rolled their eyes but decided to humor the woman. Their stolen face gazed back at them, the swirling mist within the ball distorting it. Features changed. Their true face appeared, then shifted again. The face of the guard. This too faded into another. Kazumi realized they were seeing all of the faces that they had worn, starting with the most recent and going backwards, always returning to their true self in between disguises.

Kazumi forced their eyes away from the crystal ball. The woman was burning something. Some sort of strong incense. Perhaps it had a hallucinogen of some sort to give her clients the sense that something truly mystical was occurring in the wagon. "Nothing," Kazumi said.

The old woman scowled. "Don't lie, dear. It's unbecoming. Do you want to know what I See?"

"Not particularly, no. I want to know the whereabouts of the witch named Mackenna."

"In good time," the fortune teller said. "I See a child, born in a far-off land with a rare and wonderful gift. Spirit blessed, they call it." Kazumi's spine straightened, the hand around their dagger clenching. How could the woman possibly know about that? "Great things were expected of this child. But ahh, what a disappointment. They couldn't even control their gift. And who would want a defective spirit blessed, eh?"

"So it would seem you aren't a quack after all," Kazumi muttered.

"Yes, well, some of us can actually control the gifts we are granted." The woman cackled as Kazumi tried to yank their hand away. The old fortune teller was surprisingly strong, her grip an iron vice. "So, you traveled all the way to another continent to escape your shame. Perhaps here, where magic is rare and frightening to the locals, you could make a name for yourself. Perhaps then you could earn their respect back home. But ahh, it's difficult going, isn't it? All you've succeeded in doing is becoming a mercenary for hire, hunting down bounties and killing the occasional outlaw. You need something big. Something that will get you *noticed*."

"You've had your fun," Kazumi growled. "Are you going to tell me what I need to know or not?"

"Hmm. I suppose that depends on what you will do with the information." The woman stopped speaking, though she continued to gaze into the crystal ball. "Interesting. As reluctant as I am to place one of my own in danger or to betray the trust of this child, the spirits have warned me that there is no way to dissuade you from your path. Attempting to do so would endanger all of my people."

"Glad to see you take my threat seriously."

"Know then that they have travelled north, to Calmloch, near the city of Abetheca. Their path leads them through the boglands," the Wise Woman said. "They go to find my sistren, who spend the winter there."

"Them?" Kazumi asked.

"Well, you certainly didn't think I would send her off on her own to find the elusive Fae? I lent her my own clan members to be protectors."

"How many?"

The woman grinned. "Now, now, you can't expect a lady to give away all her secrets, can you? It'll just have to be a surprise." Kazumi watched the Wise Woman silently through narrowed eyes. "I know what you're thinking. Should you trust this crazy old woman? What if she is lying to you to lead you astray?"

"Then you must know that I don't trust you and will require some assurance that you tell the truth. I think you and I will be taking a little trip together, seer. If what you say is true, I will release you with your life. If not..." Kazumi let the threat hang between them.

The fortune teller continued to grin, unfazed. Kazumi grew uncomfortable at her gaze. She seemed to look right through Kazumi to their very core. "Hmm. I think I have been more than accommodating to you. And besides, old women travel slow, and you have some catching up to do, don't you? In fact, you'd best get on the road without delay, Kazumi." The fortune teller released Kazumi's hand and held her own palm up in front of her mouth. Before Kazumi could react, the woman blew a colorful powder at their face. They shut their eyes instinctively.

When they reopened their eyes, they were no longer in the dark, claustrophobic caravan. Kazumi was lying in a field, staring up at the canopy of a tree. A brief assessment revealed no major injuries except for a pounding headache akin to a bad hangover. They sat up, their silky black hair falling in their face. Kazumi pulled out their mirror, verifying that their true appearance had returned. What the hell?

Their horse was tied to a nearby tree, munching grass as if nothing had happened. They looked around, trying to get their bearings. From their position, they could see the town not too far away. If any of the townsfolk had noticed them, they'd likely assumed Kazumi was camped there and had simply laid down to take a nap in the shade of the tree. It was midday, but it had been late afternoon when they'd entered the fortune teller's wagon, so nearly a day had passed, and the Wanderer caravan was gone.

Kazumi stood, brushing the dirt off their clothes. They noticed then that their dagger was stuck in the ground beside where their head had rested just moments before. It was stuck through a piece of parchment. Kazumi yanked out the dagger and sheathed it, then examined the note. It contained just two words: Good luck.

Mackenna

Mackenna awoke to the sound of scratching and whining at the door. She slowly opened her eyes, rolling over and glancing at Foulan in the other bed.

At some point in the night, he'd kicked off most of his blankets. His bare chest rose and fell with his breath, and she stared at the play of lean muscles across it, mesmerized by his dark skin. In the dim light of the room, she could barely see the black lines and swirls on his arms, tattoos, which all the Wanderers sported to varying degrees.

She tried not to stare at him during the day, not wanting to be rude. Growing up isolated in her small town, it had been rare to see anyone who looked very different from herself. That had to be the reason why her eyes were always drawn to his bare skin. She took in her fill now, while he slept.

Curls of thick black hair scattered across his chest caught her eye. They made a line down his stomach, disappearing beneath the blankets. A bare, muscular thigh peeked out from beneath his covers. Mackenna felt her face grow hot as she glanced over at the fireplace, where his clothes were hanging to dry. All of them.

This was improper, being in the same room with a naked man. Mackenna reluctantly pulled herself out of bed, shivering in the chill air of the room. No wonder he'd left his clothes out to dry. Her own were still damp, and they clung to her uncomfortably. She stumbled to the door, her feet numb, and fumbled with the latch.

Myst bounded in, barking happily, and jumped on her. Mackenna steadied herself and laughed, patting the wolf on the head. "Poor thing, did Foulan not let you in last night? You must have been so lonely!" Myst barked once, as if to answer yes, then rushed to Foulan's bed, jumping on it and licking his face.

"Ahh, Myst!" he shouted groggily. "Get off, you stinking mutt!" The wolf continued to lick him until he sat up, pushing her away. "Alright, alright, I'm up! Let me breathe!"

Mackenna turned her back, trying to ignore the way the blanket fell down to just his hips, revealing more of that trail of curly hair. "C'mon, Myst, let's go get something to eat," she called to the wolf. "We'll meet you downstairs, Foulan."

She headed to the outhouse first to relieve herself. Myst waited patiently outside while she did, and afterwards the two were crossing the yard back to the inn when Myst paused, her ears perked up. There were men talking nearby. Their words caught her attention, and she paused.

"I saw his tattoos, the dark-skinned one. He might not dress in their garish colors, but he's a Hinzi, no doubt," one said.

Mackenna crept to the corner of the building, peaking around it. Two men leaned against the wall of the inn, smoking pipes.

"Filthy tramps," the other replied, spitting on the ground. "How'd they get those horses, you think? Much too fine for their kind to afford."

"Stolen, no doubt," the first one answered. "They're all thieves and drug smugglers."

"What about that ginger he's traveling with? You think that boy's really one of 'em?" the spitter asked.

His companion snorted. "Claimed they were brothers, but the small one clearly ain't a full-blooded Hinzi. The thought of an Etylanian fucking one of those vagabonds is disgusting."

"Rape, no doubt. They hung one of 'em a few months ago in Norwood for rape."

Mackenna had heard enough. Fists clenched, she stepped forward to tell them off.

A soft nip at her wrist made her pause. She glanced down at Myst, who seemed to shake her head, as if warning Mackenna against her actions. How the wolf could guess her intentions she hadn't a clue, but yelling at those men would only draw unwanted attention. Mackenna took a deep breath to calm her rising anger. They would leave town today, and she would never see those men again. Who cared what they thought of the Wanderers?

She forced herself away from the corner quietly, making her way to the inn's back door. Mackenna greeted the innkeeper, who brought breakfast out to her. She stiffened when the front door opened and the two men entered. Would they attack her? Should she ask the innkeeper for help? But they simply sat at the other side of the tavern, ignoring her.

Foulan joined her a few minutes later, properly dressed now, and dug into their hearty breakfast of porridge, sausage, and eggs. She kept glancing at the men as unobtrusively as she could, and while she noticed them looking at her and Foulan from time to time, they didn't approach. Even so, she was nervous the entire time they ate, only breathing a sigh of relief when she and Foulan were outside saddling Dawn and Dusk. Oliver and Melanie joined them to see them off on their journey.

"I hope your travels will be safer from now own," Foulan told Oliver as he mounted his horse, Mackenna following suit.

"I am sure they will with two less highwaymen on the roads," the father replied.

"May Caelius watch over you on your travels," Melanie called after them as they pulled away, and they returned the sentiment. Mackenna wasn't even sure if the Wanderers believed in Caelius, the god who moved the stars and planets through the sky, creating the celestial map by which people travelled. But if Foulan was offended by the blessing, he didn't show it.

For the first hour after they left the town, Mackenna kept a wary eye out for the two men. Thankfully, no one had followed them, and she slowly relaxed again. By midday they reached Ashriver, and all thoughts of the worrisome conversation fled her mind at the sight before her. Cresting a bluff, they could see the entirety of the valley below. It was breathtaking.

Who knew that rivers could get so large? This one seemed to stretch on for leagues, so that she could barely see the shore on the other side, and that was just its width. The length of it trailed from one end of the valley to the other, disappearing into the hills on either side.

Mackenna had never seen a river deep enough for ships — actual ships and not just paddle boats. She wondered how they managed to go up the river against the current.

In the distance was a huge city. She could barely see the far bank of the river, but she could make out more city on that side as well. How did they cross it? Surely a bridge couldn't be built to span such a length?

They began their descent, the road becoming steep and winding as they traversed down the hill towards the city in the distance. The slope made Mackenna nervous, and Dawn seemed to feel uneasy as well, for she hugged the hillside as they descended. After an hour or more of picking their way down carefully, they reached the valley and came upon clusters of houses just outside the city proper. They paused to eat lunch, and Mackenna chatted idly with the locals.

She learned that what she had thought was an island in the middle of the river was in fact the spot where two different rivers converged. One came from the northwest and was called the Fisk River, the other came from the northeast and was called the Arlyn River. The Arlyn River was the one they were to follow to eventually reach the boglands from which it sprang.

As Mackenna talked with the families, Dawn leaned against her, nuzzling her head against Mackenna's shoulder. Perhaps the horse had finally come to accept her, at least enough to give her a smooth, gentle ride and not take off galloping without warning. As Mackenna patted her neck, the horse grabbed the half-eaten apple out of her hand, chewing on it loudly as she eyed Mackenna with a mischievous look. Figured. The animal was driven by her stomach.

After they had finished their lunch, they moved on. Mackenna was not sure where exactly the small villages ended and the city began. It seemed simply that the homes, taverns, and shops grew denser and more tightly packed, until she realized that they were in the heart of Arlyn proper, having never passed an actual gateway of any sort. She asked Foulan about this.

He shrugged, glancing around them. "My only guess is that they have no need for walls. They are naturally protected by the bluffs on either side of them. No army could easily storm through here and attack them. And there are so many people that I doubt they need to worry about wildlife getting close either."

They had lost sight of the river amongst the tall buildings around them, but finally it came into view once more. All along the shore were ports for those giant boats, and they were all bustling with activity.

"And besides, they're a trade city," Foulan added. "This river is their lifeblood. If they were attacked, it would be from the river itself."

"How do you know so much?" she asked him, genuinely in awe.

Foulan grinned. "I've travelled the Realms of Etylania my whole life. I've seen cities and towns of every size and variety. Eventually you begin to see patterns and discern why places are built the way they are. And anyways, I'm not as smart as you."

"What do you mean by that?" Mackenna asked. Whenever she was around him, she always felt stupid. He was always showing her new things: the best places to gather water to prevent getting ill, how to start a fire with wet wood or no flint rocks, how to read tracks to know which animals had passed by recently, how to skin and cook a hare.

"I mean, you know a lot more about plants than I ever would. I can hunt, but after a while, eating nothing but meat and the occasional fruits and vegetables bought in town or stolen from a farm gets old. I've always been too afraid of poisoning myself to eat wild plants."

"I'll keep that in mind next time you make me angry," Mackenna joked. "I know just the plant to make you sick for days without doing any permanent damage."

He frowned. "The scary part is, I can't tell if you're being serious or not."

The roads had become so crowded that they were forced to dismount and walk their horses beside them. She couldn't help noticing that she and her companions turned many heads, and more than once people backed away or cleared a path for them. Was it because of Myst? It wasn't common to see a giant wolf in a bustling city. Still, the conversation between the two men earlier returned to her thoughts. Did people everywhere think such terrible things about the Wanderers?

They came to a plaza filled with stands selling food, clothing, and other wares. "You stay here with Myst and the horses. I'm going to stock up on some supplies while we're here," Foulan said before disappearing into the crowd.

She didn't object to the chance to rest her feet for a bit. As she sat beside the horses waiting, a man approached her. He spoke to her, and from the inflection of his voice, he seemed to be asking a question.

Mackenna frowned. "I'm sorry," she said. "I don't speak your language."

The man spoke again. She realized, listening closely, that she could understand every third or fourth word he said, but that they were pronounced in a strange way she hadn't heard before. She could make out "lady," "beauty," and "bracelet." She realized he was holding jewelry in his hand, a bracelet made of silver.

"Oh, no," she shook her head, speaking slowly. "I don't have money for that. I'm sorry." She shook her head again, but he just continued to speak in his strange tongue, ignoring her. She was distracted from the conversation by a growl behind her. Mackenna glanced over to see Myst standing, hair raised, growling at two other men who had approached her horses from behind. The men paused, eyeing the wolf warily, and spoke to each other in what Mackenna assumed must be the same language as the jewelry seller.

She turned back to find the jewelry seller was suddenly standing very close, his body almost pressed against her. He was still smiling, but she realized his hand rested on her waist. Mackenna pushed him away with a yell.

Foulan appeared from the crowd, grabbing the man and yelling at him in his own language. The man yelled back, and Foulan pushed him to the ground, reaching into the man's jacket. Foulan pulled out a small sack, which she recognized as her own coinpurse, before spitting on the man. The jewelry seller looked as if he was going to start a fight, but Myst growled again, and he and his friends backed off, disappearing into the crowd.

"Pickpockets," Foulan said in disgust, handing Mackenna back her coin purse. "It's a common tactic. Keep you distracted while his friends rob the horses. I guess when he realized that was a no-go with Myst keeping guard, he decided to just nick your purse. You need to learn to be more aware of your surroundings."

Mackenna retied her purse to her belt. "You spoke to him," she said. "In his language."

Foulan shrugged. "Etylanian is the common tongue for trade between the nations. But people aren't about to give up their native languages. I've picked up a little bit here and there in my travels. Enough to get by."

"It was weird though." Mackenna replied. "Like I could understand some of it, but not much."

"Ah, it was Ecreau," he explained. "Many of the languages spoken in the different countries of Etylania are similar enough that they share common words. That's probably why."

"Are we in a new country then?" she asked.

"We will be once we cross the river. That's why we have to show our rites of passage here when we board a boat."

She thought for a moment. "Does that mean we need different money?"

"Good question," he said, and she warmed at the praise. "Thankfully no. While some countries still have their own currencies, they've all agreed to recognize Crowned Coin as the central one. Are you familiar with it? Bairnes, prinz, duques, reques, and imprars?"

She nodded. While at home they'd usually traded goods for services, coin was still exchanged from time to time. "Though I've never actually seen anything larger than prinz before," she admitted.

Foulan chuckled. "Me neither, and I doubt I ever will. Come, we need to cross the river."

After asking around and haggling a bit, he found a ferry that agreed to take them across the river. One of the crewmembers approached with a book in hand. "I'm the bosun for this ferry. I'll need to see your rites of passage." They removed the metal disks that hung around their necks, handing them over.

"Names?" the man asked boredly. Mackkena wasn't sure why he had to ask for their names when they were written right there on the disks, but they both provided their names, or rather, Mackenna gave her false name. The man didn't even bother to look up as he recorded their names in the logbook. "Country of origin?" he asked.

"None. We're Wanderer," Foulan explained.

The man eyed him, then Mackenna. "He doesn't look like a Wanderer to me."

"We don't all look the same," Foulan bit back.

"My mother was Etylanian, or so I'm told," Mackenna answered, repeating the story they'd used the day before. "She died in childbirth. I was raised by our father."

The bosun shrugged. "Fine. I'll just put Wanderer, half breed." She saw Foulan tense. Was that offensive? The man asked a few more questions about their destination and purpose for traveling, then handed back their rites of passage. "Here you are. Ferry leaves as soon as it's loaded, so don't wander off or you'll miss it, and we don't issue refunds."

Once the boat was prepared, they led the horses down the worn wooden dock, which creaked with every step. While Myst jumped onto the ferry with a happy wag of her tail and Dusk with tentative steps, Dawn refused to budge, shying away every time Mackenna tried to drag her onto the boat. She tossed her head defiantly and wouldn't even be bribed with apples or carrots. Foulan joined Mackenna, tugging at the horse while the crew watched in amusement, laughing. Then, the horse suddenly lurched forward onto the boat, throwing Mackenna off balance. Foulan managed to catch himself against the rail, but she lost her footing, falling backwards with a cry.

She fumbled in chaos for a moment, unable to discern up from down, air from water. The cold shocked her, her muscles cramping in protest. She finally managed to right herself, her arms and legs acting instinctively to push herself upwards. Mackenna broke the surface with a gasp, sputtering from the cold and water in her nose, and gazed around to find the dock much farther than she would have expected given her short time underwater. Foulan was yelling at the sailors from the deck of the boat. Myst, meanwhile, had jumped into the water and was paddling towards her.

"Good girl," Mackkena sputtered, grabbing onto the wolf's mane.

The current was unexpectedly strong. The wideness of the river had given it the misleading appearance of moving slowly. It took all of her strength just to keep her head above water as her sodden clothes and boots tried to weigh her down. There was no way she could swim back to them. What was she going to do?

Thankfully, her fall into the water hadn't gone unnoticed. A rowboat was already headed her way, the rowers expertly maneuvering around larger fishing boats and rocks and logs in the water. Within minutes they reached her, the men in it grabbing her by the shoulders and pulling her up into the boat as if she weighed nothing. "Th—thank you," she chattered. "Please help my dog." They eyed Myst warily. "She's with me. She doesn't bite," Mackenna said. Well, at least, she hoped Myst would understand they were trying to help and wouldn't bite. With some awkward maneuvering, they managed to get Myst into the boat as well. When she tried to thank them, they just nodded and spoke to each other in the same language she had heard the pickpocket using earlier.

The ferry glided up to them, and Foulan jumped down into the small boat. "Merik, you alright?" Foulan asked, his hands on her shoulders as he looked her over to see if she'd been hurt.

She nodded. "How're we going to get Myst into the ferry?" The ledge of the larger boat was easily six feet in the air.

"No worries there. C'mon Myst, same way we get up over big rocks." He knelt down on one knee, his face towards the deck of the ferry, and whistled. The wolf seemed to know what this meant and jumped onto his back. Foulan stood swiftly, and she leapt from his shoulders to the deck of the ferry above.

Foulan helped Mackenna up next, then pulled himself up into the ferry, but not before trying to pay the men who'd paddled over to rescue her. They just shook their heads and paddled away.

The bosun approached with a stern look on his face. "Wonderful. Now not only are we behind schedule with this delivery, but I'm going to have to record this incident for the harbormaster. Boys, please keep your beasts under control for the remainder of the ride, thank you."

She could see Foulan gritting his teeth at the man's snide tone, especially the word "boys." After the man had retreated, Foulan turned to Mackenna. "You okay?" he asked again.

She waved him off, glaring at Dawn. "That's it! I'm selling that stupid horse the next chance I get," she threatened emptily. "That water was freezing."

Foulan grabbed a blanket from their bags, throwing it over her shoulders and hugging her to him. She supposed he was trying to help her dry off or warm up, and she wanted to protest that she didn't need him to, but the feeling of his hard, warm chest against her face was too nice, so she kept her thoughts to herself. Once she finally stopped shivering, he stepped away to watch the river pass by beneath them, though he kept an arm around her shoulder in what she supposed was a more brotherly show of affection than a hug.

A few minutes later, they reached the other shore. Foulan got off first, guiding Dusk behind him. The boatsmen grabbed switches and gently whacked at Dawn's flank to coax her off the boat. She was more than happy to depart it, trying to run past Foulan and into the street, but he managed to grab her reigns and calm her.

Mackenna had hoped that her spill in the river meant that they might stop at an inn in the city for the night. But Foulan seemed eager to get away from the city while there was still daylight. They took off on horseback and immediately made their way out of town.

As cold as Mackenna was, she didn't want to complain. She could practically feel Foulan's irritation radiating from him at the way the bosun had spoken to them.

And besides, she didn't want him to think she was too weak to keep up. So what that she had taken a little dip in the river? She was a big girl, and she'd jumped into colder before just to wash herself. Perhaps it was the chill of dusk that kept her clothes from drying out and made the cold seep into her bones.

When they finally stopped for the night, they stayed at a local family's home, paying a few prinz pieces for warm food and a roof over their heads. The family was nice and welcoming, a young couple with their newborn daughter, but Mackenna couldn't get her spirits up. They didn't have an extra bed, so Mackenna and Foulan had to sleep on the floor by the fireplace. As soon as the family retired to their bedroom, Mackenna laid down with her back as close as she could get to the fire, Myst curled up against her chest.

"It's dangerous to sleep that close to the fire," Foulan warned her. She cracked open an eye. "What if you rolled over towards it in your sleep? Or an ember escaped and landed on you?"

"You do remember who you're talking to, right?" she muttered.

"No need to bite my head off, Spitfire." He held his hands up defensively, grinning. "The building isn't as fireproof as you are."

Mackenna's eyes had already drifted back shut. "If I catch fire, I promise to wake up and put it out before the whole building goes up..." she trailed off towards the end of her sentence.

"You sure about that?" he asked, but she was too tired to bother responding. And then Foulan was shaking her awake.

"Wha—? Can't I get some rest?" she huffed.

"Mackenna, it's morning. We need to get moving."

Mackenna's head was thick with fog as they ate a breakfast of porridge and eggs, thanked the couple, and then rode off once more. Her whole body felt sluggish and slow, like she was still stuck in the river, trying to move her limbs against the current but getting nowhere. The morning seemed to crawl by, the chill refusing to be chased away by the sun. Except, when she glanced up, the sun was high above. It was midday already? Why was it still so cold?

Perhaps conversation would help to wake her up. "What does Hinzi mean?" she asked. At the stiffening of his shoulders, she regretted her bluntness in broaching the topic.

Foulan didn't answer at first. Then he asked, "Where'd you hear that?"

"When we were in Ashriver, while you were getting dressed. I overheard some men speaking. They said that word, but I wasn't sure what it meant."

"It just means someone from Srahinza," he replied curtly.

She supposed that made sense. But why had the men made it sound like an insult? "They said some other things, too... about the Wanderers."

His lips pursed. "What kinds of things?"

"They said you were vagabonds and thieves."

He shrugged. "And do you agree with them?" There was an iciness to his tone that confused her.

"Of course not. Your people were nothing but kind to me. That's why I didn't understand. Why would they say those things?" she asked.

"Why else? They hate us."

Mackenna bit her lip. "But why? Your clan treated me better than anyone in the town I grew up in ever did."

He chuckled half-heartedly. "You really are sheltered. Many people in the Realms of Etylania hate us. They think we don't belong here."

"Why?" She wondered if he was getting annoyed by her repeated question.

"We're outcasts. Refugees. We had to flee our own country, now part of the Srahinza Empire, after it was torn apart by war. That's what Hinzi comes from; it's short for Srahinzan. Which is ridiculous because we fought against the Srahinzan tyrants who swept through the nomad lands, killing the clan leaders and swallowing everyone up into their empire. Everyone who didn't escape, that is."

"I'm so sorry," she whispered.

He shrugged nonchalantly, but she could tell from the stiffness of his posture that it bothered him at least a little. "It happened over two hundred years ago. We fled to the southernmost countries of Etylania and sought refuge. But nobody wanted a sudden influx of thousands of displaced peoples. So we continued traveling north, continued seeking a place that would take us in, and continued to be turned away. Because we came from all different tribes that were taken over by Srahinza, we just decided to call ourselves Wanderers. After a decade of seeking a new home, the Wanderers decided that their best chance was to break into small clans, each going their separate ways. Maybe then it would be easier to find somewhere that would take us in, let us settle and live there. I've heard a few clans did find permanent homes, but most didn't. And anyway, by then our people had become used to travel.

"It's why the clans work the way they do. There is safety in numbers, but if our numbers are too large, then we are seen as a threat. Some clans, like Clan Avani, live in isolation off the land and avoid any interaction with civilization. Others, like Clan Sitara, found a niche. They have become entertainers—acrobats and storytellers and actors—and they travel around performing plays and other shows for money. With Clan Drynka, we take on odd jobs when people need an extra hand: bringing in the harvest, building houses and roads, chopping lumber for the winter, things of that sort. Other clans act as trade caravans, transporting goods from town to town."

Mackenna tried to follow the conversation, but she was having difficulty hearing him over the ringing in her ears. Dawn had started to lag behind, the insolent horse always willing to stop for a snack when she thought she could get away with it. The horse seemed to be especially swaying today, making her dizzy. Mackenna tried to keep her eyes focused on Foulan in front of her, but darkness bled in at the corners of her vision until it felt as if she were gazing at him from the other end of a tunnel.

And then the world tilted sideways, and she couldn't even see that.

Foulan

"For the most part, people do little more than curse at us or refuse to trade with us, but occasionally we have dealt with violence," Foulan continued. "It's all the more reason why you need to learn to defend yourself."

Mackenna didn't answer. Perhaps he'd offended her. He didn't want to hurt her feelings, but without him, she would have died charging in against those two highwaymen, and he didn't want to feel like he had to be constantly watching both her back and his. If they ever became separated for some reason, she needed to know how to protect herself.

There was a thump of something hitting the ground behind him followed by Myst's frantic whining. He turned in his saddle, his hand going to the dagger at his belt, but there was no one there except Myst and Dawn, both staring at the limp form of Mackenna's body lying in the dirt. Foulan dismounted quickly, rushing to her side. "Mackenna? Mackenna, wake up."

She moaned, opening her eyes, then seemed to think better of it, shutting them tight. She was pale, her face clammy with sweat, and yet she was shivering despite the warm sunlight. Foulan put a hand to her head, but he already knew what he would find. She felt as if she were on fire. Dammit! This was all his fault. She'd fallen in the river yesterday, but instead of stopping and letting her rest and dry out her clothes, he'd kept pressing forward, the crowded city making him uncomfortable. She hadn't complained, so he'd figured she was fine. How stupid of him. Of course she wouldn't have complained, not after he'd made fun of her just a few weeks ago for not being able to keep up with him. And now he'd driven her to illness.

"C'mon, Mackenna," he said, lifting her up onto her horse. She slumped against Dawn's neck with a moan. "I know. We just have to find a place to set up camp. It won't be too long, I promise."

Within the hour he found a warm, grassy spot beneath some sturdy trees. He laid out her bedroll and she immediately sank into it, though she didn't sleep, only kept shivering and complaining of being cold. Foulan draped Mackenna's and his blankets over her before tending the horses and starting a fire. He cooked her dinner at noon, a potato broth, which she sipped at before collapsing against the ground again.

"Do you have anything in your pack for fever?" he asked.

She nodded weakly. "Meadowsweet... Red stem. White flowers. Sweet smell."

He dug through the bag of herbs, finally finding the one that looked right and holding it up for her to see. When she nodded, he asked, "What do I do with it?"

"Boil in hot water, like tea." She took it from him, breaking a small section off. "This much. Three times a day." He did as she asked, bringing her the tea. After she'd finished it, she whispered hoarsely, "My whole body aches."

"I know, Spitfire. It's just the fever," he said. "Try to sleep. I'll be here." He stroked her hair until she drifted off.

Mackenna

She was drowning. She tried to swim upwards, to break the surface, but water just kept washing over her, pulling her down. Her limbs were heavy and tired. Her clothes weighed her down. The water seeped in, into her eyes, her nose, her mouth, her lungs. She couldn't breathe. All was dark and heavy.

And then she was on fire. But for the first time it burned her, like it never had before. She screamed in agony, screamed like the men she had killed. She could feel it peeling her skin away, melting her eyes, burning her hair away to nothing, scorching her from the inside out. She couldn't control it, and she longed for the water to come back, to ease the pain.

She awoke briefly to realize she'd been dreaming, or perhaps she still was, only to find a young man gazing down at her. He was dark and handsome, with long black hair and lashes. He was saying something, but she couldn't understand what. She begged for water, and he held a flask to her lips, the cool liquid wetting her parched throat. She drifted off again while staring into those dark, deep, endless eyes.

Again she was on fire, but this time it was good. It was warm and burned with a sensual passion. The young man was holding her, his chest bare. She ran her fingers through those dark curls, over the tattoos. He shivered beneath her touch before capturing her lips with his. She had wanted this all along, just hadn't known it. His body was hard against hers in all the right places. When his bare thigh rubbed her between her legs, she felt a heat, a tightening, in her loins. She begged for more, but that dream too fell away.

When Mackenna awoke again, she was more lucid, more aware of her surroundings. She remembered feeling ill, falling off the horse, Foulan setting up camp and stroking her hair and her back while she lay there, sometimes shivering, sometimes crying and moaning. He lay beside her now. She could feel his chest pressed against her back, and it was indeed bare. His arm was thrown around her, and he breathed heavily in sleep.

How long had she had slept? It was pitch black, the campfire was little more than smoldering embers. She had to relieve herself. Could she even move? Her whole body felt like liquid. But she couldn't make a mess of herself, especially not with Foulan lying beside her. She pushed herself up off the ground, limbs shaking in protest. Myst leapt up when she saw Mackenna struggling, standing beside her for Mackenna to lean on. Together they made their lumbering way over to a patch of tall grass, so Mackenna could relieve herself in some semblance of privacy.

Afterwards, Mackenna collapsed back onto the bedroll, eyes already heavy. She expected Myst to lay back down, but the wolf stood at attention, her eyes focused on the giant ancient oak that they slept under.

Her massive head tilted in that way it did when someone talked to her. Mackenna heard nothing but the crickets chirping. She squinted in the direction of the wolf's gaze. The swaying of the branches in the gentle breeze had a certain mesmerizing quality to it. The longer she watched it, the more it seemed as if the tree were waving an arm at her, as if to say hello. The vines hanging from its branches reminded her of hair, and that spot of moss there could almost be a beard. Yes, that groove just above the moss was certainly a mouth, the broken remnants of a twig there the nose. And above that, those knots in the wood were no doubt the eyes.

She gasped. Had the eyes blinked at her? Was this a Fair Folk before her? Yet she felt no fear or awe, only comfort. For the eyes were achingly familiar, warm and brown like his had been, before the blindness had taken them. They even had the same wrinkles at the corners from smiling.

Mackenna opened her mouth, tried to say something. All she could manage was a hoarsely whispered, "Daddy?"

The sound of the breeze in the leaves almost sounded like her name: *Mackenna*. With a slight nod he faded away, the features disappearing into the tree.

A wave of drowsiness swept over her. She tried to fight it, to stay awake, to see if he came back, if he had even really been there at all. But soon the darkness claimed Mackenna once more.

Mackenna's fever broke the next morning. Foulan held the water skin to her lips, helping her to wet her parched throat. She assessed the state of her bedroll. While she had thrown up a few times, she thankfully hadn't done anything more embarrassing, like soiling herself. At least she had retained some dignity. After relieving and cleaning herself, she returned to camp and plopped back down to the ground. Even that little bit of activity was exhausting.

Mackenna found herself staring at the tree, seeing if she could recreate the image of her father in the daylight. She found the moss that looked like a beard, the stick of a nose, the bark wrinkles. But in the daylight, that was all it was: moss, branches, bark, vines. No matter how she stared, she couldn't make her father's face return.

Foulan must have noticed her staring. "You okay?" he asked.

Mackenna took a shaky breath. "It's just… last night. I woke up at one point and I thought… I thought I saw my father. In the tree there." She pointed. "I'm sure it was just the fever. But it just looked so real." There was pressure behind her eyes as the tears welled up, and she wiped them away quickly.

He sat down beside her, handing her a bowl of oatmeal, which she ate slowly. He didn't speak for a while, seemingly lost in thought. "Maybe it wasn't the fever. Maybe it was his spirit."

"Like a ghost?" she asked. "My people bury a body immediately, so the spirit doesn't become restless. If it is left out, it will become bitter that it's no longer alive and jealous of the living. It will turn into a ghost and wreak havoc."

"And you're afraid that might have happened?" Foulan asked.

She frowned. "He didn't look bitter or angry. He just looked… loving? Concerned? I don't know. He just looked like Finn."

"The Wanderers believe that spirits live on after their bodies die. They watch over their loved ones. But they aren't bitter or jealous. In fact, we believe that ancestor spirits can even be helpful, visiting us in times of need. At least, that's what Wise Woman Drynka says."

Mackenna wasn't sure how she felt about this. If her father was still here, somehow, why hadn't he shown himself to her sooner? Why didn't he speak to her? Why was he gone now? She needed him. Needed his counsel and his love.

"But they aren't here physically," Foulan said, as if he had read her thoughts. "They can't interact, or at least, it's very limited if they can. They observe and sometimes offer guidance to people like the Wise Women, who have the ability to hear them."

"Thank you," she whispered. She wasn't even sure if she was talking to Foulan or the tree, and maybe he knew this, because he didn't reply. They sat there in comfortable silence, contemplating the tree.

Kazumi

Before Kazumi could apprehend the witch, they needed some sort of protection. While they were adept at sword fighting and hand-to-hand combat, neither those skills nor their ability to shapeshift would help them if they were lit on fire. Thankfully, their contact Mekhag—a black market dealer in all things magical—operated out of the city of Pallanova, which was on the main road that skirted around the western edge of the boglands. From there, Kazumi could continue following the road northeast to Abetheca. While a more indirect route to their destination, it was nonetheless faster to travel by the well-tended cobbled roads than to slog through the marshes. No doubt the witch and her companions took the latter route because it was likely to be desolate.

Pallanova was a huge city, one that a newcomer could easily become lost in. Its streets and alleys wove in and out of one another, rarely forming a direct path from one location to the next. As the city had grown, the difficult terrain had forced the people to build further up rather than out, so that numerous stories of homes and businesses sat one atop another, connected by suspended archways and bridges at different levels. One could trace the age of a building by the different styles of architecture at various levels. Some of the oldest levels had had entire streets built above them, effectively closing them off underground.

It was this literal underbelly of Pallanova that Kazumi traversed now. They'd left their horse at a reputable inn far above, as the roads down here were often too narrow for anything but foot traffic. They'd also worn their armor and sword, the only two items they'd brought with them from the Isumijian Dynasty. While Kazumi carried their sword with them nearly everywhere, they only wore their armor for the most dangerous of tasks, as its uniqueness tended to stand out.

The armor consisted of a lamellar cuirass that hung to their mid-thigh worn over a pair of black, loose-fitting pants and kimono shirt. While lamellae were usually made of steel, Kazumi's were made of interconnected plates of hard leather, making it even lighter and easier to move in than the traditional armor. A pair of leather bracers that extended down to their knuckles and greaves strapped over their shins completed the armor. All of the vital organs were protected while still allowing them the flexibility to move quickly and quietly.

While Kazumi often preferred hiding in the shadows, there was little point in the underbelly of Pallanova. They knew well that every shadow hid eyes, and someone was always watching, waiting for a passerby to let down their guard. Only the smartest or bravest souls traversed these paths alone, and Kazumi hoped that they made it clear that they were neither an easy nor unwary target.

They found Mekhag's storefront easily enough. Little had changed in the year since they'd last visited. Kazumi rapped on the door in a memorized pattern. A small panel behind an iron grate slid back, a wary face peering out at them. "Who're you?" a gruff voice asked.

"A friend of Mekhag," was the only answer Kazumi gave. It was the only one needed. Only the most trusted customers ever met Mekhag in person, much less knew of his physical location. The doorman grunted and closed the speakeasy. After a series of clicks and scrapes as various locks and bars were undone, the door creaked open. "Well, c'mon then!"

Kazumi stepped inside, waiting for the doorman to finish locking the front door before following him through the old building. Nearly every conceivable inch of floor space was covered in shelves, tables, and cupboards, all housing and displaying an assortment of rare and exotic items from around the world. How Mekhag could stand such clutter, Kazumi hadn't a clue. Kazumi was careful not to brush against anything, not out of fear of breaking something or being cursed by a magical item, but rather out of a desperate need to avoid the filth. Dust and cobwebs covered everything, and Kazumi didn't doubt that spiders and roaches hid in every crevice. Thankfully they didn't see any rat droppings, no doubt thanks to the numerous cats lounging around on the priceless items and darting between their legs.

The doorman led Kazumi to Mekhag's main office, where the owner sat behind a desk as equally cluttered as the rest of his home/store. "The Isumijian is here," was all the doorman said before turning and leaving.

Mekhag looked up from a large tome he pored over with a magnifying lens. He grinned at the sight of Kazumi before him. "Ah, my most loyal customer. Come in!"

"Every customer is your most loyal, Mekhag, when they are in your shop," Kazumi said by way of greeting.

"Still, there is no need to dispense with formalities. Would you like a cup of tea?" Kazumi shook their head, eyeing the rusting teapot. "No, no, of course not. And no handshake either, I remember that, you uppity bastard."

Kazumi merely sniffed in response. "Is that cat piss I smell, or have the sewers flooded into the streets again?"

"Sometimes I wonder how you can even handle money when you can't stand to touch anything with your bare hands," the merchant taunted.

"Yes, well, thankfully that's what gloves are for," Kazumi replied dryly, indicating their own gloved hands.

"Bet you burn every pair after they become sullied. Well, at least you're keeping the Etylanian leather trade in business," Mekhag teased, and Kazumi bowed mockingly in response. "So what brings you here, friend?"

"I'm looking for a particular type of item for my current… endeavors." Kazumi never specified their particular trade, and the merchant never asked. Such was the nature of his shop. Mekhag served all sorts, from thieves to assassins to slave traders. As long as the buyer's money was good, Mekhag didn't care where it came from.

"You know I'll need a little more detail than that, chap." Kazumi was never sure if Mekhag called all of his customers "chap," or if he simply assumed that Kazumi was male under their armor. Either way, they never bothered to correct him. The less such a dangerous man knew about Kazumi's identity, the better.

"Something that will protect me from a witch, specifically one that can wield fire."

"Hmmm," the merchant sat back in his chair, stroking his thick beard in concentration. "For how long does the protection need to last?"

"Preferably permanently. But at least for as long as the person is in my presence, which could be weeks or more."

"And you are sure the person is a witch?" Mekhag asked.

"As opposed to…?"

"Ahh, not as worldly as you seem, are you, chap?" Mekhag teased. "There are three main types of magic. That which is innate, that which is learned, and that which is wielded."

Kazumi's brow furrowed. "Clarify."

"Witches have innate magic. They are born with it. It is passed down through the generations. It is also usually limited to a certain type, such as a specific element. Sorcerers learn their magic through years or even decades of intense study. They often use spells and incantations to get certain results. Finally, wizards can imbue items with magical properties, such as the many wares that I sell here. Technically anyone can wield such artifacts, but a certain finesse or skill is usually needed to do so without losing control of them. This last form of magic may be more familiar to you, as I hear it is quite common in your homeland."

Kazumi nodded slowly. "Yes, though we refer to it as science, not magic."

The merchant shrugged. "I've been to the Isumijian Dynasty a few times. There are many that would call your science wizardry."

"Are those the only types of magic?" Kazumi asked, trying to seem nonchalant. Kazumi had often wondered about the origins of their own unique ability, one that they'd never encountered outside a handful of rare Isumijians. According to the legends in their homeland, these abilities were gifted to them by a specific god, but Kazumi wasn't sure that they believed it.

Mekhag shrugged. "Well, that's all I've come across in my readings, though there do seem to be regional differences between different kinds of witchcraft. If this person you are hunting is a witch, that can make things a little more difficult."

"How so?"

"For a sorcerer, you can usually take away their voice, perhaps even tie up their hands, to control their magic. For a wizard, all that is needed is to remove the magical item they wield. Witches tend to vary more, but I have come across a particular item that seems to work well for elemental-type abilities." The merchant's eyes twinkled with some secret knowledge. No doubt he kept the whole truth from Kazumi. Giving away too many trade secrets was an easy way to become irrelevant in the trade of such rare items.

"I am interested," was all Kazumi replied. They knew this game. They had to seem nonchalant. Mekhag's prices increased the more eager or desperate a buyer seemed.

"Excellent. Follow me," Mekhag said, standing and leading Kazumi through a doorway. They travelled down more halls, Mekhag occasionally mumbling to himself in concentration. No doubt trying to remember where he'd placed the relic in this mess. Finally, he stopped in front of a nondescript looking chest, opening the lid to reveal a pile of equally unimpressive looking shackles. Mekhag picked up a pair, holding them out. "Ahh, here we are. Each pair of these shackles has been imbued with a spell that blocks elemental magics. Simply cuff them around the victim's—err, prisoner's—wrists, and they are unable to use their ability."

Mekhag rifled through a box of keys in the chest, trying a few before finding one that worked on the shackles.

Kazumi picked up the heavy shackles, eyeing them over. "They don't look particularly… magical."

"Come now, chap, you know as well as I that enchanted items can often look completely mundane. All the better to carry them in plain sight, no?" The merchant grinned. "Now, these normally sell for a hundred fifty duques or more, but since I like you, I'll give it to you for just a hundred."

Kazumi snorted, letting the shackles tumble out of their hands and to the floor, where they clattered loudly. A cat that had been sleeping nearby jolted awake, fleeing the hall. A hundred duques was a quarter of the bounty on the girl's head. "Outlandish, and no doubt a fake. I will more than likely try to apprehend the witch only to find myself burnt to a crisp."

"Now, now, you think I would sell something if I couldn't prove its value?" the merchant asked.

"How exactly do you hope to demonstrate it?" Kazumi asked. "I can't exactly return to demand a refund if I am dead."

"C'mon, have a little more faith in me, chap. I happen to know a witch we can test it on. You just have to come with me to the Arena."

Kazumi narrowed their eyes but nodded. Mekhag picked up the shackles and led the way once more through the winding hallways. They came to a stone archway blocked by a padlocked iron gate. It marked the end of Mekhag's building, the dark tunnel beyond leading deeper into the heart of the underground city. After locking the gate behind them, Mekhag removed an orb from the pocket of his robe and whispered a word. It immediately illuminated the tunnel before them with a constant, bright blue light.

"Impressive, eh?" Mekhag said as he led Kazumi down the tunnel. Kazumi made a noise of agreement. "Oh right. I forget that this magic—oh sorry, *science*—is quite common in your dynasty."

Kazumi rolled their eyes, though the merchant couldn't see it with his back turned. Kazumi owned a flameless lantern as well, though the power eventually waned and had to be recharged by a wizard after a few years.

Kazumi was silent for the remainder of the journey, though the merchant chatted enough for the both of them. Kazumi wasn't sure if it was out of loneliness or a warning to any watchers about who, exactly, he was. The merchant owned at least half the wealth in the undercity, and while there were doubtless many who wished to rob him or see him dead, none would dare attack him outright, if for no other reason than fear of what magical artifacts he might wield against them. Nonetheless, Kazumi still kept a hand on the hilt of their sword and watched every shadow for movement. Mekhag's untouchability didn't necessarily apply to Kazumi just because they travelled with him.

At last, they reached the Arena. Outside of the numerous taverns, it was one of the most popular destinations in the lower city. Anyone, no matter their class, gender, or race, could make it rich in the Arena if they were lucky and skillful enough, whether it be by betting on matches, sponsoring a gladiator, or entering the fight oneself. It wasn't uncommon for prisoners and even slaves to enter the arena in the hopes of winning their freedom.

The fighter that Mekhag led them to was undoubtedly one of the latter, judging by the leather collar around her neck. She looked to be in her mid-thirties, though it was difficult to tell under the scars and bruises. Mekhag approached a man who stood nearby, no doubt her master. They spoke for a few minutes in hushed whispers, and then Mekhag smiled and beckoned Kazumi over. "This young woman here is a witch, though her particularly element is water. It has made for some interesting battles these past few months as the Arena master has found new and unique ways to incorporate water."

Kazumi simply responded with, "Are you going to demonstrate the artifact or not?"

"All work and no fun," Mekhag said with a sigh. "Bring me a tub of water, then."

Some slaves quickly complied, while the witch watched suspiciously. Mekhag took her by the arm, leading her to the tub. "First, demonstrate for our friend here a few tricks with the water."

The woman eyed them both, then held her hand out over the tub. A perfect bubble of water lifted from the tub, floating up towards her hand. She looked over at a nearby fighter, a small grin on her face, and with a thrust of her hand, the water bubble launched at him. It must have hit with quite a bit of force because the warrior fell to the ground, clutching the back of his head. His comrades jeered, and he turned to the witch with a glare, his friends holding him back.

Mekhag chuckled. "As you can see, she can shape the water to her will. This also means that she can stay submerged underwater for as long as she wishes without running out of air. Isn't that right?"

The witch nodded, silent.

"Excellent. We're going to do a little experiment now. Please get into the tub." She hesitated for only a moment before complying. Mekhag attached the cuffs around her wrists, then snapped at the warrior she had hit, calling him over. Her eyes widened in fear. "Now, chap, I want you to hold her head underwater. If the shackles actually work to block magic, she will be unable to breathe down there and will begin to drown."

"Wha—" The woman uttered a sound for the first time, but she was interrupted by the gladiator, who replied with a grin, "Absolutely." He grabbed her shoulders and pushed her down.

She seemed to be concentrating, no doubt attempting to shape the water to keep it away from her face, but her eyes bulged wide when it did not work. The witch struggled against the warrior, but she was no match for his strength.

"Is this really necessary?" Kazumi blurted out, unable to hold back their disgust.

"You wanted evidence that the shackles work. What better evidence than this? If she truly still retained her control over the water, she would use it now to save her own life."

"You've made your point. That's enough!" Kazumi hissed.

The merchant shrugged and waved at the gladiator to release the witch, but he ignored him, continuing to hold her beneath the water. There was a maniacal gleam to his eye; perhaps she had done something to embarrass him in the arena in a previous battle. Her struggling was growing weaker. Unable to hold her breath any longer, her mouth opened, air bubbles escaping to the surface.

Kazumi didn't hesitate a moment longer. In one swift motion, they unsheathed their blade and held it to the warrior's neck. "Release. Her." Kazumi could see movement in the corner of their eye, no doubt the warrior's friends rushing to intervene, but they paused when the merchant held up a hand.

"Do as he says, chap," the merchant commanded.

"Or I will cleave your head from your shoulders," Kazumi added.

The warrior only hesitated for a second more before letting go, stepping back with his hands in the air. Keeping their sword raised defensively, Kazumi reached down and grabbed the woman's arm, hauling her up out of the water. Kazumi hit her back a few times, until water sputtered from her mouth and nose. She coughed and retched.

"Fifty duques," was all Kazumi said to the merchant.

"What is the meaning of this?!" a voice boomed from behind them. A woman nearly as tall as Kazumi and bearing more scars than any of the other warriors stormed towards them, flanked by guards on either side, though she could clearly hold her own. While one might mistake her for overweight given her well-endowed curves and round stomach, a closer look revealed thick muscles in her biceps and calves. The Arena master, though perhaps mistress was more appropriate. "Who are you to hold a sword to my warrior? And you, Mekhag, trying to kill one of my witch slaves! Give me one reason not to have you beaten within an inch of your life, merchant. Or better yet, maybe I should make you fight for your head!"

"Now, now, mistress, I was merely trying to demonstrate the usefulness of my wares, these lovely cuffs that I know you are familiar with. My customer is interested in purchasing a pair to capture his own witch." Mekhag grinned and without even glancing at Kazumi responded, "Eighty-five."

"Sixty-five is the best you'll get from me," Kazumi answered, sheathing their sword.

"The lowest I can go is eighty, chap," Mekhag responded.

"And what the hell do you think you were doing, threatening one of my best warriors?" the mistress hissed at Kazumi.

"Protecting your financial interests. Another moment longer and the witch would have been dead. Seventy. Take it or leave it, Mekhag."

The merchant narrowed his eyes for a moment, as if considering if he could get a better offer, but he seemed to want to get away from the Arena and its pissed off mistress as quickly as possible. "Deal."

"Fucking witch is useless anyway. She was novel for a time, but there's only so many tricks she can do before the people get bored. In the end she just drowns most of her opponents." The mistress spat. "Don't you dare pull this shit again without my permission, Mekhag."

Kazumi counted out the money, dropping it into Mekhag's hands. The merchant grinned and approached the slave to get his shackles back. "No need for that, Mekhag. I'll be taking her, too."

"What?" the Arena mistress and Mekhag both asked at once.

"You just said yourself that she's lost her shine. Soon she'll be costing you money to feed her. I can give you ten duques," Kazumi offered, again adopting an air of disinterest.

"I could get twenty selling her to the whorehouse," the mistress responded.

"You think they'd really want a whore they had to keep shackled all the time to prevent her from drowning the customers?" Kazumi asked.

The Arena mistress grinned. "I know quite a few lads and even some lasses that wouldn't mind, would even prefer it that way."

"Fifteen to take her off your hands right now." Kazumi had already counted out the coins and held them up to the woman. She eyed them greedily.

"Fine. She's your problem now. What you'd want with her I haven't a clue."

Kazumi dropped the coins onto the ground as a final rude gesture, and the woman's guards scrambled to pick them up. "Slave. Come," Kazumi commanded, turning and walking towards the exit without looking back.

"Do you need a guide?" Mekhag called after them.

"I can see myself out," Kazumi responded as they slipped out a different door from the one they'd entered through. Only once outside did they bother to glance back. The slave woman followed behind silently, eyeing them warily. Kazumi led her through the labyrinth of alleys and tunnels back to the surface of the city. Once in the open air, they took a deep breath, trying to calm their nerves. Thankfully the two of them hadn't be accosted on their way out of the under city.

Kazumi turned to the woman, who shrank away from them. "Attack me, and you'll be dead before I can drown, understand?" The woman nodded quickly. Kazumi reached up, unlocking the shackles and removing them. "You are free to go. Have a good life."

Kazumi turned and ascended a staircase to a higher level of the city. The sound of the woman's bare feet slapping the stone followed them. Kazumi turned, glaring at her. "You may leave in any direction you wish except the one that I am walking in."

"Why did you free me?" she asked, speaking a full sentence for the first time. "Where should I go?"

"As for the first question, because I find the institution of gladiatorial combat to be disgusting and uncultured, even more so when the fighters are there against their will," Kazumi stated. "As for the second, anywhere your heart desires, so long as it is away from me."

"A slave with no master will just end up captured and sold again. I need protection," the woman argued.

"Slavery is outlawed in the Realms of Etylania. Find any guardsman and report your story. They will see you to safety."

She snorted in response. "How do you think I ended up there in the first place? Soldiers—witch hunters—came to my town looking for those of us with magic. We paid a man who said he could help us escape, but instead he sold us into slavery. I go to the law, and they're as likely to execute me for a witch as they are to help me."

Kazumi rubbed the bridge of their nose. If the damned military would just ask for volunteers rather than using witch hunters to round up magic users, none of this mess would be happening. "The witch hunts aren't seeking out witches to kill them, they're doing it to conscript them. For the war with Srahinza," Kazumi explained. "Go to the military, and I'm sure they'll gladly accept you as a new recruit. You'll even get paid a stipend."

The woman sneered. "Just trade one form of slavery for another? I'm just as likely to die fighting for them as I was in the Arena. At least there I would have died in my homeland."

Kazumi rolled their eyes and grabbed a handful of duques, holding the coins out to the woman. "Listen. Take this. Buy yourself some clothes and food and safe passage back home. Or don't, I don't really care. But if you follow me, then I *will* hand you over to the Realm's military forces myself, no doubt receiving a nice payment as a thank you. The choice is yours."

The woman stared at the money in Kazumi's outstretched hand. After a moment of hesitation, she snatched it up, then quickly stepped back out of reach. "Thank you, sir," she said, bowing quickly before turning and darting down the alley, disappearing into the night.

Kazumi didn't bother to correct her. They turned on their heel and ascended the steps two at a time. They had what they'd come for. It was time to hunt down a witch.

Foulan

They traveled slowly for the next week. Foulan kept the horses at a gentle pace, stopping often so that Mackenna could rest. Her fever had scared him, and he felt guilty that he had been the cause by pushing her too hard. He kept a close eye on Mackenna, pleased to see her health improving and strength returning.

He'd thought she would appreciate the easier pace. She surprised him when she announced one evening, "You don't need to keep coddling me. I told you I'm fine now. It's almost insulting at this point. And honestly, I'm bored of this pace."

He thought for a moment. "Well, I think I have a solution to your boredom, at least. Do you remember what I asked you before you passed out from fever last week?" Foulan responded.

"No, not really," she admitted. "It all just blended together in my head. I heard this really loud ringing in my ears, and then the whole world tilted. Why do you ask?"

He leaned back, his arms behind him to support his weight. They sat on the same side of the campfire now. Mackenna lay back on the ground on her blanket, her head on Myst's massive bulk. The wolf had humphed once in protest but hadn't moved. "I'd asked if you would be interested in learning how to fight."

"Fight?" Mackenna asked. "I suppose it couldn't hurt, though I'm pretty sure if I was ever caught, I could just use my fire to protect myself."

"Perhaps, but you've admitted yourself that it's not very stable, and besides, you would hate to end up naked every time you got in a tough scrape." He grinned. "Though I suppose then you could just try to seduce whoever's attacking you."

Mackenna grabbed an apple from her food sack, throwing it at him. He ducked, and it soared over his head, hitting Dusk in the rump. The horse snorted, glaring at her, before bending down and eating it. "Keep your dirty thoughts to yourself, Rover," Mackenna grumbled.

"Can do," he said. "Anyway, I saw how you fought against those highwaymen. You weren't bad, but there's certainly room for improvement. You were quickly disarmed, so you clearly don't know much about using a dagger. I could teach you that, and how to shoot an arrow or throw a good punch or kick when all else fails."

Mackenna seemed to think about it for a moment, then nodded. "Let's start now," she said, springing to her feet.

He blinked at her in surprise. "Right now?"

"Why not?"

He stood as well, suddenly nervous. He'd made the offer, but he'd never actually taught someone else a skill before. Where did one begin? "We'll have to hold off on archery for the moment. You can't really start off aiming at animals, so I'll need to make a target and whittle more arrows. I lost dozens when I was first learning. So, daggers or hand to hand?"

"Daggers, I think," she said. He almost sighed in relief. Hand-to-hand combat seemed like it would involve too much awkward touching.

"Right, well, first let's look at your weapon," he said. She pulled out her dagger, handing it to him.

"One of the Wanderers gave it to me. All I had before was a cooking knife," she explained.

"It's not bad." He turned the blade over in his hands. "Simple, but when you're looking to protect yourself, how pretty your dagger looks is of little importance. It's a bit dull on the edges, so we'll have to sharpen it. But it's light, and the blade is only about half the length of your forearm, which is perfect for someone small like you. You'll have to move in closer for an attack than you would with a sword, of course, but this will do. So first, let me see how you hold it."

She looked confused as she took the dagger back from him. She stood with her feet together and the knife held limply at her side.

He shook his head. "No, your stance is all wrong. Think like you're going to fight me. First of all, a dagger is a weapon, so it should be held in front of you to protect you from attack, right?" He pulled out his own blade and demonstrated.

"Uhh, right." She held it out like he showed her.

"It's not just your arm you have to pay attention to, though," he continued. "The stance of your entire body is important. If you're standing so stiffly in a fight, you'll quickly be overpowered and knocked off balance, especially considering how small you are. You want to hunch forward like this." He rolled his shoulders forward, bending his knees. "Keep your head low to avoid attacks to it, and keep your free arm up to block incoming attacks—like this." He lifted his left arm, holding it in front of his face in a fist. "And you want your left leg in front, your weight evenly distributed between both legs, so that you can lunge forward—" He demonstrated, slicing at the air in front of him, "—or back out of harm's way." He slid back with his right foot, lifting his arm to block a blow from his imaginary opponent. "Your bracers will protect you from the brunt of their blow. And remember, your dagger's hilt is just as useful as the blade is. You can cut someone with the blade or hit them on the head with the hilt to incapacitate them."

He could tell from the look on her face that she was having trouble keeping up. "I... don't get it. I stand like this?" She tried to mimic his stance.

"Not quite. Here, let me show you." He sheathed his dagger and stepped forward, repositioning her legs. "You must learn to be light on your feet; stand on your toes if you have to so that you can move quickly." He stood behind her, grabbing her arms and moving them into the correct position. "Now, imagine an opponent in front of you just there, and attack!" He guided her, his right leg nudging hers forward, their right arms moving in tandem to thrust the dagger.

So much for not having to touch her. Foulan tried to focus on what he was teaching, but with Mackenna so close, he found himself easily distracted. Her body was warm and small, the soft curve of her backside pressed against his hips. Their position, with his arms around her, was too close to an embrace.

He stepped away quickly, needing to put distance between them. Her face was flushed, but that could easily have been from exertion. She mimicked the attack he had shown her, her gaze meeting his expectantly. "Uhh, yeah, good." He nodded and resumed the stance beside her, thrusting forward with his dagger. "Right. Again. Follow my moves."

They repeated the motion again and again, until his arm muscles burned. Then they worked on a slicing motion, and then how to pummel someone with the hilt.

After nearly half an hour of drills, he finally called a halt. "You're not bad," he told her. "You should practice those three moves every day for… oh, six months. Then they'll be second nature."

"Six months?!" she cried.

Foulan laughed. "Hey, it takes decades of practice to become a master. *I'm* not even a master with the dagger, though I must admit, I'm probably one when it comes to the bow. But what I can teach you may be enough to keep you from getting killed if I'm not around to protect you."

His words hung between them. He hadn't meant for it to sound like that but wasn't sure how to take it back. After all, once he helped her find the other clan, his duty was fulfilled, and he could return to his own. It would only be a few weeks yet, assuming their journey went smoothly.

"I see…" was all Mackenna responded before turning away from him. Foulan cursed himself for his tactlessness.

They practiced the drills again the next evening after setting up camp. He watched her repeat the motion, nodding. "Good. In addition to knowing how to move, you also need to know where to stab. You stab blindly at the torso, and you're likely to hit a bone or miss a vital organ."

He pulled his leather jerkin off, followed by his shirt.

"What are you doing?" she asked in surprise.

"It's easiest to show you." He pushed down his embarrassment at being shirtless before her. He didn't miss that her eyes travelled across his chest, pausing on the occasional scar. She seemed especially interested in the tattoos that cascaded down his arms. He gave her a moment to look before stepping towards her.

"If attacking from the front, you want to aim here, under the ribs and up. It's tempting to go for the heart, but the heart is well-protected by the rib cage, and your dagger could end up getting stuck on bone. Stabbing randomly in the stomach, though, will not kill them quickly. Not only will they suffer a slow death, but in their rage, they could still harm you." He took her hand holding the dagger, showing her the motion.

"Then, there's the back." He turned so that his back was to her. "Again, under the ribcage and up is your best bet." He indicated the spot.

He turned to face her again. "Of course, both of those options will give them plenty of time to call for backup. If you need to kill silently, you want to go for the throat. You can try slashing the throat while facing them, but it's easier to grab them, clamp a hand over their mouth, and then cut the throat." He grabbed her, quickly spinning her around so that her back was to his chest, and made the motion with his empty hand. He tried to ignore his racing heart. He was teaching her something important, something that might save her life. He couldn't deny that she felt so soft and small in his arms. Small... and frail.

"That sounds like something an assassin would do," she said after he released her.

He nodded. "I've never had to do so myself, thank the gods. But it's important to know, nonetheless." Foulan searched for something to say to fill the silence. "I haven't taught you the hardest part about wielding a dagger yet," he said. "No matter how many times you run through practices, you will never be prepared for it."

"What's that?" she asked hesitantly.

He sighed. "The day you actually have to use it."

"What do you mean?"

He grabbed his shirt, pulling it back on, and sat on the ground. She followed suit. "With the bow, there is a certain removal from the act of killing. You loose the arrow, but you do not feel it as it enters a man's body, as it pierces his flesh and organs. With the dagger…" He shook his head and looked down at his open palms. "It is all right there, in your hand, the entire time. The hardest part is the act of stabbing, thrusting it in through skin and muscle, feeling their lifeblood spill out onto your fingers, and knowing that you've just ended a life with your own hands. I hope you never have to go through with that, Mackenna, but if you do… *do not hesitate*. The killing blow must be quick and merciful, both for his sake and your own safety."

She looked away, out into the forest, where a breeze blew through the trees, loosing a torrent of red, gold, and brown leaves that swirled to the ground chaotically. "You forget," she said quietly. "I've already killed two men with my own hands."

Like he could forget. It was the reason there were wanted posters with her face on it. The reason she had met him in the first place. "Do you… do you regret it?" he asked gently.

She was quiet for a moment. "It was so easy. The flames consumed me, consumed us all. The first one caught fire and went down on his own, but the second one. The one that murdered my father…" Her hands clenched at her sides as she kept her head turned away from him. "I didn't want him to die easily. I wanted it to be painful. Very painful. I grabbed him with my bare hands and held his throat. I watched the horror in his eyes, the suffering, and I didn't care. No, that's not true… I *reveled* in it. All I wanted was for him to burn."

She paused. Foulan wanted to say something, but couldn't think of anything that wouldn't sound hollow.

"My magic took over completely, pushing away all thought, all that made me… me. I didn't feel guilt or regret," she said at last. "And… I still don't, in a way. Regret that I fucked things up so terribly? Yes. But regret at taking their lives? No." Her voice wavered. Foulan touched her chin, tilting her face towards him. Tears streamed down her cheeks. "What does that make me?" she whispered. "Am I a monster?"

He shook his head. "No. You're a grieving daughter. You watched your father be murdered, and you avenged him."

"Then why won't the pain go away?" she cried.

He didn't have an answer. Instead, he simply pulled her awkwardly into his arms, hugging her while she sobbed. With that simple action, it was as if an invisible barrier between them broke. He hadn't wanted this journey. Hadn't wanted anything to do with her. But now… Mackenna was his friend, and he would see to it that she finished this journey, that she found the peace she sought.

Mackenna

The river they had been following had grown shallower and narrower as they'd traveled. Soon it became crossable with bridges, and they no longer saw ships with sails, only smaller fishing vessels. After a week their path turned away from it, and they traveled through another wooded area for a day before emerging into the boglands.

It was the first time Mackenna had ever seen anything of the sort. She had grown up surrounded by the forests and fields of her home. But this land was much flatter and seemed to stretch on forever. They frequently came across large ponds, the reeds and grasses growing straight up out of the water. At first she had assumed them to be relatively shallow, but she quickly realized how deceptive their appearance was. A seemingly stable patch of foliage could simply be floating on the water, and if one of the horses stepped off the path to grab a mouthful of grass to munch on, their legs would immediately squelch deep into the muck. They had to travel slowly and be careful not to stray far from the path for fear of sinking into one of the hidden puddles. There were occasionally copses of evergreen trees, but these were few and far between. It made it difficult to find any privacy for relieving herself, but Foulan was a gentleman and always turned his back.

It had also grown noticeably colder since they'd entered the boglands. Without woods to shield them, the wind picked up more speed. Thankfully, the peat that grew all around them turned out to be great for burning, keeping their fire warm and roaring at night. Perhaps the worst part, though, was the smell. The whole place reeked of decay and stagnant water.

Despite their miserable surroundings, Mackenna had grown to enjoy the rhythm of their journey. They traveled during the morning and into the afternoon. In the evening they set up camp, and Foulan trained her in combat techniques. Then at night they shared stories.

To pass the time during the day, she would point out different plants they saw in their travels, telling him the properties. Doing so made her remember her father's journals, burned up to almost nothing. She ached to hold them again, to flip through the well-worn pages, to see her father's neat and precise handwriting that always made her own look sloppy beside it. It would certainly have made it easier to teach Foulan if she could show him the sketches. There were many healing herbs that she doubted they would come across in the marshes.

"Let's focus on hand-to-hand combat tonight," he said after they'd finished setting up camp that evening. "You need to know how to protect yourself if you don't have a dagger or you've been disarmed. First, make a fist." Mackenna thought it an odd request but did so. He smiled, rolling his eyes. "Yeah, that's what I thought. Never put your thumb inside your fist. It's an easy way to break it. Now show me your stance, like you would do if you were holding a dagger."

She positioned her arms and legs the way he'd taught her, left leg in back and right in front, knees bent and ready to lunge, arms held before her. "Good. The basic stance is the same. One arm before your body to protect your chest, one up higher, but not too close, or they're likely to smack your fist back into your face." He wacked her arm in demonstration. She nodded and lowered it slightly.

"Now, just like you'd lunge with the dagger, you want to lunge forward with your fist. But you're aiming differently this time." He stood in front of her, pointing to the center of his chest. "You're not likely to kill someone with just your fists, but you can still incapacitate them so that you can escape. You want to punch in the center of the chest here. Not the rib cage. That will just bruise your hand. Right here below it. This will knock the wind from them. Trust me, I've taken a few blows here before. No matter how tough they are, you hit them in the right spot with the right force, and they'll be lying on the ground struggling to breathe, might even lose consciousness."

She half hoped he would take off his shirt again to show her, but apparently the technique didn't have to be as exact as the knifework. She tried to ignore her disappointment and focus. "The other places to aim for," he continued. "The face, right in the middle. Break the nose. Or you can hit the jaw, potentially knock them out. Also, the throat, right here. Now, most of these won't kill them, like I've said. But..." He took her fist, opening it and bending her hand back so that her palm faced up at him. "If you were to jab up into the nose with the heel of your palm," he guided her hand through the movement, "you could potentially drive the nose up into the skull, killing them instantly, though it would take a great deal of force."

"What if they're too close?" she asked. "Like, if I was against a wall and couldn't pull my arm back?"

He nodded. "Great question! Now you're thinking. In such cases, use the elbows. Bring your arms in close, lift the elbow, and swing it towards those vulnerable spots on the face and neck."

"What if they've pinned my arms?"

"Then you use your legs, your knees. Anything you can. The most important thing is to break their grip and escape."

"Could you show me?" she asked, heat rising to her cheeks. Part of her wondered if she was more curious about learning or about the feeling of his strong arms wrapped around her.

He paused, then nodded, stepping behind her. He wrapped his arms around hers, pinning them to her body. "If they're behind you, you can bring your back foot up, aim for their shins, or if they're a man, in between the legs. You could also slam your head backwards, try to break their nose." He let go, then stepped around to her front, doing the same action. "Much the same if they're in front of you, but you'll want to bring your knee up. Or you can try to slam your forehead into their nose. You can even bite them, if it comes to that. Anything to get yourself free."

As he talked, she found her eyes drawn to his lips, so close to hers. She'd never noticed before how long his lashes were, or the way his throat bobbed when he spoke. She realized he'd stopped speaking, staring at her now in turn.

His arms were incredibly toned, no doubt from years of practice with a bow. Feeling them around her, she didn't think she could break free from them if he was her enemy. The thought should frighten her, and yet... she felt safe.

Foulan suddenly stepped away, leaving her cold at the loss of his body heat. "Right..." he said, his voice cracking somewhat. He cleared his throat. "Let's keep practicing."

They practiced punching the air for the next hour as the sun set, first with her aiming at him but not connecting. When he was convinced she was hitting the same spots consistently, he started to walk around her, observing her stance and offering pointers as she continued, imagining her target in front of her.

When it became too dark to see, they both sank down beside the fire. "Have you ever had to kill someone?" she asked as they ate dinner.

He was quiet for a few moments, chewing. Then he nodded slowly. "A few for sure, yeah. Maybe more. Only ever in self-defense, and my purpose was always to escape. Don't know if some of them died later or not."

"Who? Why did they attack you?" she asked, knowing that she was being nosy but too curious not to ask.

"Bandits mostly. When you travel constantly as we do, it's impossible to avoid them."

She was surprised. "Bandits would attack such a large group?"

"Not usually, no. But they have a few times when they had enough numbers. What they usually do is wait until a few people split from the group, then ambush them and take anything they have. I've been attacked a few times when hunting, but once I had Myst at my side, that took care of that problem. Most people aren't crazy enough to confront someone with a wolf protecting them."

"How did you end up with a wolf companion, anyway? I've never thought to ask."

He grinned, leaning over and scratching the canine behind her ears. "I found her. It was the middle of winter. I was out hunting for some meat, a squirrel or bird, anything I could find, when I hear this high-pitched crying. I follow the noise and find the source, a little pup sitting in the snow, all alone. There were no tracks around to indicate mother had come and gone, no sign of other pups. The best I could surmise was that she'd been abandoned by the rest of the pack because she was a runt, too weak to keep up and survive the harsh winter."

"A runt? Her?"

"Yeah, shocking as it is, she's small for a wolf. Well, there I was, with a decision to make. Did I move on and keep hunting? I wouldn't find anything there; she was making far too much noise. Did I leave her, hope maybe her pack came back for her, as unlikely as it seemed? But as soon as she caught sight of me, she ran straight up to me, begging like any pup would. I looked into her blue eyes and fell in love." He gazed at her now, and Myst returned his look lovingly, laying her huge head in his lap. They were silent for a few minutes as he stroked his hand through the wolf's fur.

"When else?"

"Sorry?" he asked.

"I mean, when else have you had to kill someone."

"Oh. The occasional tavern brawl." He sighed. "But we've also been attacked by people trying to drive us out of town. Because we're Wanderers."

"You've been attacked simply because you're Wanderers?"

He shrugged. "There are many people who hate us. Usually the worst they'll do is throw insults or the occasional rock. But there have been a couple of times where things got ugly."

"I don't understand," she said, shaking her head. "There is peace between all these different countries in the Kingdoms. The Kingdoms of Etylania have people of all different skin colors and even languages. So why do they hate Wanderers so much?"

"Maybe because we practice a different religion? Maybe because we don't come from here originally, so they see us as invaders? Maybe—no, definitely—because our homeland is at war with them. But maybe it's simply because they know they can get away with it. Most countries' laws protect their *citizens*. We're not citizens, so we aren't protected. We can't go to a local governor or constabulary and report it because they won't be bothered to do anything."

"That's terrible. Do you ever think about going back to Srahinza? The Wanderers, I mean," she asked.

He frowned. "It gets brought up at every Gathering. There are mixed feelings on the subject. Some people want to return to what was once our homeland and take it back. Occasionally a Wanderer will travel to Srahinza for a time, then come back. The stories they bring back make it clear that Srahinza is not the land we once loved. It has changed."

"How so?"

His gaze darkened. "*They* changed it. The usurpers. It was once a land of brightness and beauty. Now it is bleak and austere. They have even changed the religion, so that it barely resembles how we worship anymore."

"How do you change a religion?" Mackenna asked. "Seems like an impossible thing to do."

He shrugged. "Not really. You tell the people, 'This is how you will worship now. If you don't worship this way, you will be killed.'"

"But won't people just continue to practice their religion in private? You can tell people they can't do something, but you can't control their thoughts."

He nodded. "True, but you can rewrite the stories. Make it illegal to tell any version but your own. As the generations pass, the people will forget the original stories and only remember the new ones. Stories have power."

"So how did they do it? What did they change?" she asked.

"When the usurpers took over, killing the tribal leaders and swallowing up their lands, they wanted to break with tradition as much as possible. Because most of what is now Srahinza had been ruled by women, the Wise Women as we know them, and the usurpers were all men, they wanted to destroy any notion of women ever having power again. The best way to do that was to completely destroy the Mother Goddess. So, they replaced the goddess Adira with the god Zaman. I'll tell you first the story they apparently tell in Srahinza, then the one that we Wanderers know to be true.

"Zaman, the king of the gods, had many wives, but his favorite was Adira, whom he made his queen. However, Adira was not satisfied with her husband or the realm of the gods, and she would often travel down to the world of mortals, whom she found fascinating. There she met and fell in love with a mortal man named Khalid, and together they carried on an affair for years. They bore three children, named Maha, Isra, and Seli.

"Now, Zaman had another wife, Zarya. She was extremely jealous of Adira and longed to be Zaman's favorite wife and be made queen of the gods. So one day, she follows Adira in secret and sees her visit her mortal husband and their three children on earth. She returns to Zaman and reports what she has seen.

"Zaman is furious. He storms down to earth, where he catches them together. He strikes down Khalid, killing him, while Adira and Zarya look on. Adira gathers her three children and escapes with them, Zaman chasing after. But the people there love Adira, and they help her and her children to hide away from Zaman. Growing angry that he cannot find her, he unleashes a curse on the land, killing all vegetation before him, turning it to desert where nothing living could hide from him.

"He finally finds Adira, but by the time he does, her children have escaped to another land. He curses them to wander forever and to never find their way home. Then he takes Adira back to the realm of the gods, where he has her shamed before killing her."

"Shamed how?" Mackenna interrupted, enthralled with the story.

Foulan grimaced. "He has her stripped naked and paraded through the streets for all the gods to see. Then she is executed. The gruesomeness of her execution varies with the teller, but it is never pretty."

"How awful," she whispered.

He nodded. "According to this story, the Wanderers are descendants of Adira and Khalid, which is why we wander, never to return home to the Srahinza Empire."

Mackenna frowned, thinking about this. "But the Wanderers haven't been wandering for very long. Just a couple hundred years, right? So this story couldn't be very old, then."

Foulan smiled. "And therein is the problem. The Srahinza Empire's versions of tales are often contradictory. So now I'll tell you the true story, at least according to the Wanderers.

"Adira was the Mother Goddess, queen of all the gods. The sole ruler, mind you. She did fall in love with and marry a mortal, Khalid, and they had the three children together that I mentioned earlier. Because Khalid was mortal and her children only demigods, they could not travel to the realm of the gods, but Adira would visit them often.

"Zarya was her sister, who fell in love with the god Zaman. Zaman, however, was not a good man. He was jealous and power hungry, and he was not content with just Zarya's love. He wanted to marry Adira so that he could be king of the gods. So, he convinces Zarya that Khalid must be killed, but agrees to her stipulation that he spare their children. When Adira is away, they go to earth and kill Khalid, and then Zaman turns on the children, intending to kill them too.

"At this moment, Adira discovers him and Zarya. Though she is too late to save her husband, she steps in front of the killing blow meant for her children, sacrificing herself for their lives. Zarya, shocked that Zaman went back on his word and that he killed the queen of the gods, helps the children to escape. As in the other story, Zaman turns the landscape into a wasteland in the hopes of finding them, but he fails. Eventually, Zaman gives up and returns to the realm of the gods, but Zarya refuses to join him. She goes off into the desert and cries for a hundred years, her tears forming an oasis. There, she sinks to the bottom of the pool and dies."

"And what about Zaman?" Mackenna asked. "Is he ever punished for his crimes?"

"Adira's grown children return as adults. They go through many trials together on their quest to break into the realm of the gods. Eventually they succeed, and together they expose

Zaman and kill him. That is, according to our legends. I have heard that in Srahinza, it is different. He is no longer the king of the gods, but is now worshipped as the only God, the rest having been reduced to saints. But we know the truth. The first ruler of the gods was a woman, and she was betrayed by a man."

When they finished the last of the potatoes they'd bought at the previous town, Foulan took the burlap potato sack and a piece of charcoal, drawing three concentric circles on the sack. He put rocks in the bottom of it, then filled it the rest of the way with straw and pinecones, until it was bulging. "What's that for?" she asked, eyeing his art project amusedly.

"This is a target. For practicing archery, which is what we're going to learn today." He answered, attaching a length of rope to the sack. He went to a nearby pine tree, hanging the target from a low branch. "You will aim at it with your bow, trying to hit inside the circles. If you get inside the outer, larger circle, that's pretty good. If you get inside the smaller, inner circle, you're doing better. And if you can hit inside the smallest circle in the very middle, you've a true shot. It's how you test yourself. For now, though, just hitting the target at all is going to be our main focus."

"What, are you doubting I can do it?" she asked, offended.

He lifted an eyebrow. "Have you ever held a bow in your life?" he asked. The cocky grin on his face only annoyed her more.

"Well, no, but it can't be that hard, right?" She snatched the bow from his hand.

He handed her an arrow, showing her how to nock it. "This bow is probably a bit big for you, but it's all we've got, so might as well try it. It will just take a lot of strength to pull back the string. The trick is to not focus too long on trying to aim. The longer you hold the string back, the more your arm will tire, and the more tired your arm is, the more likely you are to shoot wide. It's best to try to pull back, aim, and fire all in one smooth motion." He stepped back so he was behind her. "Give it a shot."

She tried to mimic the actions she'd seen him do plenty of times now. She was surprised at how hard it was to pull back the string and how much her arms shook at the effort. She squinted at the target, letting loose.

The arrow didn't get close. It didn't even reach it, planting itself in the soft ground halfway between her and the target. "How?" she asked.

He chuckled from behind her. "You're going to have to put more muscle in it. Here, let me show you."

He stepped up behind her, his chest at her back, his hands on hers. They'd been in this position a few times now, but she didn't think she would ever get used to it, to the feeling of his muscular chest through his shirt and jerkin. He guided her arms, pulling the string back further, his own arms pulling most of the weight. "Like this," he said, his breath tickling the spot where her short hair met the back of her neck. She shivered, though not from the cold.

He stepped back, giving her another arrow, and she tried again. Without his arm to help, the muscles between her shoulders clenched in protest at the weight of the bow. She loosed the arrow once more. This time it zipped past the target and off into the brush behind it.

"This is impossible!" she exclaimed in frustration.

"Not as easy as it looks, eh, Spitfire?" he teased.

She stamped her foot. "Can *you* hit inside the middle circle?" she asked skeptically. It was pretty small, about the size of a plum. She didn't see how that was even possible.

"Of course," he gloated. "I'm the best shot of all the Wanderers. Probably in all of Etylania."

"I don't believe it," she said, crossing her arms over her chest.

"Oh? Care to wager on it?"

"Sure. If you can't hit inside that circle, you have to stop calling me 'Spitfire,'" she told him.

"What's wrong with 'Spitfire?'" he asked.

"Besides the fact that it's annoying?"

He shrugged. "Fine. You've got a bet." He held out his hand, and she handed the bow over. He nocked an arrow and stepped back. And then stepped further back. And then even further. How far could he shoot? There was no way he could hit that tiny target from so far away. She was sure to win this bet.

"It's usually a good idea not to be in front of an archer when he's shooting," he called to her. "Though I'm not going to miss, of course."

She snorted and moved out of the way. He drew the arrow back. He seemed so relaxed and self-assured, quite the opposite of how frazzled he looked whenever he had to speak with anyone.

"Alright, watch this closely," he said, "because the arrow moves pretty fast, and I don't want you accusing me of cheating." Under his tight wool shirt, she could see the muscles of his shoulders bunching as they held the bow taut. He squinted, his face all focus and seriousness, and released the arrow with a whoosh. There was a thump, and his face broke into a proud smile as she turned to examine the target.

It had hit the target dead in the center. Mackenna stared at it in astonishment as the sack swung on the branch, the arrow head poking out the other side.

"Well, I do believe I won that bet," he said. "Now, the question is, what do *I* want?" He sauntered towards her, and she realized with a sinking feeling that he had never actually placed his end of the bargain before shooting. How stupid of her to agree to a bet without knowing what he wanted! But then, it couldn't be anything too bad. Maybe scrubbing the dishes or cooking all the meals for a week or two. He could ask for money, but it wasn't like she had any.

"Well? What'll it be?" she asked, crossing her arms over her chest and scowling, trying to give him her meanest look.

He grinned, stepping toe to toe with her. Despite how tall she was, he was still a good head above her, and she had to crane her neck to look up into his eyes. "I think, *Spitfire*, I will take as my boon… a kiss."

Mackenna stared at him for a few seconds, waiting for him to laugh in her face and say he was just jesting. A kiss? Had he really said that? Had she just heard wrong? But that lazy smirk didn't leave his lips. "What?" she asked dumbly.

"A kiss," he repeated. "You do know what a kiss is, right? I mean, your people do kiss each other? You see, it's when two people put their lips together—"

"I know what a kiss is," she interrupted, holding up a hand. "I just… why?"

He shrugged. "Why not?"

"That doesn't answer—"

Before she could get out another word, he grabbed her shoulders, his lips descending on hers. Mackenna froze in shock, not knowing what to do. He just stood there, his eyes closed, his mouth pressed gently against hers. He didn't move or speak, and neither did she. She couldn't. She wanted to pull away, and yet she didn't. She wanted to pull him closer, she realized, and yet the thought frightened and mortified her. The truth was, she didn't know what she wanted or what she should do.

But when he pulled away, gazing down at her with half-lidded, dark eyes, she realized that what she didn't want was for him to stop kissing her.

Before she could react, he stepped away from her, out of reach. Mackenna just stared at him in confusion, wanting to ask him what that was all about, what it meant, had she done it right, and most of all, would he do it again? But then he frowned, his eyes downcast, a sudden look of anger on his face. "Sorry," he muttered and turned, walking away from her and into the trees.

Foulan

Foulan stomped through the brush, pretending to look for the stray arrow. He was such an idiot! What had he been thinking? He'd spoken before he'd had time to stop himself, telling her he wanted to kiss her. And then, when she didn't protest, he'd done it before he could lose his nerve. But it had all gone horribly wrong. She'd just stood there, not pushing him away or pulling him closer. She was obviously too disgusted to do anything. This last week, whenever they'd practiced fighting, he'd thought she'd been hinting at him, making excuses to touch him. Thought this was something she wanted as much as he did. He'd been a fool to think she was interested in him like that.

He'd been a fool to fall for her at all. Foulan froze, staring up at the dusky sky in shock. Was that it? Had he fallen for Mackenna? Just a few months ago—had it been that long already?—he'd loathed her for coming into his life and complicating it, for putting him and his family in danger, for forcing him on this adventure at all.

But as he'd spent more time with her, gotten to know her, he'd realized she was probably the first and only friend he'd ever had besides Myst. He felt like he could talk to her about anything and she would understand, wouldn't judge him. He found himself smiling and joking and even laughing around her. When she'd gotten sick, he hadn't shied away from the opportunity to take care of her, and as strange as it sounded, he had liked it. He had liked being there for her and taking care of her when she was ill. He had liked that she relied on him.

He couldn't deny he was attracted to her. He certainly hadn't been at first. At first, he'd found her appearance, well not repulsive, but foreign and odd. She was so thin, curveless, and pale. Wanderer women were all dark, curvy, and completely comfortable with bearing their skin. This girl with her bright red hair and freckles and layers and layers of clothing, men's clothing no less, was the opposite of what his people considered attractive.

And yet, he found himself drawn more and more to her appearance. He found that fiery red hair drew his eye whenever she was around. Her pale skin meant that whenever she was embarrassed, her cheeks turned a bright, rosy pink. That thin body made her lithe and graceful, and while she had very little in the way of a chest, especially with her men's garb on, her backside actually looked quite nice in breaches. And her eyes. First he had thought they were merely green, but he'd since realized he'd been wrong. They were the emerald of a forest, speckled with brown and gold like trees rising from a bed of moss.

Yes, there was no denying he was attracted to her. He hadn't forgotten that image of her lying asleep in the bath, her small breasts bared to his eyes, the water dripping off of her creamy skin. It had risen in his mind unbidden as soon as his lips had touched hers, as soon as he'd felt her small body pressed against him, so warm and delicate that he just wanted to sweep her into his arms and feel every inch of her skin with his hands, his mouth. Alongside the image of her naked had risen other images, these of fantasy instead of memory: images of her lying beneath him, her body responding to his every touch, his every kiss.

Foulan groaned, leaning against a tree, his face buried in his hand. He needed to stop this line of thought before it went too far. Already his manhood was growing hard, and if he didn't control himself, he would have to take care of himself here in the woods. How shameful and embarrassing. Besides, she clearly hadn't wanted him and never would. It was a stupid mistake to kiss her, and he would never do it again. The disgust on her face was evident, was enough to dampen his desire. But now he'd probably gone and ruined everything, destroyed his tenuous friendship with her, made it impossible for them to look at each other again without it being awkward. If he'd just thought with his head instead of letting his body rule him, he would never have gotten into this damn mess!

Foulan slammed his fist against a tree, the throb of pain reverberating through his knuckles easing his anger and frustration somewhat. If her life wasn't in danger, if he wasn't duty bound to protect her, and, yes, if he hadn't fallen for her so pathetically, he would leave now, travel to the other end of the Realms if need be to avoid ever having to see her face again. But he knew that wasn't a possibility, and even just thinking it showed how weak and pathetic he was when it came to dealing with people. No, he would return and just never speak of this again.

Foulan had reached the edge of the small cluster of trees, nothing but more swamp ahead of him. He gazed back the way he'd come, watching Mackenna's shadow in the twilight as she built a fire and began to cook. He watched her until the last of the light faded and all he could see was the campfire in the distance. Finally, he worked up the nerve to walk back, stumbling through the dark, the fire his beacon. When he reached it, he found Mackenna asleep, or at least feigning it, and for that Foulan was thankful. He was surprised to see that she had left half a pot of stew for him nearby. After eating, he unrolled his bedroll on the other side of the fire, a respectful distance for a man and woman who were not married or together in any way, and lay down. Myst settled beside him, though she kept gazing back and forth between Foulan and Mackenna, as if sensing that something was wrong. "I've really screwed things up this time, haven't I girl?" he asked. Myst just whined and dropped her head on his chest.

The next morning was the most awkward Foulan had ever felt in his life. Neither of them spoke as they ate, and they avoided eye contact altogether. Myst whined and paced between them, and Foulan snapped at her to sit still. The wolf harrumphed and trotted over to the path, sitting with her back to them. When they mounted their horses and began riding, the wolf merely followed them down the trail sullenly, refusing to look at either Mackenna or Foulan. Great. So now none of them were getting along.

Three days passed in this way. They only spoke to each other when necessary, and it was always uncomfortable. Neither brought up the kiss, as if they both wished to will it out of existence.

Sitting by the fire in the evening, the looming silence between them was broken by Myst's growl.

"What is it, girl?" Foulan asked. Myst faced away from them, staring into the boglands. Her haunches were raised, and she had flattened herself down, either afraid or ready to attack. Foulan grabbed his bow, though he wasn't sure what good it would do him in the dark, and Mackenna unsheathed her dagger.

It seemed like it took forever for Foulan's eyes to adjust to the darkness now that he was looking away from the fire. Across a pond was a small bunch of spruce trees. They looked eerie in the pale moonlight, their shadows stretching out like long fingers. Suddenly, Foulan saw a light twinkling in the trees.

"Do you see that?" Mackenna asked Foulan in a whisper.

He nodded. "Friend or foe?" he asked back, his voice also low.

He squinted into the forest, watching the light. Who would be traveling through this dangerous bog at night? One misstep and they could be in water up to their waist or even over their head. "The path doesn't go that way," Mackenna said. "I don't remember if there was any safe way to get to those trees. A boat maybe?"

He strained to listen. He could hear the fire crackling, the bugs chirping, Myst growling, and the wind blowing through the rushes, but not the sound of a paddle hitting the water. "I don't hear anything," Foulan pointed out. Even if the person or people were in a boat, the light was moving much too quickly, dimming and brightening, bluish in color.

Myst was at the edge of the pond's bank now, and the light seemed to be growing closer. And then suddenly it winked out. They all continued to stare, searching for it. It wasn't until Myst stopped growling that they finally relaxed some. When the light didn't reappear for a few more minutes, they returned to the fire, both wary. "A bug, maybe?" Mackenna asked.

"Maybe," Foulan agreed, though he didn't seem convinced. Myst returned to the fire, curling up next to them. Eventually he heard the sound of Mackenna breathing deeply in sleep, but sleep eluded him as he stared into the darkness.

Mackenna

The strange lights continued for the next few nights. They always appeared late at night, around the time that Foulan and Mackenna would normally go to sleep. They were not accompanied by any discernible sound, and Mackenna and Foulan likely wouldn't have noticed them at all if it weren't for Myst suddenly alerting them. The first night it had only been a single light, but with each continuing night, more would appear. They were always far off in the distance, and they often moved sporadically.

Mackenna and Foulan took shifts during the night, afraid they were being stalked by someone. Was there a pack of bounty hunters following them, waiting until the right moment to strike? It seemed unlikely. After all, it was just the two of them and Myst—easy targets, unless they somehow knew of Mackenna's fire magic. It was the only reason they kept a fire burning through the night. While it made them easier to spot in the boglands, it could serve as a reminder to those who might think of attacking.

If that even was the cause of the strange lights. They often disappeared as quickly and silently as they appeared, and afterwards Myst would circle their campsite a few times, sniffing the air, before returning to the fire and lying down. Mackenna had grown to trust the wolf's keen senses and her ability to wake suddenly whenever danger was nearby.

After a week in the boglands, haunted by the strange lights, Mackenna and Foulan were both relieved to find the lake they had sought. Just as Wise Woman Drynka had predicted, there they found Clan Halah. The area around Calmloch was too soggy for a camp, so the clan had set up on a rocky highland nearby. From their vantage point, the Wanderers saw Foulan and Mackenna approaching long before they arrived and came to greet them.

"Foulan!" a warm feminine voice called. Mackenna found a middle-aged woman hailing them. She had short-cropped hair and wore breeches but did nothing to hide her cleavage, making it quite clear that she, unlike Mackenna, was not attempting to disguise her femininity. "When I saw that beast you always travel with, I knew it was you. And who's your friend?"

Foulan dismounted from his horse, smiling. "This is Mackenna," he said, not bothering with her assumed identity now that they were among friends again. "I brought her here at Wise Woman Drynka's request to speak with Wise Woman Halah."

The woman frowned. "Well, I suppose you arrived just in time," she said, "though I'm not sure how much wisdom you'll get from her."

"What do you mean?" Foulan asked, pausing in his unpacking of Dusk.

The woman shook her head sadly. "Halah is dying. She told me so a few months ago. It was the last clear thing she told me. Since then her mind has…" The woman paused, as if trying to find the right words. "She is very confused now. Often speaking nonsense. Her mind is gone, I fear, and I believe her body will soon follow."

"I'm so sorry," Foulan whispered.

The woman shrugged. "Well, you've come this far, and I'm certainly not going to turn you away. See to your horses, and I'll see if we can find some lunch for you."

Mackenna and Foulan unloaded their horses and brushed them down, then left them to mingle with the clan's other animals. As Mackenna greeted the other members of Clan Halah, she noticed something different about them. The clan was about half the size of Drynka's, and there were very few children. She also didn't see any men.

The woman, who Mackenna learned was named Fatimah and was the clan leader, invited them into her wagon, grabbing a hot tea kettle from beside the communal fire. Foulan and Mackenna settled onto some cushions on the floor. Like most wagons, there was little in the way of actual furniture.

"Where are your men?" Mackenna asked. "Are they off hunting or working somewhere?"

Fatimah seemed surprised. "Foulan didn't tell you?" She cocked her head to the side and gave a small smile. "There are no men in our clan. It is for women only. It has been so for many generations."

"What do you mean?" Mackenna asked in confusion. "Don't you have fathers, brothers, sons?"

Fatimah poured them each a cup of tea and then sat before them. "Some of us do, elsewhere. Others do not. But this clan has always been women only. Wanderers can change clans whenever they wish — usually at a Gathering, as we are seldom together otherwise. Different clans operate differently depending on their Wise Woman and her rules. This is our rule. The women here all abide by it and have different reasons for being here. Some are orphans. Some have lost their husbands.

Some are victims of the violence of men. It matters not their reason."

"Then none of you have children?" Mackenna asked.

"I didn't say that. When the clans meet, some of our women will go off with a man. Being a member of this clan does not require celibacy." Fatimah sipped her tea. "Anytime a woman wishes to go into a town and take a lover, that is her prerogative. But those men are not welcome to join the clan. And if she has a son, she is welcome to raise him until he becomes a teenager. Then, she must decide if she wants to send him to a different clan alone or go with him."

Mackenna eyed Foulan. "But he's here…?"

Fatimah smiled gently. "Wanderer men may visit, like Foulan is now, but they cannot stay more than a few days, and they must camp away from the clan at night."

Mackenna wanted to ask more, but Foulan interrupted her. "About Halah. Will she be able to speak with us?"

Fatimah shrugged sadly. "I wish I knew. Some days are better than others. On a good day, she will recognize me or another clan member, even talk to us. But most of the time she is nonsensical." Her eyebrows furrowed. "I hate to say this, but I think it would be easier if she was weak of body, as well. When she gets… confused, it is very difficult to calm her down. She tries to fight us, tries to wander off. Someone has to be with her constantly." She rubbed her face, and Mackenna noticed for the first time how tired she appeared, with dark shadows under her eyes. "What did you come to speak to her about, anyway?"

"It's a bit of a story," Foulan said, his eyes landing on Mackenna. He told Fatimah of how he stumbled upon Mackenna, of the men who were chasing her and why, of the bounty hunters who attacked them in Hartland, and their ensuing quest. "Wise Woman Drynka said that we should seek out Halah, that she would be able to tell us how we can find the Fae Folk," he finished.

The color drained from Fatimah's face. "You seek the Fair Ones?" She shook her head. "You should end this quest now. No good will come of it."

"What do you mean?" Mackenna asked. "I mean, are they even real? Or are they just children's stories?"

Fatimah took a deep breath. "They're real, or at least, I believe they are. Wise Woman Halah claims to have known one, when she was younger. She wouldn't speak of it often, but she mentioned it from time to time, even before her mind started to go. But that's not the only reason I believe. In these parts, many locals claim to have seen the Fair Ones. Here they call them the Wee Folk, for they are diminutive. But don't let their small size fool you—they are dangerous creatures."

"How so? What do they do?" Foulan asked.

"They lead people to their deaths," she replied. "The boglands are dangerous enough as it is, but the locals will tell you that you should never venture out after dark. And if by chance you do, never follow the fairy lights."

Mackenna's body went cold. "Fairy lights?"

Fatimah nodded. "That's what they call them. Little blue lights that appear in the distance. Nobody can seem to agree entirely on what they are. Some say the lights themselves are Wee Folk. Others say they are lanterns being held by invisible Fae. Others claim that they are lost souls. But all agree that they are dangerous. They lead unwary travelers away from safe paths, until the person becomes lost or, most often, falls into a deep pool and drowns. Or perhaps the Wee Folk drag them down. Nobody is certain. What is certain is that you don't want to seek them out."

"But I have to," Mackenna whispered. "Drynka said that that was the only way I could be free. If I don't…"

"I urge you to give up your quest, for your own safety," Fatimah said. "I am sure Drynka had good intentions sending you here, but I don't think she knew just how dangerous the Wee Folk are."

"You don't understand," Mackenna argued, close to tears. "You don't know what it's like to live with something you can't control, something that feels like a… a curse. I will be hunted for the rest of my life if I can't find some way to get rid of the fire. It has ruined my life. I want nothing more than to snuff it out."

Foulan frowned, his eyes filled with pity, and Mackenna forced herself to look away, hating how pathetic it made her feel.

"Is that really what you seek?" Fatimah asked. When Mackenna didn't answer, she continued, "I can see that you won't be swayed from your path. Of course you can speak with Halah, for what little good it will do." She stood. "My wife Samar is with her now. Let me check and see how she is doing today."

After Fatimah left the hut, Mackenna asked aloud, "Did she say wife?"

"Yep," Foulan answered.

Mackenna turned to him with an irritated frown. "Do you enjoy making me feel ignorant?" she asked.

He quirked an eyebrow as if in confusion, but she didn't miss the twinkle in his eye. "How so?"

She threw her hands in the air. "You could have told me that we were going to visit a clan of all women. And that they marry one another."

"Is there a problem with that?" he asked, swirling the remaining tea in his cup.

"No, of course not." She shook her head. "That's not the point."

"Then what is?" he asked.

Mackenna sighed. "I always feel like a fool around you. I understand that I don't know much of the world and other people, but you could help prevent some embarrassment on my part."

"I see," he said slowly. "I apologize, Mackenna. It was never my intention to embarrass you. I suppose sometimes I just forget that you are not as well traveled as me, that so much of the world is new and different to you." He smiled at her, and she found her irritation cooling.

Fatimah returned soon after, an apology on her face. "Today is not good. Wise Woman Halah is in one of her moods. She has been very insistent as of late on going swimming in the lake, despite the cool temperature. She is angry that we won't allow her to. Maybe try again tomorrow."

Foulan and Mackenna nodded and left the wagon. Wanting to contribute to the clan's food store, they decided to go hunting. Foulan took down two rabbits and three geese. With each one, he approached the poor dying creature, its legs kicking, eyes wild, whimpering in despair, and sliced its throat quickly and efficiently. He then whispered a small prayer over it, thanking Prasamundi, the goddess of the hunt. Foulan even let Mackenna try her hand at shooting the bow. It was a good thing that he had already caught enough for dinner and to share with the others, because she didn't manage to hit a single thing she shot at.

They returned to the camp at dusk and cooked dinner, sharing their game with the clanswomen in exchange for soup, bread, and even some cheese. After dinner they told stories until Mackenna began to nod off. She made her way to Fatimah's wagon, bidding goodnight to Foulan and Myst, who left the camp to sleep alone.

The next morning, Foulan looked haggard, like he hadn't slept a wink.

"Are you alright? Did something happen?" Mackenna asked as they broke their fast.

He sighed, rubbing at his eyes. "Last night, the fairy lights were back," he told her. "I didn't think I would have to worry about them, with the caravan within sight. And there were more of them, hundreds. All around the camp." He frowned, glancing at Myst, who slumbered nearby. "Myst took off after them, out of my sight. I kept calling her, trying to get her to come back. And then I heard her yelp in pain. I grabbed my bow, was starting to panic, when she came running back to me. And those lights were following her. Getting closer. I freaked out, shot an arrow at them."

"Did you hit one?" Mackenna asked.

He shook his head. "I don't think so. They scattered after that and all faded away. I couldn't sleep most of the night, wondering if they would attack. I finally fell asleep around dawn. I woke up with this lying next to my head."

He held out one of his arrows, a third of the shaft caked in mud. Mackenna gasped. "You're sure it's the same one?" she asked. "Maybe you just dropped it in the night?"

He shook his head. "I count my arrows when I shoot. It's important to know how many you have on you at all times, and how many you've fired. And besides, it was right beside my face." His hand shook. "What bothers me most is... how did they get close enough without waking Myst? She stayed by my side all night."

Mackenna didn't have an answer for him. However, after breakfast, she requested once more to speak with Halah. When Fatimah tried to dissuade her, claiming that Halah was being difficult, Mackenna refused to turn away. Finally, Fatimah allowed her into the Wise Woman's wagon after lunch. "She's usually a little calmer after she's had a meal. Just you though, if you don't mind. I don't want a man in there to confuse her even more."

The Wise Woman's wagon was more furnished than the others, showing her higher status. Mackenna counted three cats, each lounging on the furniture and eyeing her coolly, as if in fact they were the clan's rulers. Halah sat in a rocking chair, petting one of her cats and murmuring idly to it.

"Wise Woman Halah, there is someone here to see you," Fatimah said, speaking loudly and enunciating. "She is an outsider, but she is our friend, and has come seeking your advice."

The Wise Woman did not respond, just continued rocking. "May I sit with her for a while?" Mackenna asked.

Fatimah nodded slowly. "I have work to do, but if she gives you any trouble, just yell." With that she left, closing the door gently behind her.

Mackenna made herself comfortable on a rug on the floor. One of the cats immediately jumped down from its perch and rubbed against her, demanding pets with a loud meow. "Wise Woman, I'm not sure if you can hear or understand me," she said quietly as she stroked the cat. "But I need your guidance. I am... cursed. By a magic that I cannot control."

At the word magic, Halah stopped rocking, her head cocked in Mackenna's direction. Mackenna took it as a sign and continued speaking. "My father died. I burned my village and the men who killed him. Now there are witch hunters after me. And I... I am afraid. I think if only I could fix this fire burning within me, if I could be normal, then I could be free of all of this."

Halah said nothing, just continued petting her cat. "Foulan took me to Wise Woman Drynka," Mackenna continued. "She said that I need to learn to control it. If that's all that I can do, at least it would be something. She said that you could help me. That you have knowledge of the Fae—"

As soon as Mackenna mentioned the Fae, the Wise Woman perked up. She mumbled in her native tongue.

"Please, slow down," Mackenna said, "I can't understand you."

Halah paused with a frown, then began to speak again, slower and more clearly, this time in Etylanian. "The Fae. Yes. The Fair Folk. Yes yes! The Wee Ones. Friends, yes."

"Yes. Do you know where I can find them?" Mackenna asked.

The Wise Woman smiled, her few remaining teeth peeking from between her lips. "The Lady, yes. Such fun we had! Swimming… swimming all the time! Shiny scales."

"I don't understand," Mackenna murmured.

"I can hold my breath forever!" Halah puffed her cheeks out, then held her breath until her face started to turn blue.

Mackenna panicked. "Wise Woman, please, you have to breathe!" she cried, rising from her seat on the floor. "Tell me more about the Fae, won't you?"

Halah took a breath. "She's going to take me home," she gasped. "To the bottom of Calmloch. She promised to when the time came."

She would get no sense from the woman. "The bottom of the lake?" she asked, just to humor her.

"Yes, that's where she lives. In the lake! I have to get there soon." She began rocking again, although it seemed more frantic than before. "I'm going to die soon. I have to get back to my beloved in the lake. Won't you take me?"

Mackenna shook her head. "I don't think that would be for the best, Wise Woman. You might get hurt or fall in the water."

"Yes! The water. She can't leave the water. That's why I have to go to the lake. Won't you take me swimming?" she begged.

"I'm sorry, Wise Woman. I can't. And it's too cold besides—
"

"Bah! Forget you then! I will go by myself. Just have to ask the fairy lights. They will lead me to her." She returned to murmuring to herself. Mackenna tried a few more times to get her to speak, but the Wise Woman ignored her. Mackenna finally left the wagon, her heart heavy. While she pitied the poor old woman whose mind had gone, she couldn't help feeling frustrated as well. Had she come this far for nothing?

Foulan was waiting for her outside of the Wise Woman's caravan. He frowned at the look on her face. "That bad, huh?"

Mackenna shook her head. "There's no getting sense from her. I'm sorry, Foulan." Tears sprang to her eyes. "I made you bring me all this way for nothing. I'm sorry to have wasted your time."

Mackenna found herself suddenly enveloped in his arms, her face against his hard chest. "Don't say that," he whispered. "It wasn't a waste of my time."

"But… but you never even wanted to come…"

He smiled down at her. "That was then. Things have changed. Or, maybe I've changed. You're my friend, and I will do whatever I can to help you gain control of your magic."

She had to hide her face so that he wouldn't see how his words made her mouth tremble. "Thank you," she said. "But I don't even know what to do anymore."

He sighed, stepping away from her, and she suddenly felt cold. "We'll figure that out. For now, let's make ourselves useful to repay Clan Halah's hospitality."

By the time night fell, a thick fog had rolled in off of Calmloch, obscuring the entire camp. Most of the women went into their caravans to escape the cold, leaving just Fatimah, her wife Samar, Foulan, and Mackenna sitting around the communal fire and discussing what they should do now about Mackenna's powers and the bounty on her head. They hadn't come to any definitive conclusions by the time night neared its apex and they decided to go to sleep.

"Let me go and check on Halah one more time," Samar said as she rose from her spot. The outline of Halah's caravan was barely visible through the fog, despite the short distance.

"I'm sorry that you did not find what you were looking for," Fatimah said. "I can only allow Foulan to sleep outside the camp for another night or two. After that, he will need to move on. But you, Mackenna, are welcome to stay longer if you would like."

Mackenna shook her head. "Thank you for the offer. But I will go with Foulan, once we figure out where we're going."

"Be careful tonight, Foulan," Fatimah cautioned. "Don't go too far from camp. If you start to feel threatened again, yell to wake us—"

"Fatimah!" Samar screamed. The three of them shot to their feet and ran towards the Wise Woman's caravan. Samar stood in the open door.

"What is it?" Fatimah asked nervously. "Is she—"

"Missing!" Samar gasped.

"What? You are sure?" Fatimah ran inside, but Mackenna could see from where she stood that the tiny wagon was empty. "But how?"

"I don't know. I gave her her sleeping draught with her nightly tea, as usual." Samar picked up the cup by her bed, tea sloshing over her shaking fingers. "She didn't drink it. But how did she leave without us noticing?"

"Check the other wagons, in case she got confused and wandered into one," Fatimah commanded, and Samar nodded, picking up her skirts and heading off to the nearest one.

"She mentioned the lake. When I talked to her today. She begged me to take her to it," Mackenna said.

Fatimah said something in her native tongue. Judging by the inflection, Mackenna assumed it to be a curse. "The lake is huge! It can take days to walk all the way around it. Foulan, can your wolf track?"

Foulan nodded. "She's done it to hunt game, but never to track a person. But we can try."

Samar returned, shaking her head. "She's not in any of the caravans. Nobody's seen her."

Fatimah grimaced and grabbed some of Wise Woman Halah's clothing, holding it in front of Myst's nose. The wolf sniffed it intently, then turned from the caravan, heading away from the camp.

"I will stay here in case she returns," Samar said, kissing Fatimah quickly on the lips. Mackenna blushed and turned away to give them privacy.

"We will follow her trail together," Foulan said to Fatimah and Mackenna, and she was surprised at how easily he felt into leadership in the heat of the moment. "We'll each take a torch. Whatever you do, do not become separated! In this fog, we could easily become lost. If you do get separated, sit down wherever you are and wait for someone to find you or the morning sunrise to clear it. Understand?"

Fatimah and Mackenna nodded, and the three of them set out after Myst, who walked intently with her nose to the ground.

They blindly followed Myst into the fog. Within a few minutes, the light and sound from the caravan circle was swallowed up. Mackenna tried to orient herself, guessing where she thought the lake might be, but it was impossible. The fog blocked out any moonlight, and anything more than a few arm's lengths away was nothing more than a silhouette in the darkness. Only the light from their torches helped Mackenna to keep track of Foulan and Fatimah. They called out Halah's name into the night, but the fog seemed to dampen sound as well as sight.

Mackenna stumbled over a tree root, barely managing to catch herself. Her torch tumbled out of her hand and rolled away, and she cursed, scrambling after it. She thankfully managed to get it back before it could snuff out. Mackenna stood, looking up only to find that the torches of her companions had vanished in the fog. She heard movement and stepped towards it. She had walked only a few paces before a giggling came from her right. "Wise Woman?" she asked. The laughter continued as she stepped forward. "Is that you, Halah?" This time the sound came from her left. She turned, wielding her torch before her, but could see nothing. Once more it came, now from behind her. She had by now become completely disoriented.

Suddenly, a light flickered before her. She moved towards it, thinking it must be one of her companions' torches, but it went out again. Then another appeared beside her. Soon she was surrounded by winking lights, all with a bluish hue. The giggling was all around her now, and Mackenna went cold, remembering Fatimah's warning about the fairy lights.

"Mackenna! Where are you?" It was Foulan's voice, but it sounded far away. How had they gotten separated so quickly?

"Foulan! I'm here!" Mackenna cried. He didn't respond. "Can you hear me?" she called again.

Can you hear me?

…I'm here!

The voices came from all around her, mocking her words. They were high pitched and echoed as if many people were speaking at once.

I'm here!

Mackenna…

Mackenna turned in circles, brandishing her torch in one hand, trying to keep the lights away. But they kept moving closer.

"Get back! Leave me alone!" she yelled at them.

They ignored her. *Where are you? Mackenna!* Was it his voice in the distance or theirs? She had no way of knowing for sure.

"What do you want?!" she shouted at the lights.

The whispers stopped. She was now completely surrounded by the fairy lights, little blue flames bobbing up and down, all around and above her. There had to be at least twenty of them. Then one moved forward from the group, growing closer, pausing just before her face.

She squinted at the light. The blue flame was about the size of her fist, and inside of it was a tiny person. Or rather, the blue light was a tiny person encased in flames. It was completely naked and appeared to be genderless. Its skin was the blue of its fire, and it had delicate wings, like those of a dragonfly, sprouting from its back.

"Wha—what are you?" Mackenna whispered, her hand reaching out instinctively toward it.

The creature landed in her palm. She almost flinched away, expecting it would burn her, but while it was warm, it did her no harm. Was it because of her own affinity for fire or something else? She wasn't sure. "I could ask you the same question," it said in a small voice.

"What?" Mackenna responded stupidly.

The creature's face had an uncanny sharpness to it, as if its skin was pulled too tight around its skull. The narrow eyes it trained on her were entirely black. "Though I suppose you asked first," it said. "I am a will-o'-the-wisp. A fairy light. A jack-o'-lantern. We have many names we are known by. But you will know me as your guide."

"My guide?" Mackenna repeated.

"You sure ask a lot of useless questions. Yes, your guide. You're looking for the Lady of the Lake, yes?" The wisp phrased it more as a statement than a question.

"I don't know what that is. I'm searching for Wise Woman Halah, who has gone missing." Mackenna narrowed her eyes. "Are you creatures to blame?"

The wisp smirked. "Blame? That's a strange way of putting it. We merely guided her where she asked us to." It jumped up, fluttering above her hand. "But you're in luck. You will find them together. Come."

"Wait!" Mackenna eyed the small creature warily. "I've been told you are not trustworthy. You lead people to their deaths in the bogs. How do I know this is not a trick?"

The creature paused, glancing back at her. "The fact that you are asking at all seems to me that you don't believe it to be a trick." As Mackenna tried to follow its logic, it continued talking. "Besides, we only play those tricks on the bad humans. You would always see through them."

What exactly did the creature mean by that? She didn't have time to contemplate as it darted away. She followed it, stepping carefully with an eye on her path to make sure she didn't suddenly fall into water. Did it mean it would not trick her because it believed she was not a bad person, or did it somehow sense that she had magic of her own? How would it even know either of those things?

She had to remind herself that she and Foulan had been followed by these wisps for over a week now. The creatures had most likely been spying on them, gathering information about them. But to what purpose?

A glance back showed that the other lights followed behind her, but they kept far enough away that she couldn't make out their details. If she tried to turn and walk away, or to sit down and ignore them until sunrise, would they descend upon her and attack like wasps? She didn't want to find out.

Mackenna was not sure how long she followed the creature through the fog. As with her sense of direction, she had lost all track of time. After what had perhaps been just a few minutes of walking or hours, the sound of the waves lapping the shore reached her ears. Gravel crunched under her boots. The wisp stopped at the edge of the water, turning back to her. "We're here. I will accept my payment now."

"Payment? What kind of payment?" Mackenna asked.

The wisp rolled its eyes again. "We don't guide for free, you know. I just need something small, but it has to belong to you and you alone. A strand of hair, a tear, a kiss. Any of those will do."

Wait, was it being serious? "Uh, okay..." she plucked a strand of her short hair, holding it out between her thumb and finger. The wisp leapt forward, snatching it eagerly.

"Much thanks!" it cooed, then turned, glancing out at the water. "Ahh, she's here to see you. The Lady! If you don't mind, I think I'll stick around and watch. This should be interesting."

Mackenna squinted into the fog that hung over the lake, where a figure slowly appeared. It had the shape of a woman, but as the fog cleared around her, Mackenna saw that she was clearly not human. The long hair flowing around her body like water did little to hide the fact that she was nude, and her skin sparkled in the light of Mackenna's torch. Peering closer, Mackenna realized it was because her skin was sprinkled with patches of scales, like those on a fish. And from the waist down, she had the tail of a fish as well.

Like the wisp creature that had led her here, this Faerie also had tall pointed ears and narrow eyes. Her eyes, however, were fathomless pools of blue.

The creature opened its mouth and spoke. Where the wisp practically squeaked when it spoke, her voice was calm and lilting, like water bubbling over rocks. "I am the Lady of the Lake, though you may know me as an undine, a siren, or a mermaid. Why do you seek me out, little fire?"

Mackenna tried to follow this. "Um, I'm sorry," she said, "which of those is your name?"

The Lady frowned, her eyes narrowing in irritation. The wisp beside Mackenna piped up, "Oh no, you mustn't ever ask a Fae their name. That is sacred, and only given to those very close to us. Instead, we can tell you what other humans call us." It bobbed around in front of her as it spoke. "That changes from place to place and tongue to tongue, so she listed a few, hoping one might sound familiar. But in this case, you should call her by her title, Lady of the Lake."

Mackenna was not sure what she had expected from this encounter, but a lesson on etiquette was not it. "Oh, I see. Umm, I apologize, Lady of the Lake."

The siren nodded and waved away the insult. Mackenna noticed that her fingers were webbed. "Your ignorance is forgiven, given your circumstances," the Lady said. "Now then, what did you seek from me?"

Mackenna looked between the siren and the wisp. They gazed back expectantly. "Well, the Wise Woman Halah has gone missing," she told them. "That is why I am out tonight. To bring her home."

The Lady of the Lake tilted her head to the side, but Mackenna could not read her expression. "And what makes you think she wants to go back to her clan?"

"She is very old and is losing her mind. She is likely lost and alone at this very moment…" Mackenna trailed off, feeling as if she were missing out on some clue.

"She is not alone at all," the siren answered. "She is here with me. No need to hide, Halah. Come out and say hello to Mackenna."

The Wise Woman peeked out from behind a large boulder protruding from the water, grinning mischievously. "You wouldn't bring me to the water," she accused, "so I had my friends guide me." She waved at the wisp, who bounced up and down in response.

"Wise Woman Halah, your clan is worried about you," Mackenna said. "We've been out searching for you. Aren't you freezing? You should come back with me."

Mackenna stepped forward, but the moment her boot toe touched the edge of the water, the siren suddenly leapt forward in front of Halah, hissing at Mackenna. The gills on her neck flared in agitation. "Get away from my lake, little fire!" she growled. "You are not welcome in it. Halah is my beloved, and she promised to come home with me at the end of her mortal life."

Mackenna stepped back, her hands in the air. "I don't understand," she said. "Halah?"

The Wise Woman smiled, stepping out and wrapping her arms around the Lady, who relaxed her defensive posture. "When I was a young girl, my clan camped beside this lake for the summer. That's when I met the Lady. We became friends. As the years went by, whenever we were in the area, I came to visit. And she became more than my friend. She became my beloved undine."

The Wise Woman nestled her head into the Siren's shoulder. The Faerie ran her webbed fingers through the old woman's hair. "When I swim with Halah, I can breathe for her," she said. "We would swim down to my home and spend days together making love."

Halah smiled. "I promised that when I neared my death, I would return, and we would go down to her home at the bottom of the lake. And even though my body may die, and the fish eat away my skin and organs until all that remains is bones, my soul will be here with my beloved for all eternity."

Mackenna gazed between them. "I'm... I'm not entirely sure I understand."

"You don't need to understand, fire child," the siren snapped. "Not about this, anyway. Now ask the question you truly came here to ask."

Mackenna glanced between the siren, the wisp, and the Wise Woman, but they only stared back in silence. "I would like to know how to get rid of my magic, or, barring that, how to control it," she said. "I was told to seek out the Fae. Would you, either of you, be willing to help me?"

The siren shook her head. "That is not something I can teach you," she said. "You are of fire, and I am of water."

"And you? You're fire, right?" Mackenna asked the wisp.

It bobbed in agreement. "Of a sort. My fire is part of me, but it's not fire, not like yours. It can't catch or spread. It is just my body." The creature looked contemplative. "It would be like you trying to teach a human how to breathe, or make their heart beat. It's not the same."

"Then what was even the point in bringing me here?" Mackenna muttered.

"I said that I cannot teach you," the siren replied. "That does not mean that I can be of no help. You must go to the Faelands, the seat of the Faerie Court. I believe that there you will find someone who can be your teacher."

"The Faelands?" Mackenna asked. "Where is that?"

"At the top of the world, of course!" the wisp replied with a grin.

Mackenna glanced up at the sky in confusion. "Not quite," the siren replied. "You must go north, to the land of snow, where the sun does not rise for a season, where the night sky is lit by rainbows. There you will find an island encased in ice. That is the seat of the Faerie Court."

"Does such a place truly exist?" Mackenna whispered.

"After all you've seen tonight, you doubt *this*?" the wisp replied.

She shook her head. "I suppose I should not. But it sounds so… fantastical. I thank you, Lady of the Lake and will-o'-the-wisp." Mackenna bowed, as her father had taught her to do when showing respect to her superiors. To the wisp she said, "You guided me here. Would you be willing to continue to guide me to the Faerie Court?"

The wisp tittered. "Trust me, fire child, you don't have enough hair on your head or blood in your body to pay me for that long of a journey. And I don't care to leave my boglands, besides. You're on your own." With that, the wisp fluttered away, followed by the rest of its kind.

Mackenna watched the lights wink out, then turned to Halah. "Wise Woman, is it truly your wish to stay here?" she asked. The old woman grinned at her and nodded. "Then, I suppose I cannot dissuade you."

"Let us go home, beloved," the siren said. She embraced the old woman and kissed her, and they sank into the water together.

Mackenna glanced around her, trying to determine where exactly along the lake's shore she was. Her torch had gone out, and the fog was still thick. Realizing it would be smarter to sit and wait for morning, she climbed up onto the grassy bank and curled up in her cloak, her back to a boulder.

Foulan

Dawn was breaking when Foulan and Myst finally found Mackenna sleeping near the lake, shivering in her cloak. "Mackenna!" Foulan yelled. "Thank the gods you're alright. Fatimah made us stop searching for Halah after we lost you as well. I spent all night worrying about you."

Mackenna sat up groggily, clutching Myst for warmth while Foulan called to Fatimah, who was combing the beach nearby. "I'm so sorry, Foulan," Mackenna whispered.

"What do you mean?" he asked, helping her up. He was surprised when she wrapped her arms around him, sinking her head into his chest.

"I tried to get Halah to come back with me, but she wouldn't. I didn't know what to do but let her go. She seemed so happy," Mackenna whispered.

"You found Halah, then?" Fatimah asked, jogging up to them. "Where is she?"

Mackenna pointed out to the water. Fatimah and Foulan both stared at it in confusion. "Last night, a will-o'-the-wisp led me here. This lake is the home of a siren. She and Halah were— are—lovers. And Halah insisted that she wanted to be with the Lady of the Lake when she died." Mackenna looked at Fatimah miserably. "I am sorry that I did not stop her, but it was her dying wish."

Fatimah fell to her knees, staring out at the water. "She is dead, then?"

Mackenna nodded, her gaze returning to Foulan. "Thank you for everything you have done for me," she said. "But you should go back home to your clan now."

Foulan's heart sank. Mackenna didn't want him around anymore? Had he done something to drive her away? "I don't understand," he replied. "Why?"

She shook her head. "I know you never wanted to accompany me in the first place. Thank you for taking me this far, but it seems it was a fruitless journey. I will figure something out, find somewhere to live until I'm caught." Her mouth trembled as she attempted to smile.

"Why would you do that? You can't be ready to give up," he said.

"I don't know what else to do," Mackenna whispered. "The siren told me I must make an impossible journey. I don't know how I would even get there, and I would never ask you to help me. This should never have been your burden to bear."

"And where did this siren say you must go?" he pressed. "How is it so impossible?"

"She said I must go to the top of the world, to a frozen island north of the Realms of Etylania." Mackenna described a world of endless winter nights lit by rainbows and of frozen oceans. "I'm not sure such a place even truly exists, and if it does, it is surely no place for humans."

Fatimah stood, wiping at her eyes. "It does exist," she interrupted. "At least in legend."

"How do you know this?" Mackenna asked.

"Let me show you."

They followed her back to the camp, the walk taking a little over an hour. Fatimah invited them into her caravan. Opening a chest, she pulled out a rolled-up piece of leather, spreading it on the table before them to reveal a map.

"The map in your possession ends here," Fatimah said, drawing a line with her finger along the middle of the leather. "This one goes further, to the northernmost countries of Etylania. This is the edge of the continent," she said, pointing out a jagged line towards the top of the map. "Here it meets a sea. Ships can sail through it during the summer, but in the winter, it turns to ice." She tapped her finger on the table above the edge of the map. "There is legend about an island in that sea, a landmass that is nothing but ice, where no plants grow and no people or animals can live. According to this legend, the Fae live on that island, and they will grant the wish of whoever can reach it alive. Every few decades, some fool gets it into their head to try to find this treasure. They depart from the port in Icedell, and they almost never return. This may be the Faelands that the siren spoke of."

"How would we get there?" Foulan asked, studying the lines winding across the page that marked the roads and countries.

"It certainly wouldn't be easy," Fatimah answered. "From here, you could go around the western edge of Calmloch until you reach the town of Abetheca. Then you can take this trade road north. The further you go, the less cities you will find, and you will have to skirt along this mountain range, the Stenfrysta Mountains. It runs the border between four different countries that you'll pass through, but out there in the wilderness, you at least won't have to present your rites of passage to anyone. That will get you to the port city of Icedell. From there, you would have to find a ship to take you to the island. Whether these really are the Faelands, or how you will gain access to them, I know not."

Mackenna had slumped to the floor as Fatimah spoke, her head in her hands. "It is no use," she said. "We would never reach it, and there is no guarantee if we did that we would find the Fae."

"How long?" Foulan asked.

"To reach Icedell?" Fatimah shrugged. "Assuming you can get through the Stenfrysta Mountains before the snows hit, two months would be my guess. But if the snows come early, you will get stuck in the mountains, which can be extremely dangerous."

"Then we'll have to stop in Abetheca to buy winter furs and a heavier tent," Foulan thought out loud.

"Foulan, stop," Mackenna groaned. He glanced over at where she sat. "I can't make you do this."

He sighed, stretching his arms over his head. "It's a good thing you're not making me, then, isn't it?" When she looked as if she might protest further, he knelt down before her. "Mackenna, I have come this far with you. I will see this to the end. If for nothing other than to satisfy my own curiosity about these Fae creatures. Now, I suggest you get packing, as we need to leave within the hour."

Fatimah traced a rough copy of her map onto a piece of parchment for them to take. When she was finished, she rolled it up and handed it to him, then pulled him into a hug. "Please be careful, Foulan. I hope that I will see you at the Gathering next spring, and you can tell me all about your adventure." He realized that it would not be Clan Halah anymore when next he saw them, and wondered who among them would be the next Wise Woman.

When they reached the town of Abetheca a few days later, they found it surprisingly busy and festive. Herdsmen were leading their cattle into town in large numbers, and many of the cows were being butchered. Farmers were carting in their final harvests of the year. Winemakers had brought out and opened large casks. All around, the smell of food cooking permeated the air.

All of that in itself was not so strange, for summer had ended, the days growing shorter and the nights longer. But what Foulan did find strange were the decorations adorning the houses and people. "What festival is this?" he asked Mackenna.

"The harvest festival," she explained. "They usually happen around the equinox. Have you never been to one before?" She seemed surprised that there was something he didn't know.

"A few, but none that looked like this." He pointed to a windowsill, upon which sat a gourd with a misshapen face carved into it. They adorned many of the houses and buildings. "What is that?"

"A lantern. A candle will be lit inside it at dusk. The equinox is the beginning of winter, when the nights start to become longer than the days. The death of nature means that the dead can cross back over into our world," she explained.

"And your people definitely don't like that, right?" he asked. "Yet, nobody looks especially afraid."

She shrugged. "It is said any dead souls can cross over, even relatives and friends. It only lasts a night, then they go back. So we don't have to worry about them becoming twisted with jealousy and turning into ghosts. But it means that the souls of bad people can also come back. Thus, a lantern is carved that looks like a human face. The spirits are drawn towards it, and they get trapped in its flame, preventing them from wreaking too much havoc. With dawn the flame dies down and they are released, but by then they must return to the realm of the dead."

"And these people? In the robes? What are they doing?" he asked. He had noticed many people in long white robes with white hoods going from door to door.

"They are begging for food for the communal feast. Everyone is expected to contribute. It is said the better your contribution, the more luck you will have next year. People have already sacrificed the animals and begun cooking them. Tonight everyone will feast."

"Your people really are confusing. They're scared of spirits, so you would think everyone would be locked up in their houses hiding. But they're all out celebrating."

Mackenna shook her head. "I don't think most people really put stalk in all the talk of ghosts and spirits. It's just a fun way to celebrate the harvest with food and drink while trying to give your friends a scare. Come, it will be fun."

They rented a room at an inn, stabled their horses, then walked through the town. Many people had begun to build fires in the streets, and others had set up stalls selling wares, food, and celebratory items. They bought meat roasted on sticks and drank spiced apple wine. Foulan noticed that many people had their faces painted with white and black ink, resembling skeletons. "To confuse the dead," Mackenna explained. "I guess if they think you are one of them, they won't hurt you."

"So spirits are also really stupid?" he asked.

She laughed. "I didn't say it made any sense."

"What about the masks?" he asked. Many people were wearing them; some were frightening, others beautiful and brightly painted. Some appeared to have taken weeks or even months to make, while others were as simple as a sack with the eyes and mouth cut out.

"The same reason, to fool evil spirits. At least, that's what people say." Mackenna grinned mischievously. "Most people wear them so that they can play tricks without getting caught. The next day, everyone agrees that the tricks must have been committed by bad spirits or wicked Fae."

"And what kind of tricks would that be?"

"Harmless stuff mostly. Stealing a neighbor's pig and putting it on a roof. Setting livestock free. Running through the streets in *just* a mask. Coating doorknobs in sticky honey. Drawing on drunken fools who've passed out. And, of course, trying to scare the wits out of your friends. Would you like to buy one?"

They found a stall where a woman was selling masks that they could afford. They appeared to be made of some sort of paper hardened with plaster. Mackenna picked out one with leaves glued to it, saying that it reminded her of her father. Foulan found one with a long snout and tufts of fur, resembling a wolf. He put it on and turned to Myst. "Well, what do you think? Do I look like you?"

The wolf just groaned and tucked her nose into her paws.

As the sun set, people started to play instruments: drums and lutes and the occasional flute. They made their way to the center of the town, where the largest bonfire Foulan had ever seen roared in the plaza. It was easily wider than a caravan, and its flames licked nearly as tall as the roofs of the buildings around it. "Will you dance with me?" Mackenna asked Foulan.

"I don't know the steps," he answered honestly.

She laughed. "Neither does anyone else. There are no steps. You just let the music and the fire guide you." A bartender stood outside a tavern, filling people's mugs with mead. Mackenna tossed the woman a coin, and she filled their cups. "Here, this helps."

They drank and danced, though it seemed to be mostly jumping and spinning. Some people danced in pairs, others in larger groups, sweeping a partner or two up in their arms for a few moments before moving on. Foulan glanced around for Myst on occasion, always finding her sitting with her back to a building, not wanting to get stepped on in the fray. Thankfully, nobody seemed interesting in bothering the large wolf.

Foulan's head grew light from the drink and dancing and the heat of the fire. Mackenna must have been feeling it too, for she danced closer to him now, their bodies almost touching. Somehow, his hand had found its way to her hip. With her mask on, all he could see was her eyes and her lips. He suddenly had an overwhelming desire to kiss her once more, to taste the sweet honey wine on her lips.

"I need something to drink!" Foulan shouted over the music and revelry, indicating the tavern. His throat was parched, and sweat trickled down his back from dancing. But most importantly, he needed to step away from Mackenna, before he did something stupid. She simply nodded and waved him away.

He slowly sidled through the throng, dodging drunken revelers and dancers. It took a while to find any establishments that had something other than wine or ale, but finally he discovered one with apple cider. He downed a mug of it in a few gulps, sighing in relief.

Foulan glanced up to make sure he could still find Mackenna in the crowd. Unfortunately, she was nowhere to be seen.

Kazumi

Kazumi reached the town of Abetheca just as the harvest festival was getting underway. From here, it would just be a day's journey south to reach Calmloch. The difficult part would be getting ahold of the witch. Kazumi didn't doubt she and her companions had found the other clan by now. There would be no way for Kazumi to attack them directly to get at the girl. Perhaps they could be bribed with part of the bounty money? Kazumi wandered through the streets of the little town as they mulled over the options. There was nothing more to do for tonight but rest, then venture out on the morrow. Still, Kazumi knew they'd be too distracted thinking about a potential confrontation to relax, so they decided to partake in the festivities.

Kazumi was enjoying a pastry stuffed with apples when a flash of red caught their eye. They glanced up, zeroing in on the color. The hair belonged to a boy, or perhaps he was a young teen. He was thin and had yet to sport any hair on his face. Beside him stood a young man, who looked close to Kazumi's age. The young man was clearly a Wanderer judging by his dusky skin and tribal tattoos.

Kazumi stepped forward, studying the pair. They were looking at paper mâché masks for the festivities. The younger boy turned towards his companion, grinning as he held up a mask with leaves, and Kazumi reached into their pocket, pulling out the parchment they carried with them everywhere now.

Kazumi had long since memorized the image, but they had to be sure they were not being overly hopeful. While the sketch of the girl on the page had long hair, there was no doubt that the face was the same. Clever of her to try to disguise herself as a boy.

How many Wanderer companions did she have? Kazumi watched them as they put on their masks, and the Wanderer looked at the ground, speaking to someone. Through the crowd Kazumi spied a furry form. A large dog. Were these the only companions who traveled with her, or were there more? Kazumi followed them discreetly as they moved on, sampling the food and cider. They drank and danced in the town's main square around a roaring bonfire.

So far, Kazumi had spied no other Wanderers with them. There would be no better time than now to act. But they'd left everything back at the inn, including the shackles...

Kazumi raced back to the inn, not bothering to avoid attention as they did so. Most of the people were too drunk to notice anyway, giving little more than a surprised yelp when they pushed past someone. Kazumi grabbed the shackles, pausing for a moment to glance at their armor and sword. They certainly didn't have time for the armor, but should they take their weapon? It would attract more attention, but they didn't know yet if she had other bodyguards among the crowd.

No, it would be better to whisk her away from her companions as quickly and quietly as possible. Shackles hanging from their belt, Kazumi rejoined the crowded streets once more, retracing their steps back to the town center.

Night had fallen when they found the couple in the town's square, still drinking and dancing. Kazumi scanned the crowd again, locating the dog, which sat nearby out of the fray, watching the revelry.

That was at least one less complication. The other was the girl's traveling companion. While the Wanderer did not look particularly intimidating, Kazumi knew that looks could be deceiving. He didn't appear to carry any noticeable weapons on him, though Kazumi wouldn't doubt that he kept at least a dagger or two hidden on his person.

Kazumi studied the Wanderer's features from the shadows, trying to record them to memory. Ducking into a dark alley, they took out a pocket mirror and stared into it, willing the Change to come. The long black hair turned coarser and shortened. The skin darkened from a pale moonlight color to a warm brown. Stubble sprouted from the chin and upper lip. Satisfied that they now passingly resembled the girl's companion, Kazumi waited for the right moment.

When the Wanderer went to get a drink, leaving the girl alone in the crowd, Kazumi knew they wouldn't get a better opportunity than this to strike. They stepped out of the shadows and into the town square. Their clothes were different from the Wanderers', but hopefully the dark and press of bodies would conceal that. Kazumi wove through the crowd, stopping before her small form. Now that they were closer, they weren't really sure how anyone could mistake her for a boy. It was obvious from up close that she was a woman in breeches. While upper-class ladies almost always wore expensive gowns, it was not uncommon for lower-class women to wear whatever clothing was suitable for the weather and task at hand. Perhaps Kazumi was just better at deciphering a person's gender than most, considering their own unique ability.

"Let's dance!" Kazumi said to the girl, grabbing her hand and sweeping her towards them. She blinked blearily up at them, swaying on her feet. Perfect. Her inebriated state should only make things easier.

Kazumi didn't give her time to respond before pulling her into the fray of dancing bodies. They spun her around a few times as they moved through the crowd, both disorienting her and situating them on the other side of the bonfire from her companions. "Whoa there, you look a little dizzy," they chuckled. "Why don't we get you some fresh air?" Knowing her abilities, they wanted to get her away from the fire as quickly as possible.

The girl mumbled something over the din, eyeing them in confusion. Perhaps not as drunk as they'd thought. Kazumi led her towards a dark alley between two pubs. Save for a passed-out reveler and a couple using the shadows for intimacy, it was empty.

"Foulan, what's going on? You sound funny," the girl muttered.

"Sorry, must be the wine getting to me." Kazumi kept their face turned away from the girl.

"But… where'd you get those clothes?" she asked.

"Do you like them? A merchant was selling them, and I though they looked unique."

"Well, let me get a better look then," she said, pulling back on her arm. Kazumi paused, and she turned them around to face her. The girl eyed his baggy trousers and kimono top in appreciation. "They are nice, though I'm not sure how practical they'll be for a place as cold as Icedell. How much did that cost, anyway? I thought we needed to buy firs."

"I can always sell them later. Come. You look like you need to rest. You can barely stand!" As if to prove their point, she fell against them, giggling.

"I don't want to leave yet, though. It's so nice to forget our quest, if only for a moment." Her voice was muffled as she buried her face in their shoulder. She gazed up at them, her cheeks flushed. "Foulan… will you kiss me again?"

They froze. Well, that certainly wasn't what they had expected. So the two were lovers, or at least near to it. She had closed her eyes and was leaning her face towards them, her breath reeking of alcohol. "I think you've had too much—"

She doubled over, cutting them off mid-sentence. Kazumi felt something hot and wet soak into their sleeve as the smell of regurgitated alcohol filled the air.

They closed their eyes, taking a second to tramp down their irritation and disgust. A puker. They hated vomit. Hated bodily fluids of any sort, really. It was part of the reason they preferred not to kill a bounty or bystanders. They didn't necessarily have a moral issue with killing, but the thought of a stranger's blood getting on them repulsed them to no end. And now this damn girl had puked on them.

They tried to hold onto their façade, but they could feel it slipping as their disgust overwhelmed them. Dammit! They needed to get her out of here quick, before she noticed.

"I'm sorry," she cried, clutching her stomach with one hand. "I think I need to lie down."

"Of course, of course," they soothed, trying to force a pleasantness that they did not feel into their voice. "Here, just come with me."

Kazumi continued to lead her down the alley, keeping their face turned away from the girl. As quietly as they could, Kazumi lifted the shackles from their belt. They would need to clamp her mouth at the same time as the shackles to keep her from screaming and drawing attention. The thought of touching her mouth, likely still covered in vomit, sent a shiver of revulsion down their spine.

The girl suddenly dug her feet in, pulling them to a stop. "Wait, who... you're not Foulan."

Fuck. The jig was up. Kazumi lunged towards her, shackles in one hand, the other outstretched to silence her.

They didn't make it in time. "Foulan!" she yelled out. "Help!" Kazumi slapped their hand over her face and wrapped their arms around her.

"Hush! I was trying to do things the easy way..."

She struggled against them, her small form surprisingly dexterous. Kazumi felt a stabbing pain in their leg and unconsciously released her. The girl stepped away, a dagger in her hand. It was dripping with blood — their blood.

Kazumi grimaced and held up the shackles, limping towards her, hoping they looked menacing and not pathetic. Unfortunately, she didn't drop the dagger, though she did step backwards away from him. "I need you to come with me, witch. Now."

"Get the fuck away from her!" a man's voice yelled. Kazumi glanced behind the girl to see her companion in the alley, his dog beside him. He too had a dagger drawn, but Kazumi was more concerned by the bared teeth of the very pissed off canine barreling towards him.

Not a dog at all... it was a fucking wolf.

Kazumi quickly sized up their options. Had the wolf not been present, or had they not just been stabbed in the leg, they might have a chance to kill the intruders and escape with their mark. However, they couldn't fight three at once with an injury, and despite her inebriated state, the girl still had dangerous magic.

This was no longer an issue of getting away with the girl. Now it would be a trial to simply escape with their own life. They could make it to the end of the alley and away before the man could reach them, but should the wolf decide to pursue, there was no doubt it would be faster.

Kazumi didn't wait another moment to ponder. They spun on their heels, running away from the pair and their beast. They knew the skin of their leg must be ripping open further open as they ran, but thankfully the adrenaline kept the worst of the pain at bay. They reached the end of the alley and emerged onto another street, though it was much less sparsely populated than the town square had been.

And the clacking of nails on cobblestones continued behind them, growing louder.

What they needed was a distraction, something to keep the three occupied while Kazumi made their escape. Thankfully, an opportunity presented itself in the form of a guard on patrol. He carried a torch and was currently occupied dealing with a group of rowdy revelers throwing eggs at a house.

Kazumi raced towards him, yelling, "Witch! Help! I'm being attacked by a witch!"

The guard looked towards them in confusion, trying to discern Kazumi's yelling. His eyes fell on the open and bleeding wound in Kazumi's leg, and he rushed towards them, drawing his sword.

Kazumi heard a low whistle from the alley, and a glance back revealed that the wolf had stopped just at the edge of it, chest heaving, muscles straining against its instincts to protect its companions. There came another whistle, and it turned and ran back the way it had come, out of Kazumi's line of sight.

"What's all this now. What happened, err, miss?" The guard asked, his voice betraying his uncertainty.

Kazumi didn't bother to correct him. A guardsman was more likely to take pity on a woman than a man. "Please, sir, I was attacked!" Kazumi fell into his arms.

"Who hurt you? What was that about a witch?" the guard asked.

Kazumi froze. Damn. Kazumi had said the first thing that had come to their mind, suspecting that the couple would want to avoid law enforcement at all costs. But the bounty hunter couldn't reveal that their attacker was the same witch on the wanted poster and start a witch hunt in the town. If the townspeople caught her and turned her in, Kazumi wouldn't get paid.

"A crazy bitch! She stabbed me in the leg!" Kazumi yelled, making their voice sound as hysterical as possible. It wasn't exactly difficult, given that the pain had started to catch up to them.

"Who did this to you? Someone you know?" the guard asked.

Kazumi shook their head. "I've never seen her before."

"Stay here. Will you be okay for a moment?" the guard asked.

Kazumi nodded, and the man approached the alley, weapon drawn. He returned only a moment later. "Well, she's gone now. I need to get you to a medic. This is definitely going to need some stitches. Can you walk?"

Kazumi nodded, and the guard put their arm around his shoulder, supporting them as he lifted them off the ground. Kazumi swayed, playing the damsel, though it wasn't entirely an act. They were actually starting to feel lightheaded from the blood loss.

"Steady now, miss. Describe the woman who attacked you to me while we walk. Can you do that?"

Kazumi nodded and gave the most basic description they could. A woman of average height and build, with brown or perhaps blond hair, and no remarkable features. Ten minutes or so of hobbling later, they arrived at the town medic. The guardsman rapped on the door, and the doctor opened it immediately, a few other patients inside, no doubt revelers who had partied a little too hard and hit their heads or gotten into a brawl.

The guardsman briefly explained the situation, then handed Kazumi off to the doctor. "We'll keep an eye out for your attacker, miss, but I wouldn't hold your breath. Lots of people come from all over for the festival, so she'll likely be gone come daylight."

"Just do your best, please," Kazumi whispered, and he nodded, closing the door behind him.

The doctor led Kazumi to a private room, where she set out the items she would need to stitch them up. She took a seat on a stool beside the cot, her eyes falling to Kazumi's hip.

"What's this?" the doctor asked, noticing the shackles that hung from Kazumi's belt. Kazumi felt the heat rise to their cheeks and tried to stammer out an explanation, but the doctor merely grinned.

"Ahh, no worries. You wouldn't be the first patient I've seen that got injured having a little too much fun in the bedroom," she winked at Kazumi, then turned her attention to the gash. "This does, however, look a bit extreme for bedroom play. You're not being forced to do this, are you? For a brothel?"

Bless her kind heart, the doctor thought they were a whore.

Kazumi shook their head. "Oh, nothing like that. Just a misunderstanding as to who would be wearing the shackles is all."

"Well, maybe choose your lovers more carefully next time, yeah? Have someone else in a room nearby who you trust should things go south?" the doctor advised.

"Yes, well, I certainly won't be seeing that woman ever again. I just hope the guards catch her."

The doctor gave Kazumi a pitying look. "Not likely." She handed Kazumi a bottle. "Here, a drink of this will help with the pain."

Kazumi swigged it, then laid back on the cot. They felt their eyes growing heavy as the needle pierced their flesh. Perhaps they'd lost more blood than they'd realized. How the hell were they going to catch the witch now? What had she even been doing in the town instead of at the lake with the other Wanderer clan?

Kazumi thought back to the interaction, before everything had gone south. She'd mentioned the cold—and a name. What was it? Icedell. It sounded like the name of a town. Why the two were heading there, Kazumi hadn't a clue. The old woman had said something about searching for the Fae.

Kazumi would have to follow the road to Icedell and hopefully catch them before they got there. But for now, they needed to sleep.

Foulan

Foulan closed the door to their room, leaning against it with a sigh of relief. They had made it back without being caught by the guards or the strange man who had accosted Mackenna. It didn't help that they'd had to stop twice so that Mackenna could vomit.

Mackenna sank to the floor, curling into a pathetic ball. Myst licked her face with a whine until Mackenna pushed her away. "Okay, I'm fine," she grumbled. "I'm fine, I said." The wolf laid down next to her, and Mackenna wrapped her arms around the furry body. Foulan sank into a chair. "How did you find me?" she asked.

"I lost you in the crowd and started to worry," he said. "Then suddenly the bonfire erupted, grew twice its size, and I knew you were in danger."

"I didn't mean to… is everyone alright?" she asked.

Foulan glanced up from unlacing his boots to see the look of horror on her face. "Everyone's fine, relax," he said. "They all thought it was cool, that some spirits had done it to make their presence known. A cart caught fire but was put out quickly, and nobody was hurt." He pulled off his boots and frowned at her. "I was worried sick though. What happened?"

"I'm sorry," she whispered, rubbing her face in Myst's fur. "Truthfully? I'm not entirely sure… I was dancing with you, and then you were pulling me down an alley, but then it wasn't you. It was that… person." She took a shaky breath. "I struggled and I… I stabbed… him? Her? I'm not even sure in the chaos. I didn't even know I'd done that to the bonfire."

"Why didn't you just catch fire? Light him up with you?" Foulan asked.

She shook her head. "I couldn't. I think… the alcohol was confusing me. I don't have good control of my magic even when I'm sober."

He knelt down in front of her, taking her face in his hands. "I'm proud of you. You protected yourself when I could not, and I'm so sorry I wasn't there."

She nodded slowly. "I was afraid that you wouldn't find me."

"I wouldn't have if it weren't for her nose," Foulan said, poking Myst's furry rump with his toe. The wolf glared at him but didn't move, not wanting to disturb Mackenna. Foulan sighed, laying his face in his hands in exhaustion. "What did that guy want with you? Was he… was he going to rape you?"

Mackenna frowned. "I don't think that was his intent. He never made any lewd comments or attempted to touch me. He only grabbed me after I tried to fight him off. I just don't understand. How did he have your face?" she asked, her voice breaking.

"You're certain that's what you saw? That it wasn't just the alcohol?"

"Not anymore, but… Could it be another faerie trick?" Mackenna asked.

Foulan shook his head. "He seemed human enough to me, and he bled red when you stabbed him. Perhaps some sort of magic? Or a drug to cause confusion? That still doesn't explain what he wanted with you."

"He called me a witch," Mackenna realized. "And he had shackles that he was trying to get on me. He must have recognized me and wanted the bounty."

Foulan thought about it for a few minutes. "I checked for bounty fliers when we arrived. I didn't see any. I assumed that they hadn't made it this far north. So he couldn't have been a random person who saw it and decided to try his luck."

"Then what was he after?" she asked.

"I think you're right, about him being after the money. I think he must be a bounty hunter. A professional, not like that gang back in Hartland. How long he's been tracking us, waiting to strike…" Foulan shuddered. "And he's clever. To wait until you were alone and inebriated, then to attempt to lead you off quietly so as not to cause a scene. Not to mention that he tricked a guard so he could escape when his plan failed. This guy isn't your average thug."

"So what should we do?" Mackenna asked fearfully.

Foulan sighed. "For now, we need to get out of here. For all we know, the guard is scouring the whole town looking for us. Now would be the best time to sneak out with the festivities." She groaned, no doubt queasy at the thought of getting on a horse. "An then tomorrow we'll on our planned route and hope we don't ever see him again. This is a big continent. Hopefully we can elude him."

"And if we can't?" she asked.

Foulan stood and helped Mackenna to her feet. He assessed the scrapes and bruises she had gotten. Thankfully, they were all superficial, nothing that a bit of cleaning and bandages couldn't take care of. "Then we fight," he said.

After a week without any sign of the bounty hunter, Foulan and Mackenna began to relax. As they travelled farther north, the land became hilly, then mountainous. Thankfully, the road they followed, designed for horse- and mule-led carts, was not particularly steep. Even so, snow capped the highest peaks in the distance, winter descending faster upon the forested foothills than the rest of the country. They had begun to wear their fur coats and hide pants, and they were forced to sleep in a tent at night.

It was uncomfortable at first, being crammed into the small space together with Myst lying across their feet. However, Foulan couldn't deny that he enjoyed the warmth of Mackenna's body lying beside him. It actually became so warm that he had to return to sleeping shirtless and she in her underclothes. He loved the way her face lit up bright red whenever she saw him half-naked. He pretended not to notice her poor attempts at stealthily snatching peeks at him. It was the closest either of them came to acknowledging the awkward kiss between them.

As much as Foulan wanted to bring it up, to explore the unspoken desire between them, he didn't dare. He feared being wrong about her feelings for him, and if he was, would she allow him to continue accompanying her on her journey? He didn't want to risk possibly losing the comfortable companionship that had developed between them.

Though it certainly wasn't always comfortable, most especially when they sparred. He insisted on continuing her lessons. They seemed even more dire now that they knew a professional bounty hunter was after them. Foulan hadn't realized until she'd been attacked that night just how much he worried about Mackenna, about her ability to protect herself. The thought of someone hurting her squeezed at his insides and made him feel sick.

So he forced her to train with him every evening, despite their exhaustion from traveling, and he refused to go easy on her. He started teaching her different ways to break away if she'd been grabbed by her attacker, whether they had her by the arm or pinned against them or on the ground. That was the most uncomfortable to do, to pin her to the ground like someone would if they were intent on raping her. His heart would race and breath quicken, and more than once he would have to clear his throat to steady his voice. As he showed her where to hit and kick from this position, he reminded himself that this was likely the situation where she felt most vulnerable, that he needed to act professionally. But his traitorous body still could not help responding, making him feel disgusted with himself. Thankfully she didn't notice, or if she did, she didn't comment.

One day they came across a hill covered in mushrooms. They grew out of broken and fallen trees and brush. Mackenna gathered them into a satchel. "Wood Ear mushrooms. They make wonderful soup," she told him. "Father would always buy dried ones from travelers that came through town. They usually only grow on broken Elder Trees." She paused, staring down at the mushrooms in silence, her head hanging.

"Are you alright?" Foulan asked as she slumped onto a rock. Myst, noticing her sudden change in mood, leaned against her, laying her head in Mackenna's lap.

"Most days," she began. "Most days I am alright. It's almost like I forget that his death is what started this journey. As if he might be waiting for me back in our village, to welcome me home. And then other days, I am suddenly reminded that I will never see my father again. At least, not in this life."

She wiped at her tears. Foulan wished he could say something to cheer her up, but he could think of nothing. He followed Myst's lead, sitting beside her and wrapping an arm around her shoulder. He had no words, but at least he could comfort her with his presence.

"I had hoped to see him again," she said after a moment. "At the harvest festival, when the veil between life and death is thin. I had hoped he would come to visit me, like he did when I was sick. Assuming that was even real, and not just a fever dream."

"Even if it was a fever dream," Foulan said, "that doesn't make it any less real." She gave him a quizzical look. "There is a certain sect of my people that use hallucinogens to have visions. Visions of the future, or of the gods, or the dead."

She nodded. "I have heard of such. Sometimes father's medicines would cause people to see things that weren't there, but it always went away after they got better."

"But who says that whatever they saw wasn't really there?" he asked. "Perhaps there are invisible spirits all around us, but we can only see them when our minds are opened to them.

Through fever or drugs… or even magic." Foulan shrugged. "I don't know. I've never tried it myself. Perhaps these Fae, when we find them, will know more about the realm of the dead."

"If they even exist," she said. "What if they don't? What if we get to that island and it's nothing, just stories? What if I am meant to wander forever, never finding answers, never freeing myself from this magic?" Her voice was small and miserable, and Foulan's heart broke. How lonely she must feel, an orphan with no home, no family, no clan.

"Then I would wander by your side. Myst and I, we would be your family, as would all of Clan Drynka." He wasn't sure if he'd meant it as a declaration. But when she gazed up at him with wide eyes, he realized that it sounded like one. A declaration of love? Of friendship? He wasn't sure himself.

But he couldn't stop gazing into her eyes, glistening with unshed tears. He had promised to accompany her to the end of this quest, but he realized now that would not be enough. He wanted to go with her wherever her journey took her. Suddenly, he couldn't imagine her not being beside him always.

He couldn't bring himself to speak the words. They were far too embarrassing. What if she did not feel the same way? And yet, it seemed as if he somehow conveyed them unspoken, for before he knew what was happening, she had moved closer, pressing her lips against his.

Foulan froze, afraid to move, afraid to end the moment. She pulled away, frowning. "I'm sorry, I shouldn't have—"

Before she could finish apologizing, he captured her lips in another kiss. There was no more doubt. He could see in her eyes that she felt the same as him, that the tension between them was not one sided. She wrapped her arms around his neck, deepening the kiss, and Foulan felt like he was soaring.

Unfortunately, it couldn't last forever. Annoyed at being ignored, Myst shoved her head between them, leaving a sloppy kiss of her own against their cheeks. They broke apart, scolding her, and the wolf looked oddly amused, if such a thing were possible.

"We should probably get back on the road," Foulan pointed out, though he would rather have stayed there all day kissing her. Mackenna nodded slowly, biting her lip. He knew she meant nothing by it, a contemplative gesture, but he barely managed to avoid groaning as he fought the urge to swoop in and capture her lips once more. Instead, he collected his composure and stood, helping her to her feet. They mounted their horses and were off once more.

Mackenna

They did not make it to Icedell before the snows hit. They were still skirting the base of the Stenfrysta Mountains when the weather turned bitterly cold. At midday, soft flakes began to fall, and by that night, a gentle blanket of white had coated the landscape. Thankfully the road through the foothills was scattered with shelters for travelers. They weren't as nice as a bed at an inn, with no baths or hot meals; some were little more than barns with cots in the lofts. A few of them even had homeless vagabonds living in them, who would offer to groom travelers' horses or wash their clothes in exchange for food. But they were warm and free, and that was really all that mattered when the weather turned.

After a week of riding through wet snow and sleeping in crowded shelters, Mackenna was relieved when they finally reached Icedell. At least it wasn't snowing as they made their way into the city, but it was still bitterly cold, the sun's weak rays doing little to warm the frosty air. They found an inn called The Boatman's Reprieve, where they rented a room and got the horses settled. Foulan insisted that they immediately head to the harbor to inquire after any boats. Mackenna wanted nothing more than to sit in the inn's warm tavern near the fire and sip at a hot tea until the numbness left her fingers, but she understood the necessity of looking right away. After all, if they didn't book passage soon, the waters would freeze over before they could.

The town was larger than Mackenna had expected, and beautiful in an austere way. Everything was made of cold, dark stone, slick with ice. Some of the town was situated in the bay, while the rest was built into the stone cliffs around it. Many of the buildings and walkways were carved directly into the cliffside. Those closer to the level of the bay had thick wooden doors to keep out the cold, but those higher up were clearly for the wealthy, with large metal doors glinting gold or silver in the sunlight.

The harbor was enormous, spanning the length of the city along the shoreline. Like everything else in the town, it too was made of black stone, polished by centuries of salt water. Boats and ships of every size were docked along it, bobbing in the waves. As they walked along the shore, Mackenna was thankful that their path had waist-high stone walls to protect pedestrians from slipping and falling into the sea.

They came across a man mending nets near his fishing boat. Foulan approached while Mackenna stayed back with Myst, not wanting the wolf to intimidate him. After Foulan and the man talked for a few moments, Mackenna noticed Foulan's distraught face and the man shaking his head. She decided to approach, Myst tagging behind. The sailor nodded to her politely. "I'm sorry miss, but I'll tell you the same thing I told him," the man said. "It's too late in the year. No ships will go out to sea, and most especially not to that godsforsaken isle."

"Too late?" Mackenna asked, gazing at the water. While it looked dangerously cold, it seemed navigable to her, with what little knowledge she had.

"Aye miss. The ice has already started to form out past the bay. Some small boats, like my vessel here, can still go out a ways to catch fish. But the island you speak of, it's too far in this cold. We'd run up on ice and crash." He shook his head. "Don't know why two young people would want to go there anyway. It's empty. Cursed. Most who go off searching for the treasure never come back. Died looking, no doubt. All over some crazy stories."

"Stories like what?" Foulan asked. "Can you tell us more?"

The man narrowed his eyes. "No. No need to fill your heads with more ideas. You and your wife would do best to return home and enjoy your time together. No need to end it prematurely."

They didn't bother to correct him, and he would elaborate no more. They continued down the harbor, stopping to ask the few sailors and captains they met. Most were mending their boats or preparing them for the winter to come. None were heading back out, and they all reacted much the same to the request to visit the empty island off the coast. Some laughed at them, calling them fools. Many more gave Mackenna and Foulan pitying looks but would speak no more. All were adamant that they would not venture out so far until after spring had come.

They returned to the The Boatman's Reprieve, downtrodden and hopeless. They had come so far, only to arrive too late. The soonest they could strike out to continue their journey would not be for many months. This far north, the mountains and ocean could still be frozen over well into the spring.

As they sat in their rented room that night, Mackenna asked aloud what they should do next. Try to return south before the mountain roads were impassable? Seek out a clan and beg to be taken in?

Foulan shook his head. "We can't turn back now. Not when we've come this far."

"We don't have enough money to stay here through the winter," Mackenna pointed out.

He sighed. "That is, unfortunately, very true. Which is why tomorrow I'll head back out and ask around for work. I doubt that there's much game hunting around here, but I'm sure I can find something to make myself useful. And when the spring does come, we'll hire one of those ships to take us out to sea."

"Then I'll work too," Mackenna chimed in. "And we'll have that much more when the winter ends."

Foulan smiled, a thoughtful look in his eyes. "I think we should maybe give up trying to pass you off as a boy, though."

She frowned at him. "Why so?"

"That sailor was not the first to see through your disguise, even with your trousers and all those furs on. Didn't you notice? He thought you were my wife." She blushed, looking away. "I don't know that anyone we've met in our travels truly believed we were brothers."

"Why are you bringing this up now?" she asked.

"I was just thinking, it might be easier for you to find work as a woman. Most laborers would see your small frame and refuse to hire you, thinking you're either too young or too weak. But there are plenty of inns and taverns around here. I'm sure they need barmaids, and they usually prefer pretty ladies. They should even let you keep any tips from customers." He shrugged. "If you wanted to, of course."

She thought about it. "I guess I could. Though that's not to say I couldn't do the same work as any man."

"Of course, of course!" he laughed, holding his hands up to placate her. "It just might be best to branch out with our job searches." They sat quietly for a few moments, until he spoke again. "There is another reason too."

"And that is?" Mackenna asked, leaning against him.

"I think if we keep trying to pretend we're brothers, and people keep seeing through it, they'll just get suspicious. Wonder what we're trying to hide. That would just cause more undue attention, and I don't think we could keep the facade up for long, not if we'll be living here. But that sailor gave me an idea today." He took her hand in his, rubbing it gently. "He thought we were husband and wife. Why not play the part? Nobody would blink an eye at us living together if they believed that."

Mackenna wasn't sure why, but her heart fluttered at the thought. They had kissed, yes, and that kiss had promises of more. But to pretend to be married?

"Nothing has to actually change," Foulan insisted, staring at their entwined hands. "I can sleep on the floor if that makes you more comfortable."

"Sleep on the floor?" Mackenna chuckled. "We've already been closer than that in our tent."

"True," he nodded. "But it would only have to be for show. I wouldn't expect anything… else."

He kept his gaze down, giving her time to study him. He had started to let his beard grow in thicker with the cold. Even so, she didn't miss the flush in his dark cheeks. She leaned closer, feeling brazen, and whispered in his ear. "What if *I* expected more?"

Foulan's head shot up so quickly that it collided with her own. She cried out in pain, jumping back and landing on Myst's tail, who startled awake. Mackenna clutched her nose gently as Foulan panicked, apologizing with every other breath. "I'm so sorry, is it broken? I didn't mean to. Are you bleeding? I'm terribly sorry. Myst, be quiet, you're fine. Mackenna, can I see please?"

After the pain had dulled somewhat, she lowered her hands, letting him look at her face. "Just stop apologizing," she hissed out as he prodded gently at her nose.

"Sorry," he said again. "I don't think it's broken, though, since there's no blood. Just a little bruised, maybe." His shoulders slumped. "I'm quite terrible at courting, aren't I?"

She giggled. "Maybe a little."

"So, um... what was it you were saying? About expectations?" he asked, voice hopeful.

"I can't remember now, after that blow to the head," Mackenna replied with a coy grin. "Maybe try asking me again some other time."

"Ahh, but there will be another time? That bodes well." He leaned down, kissing the tip of her nose gently. "Well then, I'll try to be less... enthusiastic when the time comes."

Mackenna had little trouble finding work. All she had to do was inquire with the innkeeper the next day. As with most inns, the upper floor was guest rooms, while the lower floor was a public tavern that sold food and drink. The woman, whose name she learned was Hilda, looked her up and down. "Have you any experience?"

"In a tavern, no, not exactly," Mackenna said. "Until recently I worked with my father. He was an herbalist. I helped him make potions and deliver them around town."

"Was?" the woman asked.

Mackenna glanced down at her hands. "He died recently."

"So what's brought you here?" Hilda asked. "I can tell you're not from around here."

"You can?" Mackenna asked. "How?"

The innkeeper smirked. "Your accent. You're clearly from the south."

Mackenna nodded. "After my father's death, we travelled here, my… husband and me. We were hoping to book passage across the water, to the island, where they say the faeries live." Mackenna sighed. "Unfortunately, we got here too late, and now no one will venture out past the bay."

Hilda frowned. "Chasing the old tales, I see. Take my advice, girl, and give up. That island is nothing but barren ice and rock. So what is it you're looking for?"

"What do you mean?" Mackenna asked.

"Your heart's desire," the innkeeper asked, rolling her eyes. "They say if you can make it to the island and strike a deal with the Fae, they will grant you your heart's desire. Wealth, love, power, immortality, beauty. Sadly, the few who actually make it this far are usually desperate, looking to cure a loved one or themselves of a wasting illness or to bring the dead back to life. They throw their lives away seeking to change fate. Rarely any who venture out make it back, and those who do were the smart ones who gave up."

Mandy Burkhead

"And the rest?" Mackenna asked.

"Died, no doubt. Fell trying to climb the sheer cliffs, or perished from the cold, or hit ice with their boats and sank. It's a death sentence, but many of them are so desperate, or already dying, that they don't care. So… what are you seeking?" she asked again.

Mackenna thought for a moment. "To break a curse," she whispered. "To be honest, I'm not sure I ever would have believed in this island of faeries, but then I met some of them and learned they're not just legend. And if they really exist, is it so impossible to believe that they have a home out in the ocean where they hide away from humanity?"

"Hmph," was all the innkeeper responded. "I've never met one myself, but there's a lot I haven't seen in this world. But you're young, and if you aren't dying, I think you should just try to live with whatever curse you have, rather than throw your life away chasing a cure."

"I've come this far. I can't just give up. And… I have nothing to go back to," she answered honestly.

"You've got that nice young man of yours," Hilda noted.

"Yes," Mackenna said. "But even if we wanted to go back, I'm sure the mountains to the south are impassible by now. Either way, we're stuck here for the winter, and we need a place to stay and work to do."

"Are you a hard worker?" the innkeeper asked. "Can you take orders? Work with people?" Mackenna nodded at each question. "You seem like a good kid. I'll take you on for a week here. If you can do good work, then you can stay the winter. The pay, after your room and board, will be fifty prinz a day, plus you can keep any tips you get. Do you own a dress?"

"Umm, not at the moment," Mackenna replied. "All I have are my traveling clothes."

"Visit The Duchess' Castoffs. It's a clothing reseller. The owner will probably have something that fits you close enough. We have good customers here. They know not to get too rowdy or handsy. But they always tip the cute girls better, and I say there's no harm in exploiting that if you can."

By the next evening, Mackenna was waiting tables in the tavern in a pretty lavender gown with ribbons and ruffles. It was not something she would have normally worn, but the owner of the resale shop had insisted that it suited her red hair. He had even let her buy it on credit, saying she could pay him once she got her feet under her.

Halfway through the evening, Foulan returned, a look of disappointment on his face. When she brought him his dinner, he explained that he hadn't found any work. "As I suspected, there's no use for a huntsman in a coastal town. I've asked around to see what kind of labor there is to do here, but everyone informed me that the town is busiest in the summer, when the port is open. The rest of the year, it's fairly quiet. I'll try again tomorrow."

Tomorrow wasn't any better. When Foulan returned then, his mood was dark, his eyes clouded. "Still no luck?" Mackenna asked him.

He shook his head. "I'm not sure I'll be able to find any work." She noticed that his fist was clenched, and she sat down beside him, laying her hand on his. "I went down to the docks to ask for work with some of the small fishing vessels," he said. "I was able to speak with a few of them once we found a common tongue, but they could tell right away that I'm a

Wanderer. The nicer ones laughed at me, saying I wouldn't last a day on a boat, and would likely be retching over the side the whole time."

"And the not-so-nice ones?" Mackenna asked.

"They called me a vagabond and a Hinzi. Said my kind wasn't welcome here."

She frowned, wishing there was something she could say to lift his spirits. As much as he tried to brush it off, she could tell the insults to his people hurt him.

Mackenna had noticed as they spoke that a customer at the next table was watching them. He seemed oddly familiar, though she couldn't place him. When he stood and approached their table, she asked if he needed another pint of ale or bowl of stew. He shook his head, frowning, his gaze on Foulan. "You looking for work?"

Foulan nodded slowly. "I'm sorry, have we met?"

"A few days ago, you asked me if I would give you passage across the waters." He raised a hand. "Before you ask, my answer hasn't changed. It's too dangerous to leave the bay. But I *can* give you a job."

"What would I need to do?" Foulan asked.

"Before the winter, most of the fishermen head south and don't return until spring. Myself and a few others stay behind to fish the bay and feed the town. I won't lie, it's tough work. Miserable and cold most days. But the townspeople need to eat in the winter." He stroked his rough, bushy beard. "I could use some help hauling in the nets this winter. In addition to your pay, I can teach you how to sail."

Foulan nodded. "I'm not afraid of hard work," he said. "But I asked other captains at the wharf, and they all laughed at me.

Said I'd probably fall off the boat and drown within a week. None of them even bothered to ask if I knew how to swim."

The sailor shrugged. "It doesn't really much matter if you can swim or not, and those captains know it. Even the most seasoned sailor would perish if he fell into the sea in winter. The water stabs into you like a thousand needles. Most who fall in get so shocked that their limbs can't move, and they drown within minutes."

"How do you know?" Mackenna asked.

He smiled, and Mackenna noticed that most of his teeth were black, though a few had been replaced with gold. "I fell in meself, once," he said. "Would've died too, if I hadn't been lucky enough to get tangled up in the nets. They were able to haul me in like a fish. I don't remember much after goin' in the water, but they told me that as they sailed back to shore, they were afraid I was already dead, my skin was so blue."

The more Mackenna heard, the more she grew afraid. "I don't know, Foulan. Maybe you should just keep looking for something else. This seems too dangerous."

It was the wrong thing to say. She realized it as soon as his eyes narrowed and his shoulders squared. He was determined to prove to the sailors who'd laughed at him that he could do their job, vagabond or no.

"I'd be happy to work for you," he told the man. "When can I begin?"

Foulan

They fell into a new routine. Foulan got up before dawn each morning, dressed in layers of furs, ate a quick breakfast, and then walked to the pier as the sun rose. The days were short this far north, and the old sailor, whom Foulan learned was named Skári, warned that they would only get shorter, until in the middle of winter there would be whole weeks where the sun never fully rose and they fished in twilight. Such a thing sounded impossible to Foulan, but Skári informed him that the opposite would happen in the summer, when the sun would shine even at night.

Whenever Foulan returned to The Boatman's Reprieve after a long day of fishing, he would find Mackenna serving the patrons in the tavern, her shift having started just an hour before he arrived. He would eat dinner and chat with her when he could, then head off to bed. He would awaken in the night as Mackenna crawled in beside him and Myst settled at his feet, before falling back asleep for a few more hours.

Their different schedules left Mackenna and Foulan little time to spend together, and even had Foulan wanted to further explore their romance, he was too exhausted at night to do so. Skári hadn't been exaggerating when he said it was miserably cold on the boat. Even though they always remained within sight of the shore, once they were out in the bay, the wind picked up, stinging his cheeks and eyes, the only part of him that was exposed. It was impossible not to get splashed hauling in the net, but thankfully the old sailor had an extra pair of what he referred to as wet boots, which went over Foulan's own boots and were heavily oiled in lard to keep out any moisture.

While they worked, Skári taught Foulan how to sail. It was surprisingly easy to learn. Skári showed him how to discern the direction of the wind, ensure the ropes were pulled tight, and steer the wheel. It helped that it was a small boat with just a single sail, barely large enough for the two of them and a haul of fish. Within a week Skári let Foulan take the wheel and sail them around the bay with their nets dragging behind them.

Foulan also learned that Skári loved to sing sea shanties and tell tales. One day, he asked the sailor for more stories about the island, hoping to learn its secrets. The old man frowned. "I had hoped you two would turn away from that dream," he said, "but I can see from the look in your eyes that you won't. It's the same look I had as a young lad, when I went out to sea seeking adventure."

"It's not adventure we seek," Foulan replied. "It's help. For Mackenna."

"I figured as much," said Skári. "You don't have to tell me, but I do want to know. Is she well?"

"Yes. Not ill, or anything like that," said Foulan. "But… she believes the Fae are the only ones who can help her. Do you believe they really live there? On that island?"

"Us sailors tell many tales. With time, the same story can be told so many times that it changes, grows in wonder and majesty. But even so, we know they all have a start somewhere." The old man gazed silently out at the open sea for a few minutes. "This is the story I've always heard, and you can make of it what you may.

"Long ago, there was a sailor, a young man with a beautiful wife and three children. He sailed these same waters that we do now. While out to sea, a terrible storm came upon him, tossing his ship about on the waves, which had grown as large as mountains. He found his boat dashed upon the rocky cliffs of that island, crushing him between the water and the stone. He was lucky to survive, though he nearly perished.

"When next he awoke, he lay in a soft bed made of leaves, surrounded by wondrous creatures, who seemed to find him as strange as he found them. They brought him to the Faerie king and queen. The queen explained that her scouts had found him alive, though barely, and brought him to her. Her people had healed his wounds with their magic, saving his life.

"The sailor fell to his knees, thanking her, asking how he could repay the debt. The woman told him that he must labor for the Fae for a year and a day. After such time, he would be free to leave the island and return home. He gladly did so, though he missed his wife and children terribly, and knew that they likely thought him dead. He hoped that his wife would still be waiting for him when he was freed.

"After he had repaid the Faerie queen, she gave him a boat with no sails or oars, and informed him that it would take him back to the land of men. He seated himself in the boat, and it started gliding through the water of its own accord. Not long after, he saw land in the distance, a large city before him that he did not recognize. The boat landed on the shore, and as soon as he disembarked, it glided back out into the water. The man approached the city, explaining that he had been shipwrecked and knew not where he had landed. The sailors that he met all said the same name: Icedell."

"Where we are now," Foulan interrupted.

"Yes, but there was a bit of a problem. You see, the man's own hometown had also been called Icedell. And yet this clearly was not the same place, for it was much larger and grander, spreading across the bay and up into the mountains above. But they all told him the same thing. Finally, one sailor had the idea to ask the man his family name. When he replied, the man gave him directions to a house, and said that his kindred lived there, and perhaps they could help him to get home.

"He followed the man's instructions. As he wandered through the city, a sense of unease overcame him, for slowly he started to notice things that seemed all too familiar in this unfamiliar place. The man's directions led him to the oldest part of the town, where the stone buildings were crumbling with age. When he came to the house, his dread overcame him, for he recognized it as his own, though it looked ancient to him. He knocked on the door and was greeted by a beautiful young woman. Not knowing how to explain his predicament, he simply asked for his wife by name, hoping she still lived there.

"The woman shook her head, confused. 'I don't know anyone by that name, but that was the same name as my great grandmother, entombed in a crypt these past five decades.'

"The man feared to ask the next question, but knew that he had to. 'Her husband, do you know what his name was? Is he laid beside her?' She shook her head. 'He was lost at sea, so there was no body to place in the crypt. For the rest of her life, my great grandmother waited, gazing out to sea from the roof of our home, longing for his return. Even when she died, an old woman with many grandchildren, she was a widow, still mourning her lost husband.'"

They sat in silence for a few moments, Foulan absorbing what he had heard. "What happened to the sailor after that?"

Skári shrugged. "Most of the stories don't say. Of course, they're all somewhat different."

"Different? How so?"

"In some of them, he stays but a day on the island, only to return home and find that decades have passed and his wife has remarried. In others, he did not love his wife, and while on the island, he falls in love with the Faerie queen. However, she casts him out for some transgression, usually minor. When he returns to the world of men, a hundred years or more has passed. As soon as he steps foot onto land, however, the Faerie magic wears off, and he crumbles to bone and dust.

"But one says that while working for the Faerie queen, he discovers a secret well on their island, and learns that it is the source of their longevity. So he steals water from the well and escapes the island, bringing it back home to his people. In that version, only a few decades have passed, and the townspeople are filled with wonder to find him returned and looking as if he has not aged a day. He intends to give his wife—there's no mention of children in this one—some of the elixir, but finds that she has grown old and no longer pleases him. What's more, he quickly becomes ill upon his return, when on the island, he never dealt with illness or pain. Realizing that his immortality is not assured now that he has left the land of the Ancient Ones, he abandons his wife and the town and disappears into the mountains, hoarding the water of youth for himself."

"What do you think, Skári?" Foulan asked. "Do you think the Fae really live there?"

"I don't see why not," the sailor answered. "I did my fair share of traveling as a lad. Visited far off lands, met fascinating people, saw strange and wondrous things. Some of those things were neither beast nor human, but somewhere in between. So do I believe it's possible? Aye. But even if you find them there, there's no telling if it would do you any good. In my experience, the Fair Folk are just as likely to hurt as they are to help, and they don't seem to have any guide for which they choose except their own whims."

Foulan had a feeling the old man wasn't telling him everything, but he had come to realize that pushing the sailor would get him nowhere. When Foulan returned to the inn that night, he shared the stories with Mackenna. Instead of frightening her, they seemed only to steel her resolve. "When the spring comes, we will seek them out," she declared. "We will strike a bargain with them to get rid of my magic."

He didn't try to convince her that she didn't need to be cured, that she was not sick or cursed. He had tried before, and she wouldn't hear of it. He supposed he couldn't blame her for thinking so, after everything she had been through.

Kazumi

Kazumi woke in a strange bed, the ceiling above their head unrecognizable. Where were they? How had they gotten here? Slowly, memories returned. They had left the day after the festival, despite the medic's advice that they rest and recover. There was no rest when Kazumi was on the hunt. One could almost say they became… obsessive.

They'd made good time at first, but then after a few days, Kazumi had begun to feel weak with fever. Investigating the wound revealed it to be infected. Perhaps they should have listened to the medic after all. Kazumi set up their tent and laid down, hoping the fever would pass by the morning.

It had not. For three days they'd laid sick in the tent, barely able to eat, the wound seeping a foul-smelling pus. The worst part by far though was the vomiting. Kazumi hated vomiting more than anything.

The last thing they could remember was the sound of horse's hooves crunching through the snow as someone approached. Kazumi was pretty sure they'd called out weakly, begging for help, before darkness had taken them. How pathetic. But here they were, presumably alive, so perhaps it was not all bad to have begged.

Kazumi heard footsteps approach and struggled to sit up. The door was opened by a woman who looked to be in her forties. Her long brown hair was tied in a braid, and she had wrinkles around her eyes and lips. Had she lived an easier life in a city, she would be considered quite pretty, but the harsh life of the frontier had left her face wind bitten and scarred and her hands callused. She walked with a slight limp indicating an old injury.

The woman smiled at them. "Ahh, you've finally woken. I wasn't sure the fever would ever break."

"Where am I?" Kazumi asked.

"I found you while out checking the traps. You were near death, but I've tended your wound and cared for you this past week."

"Week?" Kazumi nearly cursed aloud. To have lost so much time to a damn knife wound. They pushed the blankets away and made to get out of the bed, only to realize that they were naked. Kazumi quickly pulled the blankets back up over them.

"Where are my clothes?" they hissed.

"They were quite soiled. I washed them and you."

How mortifying. She had seen them naked? Kazumi never let anyone see them naked. "Have I been soiling myself for a week?"

She seemed to sense their embarrassment. "Well, I've helped you with that. I'm sure you don't remember with the fever. All you've been able to keep down is liquid anyway, so…"

"Please, stop." They held up a hand, unable to listen to any more. "I need a bath."

"Of course. I'll heat some water."

Kazumi sat up in the bed, hugging their knees to their chest. The woman had no doubt seen them in their entirety, but she hadn't commented on what she had or hadn't noticed. The woman returned when the bath was ready.

"Do you have a robe or towel I could wear?" Kazumi asked.

"You are quite modest, aren't you? I told you I've already seen—"

"Please," Kazumi begged, the word tight in their throat.

"Of course. Here." She handed them a loose night dress, her own, no doubt, and Kazumi pulled it on, then pushed themself out of the bed.

Only to wind up on the floor. "You're still far too weak to get up on your own! Let me help you." The woman put Kazumi's arm around her shoulder and helped them to stand. Together they hobbled to the kitchen, which also appeared to be the main room of the house, where a hot bath sat waiting in the corner by the fireplace. Kazumi sank into it, gown and all. They sighed in relief, their eyes slipping shut.

Only to shoot back open at the feel of the woman stroking their hair. Kazumi sat up, glaring at her.

"I told you, I've already helped bathe you and cared for you this past week," she said. "And you are still weak. Let me wash your hair at least. You just relax."

As if they could. But they were quite exhausted, so Kazumi settled back down against wooden tub, letting the woman wash their hair. The enjoyable sensation of her hands in their hair battled with their extreme discomfort at being touched, especially in such a vulnerable position.

"I can wash your body too, if you wish," she offered.

"No! Please... I would like some privacy," Kazumi muttered.

Was that a look of disappointment in the woman's eye? "Of course," she replied. "Let me fetch you your clothes." She left the room.

Kazumi pulled off the dressing gown and washed as quickly but thoroughly as they could. Kazumi was finally able to relax somewhat once they were dry and dressed in their own clothes again. The woman helped them to the table and then bustled about the kitchen, heating up a stew in a big pot over the fire. The smell made their mouth water.

"I'm Gerda, by the way. What's your name?" she asked.

"Kyoko," Kazumi lied, choosing a popular Isumijian name.

"A lovely name. It is fitting for such a beautiful person," she said, setting the bowl of stew before them. Kazumi noticed that she hadn't said "man" or "woman." "Eat slowly, now. Your stomach hasn't had solid food in some time and may get upset."

A few minutes into eating the hot soup, Kazumi got the uncomfortable feeling of being stared at. They looked up to find the woman watching them. Her face seemed a mixture of curiosity and something more. Something dangerous.

"You're staring," Kazumi accused.

"I apologize. It's just... I've never seen anyone like you before."

Kazumi wasn't sure if she meant Isumijian or something... else. They didn't ask. "Yes, well, it's quite rude to stare."

"My apologies," the woman smiled. "I forget my manners sometimes, living out here alone. In the winter I can go whole weeks, months even, without seeing another soul."

"Alone? You've no family?" Kazumi asked. They didn't care, but they wanted to change the topic away from them.

"I've been a widow some years now. No children. It can be lonely at times, but I enjoy the freedom." She placed a hand on Kazumi's arm, stroking it gently. They barely managed to avoid jumping and yanking away. "What about you?"

"What do you mean?" they asked.

"Have you family? A… lover?" she questioned.

This was getting to be too much. "I apologize, but I am growing quite tired. I think I need to rest some more."

"Of course. Let me help—"

"It's fine. I can do it myself." Their limbs shook, but they were able to stand on their own. Kazumi shuffled to the bedroom, collapsing onto the bed. It hadn't been a complete lie; they were exhausted.

After a few more days, their strength had returned enough for them to move about the small cabin on their own and keep down solid food. Most importantly, they could take care of relieving and cleaning themself without help.

They didn't miss the way the woman watched them, the curiosity in her eyes. Or how often she tried to touch them— their hair, their arm, their shoulder. They shrugged her away uncomfortably every time, and if it disappointed her, it didn't seem to deter her any.

Kazumi was thankful that at least she had also cared for their horse, keeping it groomed and warm in the barn. There they also found their saddle bags with their money, tent, food, and blanket. What they didn't find was their armor or sword. The house was tiny, just a few rooms, and the barn wasn't much bigger, yet their sword and armor were nowhere to be found.

Kazumi asked about it at dinner that night. "Armor? Sword? I did not see such when I found you. Just you, your horse, and your tent," she replied.

"It should have been in my tent with me. Would have been pretty difficult to miss," Kazumi muttered.

"Perhaps you were robbed while you lay ill…" the woman seemed deep in thought. "I know. Tomorrow we'll return to where I found you and search together. How's that?"

Kazumi nodded reluctantly. After dinner, Kazumi made their excuses and went to bed.

They awoke in the night to the feeling of hands caressing their body. Instantly awake, they grabbed the woman's wrists, stopping her exploration. "What are you doing?" Kazumi hissed.

"I'm sorry. I just couldn't help myself," the woman whispered, snuggling her face against Kazumi's neck. While Kazumi slept in their clothes, they could tell that the woman was naked. "I know you must leave soon. But first… won't you spend the night with me?"

"I am in no mood. Please leave," Kazumi muttered.

"Do you know, while you were ill, I slept beside you, keeping your body warm with mine?"

"You overstep your bounds doing so without my consent," Kazumi said, grip tightening on her wrist. The woman gasped, though it didn't seem to be completely from pain.

"No, no, I did not touch you, no matter how much I wanted to. I only held you. But I come to you now to ask you to let me. Let me touch you. Let me feel you."

"You lied about my armor and sword, didn't you?" Kazumi realized. "You have them hidden somewhere." They had suspected as much, but now it was clear.

"Yes. I'm sorry. And in the morning, I'll return them. But let us be together for tonight. When I was married, my husband never satisfied me as he should. I wondered for many years if perhaps I was meant to be with a woman instead. But I'd never imagined that I would meet anyone… like you."

"Stop touching me!" Kazumi growled, pushing her away and jumping out of the bed.

It had not been the first time Kazumi had drawn the interests of people curious about their exotic and androgynous appearance, nor did they doubt it would be the last. Kazumi usually turned them down. The few times they'd been intimate with another, they had found it unenjoyable. The smells, grunting, sweating, and not to mention the fluids. Kazumi hated bodily fluids of any kind. And what if their partner turned out to have a disease? Or gods forbid if a child was somehow produced?

"Please, just one night! Let me know what it's like—"

"Enough!" They yelled, grabbing the woman by the throat and pushing her against the wall. "I am not some whore for you to satisfy your curiosity with."

"If it weren't for me, you'd be dead," she hissed.

"And I am more than willing to pay you for your troubles, but with coin, not my body. Now, I will only ask this once more. Where. Are. My. Things?"

They tightened their grip on her throat, until the desire in her eyes was replaced with fear. She gasped and beat at their arm. Kazumi loosened their grip enough for her to speak.

"Under the rug in the kitchen. The floorboards are loose. You'll find it all there."

Kazumi released her and followed her instructions. Sure enough, their armor and sword were where she'd said. They strapped on the armor quickly and no doubt sloppily, then secured their sword at their hip. As Kazumi saddled their horse, the woman came outside, thankfully clothed. "At least don't leave now. It's the middle of the night and snowing. You're likely to hurt yourself."

"How do I get back to the main road?" they asked, ignoring her.

"Just follow the path there. It's the only one to my little homestead."

Kazumi swung up onto the horse, feeling the scabs on their thigh pull tight. They reached into their saddle bag, grabbing a few coins blindly and tossing them at the woman's feet. "For your troubles. My debt to you is paid."

With that, Kazumi rode off into the night.

Kazumi reached the city of Icedell a few days later. Once there, it was surprisingly easy to find the witch. They'd only had to ask at a few taverns before they were directed to the one where the witch had apparently gotten a job. Why would the witch and her Wanderer friend travel all this way to such a remote city and then immediately get jobs? Perhaps having reached the northern coast, they figured they should stop running and start new lives?

Determined to find out, Kazumi Changed their appearance and entered the tavern in the evening, when it was the most crowded. They took a seat in the back corner, watching the girl as she served drinks, brought food, and chatted with the locals. But they became distracted by the sensation of being watched.

Kazumi glanced over to see the wolf staring at them from across the room, its teeth bared. Its growl was low but nonetheless discernible as it cautiously approached, hackles raised.

Fuck. Apparently the canine recognized their smell, if not their appearance. Its confusion at their disguise was no doubt the only reason it hadn't already attacked. But it appeared ready to lunge at any moment.

The tavern had grown quiet, the other visitors now aware of the standoff. Kazumi didn't dare take their eyes off of the wolf's, hoping that a show of dominance would force it to stand down. Out of the corner of their eye, they could see a flash of red as the witch ran towards them.

"I'm so sorry, she's never done this! What has gotten into you, Myst?" she hissed at the wolf in embarrassment. "C'mon, if you can't behave, you're going up to my room. Myst… I said come."

Begrudgingly the wolf obeyed, though not without throwing one last look over its shoulder in Kazumi's direction. The witch returned a few moments later, apology clearly written on her face. "I'm really so sorry. What can I get for you?"

Kazumi set down the pocket mirror that they had glanced into to make sure their disguise still held despite their nerves.

Thankfully, it had not wavered. They pitched their voice low, doing their best to imitate the local accent. "Stew, please."

"And to drink?" she asked.

"Just water." An odd request, no doubt, but Kazumi never drank while on a mission.

The girl curtsied and disappeared once more. The chattering in the tavern resumed as people went back to their food and drink. After a few minutes, she returned with a bowl of stew and a mug of water. "Anything else you need, sir?"

"I've never seen you around here before. Are you new to town?" Kazumi asked.

"Oh, yes. I only arrived a fortnight ago."

"What would bring you here at a time like this? We don't usually get tourists until summer."

She smiled, no doubt used to this line of questioning from the locals by now. "Oh, my… husband and I just wanted a change of pace is all."

Kazumi could tell she wasn't willing to give up anymore, at least not right now. She was a fugitive, after all. They nodded, letting her get back to work. They watched her surreptitiously, planning out their next move.

They suspected they could take the Wanderer in a fight, though he was nowhere to be found at present. For the girl, all they had to do was get the magic-suppressing cuffs onto her before she could react. The real problem was the wolf.

Kazumi was not too proud to admit that the creature frightened them. They didn't care for dogs, and this thing was much worse. It was easily twice as large as most dogs, but despite its size, it had been surprisingly swift and light on its feet that night in the alley. Not only that, but it was clearly more intelligent than a pet, seeming to understand and obey anything that the girl said to it. Even if they returned in a new disguise each night, the dog would recognize their smell, drawing suspicion from the tavern's patrons. It might even attack them. Kazumi wasn't fond of the thought of that beast sinking its deadly fangs into them and ripping them apart.

While they were curious as to what exactly she was doing in Icedell—besides simply hiding from her problems—they supposed that didn't really matter. All that mattered was getting to the girl when neither the wolf nor her "husband" were around.

For now, the best course of action would be to wait and watch from a distance. Like a spider, they would spin their web and wait quietly for the little butterfly to flutter into it.

Mackenna

Mackenna stepped outside, taking a deep breath of the cold air. It was only mid-afternoon, but twilight had fallen already. Soon, the tavern would be swarming with townsfolk. With the cold and lack of sun, there was little for people to do for fun besides hang out in the taverns. They were a fun crowd, drinking, singing, and playing dice. But having grown used to the quiet of the open road, the busy tavern and its roaring fire often felt overly warm and crowded. Hilda seemed to realize Mackenna's restlessness and had sent her out to pick up an order of bread from the baker for dinner that night.

Even though the baker's wasn't too far, it was bitterly cold out, so she'd changed out of her dress and into her hide pants and fur coat. Mackenna was down the street when she realized she'd forgotten her hat and gloves. She considered turning around to get them, but she didn't want to waste any more time, as she'd still have to change once she got back before she could start waiting on the customers.

It felt odd to not have Myst beside her, but after the wolf had growled at a patron last night, she'd asked Foulan to take her with him on the boat. Her best guess for Myst's strange behavior was that she too had started to get cabin fever from being cooped up in the tavern instead of out on the road. Myst couldn't exactly run around on a small fishing boat, but perhaps the open air and spending time with her master would help to calm her.

Mackenna noticed a figure approaching from her left, and she tensed instinctually. The person appeared to be elderly, walking with a hobble. She couldn't see their face; in this cold, everyone had to bundle up until everything but their eyes were covered. "Do you have any food," the person croaked, and she guessed her to be a woman from her voice.

"I'm sorry?" Mackenna asked. She tucked her hands into her fur coat to warm them.

"I'm so hungry. My kids left to find work, but they haven't been back in weeks. I don't have any money for food. Please, miss," the woman begged, holding out a hand.

"If you come back to The Boatman's Reprieve after we close tonight, I can see what we have left over. I'm sure the owner wouldn't mind—" She was cut off by the woman suddenly collapsing. Mackenna rushed forward to catch her. "Are you alright?" she asked.

Something icy cold closed around her wrist. Mackenna looked down in confusion to see a band of thick iron wrapped around it. A shackle, and the woman was reaching for her other hand.

She didn't have time to think. Everything that Foulan had taught her kicked in, and she struggled against the old woman. She tried to yell, but the woman clasped her hand over Mackenna's mouth, blocking out any sound. Biting her hand proved ineffectual with the thick gloves that she wore. The stranger started pulling her away from the inn. She was surprisingly strong for how frail she'd looked. The woman was still trying to get at her other wrist, but Mackenna refused to let her have it. She kicked backwards, but found it difficult to land any hard blows with all the padding.

She could feel the panic rising, and with it, her flames. Normally she would fight to keep them contained, but she didn't know who had her or what their intentions were, so she gave in, letting them take over. The heat rushed across her skin, her blood singing with it.

Nothing happened. She could feel the fire at her core, where it always sprang from. It danced under her skin, ready to burst free, but it wouldn't come out. It was as if there was a barrier blocking it, holding it within her. In her shock, she stopped struggling and found herself pulled into an alley. Mackenna managed to turn to face her assailant. She grabbed at the old woman's scarf, ripping it away from her face.

A face she recognized immediately. Not an old woman at all, though Mackenna could have sworn she'd seen wrinkles around her eyes just moments before. It was the bounty hunter who had attacked her before. Up close, they appeared to be about her age, give or take a year or two. They were also beautiful, with a mixture of masculine and feminine features that left Mackenna still uncertain as to whether her attacker was a woman or a man.

Well, it didn't matter either way. What mattered was that they were here, and Mackenna was alone.

"I'll thank you to please stop struggling," they said with a grin, dropping the frail act they'd adopted earlier. "And you can try to light me on fire all you want, but this little accessory," they held up her wrist by the heavy shackle, "will prevent you from doing so. Now, give me your other wrist to secure you, and then we can be out of this horrible town and headed somewhere warmer."

Mackenna knew if that she wanted to have any chance of escape, she couldn't let them bind her hands together. Unfortunately, they were far stronger than her physically. She did the only thing she could think of at the moment and slammed her head into her assailant's. It hurt like a bitch, but she could tell from their sudden yell and the blood pouring down that she'd likely broken their nose.

Mackenna kicked them as hard as she could in the stomach, causing them to release her. She turned and ran, not caring which direction she went in, only knowing that she had to put as much distance as possible between them and her. She turned through the narrow alleys randomly, hoping to confuse them. Nobody else seemed to be outside in this cold. Should she bang on doors and beg for help? With a shackle on her arm, they might think her an escaped prisoner, and they wouldn't be far from the mark. She had a bounty on her head, after all. Anyone had the right to arrest her.

She quickly realized that she was lost. Mackenna wasn't sure how to get back to the inn from here, and even if she did go back, she didn't know if the innkeeper would protect her or turn her in. If she were to follow the gradual downhill slope of the road, it had to lead her to the bay and Foulan.

Foulan

"A good haul today," Skári commented as they finished emptying the contents of the fishing net into a barrel. "That wolf of yours makes a good fisher dog. In warmer months, some fishers will have their dogs jump into the water and haul the nets in by their teeth."

"What do you think, want to swim around in the bay when the water warms up?" Foulan asked Myst, who eyed him with what seemed to be suspicion. The wolf licked her chops and pawed the barrel impatiently. "Yeah, yeah, here's your pay." Foulan tossed her a fish, which she caught in the air and immediately began to tear into.

"I'll haul this over to the market. Would you mind cleaning up the boat for tonight?" Skári asked.

Foulan nodded. "I'll meet you at the inn when I'm done," he replied. After working with him for a while, Foulan had realized that Skári was a lonely man. He had no wife or children of his own, and the only thing he seemed to care about was fishing. So Foulan had offered to buy the old sailor a drink one night. It had turned into an open invitation to visit the tavern together in the evenings and share stories.

Foulan noticed that the townspeople would sometimes send them odd looks. At first he thought their stares had been directed at him, but Skári told him the others were just surprised to see him there. He'd been a reclusive hermit for many years, providing the city with food but rarely spending time with the townfolk. Foulan could relate. Just as he loved to be alone amongst the trees and the wild beasts, Skári preferred the loneliness of the sea. Even so, the fisherman seemed to enjoy their evenings at the tavern.

Foulan had almost finished gathering the nets when the sound of footsteps racing across the cobblestones caught his attention. He turned to see Mackenna running towards him, her face panicked. Foulan grabbed his bow and quiver of arrows. Skári had found it odd that he always took them with him on the boat, but he felt naked and vulnerable without them. "What is it? What's wrong?" Foulan asked. Myst immediately positioned herself beside Mackenna, growling in the direction she'd come from.

Mackenna fell into his arms, struggling to catch her breath. "The bounty hunter… found us," she gasped.

Foulan cursed and notched his bow. "Are you okay?"

"No. They… they did something to me. To my magic. It's not working!" Mackenna's eyes were wide with panic.

"We'll figure it out," he soothed. "For now, where is he? Is he still following you?"

She didn't have to answer. Myst suddenly howled in warning. Foulan looked up to see a cloaked man running towards them. There was a flash of metal, and Myst's howl was cut off with a whimper.

"Myst!" Mackenna knelt by the wolf's side. There was blood on her fur, and a strange knife, in the shape of a star, embedded in her side. The wolf cried in pain, still alive, though Foulan didn't know for how long.

A wave of cold fury and fear washed over Foulan. He drew back the arrow, the rest of the world falling away. All he could see was the man before him, brandishing his strange sword, a lethal grin on his face. Foulan had never felt so focused, his head so clear. Time seemed to pause as in one smooth motion he lined up the arrow, aiming for the heart, and then released.

The man brought down his sword at the same time. Foulan expected the arrow to land, blood to bloom from his chest. Instead, the man stood unharmed, the arrow cut down at his feet. He'd never seen anyone move so fast in his life.

"Foulan, the boat!" Mackenna cried. "We have to escape! We can't fight them, and Myst is dying! But the Fae, maybe they can save her!"

"Are you crazy?" he asked. "We don't even know where the island is, if it's even real. Mackenna, it's not safe—"

"It is real!" she yelled, grabbing him. "It has to be! I've met them! I've talked to them!"

"The ocean is frozen—"

"I don't care! We're getting on this boat, and we're going to that island. Now!" she yelled, trying to lift up the wolf.

Another one of the knives came sailing at them, embedding itself in the wood of the mast with a thunk. Foulan bent down and helped Mackenna lift Myst into the boat. He could keep firing arrows, one after the other. There was no way the man could stop them all. But he risked Mackenna's and Myst's lives in the process. They had to get away as quickly as possible, and with Myst injured, the only way to do that would be on the boat.

It took only moments to unfurl the sail and pull it tight. He barked orders at Mackenna, who dashed to do what he said without question. The wind grabbed the sail, quickly pulling them away from the shore. "What the hell is going on here?!" a voice yelled from the dock, and he glanced up to see Skári confronting the bounty hunter.

"Get away from him Skári! He's dangerous!" he called out, but the boat was quickly retreating from the docks, and his voice was lost to the wind. As worried as he was for the old sailor, he needed to focus all of his attention on the task at hand. Foulan grabbed the wheel, steering them towards the open ocean. Mackenna knelt down beside Myst, who breathed heavily and continued to whine. "It's okay girl," she cooed. "It's going to be okay."

"There's needle and thread in that box," Foulan said, gesturing with his head. "For stitching the sail. Can you sew her up?"

"I can try," Mackenna answered. Her hands shook terribly as she attempted to thread the needle, and he realized that she wore neither a hat nor gloves. She finally managed to thread it and put a hand on Myst's head. "Please, I need to you be calm," she told the wolf. "If you move too much, it will just make it worse." As if the wolf understood her, she held as still as she could, not even flinching when Mackenna pulled the star-shaped blade from her side. Mackenna stitched as quickly as she could. "Why do you have to have so much damned fur?" she asked, laughing despite the tears streamed down her face. She finished off the stitches, then wrapped her scarf around the canine's midsection, tying it tightly to hold back the bleeding.

All the while, Foulan steered them through the icy sea. He didn't even know if he was going in the right direction, so he focused only on keeping them afloat. He tried to remember the map that Fatimah had shown them. On it, the island had been directly north of the city of Icedell. Assuming that was true, all he had to do was keep the rising moon to his right. Even so, panic gripped him. He could see the ice for the moment and steer around it. But what if the moon went behind a cloud, and they had only the boat's lantern to see by? What if they missed the island and ended up lost in the open sea? Had they run away from a dangerous bounty hunter only to slowly freeze to death?

After what felt like an hour, he glimpsed moonlight glinting off of something in the distance. He kept them pointed towards it, recognizing it as ice and snow. "Mackenna, look," he breathed. "The island."

The mass of ice grew larger and larger as they came nearer. For some reason, he had expected it to be small, no larger than a town perhaps. This island was a land mass in its own right; he could barely see from one end of it to the other, and it appeared to be made entirely of sheer stone cliffs covered in ice. He saw no flat land on which to dock, nor did he expect that anything could possibly live here. There was not even a tuft of grass or scrap of lichen to be seen. Even so, he turned their boat so that it slowly coasted along the perimeter of the massive island, keeping them far enough away to avoid any rocks hidden beneath the waves that crashed against the cliffs.

Neither of them spoke. What could they say? Myst had stopped whining, but her breathing was labored, strange wheezing sounds coming from her lungs. Suddenly, Mackenna's voice broke the silence. "There. Head for that cave."

Foulan's gaze followed where she pointed, but he saw nothing. Nothing but more ice towering above them. "I don't see it."

"There. It's *right there*. Between the rocks." She continued pointing, but still he saw nothing.

"Mackenna, there's nothing there. The cold is getting to you. Here, take my hat and gloves. We'll take turns wearing them." He pulled them off, holding them out to her with one hand, the other on the wheel.

"I'm not hallucinating," she argued. "How do you not see the giant cave in the rocks? It's right in front of us! Look!" She grabbed his bow and an arrow, knocking it and firing at the cliff.

It went through the ice. Not into it, lodging or breaking against it. Just through it, as if it wasn't there at all, and then disappeared. "What?" he asked dumbly. "How is that possible?"

She shrugged. "An illusion? Maybe I can see it because of my magic. I don't know, but head in that direction."

His did as she bid him. He'd seen the arrow disappear. And yet his mind yelled at him that he sailed them straight towards rocks, towards their doom. He braced himself for the impact, but it never came.

Darkness descended as the moonlight was cut off. He looked back, finding himself gazing out of the mouth of a cave that hadn't existed a moment before. The tiny lantern of their boat did little to illuminate the darkness, but he could tell from the echoes that the cave must be massive. The wind had gone out of the sails, and they bobbed on the waves, which were surprisingly calm inside the cave.

"Hello?" Mackenna yelled into the darkness. "Is there anyone here? We come seeking help from the Fae!" Her voice echoing back at her was the only answer.

"What now?" Foulan asked. He heard sobbing, and looked down to find Mackenna curled onto the floor of the boat, her body wrapped around Myst. He sat down beside her, resting a hand gently on her back. Neither of them had an answer.

277

Mackenna

Mackenna woke from a light doze to find three creatures staring at them. At first she believed the darkness and her drowsy mind were playing tricks on her. One appeared to be a giant with stone for flesh. The other was a knight on horseback in full armor, but it had no head. The third was a woman from the waist up, but below that appeared to be a horse.

"We are here to take you to the queen," a masculine voice proclaimed. Neither the stone creature nor the half-horse woman had moved their lips, as far as she could tell. She realized the voice was coming from the headless rider.

She glanced at Foulan, who was also staring at the creatures in shock. His mouth opened and closed, unable to form words. "Who… who are you?" she asked, her voice raspy from the cold.

"We are the Ancient Ones. You have come here seeking our queen's favor. We have been sent to fetch you to her." Mackenna realized that the headless rider held a helm under one arm, and that it was not empty. It appeared that the voice was coming from inside.

Mackenna and Foulan looked at each other before standing slowly. The headless rider reached a hand to Foulan, pulling him up behind him. The horse woman likewise held out an arm to Mackenna, but despite her feeble attempts, Mackenna's body was too numb from the cold to pull herself up. Suddenly, she found herself being lifted into the air by a hard and unyielding force and placed on the horse part of the woman. She looked back to the see the stone creature that had placed here there bent over their small boat, lifting Myst gently in its arms. The wolf did not move, and Mackenna feared she was already dead.

They set off without another word. The Fae offered no conversation, and Mackenna was too tired and overwhelmed to speak. They travelled through the darkness of the cave without any kind of light to guide them. Either the Fae had very good vision, or they knew the path by heart. Mackenna was colder than she had ever been in her life, and she wasn't entirely sure it was due to their arctic surroundings. There was a hollowness inside her. She knew her magic was still there, deep within, but she couldn't tap into it, the cuff cutting it off from her. All her life she had hoped for a way to control it, or, barring that, to be rid of it entirely. But now that it was suddenly gone, she ached to have her fire back, to feel its heat once more.

Finally, they emerged from the dark void of the cave, and Mackenna gasped. She had expected a wasteland of ice and snow, but what they found before them was a beautiful wooded valley hidden inside a ring of mountains. The air was calm and unnaturally temperate, the trees lightly dusted with powder and sparkling in the moonlight. In the distance below, she could see a lake at the foot of an enormous tree that towered over everything else on the island save the mountains themselves.

They gradually descended a pathway cut into the rocky cliff. Soon they reached the forest floor, the Fae never making a sound as they moved across the mossy earth. Mackenna had the uncomfortable feeling, however, that they were not alone. Flashes of movement at the edges of her vision caught her attention, and she would look over to see eyes peeking at her, but they would quickly vanish. The tinkling of bells (or was that laughter?) echoed through the forest before quickly fading. It reminded her of being stalked through the bogs by the will-o'-the-wisps. Their Fae guides seemed unconcerned, however, and continued their steady parade.

The forest fell away, and they found themselves in a clearing. Before them was the giant tree, larger than any Mackenna had ever seen, larger than a castle. As they made their way up the tree's trunk, she realized that it *was* a castle. They climbed the roads created by its roots, passing entrances into what appeared to be buildings and homes built directly into the trunk. Instead of doors, the entryways were hung with ivy, and moss formed the roofs. Bridges made of vines criss-crossed between the buildings. Eventually they reached the spot where the branches of the canopy met the trunk. There, a huge archway led into the tree itself.

Mackenna thought she had felt overwhelmed before, but it was nothing compared to what she experienced once they entered the heart of the tree. Inside was the throne room of a royal court. Their Fae guides stopped, helping them down. Mackenna could only stare dumbly at the creatures that filled the throne room.

There were some that looked mostly human. Short, stout men and women with thick beards. Others that were thin, tall, and pale, with dark red eyes, whose smiles revealed sharp fangs. Small green creatures, no larger than a toddler, with enormous ears and leathery skin. There was a person covered in fur, with a bushy fox tail and ears.

More often than not, however, they seemed to be some strange mixture of a human and a beast. A woman with bright red feathers for hair and wings instead of arms. Merfolk, like the Lady of the Lake, with scales and gills and webbed fingers.

Another who was a man from the waist up, but instead of legs, he had the long coiling tail of a snake. There were Fae with bark for skin and leaves for hair. Mackenna flinched away from an enormous spider, larger than a horse. Sprouting from its back was the torso of a woman, who turned, gazing at her with eight eyes.

Tiny creatures with firefly wings darted between the larger Fae. There were others, only the size of her hand, that she had mistaken for small rocks until she saw them scurry across the floor. There was a man who walked on two bull legs, his body a wall of muscle, giant horns and a bovine snoot sprouting from his skull. A skeletal corpse in rusted armor reached out its bony fingers towards her.

"Make way for the humans," a feminine voice called through the room. The Fae creatures stepped aside, clearing a path to the throne. It was carved—no, she realized that it was naturally grown—from the wooden walls of the tree itself. On it sat the most beautiful woman Mackenna had ever seen. She had skin that was so pale it was tinged blue. Hair as white as snow hung to her waist, and shimmery, delicate blue butterfly wings sprouted from her back. Her gown and crown appeared to be made of ice. There was no doubt that this was the queen.

A giant of a man stood beside the throne. He had the legs of a goat, and massive antlers sprouted from his head. Fur covered his back, arms, and legs, and the only clothing he wore was a loincloth. The large muscles of his chest and arms gave Mackenna the distinct impression that he could crush her with one hand. Wild, unkempt hair flowed from his head, and he sported a braided beard. "Kneel before Queen Titania," he commanded.

Mackenna and Foulan approached her throne and knelt uncertainly. "Humans," the queen spoke. "You have come to the Faelands seeking aid."

It was not a question, but Foulan replied anyway. "Yes, my lady. Myst, my wolf, is gravely injured."

"Bring the creature here," the queen called. The stone Fae did as she bid, laying the wolf at her feet. She reached a hand down, running it through Myst's fur. "Yes, she is mortally wounded, but she is not too far gone. We can save her."

The stone man picked her up again, carrying her away. Mackenna could only assume they took her to a healer.

"I doubt that is all that you wish to request of me, children," Titania continued, "for that wound is fresh, and I sense that you are a long way from home." When her eyes fell on Mackenna, it felt as if the queen was looking through her, into her very soul.

"I seek help. I am… cursed," Mackenna whispered.

"Cursed?" the Faerie queen lifted an eyebrow. "And what is the nature of this curse?"

"A fire burns within me. One which I cannot control," she explained. "I destroyed my village. I… killed people. I seek a way to… to control it."

"Would you demonstrate your curse for us, child, so that we may see it?" the queen requested.

Mackenna stood slowly, pulling off her fur coat. It was a relief to have it off, as it was rather warm in the throne room. "I can't at this moment. The person who attacked our wolf… they used something to block my magic." She held up her right arm, showing the shackle around one wrist. A collective intake of air seemed to echo through the entire room. Mackenna lowered her tired arm in confusion, gazing around her at the Fae, who were all staring at the shackle as if it was a snake that might bite them.

"Tell me, child, is that iron?" the queen asked.

"I think so? I'm not certain," Mackenna answered.

"That is a very dangerous object you have brought into our land, child," said the queen. "Iron is deadly to us. If it stays in our land for too long, we will all become terribly ill. It must be removed. Immediately."

"I don't have the key," Mackenna said. "Or I would have, Your Ma—"

"Cut her arm off." The suggestion came from the man who stood beside the queen's throne. When he spoke, it was with an authority that it made it quite clear that he was just as important as the queen herself.

Murmurs of agreement rose in the crowd. "Yes, it will be the quickest way," someone called.

"What?" Foulan yelled, jumping up beside her. He reached for his bow, then seemed to realize that he did not have it with him. In their exhaustion they must have left it in the boat. He positioned himself between Mackenna and the queen, but they were surrounded. There was no way he could protect her from them all.

"Bring me Sneak," the queen called out. "If he can't remove it, then we will do so."

A few minutes later, a man appeared, bowing before the queen. She commanded him to remove the shackle, and he pulled a lockpick kit from a bag at his waist, setting to work on it. Mackenna watched him as he did, trying to discover what strange Fae he was. From what she could tell, he appeared to be completely human.

With a click, the shackle opened, crashing to the floor. The man picked it up, smirking at the queen. "I was hoping for something more challenging," he said. "What should I do with this?"

"Toss it into the sea," the queen commanded. "I will send a guard with you to take you there."

He shrugged as if bored and was led away by the half-horse woman that Mackenna had rode on earlier.

Once he was gone from the room, taking the shackles with him, the mood lightened, as if the Fae inside had been too afraid to even breathe. The queen turned back to them with a smile. "Now that that is taken care of, I can perhaps be of aid to you. Come here child. Take my hand." She held her hand out to Mackenna, who stepped forward hesitantly. Mackenna's hand, dirty and bloody from tending Myst's wound, contrasted sharply with the queen's delicate one, but the Faerie woman didn't seem to care. "Ahh, yes, now I understand. I could not sense it with that iron on your arm. You are not cursed at all, child. You are Fae touched."

Once more the room reacted, the Fae murmuring amongst themselves. "I don't understand, Your Majesty," Mackenna whispered.

The queen held up a hand, tracing a finger gently down Mackenna's cheek. She ignored what Mackenna said, seemingly engrossed in staring at her face. "In fact," she said, "I would say that you seem to be equal parts Fae and human." Her lips pinched, a slight furrow forming between her brows.

"You think she could be Shaelyn's," the man beside the queen stated.

"There is only one way to find out," said the queen.

Once more they seemed to be waiting for someone to appear. Mackenna backed away towards Foulan, gripping his hand tightly. Even though they both shook, the feeling of his hand in hers comforted her a little, lending her the strength to keep standing. At least they did not have to wait long. A woman entered the room. While she wore no chains, it was evident from the way two other Fae flanked her like guards that she was a prisoner of some sort. She knelt before the queen, her back to Mackenna and Foulan. Her movements were mechanical, as if she bowed merely out of protocol and no actual respect.

It was not the queen who spoke, but the man beside her. "You know the punishment for lying to the Queen of the Fae."

"Might I ask what it is I have lied about?" The woman's voice was a monotone. There was neither fear nor hatred. She seemed to be completely devoid of any emotion.

"Nineteen years ago, you returned from traveling amongst the humans," the queen began. "During your travels, you broke a number of rules. However, you assured me that you had left no evidence of your transgressions." The woman stiffened, seeming for the first time to show any emotion, though what exactly she felt Mackenna couldn't tell. The queen leaned forward. "You told me the baby had died. And yet, behind you stands a young woman of the appropriate age with a startling resemblance to yourself."

The woman's head shot up suddenly. She jerked to her feet, turning towards Mackenna and Foulan. Mackenna was able to get a good look at her now. She had light brown skin, chestnut colored hair, and high, sharp cheekbones. Her ears were long and pointed, and two goat horns sprouted from her head, curving back along her skull. Besides those features, she could have passed for a human. Her eyes were what struck Mackenna the most. A brilliant emerald green, they seemed impossibly sad.

"Look at her and tell me that your child died," the queen hissed.

"I… I cannot," the woman replied, her voice breaking. A single tear slid silently down one cheek. "She is my daughter."

Mackenna was reminded of the day she'd fallen into the river, of the momentary chaos and confusion as the cold hit her. The air left her lungs, her mind going blank. Heat and cold washed over her in alternating waves. Her vision narrowed, so that all she could see was this woman.

This liar.

"Tell me, love," the woman said. "What did Finn name you?"

How did she know her father's name? What sorcery was this? "My mother is dead," Mackenna hissed, stepping back from the woman. Foulan's hand rested on her shoulder, protective. Supportive. "She died giving birth to me."

"It appears we were both lied to," the queen said.

"I am so sorry," the woman whispered, but it was directed at Mackenna, not her queen. "I wanted to protect you. To keep you away—"

"Shut up!" Mackenna yelled, covering her ears. "This is a trick! A Faerie trick! My mother is dead! I killed her! I destroyed her with my flames, just like I destroy everything!"

"If I had known you would have had such powers, I would never have left you," the woman whispered. "I thought yours might be gentle, like your father's hedgewitch magic—"

"Get out of my head! Stop pretending to know him! Stop pretending you're my mother!" The fire was rising within, heating her blood. She was trapped. An animal in a snare. Horrendous monsters surrounded her. Her only friend, her love, was trapped here with her. She had to get away from him. She didn't care what happened to the others, but she couldn't hurt Foulan. Mackenna turned, rushing towards the crowd.

A hand grabbed at her, the wild man who had stood beside the queen only moments before. His face was contorted in rage. Mackenna's own rage rose up to meet his, and the fire burst forth, her hair alighting. Smoke quickly blinded her, the stench of scorched clothing filling her nose. Certainly she was hurting the man, but he didn't seem to feel the pain. "Don't hurt her!" a voice cried, but Mackenna didn't know if it belonged to the queen or to Foulan or to the imposter who claimed to be her mother. Perhaps all three.

"Zephra!" the wild man yelled, and another Fae was suddenly beside him, as if it had appeared from thin air. "Snuff her out," the man commanded.

"Let go of —" Mackenna's protest was cut off as all of the air left her lungs and her fire extinguished. It was like she had been punched in the chest, but no matter how much she gasped, she could not get any air. Somehow, the Fae he had summoned was choking her. Panic set in, making her fight harder. But no matter how much she struggled, the man's grip was a vice. Her strength quickly left her, her body growing weak with each passing second. Black spots formed on the edges of her vision.

Had she come this far just to be murdered? Were her final moments going to be filled with fear and horror? What about Foulan and Myst? What would happen to them?

She had to remain conscious. She had to…

Kazumi

As Kazumi watched their target escape, they turned on the man who had attacked them. "You just cost me a great deal of money!"

The man, either a fisherman or boat hand by his clothing and smell, simply shrugged. "I don't appreciate people attacking my protégé." He straightened up, stroking his scraggly grey beard, wielding a harpoon before him. "I also don't care for violence. You have one minute to get out of my sight before I call the guards."

Kazumi's eyes narrowed. The man had said that one of them was his protégé. He could only be referring to the boy who traveled with the witch. Kazumi had watched him head to the docks that very morning with his wolf in tow. He'd seemed to be on his way to work. Which meant the man before him was likely a sea captain. And a sea captain should certainly know how to sail.

Kazumi didn't wait another moment. They lunged forward, knocking the harpoon aside. Drawing a dagger, they brought it to the man's throat. "You are going to fix this little mess for me. Now drop your weapon." The old sailor seemed to contemplate his choices for a moment before doing so, lifting his hands in surrender. And yet his face remained stoic, no fear in his eyes. Kazumi glanced around, their eyes landing on the nearest sailboat. They nodded towards it. "Get in."

"That's not my boat," the sailor protested.

"Did I ask?" Kazumi hissed, pushing the man towards it.

"People tend to frown on boat thieves. Some even call it piracy," the sailor said.

"Well, if you do everything I say, you might survive long enough to explain to them the circumstances." They kicked the man off of the dock and into the boat. The sailor regained his feet easily. Kazumi jumped in behind him, but they nearly fell over as the boat rocked. "Now follow them."

The sailor shrugged. "It will go faster if you help me." He set about hoisting the sail, ordering Kazumi to pull on this rope or that. Kazumi kept his eye on the man as he did so, expecting a trick, but none came. Soon they were out on the water, their prey a speck in the distance.

It felt as if they moved achingly slow. The sailor had begun to sing sea shanties, seemingly unperturbed by the fact that he had been kidnapped. "Can't you make this thing go faster?" Kazumi complained, interrupting him.

The sailor's smile pulled at an old white scar on his weathered cheek. "This is as fast as she goes. She's designed for leisurely strolls on the water."

"You couldn't have told me that before?" Kazumi growled.

The man shrugged. "I don't recall having a say in the matter."

Kazumi scanned the horizon, searching for the bobbing light that indicated their prey's boat. It was nowhere to be seen. "We've lost them!" they hissed, turning on the man. "You did this on purpose." They loomed over the sailor with dagger drawn. "If we don't find them, you'll be fish food, do you understand?"

The man simply smirked, as if amused. "And then how, exactly, would you return to shore?"

Kazumi's hand tightened on their dagger. Idiot! They were always methodical, always two moves ahead of their adversary. What was it about this particular mark that had them acting so foolish?

"What exactly is your intention with my friends? Are you an assassin?" the sailor asked.

"I have been in the past," they answered. "But in this particular case, I have to bring that witch in alive. I don't know how well you know them, but that girl is a murderer." Perhaps they could turn the sailor against the two. Appeal to his morality, assuming he had any. "She killed soldiers that were on their way to protect our lands from the Srahinza Empire."

The sailor shrugged. "We are a long way from the southern border."

"She burned down her village," Kazumi said. "She's uncontrollable. A powder keg about to burst at any moment. I'm doing the kingdoms a favor by bringing her to justice. If she escapes, who knows what devastation she could cause." The sailor seemed unimpressed. "But if we can't catch up to her, it will be on your head."

The man snorted. "We don't have to catch up to her. I already know where she's going."

Kazumi's eyes narrowed. "And where is that, exactly?"

The sailor grinned. "The Isle of the Fae."

An old fairy tale niggled at the back of their mind. "Then you really believe that nonsense? That there is a whole civilization just sitting out on a piece of ice in the ocean?"

The sailor shrugged. "I guess you'll see soon enough."

Soon enough apparently meant in an hour. Kazumi hunched uncomfortably in the cold boat, keeping an eye out for their mark but never letting the sailor out of their sight. They didn't doubt the man would try to throw them overboard and drown them the first chance he got. They kept their dagger tightly gripped in one hand the entire time.

"Ahh, here we are," the man said, and Kazumi looked up, startled to find a sheer wall of ice before them. In their fascination, they almost didn't notice that the boat was heading straight at it, showing no signs of slowing down.

"What are you doing?" Kazumi yelled. "We'll crash into it!"

The captain continued smiling to himself, ignoring Kazumi's screams, as they sailed straight at the wall. The crazy man was going to kill them both! They hunkered down, bracing for the impact. After a few moments, Kazumi peeked an eye open to find that they were inside a cave of some sort.

With the sudden lack of wind, the boat glided to a slow stop beside another boat, and Kazumi grabbed the lantern, peering over. It was empty save for the Wanderer's bow and arrows and a dark spot of blood on the floor. Either Kazumi's quarry had landed here safely and left it, or they had perished in the sea.

"What the hell do we do now?" Kazumi asked.

The sailor jumped ashore, not bothering to tether his boat. There was an opening in the cave wall before them, a tunnel leading off into the mountains. "We take a little walk."

Foulan

Foulan rushed forward to protect Mackenna, only to find himself being held back by the woman who claimed to be her mother. For as delicate as she appeared, her grip was surprisingly strong. "He won't kill her," the woman whispered in his ear. "But if you wish to live, you *will not* intervene."

He wasn't sure if it was the urgency in her voice or her tight grip on his shoulder that made him pause. As soon as Mackenna went limp, the man nodded to the creature beside him, who held its hand to its lips and motioned like it was blowing a kiss. Mackenna gasped loudly, her eyes shooting open. Her eyes darted around in panic for a few seconds before she passed out once more.

"Now, you must keep quiet and follow my lead," the woman whispered, turning to the queen. "Your Majesty," she said, bowing to the queen, "please forgive my daughter's actions. I believe she was quite overwhelmed."

Titania glowered at the woman. "It is not your daughter's actions that anger me, Shaelyn. It is your deception that I take offense to."

"The deception would not have been necessary had my request been granted, Your Highness," was the woman's only reply. While Foulan wasn't sure what she meant, he noted that she did not apologize to the queen.

"What do you command, My Queen?" the giant, antlered man asked, still holding Mackenna by her neck. Foulan's fists clenched at the sight, but Shaelyn kept him from acting.

"For now, you will find quarters for our guests while I… deliberate on this revelation," the queen commanded. The giant man nodded and threw Mackenna over his shoulder like a sack of potatoes. Shaelyn guided Foulan after them, but the queen spoke once more. "I did not dismiss you yet, Shaelyn."

She paused, not looking back. "Would you deny a mother the chance to meet her daughter, Your Majesty?"

Foulan glanced at Titania. Her lips were pursed, her eyes narrowed. He would no doubt have frozen on the spot had her icy glare been directed at him. She gave the slightest nod, and Shaelyn continued walking, pushing Foulan along before her.

They were led down numerous hallways. The walls were smooth, uncut wood. It seemed that somehow these hallways and rooms had been shaped from living wood. He had little time to marvel, however, for they were quickly led to a door. Inside appeared to be a sitting room, with two other doors leading to what he guessed were bedrooms. It was sparsely furnished, with just a few sitting chairs and a lounge, on which lay a giant mound of fur. Foulan rushed forward, sinking down beside Myst, burying his head in her side. Her fur was soft and damp; someone had cleaned her. But most importantly, she breathed easily under his head, not the gasping rasps from earlier. He felt along her side, expecting to find Mackenna's jagged stitches. Instead, he found a scar. How was there a scar when the dog had been stabbed just hours ago?

The beastly man entered one of the bedrooms and laid Mackenna down on a bed, then turned and glanced between Foulan and Shaelyn. Foulan wondered if he would say something, but he merely glared at them before clomping away.

Foulan watched through the doorway as Shaelyn stepped towards Mackenna's prone form uncertainly, dropping to her knees beside the bed. She brushed Mackenna's hair from her face before leaning over to kiss her forehead gently. "What is her name?" the woman asked, her eyes never leaving her daughter's face.

"Mackenna," he answered. "And I'm Foulan."

"Mackenna," she repeated, as if testing the word. "A fine name. A strong name." The woman stood slowly, returning to the sitting room. However, she seemed too nervous to sit, and instead approached the window and opened the drapes. The window was really just a hole in the wall. There was no glass or shutters, nothing to prevent the cool night breeze from entering. Although the opening stretched from knee height up to the low ceiling, the woman seemed unconcerned by the enormous precipice before her. Glancing out at the lights of the homes below made Foulan feel dizzy from the height, so he looked away. "Now may be the only time we have to speak," she said, "so you must ask any questions that you have."

"I… I honestly don't know where to begin," he replied. "Are you really Mackenna's mother?"

"If you ask if she came from my womb, then yes," Shaelyn said. "But I also abandoned her when she was but a few days old. So I am not sure I have the right to claim such a title."

"Why?" he asked. "Why did you abandon her?"

Her strong brow scrunched in the moonlight, but other than that, her face remained stoic. Foulan had a feeling she had perfected the art of hiding her emotions. "It was not by choice. The queen finally found me. I had hoped… well, it doesn't matter what I had hoped. I did not wish for the queen to get her hands on Mackenna, so I hid her. I could not, however, hide the fact that I had recently given birth. So I claimed that Mackenna had been stillborn." She rested her hand on her stomach gently.

"Why?" Mackenna's voice came from the doorway. Foulan glanced over, surprised to see her awake. She refused to look at her mother, instead approaching the lounge where Myst lay. Foulan stood so Mackenna could take the seat. "Why did you have to leave? Why did father tell me you had died?" she asked as she stroked the wolf, her eyes on the creature as she avoided looking at her mother.

Shaelyn stepped forward with one hand outreached, but Foulan caught her eye, shaking his head. He knew Mackenna well enough to know that Shaelyn should keep her distance for now. Shaelyn lowered her hand slowly. "To tell you everything would be a very long story, and I do not know how much time we have. We are a reclusive folk, but occasionally those of us who appear more human than the others are sent out into the world to scout. We are supposed to return within a year. I was sent on such a mission, and during that time I met your father, and we fell in love. I thought… I thought I could hide from the queen. That perhaps if I did not return, she would believe me dead. But I was wrong. Finn… how is he?"

"Dead," Mackenna said bluntly. Shaelyn froze, the hope on her face dying as sorrow took its place. She collapsed onto the windowsill as Mackenna continued, "Witch hunters came looking for him. He tried to fight them off, and they killed him." Mackenna's voice was bitter as she spoke. "You still haven't said why you had to hide in the first place."

Shaelyn paused, as if uncertain of what to say next. "I did not return as I was meant to; instead, I stayed among the humans. I married one and became pregnant with his child. By doing so, I broke our laws, and thus I became a fugitive. I knew that if the queen learned of your existence, you too would become her prisoner. I had revealed my nature to your father some time before I was taken. When they came for me, I made him take you and run away so that they would not find you. Before he left, I begged him to tell you I was dead. I believed it would make things easier for you. I didn't want you to grow up wondering about me, about who and where I was. I didn't want you to discover… this…"

"I always believed that it was my fault," Mackenna said, her voice breaking. "That I had killed you with my fire. That I had burned you from the inside out. Father always denied it, but I still believed it. I would have nightmares about it as a child."

"I'm so sorry. I didn't know if you would have any magic, or if you did, what form it would take," Shaelyn explained. "Fae magic is wild and often random."

Foulan longed to go to Mackenna, to hold her, but she would not want that, not in front of her mother who was still a stranger. "What happens now?" he asked instead, breaking the awkward silence.

"The queen is deliberating on what to do with you and how to punish me," said Shaelyn. "I know not what she has planned for me, but as for you, I can at least give you some guidance. Mackenna, despite having a human father, you are one of us. You will be given the same respect and treatment as any Fae. However, your companion is human. Therefore, you must listen closely. If you ever hope to have a chance at leaving this island with Foulan, you must claim him as yours."

"What do you mean?" Mackenna asked, finally meeting her mother's eyes. She drew her knees to her chest.

"There are humans in the Faelands. They live here as servants. In exchange, they are provided for and live much longer lives than most humans, many for hundreds of years." Shaelyn looked uncomfortable. "Sometimes they work long enough to pay off their debts and are free to leave. Sometimes they die before then. The scouts… our job is to go out and find more humans to bring back to the Faelands. That was what I was supposed to be doing when I deserted."

"You're talking about slavery," Foulan hissed, his fists clenching. "You enslave humans."

Shealyn shook her head. "It is not exactly the same. These humans are not taken against their will, I assure you. We find those who need something from us, who wish to make a bargain with us. How many years they must bargain depends on what they wish for. And you already owe a few years in exchange for your wolf's life." She gestured to Myst on the couch.

"Do you mean they're going to make Foulan a slave?" Mackenna hissed.

Shaelyn nodded. "However, there is a tradition that whoever brings the human to the Faeland can choose to claim that human as their own. Most just offer the human to the queen to command as she sees fit. However, if you claim him, then he will belong to you and not her. It will be the best way to keep him close."

"Myst is not the only reason we came here," Mackenna said. "We traveled all this way so that I could find someone to get rid of my magic. I've… I've killed people with it. Burned down homes. I'm wanted as a criminal."

"A criminal? You take after your mother after all then," Shaelyn said with a sad smile. "You cannot be rid of it, child, any more than you can be rid of the blood that flows in your veins. It is who you are. But you can learn to control it. I know of a Fae you can ask. As with any request, you will have to make a bargain with him. Once we have heard the queen's verdict, I will speak with him."

Kazumi

Kazumi followed the sailor through the darkness for what seemed like forever. At least their broken nose had finally stopped throbbing, the pain fading to a dull ache. The path never split or veered. They wondered how deep they were in the mountain, how much earth and rock hung over their heads. It had been here for millennia. It surely would not cave in now. Even so, their throat was tight, nausea rising the longer they walked.

They needed noise or a distraction of some kind. Even the sailor's obnoxious singing would be better than being alone with their thoughts. Kazumi broke the silence. "How did you know all this, anyway? How to get to the island? About this path?"

They could not see the sailor's face, but they could hear him smiling as he answered, "How else? I've been here before."

Kazumi nearly stumbled in surprise but caught themself. "You didn't care to share this information with me earlier?"

In the lantern light they could just barely see the man's shoulders rise and fall. "You didn't ask."

"Well, I'm asking now. What should we be expecting ahead? And don't leave anything out this time." They tried to make their voice sound threatening, but it wavered.

"By now the Fae will have realized that more strangers have landed on their island and sent an envoy to greet us. I figured we could save some time by meeting them halfway. They will take us to the Faerie Court, where the queen will decide what to do with us."

"What do you mean by 'do with us'?" Kazumi asked.

"Well, the last time I was here, I was brought by the Fae," he said. "I worked for them for, oh, fifty years or so. That paid off my debt, and I was freed." The nonchalance in the sailor's voice was nearly as shocking as what he said.

"You're saying we're going to be enslaved?!" Kazumi yelled.

"Think of it more like a contract" the sailor said. "After all, people generally only come to or are brought to the Fae if they want something from them. But the Fae don't give anything away for free."

"I'm not here to ask them for anything!" Kazumi growled.

"No, you're here to hurt one of their own," the sailor replied. "You'll be lucky if they don't kill you immediately."

One of their own? What did the old man mean by that? Surely he couldn't be referring to the witch? But if he was, then Kazumi was thoroughly screwed, suddenly in enemy territory having hunted a Fae across the continent. The sound of footsteps came from ahead. They had only moments before the Fae would be on them. They doubted their tenuous ability to Change would do them any good here. If the stories were true, Fae were magic incarnate. They would likely see right through it, assuming Kazumi could even hold a façade through an interrogation.

They wore their armor and carried their sword, but they hadn't a clue how many Fae they were up against. An entire court's worth. And even if they did escape, where would they go? They were stuck on a hunk of ice in the middle of the ocean.

A tight band had wrapped around their chest, quickening their breath. Kazumi recognized the overwhelming dread that came with fits of panic. Fuck. The last thing they needed right now was to collapse to the floor as a sobbing, hyperventilating mess. They reached into their pocket, pulling out a vial and quickly downing it. It took a few minutes to work, but it took the edge off just enough that they could think clearly. And they needed to be able to think clearly if they wanted to get out of this alive.

Mackenna

"The queen requests your presence," came a gravelly voice from the doorway. A Fae stood there, another one of the giant ones that appeared to be made of stone (or perhaps the same one?). The three of them made their way to the door. The Fae let Mackenna pass, but blocked the door after her, leaving Foulan and Shaelyn inside. "Not you." They both threw worried glances at Mackenna before nodding and stepping back into the room. The Fae led her away, back down the hallway to the court.

She stood before the queen once more, who said, "You did not inform me that there were others joining you."

"My lady?" Mackenna asked in confusion.

"Two more humans arrived on our island. I believe you may know them." The queen nodded her head to the crowd, which parted. Two figures stepped forward, and Mackenna recognized them indeed: the old mariner who had employed Foulan and the bounty hunter who had stalked them for months.

Mackenna took a deep breath, wondering if the bounty hunter would attack her. The queen claimed that Mackenna was Fae, was one of them. Would the Fae protect her from the hunter?

"Poet?" the queen spoke, surprise in her voice. "We did not expect to ever see you again, once you'd bought your freedom and left. To what do we owe this pleasure?"

Mackenna glanced between the Faerie queen and the sea captain in confusion. These two knew each other? Skári bowed to the queen. "My queen," he said, "I did not expect to ever return, especially after so many years. But it would seem fate had other plans for me."

"And who is this human with you?" the queen asked.

Skári glanced at the bounty hunter and shrugged. "No friend of mine. In fact, she made me sail her here at knife point."

The queen was thoughtful for a moment. "Is 'she' the correct way to address you, human?"

The bounty hunter seemed surprised. "I prefer 'they,' if you don't mind."

"And what, pray tell, would compel them to do such a thing?" the queen asked.

"Because they're hunting me," Mackenna interjected. "They have been for months now. They're the one who hurt Myst. They are trying to kill me!"

"If I may speak in my defense?" the bounty hunter asked. The queen gazed at them coolly before nodding. "I am a bounty hunter. There must be a bounty for me to hunt, and those are only offered for criminals. The bounty on *her* is to bring her in alive. I never sought to harm her, only to bring her to justice."

"Human laws and justice have no meaning here," Titania responded, and Mackenna took a deep breath in relief. "Not only have you wasted your time in coming here, but we take particular offense that you would seek to exact your human justice on one of the Fae."

"I was not aware — " the hunter began.

"Your awareness is not important. Only that you have moved against one of us. The penalty for what you have done is death." The queen's voice had turned to ice. The bounty hunter would not survive this night.

They knelt, head bowed. "If you would spare my life, I will leave here and give up this bounty. She need not fear harm from me again."

"Mackenna," the queen spoke. "You are the injured party in this. What vengeance would you seek?"

Mackenna thought for a long moment. This bounty hunter had made her life miserable for the past few months. She had spent many sleepless nights jumping at every sound, afraid it was the hunter in the shadows. The person had struck Myst with a knife, nearly killing her. And yet... the well of rage within her had burned out. There was no fuel for the fire at present, and now she felt only tired. Tired of death and destruction. She had come here hoping to change things, so that no one would die because of her again. "Let them go," Mackenna finally said. "As long as I never see their shadow again, I will be content."

"It would seem Mackenna is more magnanimous than I." The queen's lips pursed. "You seek to bargain, then? Very well. But you will have to pledge more than that. You will give the next thirty years of your life in service to me."

The bounty hunter's head lifted, eyes wide in shock. They glanced around at the Fae surrounding them, clearly outnumbered, before their hate-filled eyes landed on Mackenna. "It would appear I have no other choice..." they said.

"Of course you do," the queen interrupted. "Your other choice is death."

The bounty hunter nodded. "Yes, well, I quite prefer to be alive."

"What is your name?" the queen demanded.

"Kazumi, your majesty," they replied.

"No longer," the queen proclaimed. "You will now be addressed by your job title. You will be put to work cleaning. Someone remind me, what names are already in use for this job?"

"Washer," a Fae called.

"Scrubber," said another.

"Cleaner, I think?" came a third voice.

The queen nodded. "Hmm. A chambermaid… Chambers will be your new name. Rise and kiss your queen." Kazumi stepped forward tentatively, reaching for the queen's hand. Titania took the bounty hunter's chin between her fingers instead, bringing their lips together gently. Kazumi collapsed to the floor, clutching at their head.

"What—" they sputtered. "What did you do to me?"

"I took your name. It will be returned to you when you have completed your servitude. Take them away." Two Fae stepped forward, lifting the bounty hunter from the floor and leading them out of the room.

The queen turned to the fisherman. "You earned your name back many years ago, Poet. Unless you wish to pledge yourself to me once more?"

"Ahh, no, my queen. I do think I will keep my name for now," Skári replied.

"Then you must leave. We cannot have an unclaimed human amongst us," Titania said.

"Unless, of course, Mackenna wished to claim me," he said.

Claim him? Her mother had mentioned that as well. That she should claim Foulan to protect him. "Umm, yes. And

Foulan, too! The other human who was with me. I claim them both," she stammered.

There was a soft murmur amongst the crowd. The queen lifted an eyebrow. "You have known of your Fae heritage for less than an hour and now wish to claim two humans at once? How interesting." She seemed to contemplate for a moment before nodding. "Very well, then. Let it be known to the Court."

A murmur went through the crowd. The queen waved her hand. "You are dismissed for now, Mackenna."

Skári bowed to the queen, then turned to Mackenna. "Well, my lady, if you would show me back to your quarters, I shall attend you."

Mackenna stared at him for a moment before nodding. "Of… of course." She turned and made her way through the crowd, exiting through the enormous archway that led deeper into the tree. Once they were alone, Mackenna asked, "Did I just make you my slave?"

Skári chuckled. "In a sense, yes, though it's more than that. By claiming me, I am your responsibility. You must make sure that I am fed and cared for humanely. And I must serve you. Furthermore, you are responsible for my behavior. If I break any Fae laws, then you must deal with the consequences. But if a Fae were to hurt me, they would be subject to your wrath."

"I'm so sorry. Should I not have done that? This is all very complicated," Mackenna murmured, wrapping her arms around herself. "And what was that the queen did to… to Kazumi?"

"Chambers now, remember?" He pursed his lips. "Names are a powerful thing, especially when magic is involved. The queen took her—their name. They will try to remember it, but won't be able to, not until the queen has returned it. It can be very frightening, to suddenly lose a part of your identity like that. It is how the queen keeps control of the humans she's claimed."

"I… I didn't do that to you, did I?" Mackenna gasped.

He shook his head gently. "No, that power is solely hers. For what it's worth, I trust you," Skári said, laying a hand on her shoulder gently. "I was offered the chance to leave, but I wanted to stay. To help you and your young man."

"My young man?… Oh, he's not… I mean…" she stammered.

"He is now," Skári said with a wink. Mackenna felt a flush rise to her cheeks. "If you hadn't figured it out already, I was indentured to the queen once, many years ago. I eventually earned my freedom and had my name returned. I can help you navigate the Faerie Court."

"Uh… thank you," she said. "Though I've recently met my… my mother, as well. She's filled me in on some of it."

"I see," he chuckled. "Perhaps you didn't need my help after all."

"No! Please don't think that. I welcome all the help I can get," she said with a nervous chuckle. "In fact… I'm pretty sure I've gotten us lost."

"Describe the room to me," he said. "Perhaps this old brain of mine can still remember the layout of the palace."

Mackenna awoke to her mother's voice saying, "The Fae I told you about is here. Do you wish to speak with him?"

She sat up groggily, nodding. As much as she'd wanted to spend more time talking to her mother last night, she'd been so exhausted when she and Skári had finally found their way back to her mother's rooms that she'd fallen immediately asleep. Foulan was still fast asleep beside her, but to her relief, Myst was awake. She hugged the wolf, who gave her a slobbery kiss. After dressing and untangling her hair, she entered the sitting room to find the Fae waiting for her.

He had bright pink skin and hair made of fire. His body radiated warmth that she could feel even from the other side of the room. She found herself staring at him in fascination as he spoke. "Your mother asked me to teach you. To help you learn to control your magic. My name is Somerlad." He bowed extravagantly.

"Oh, nice to meet you." Mackenna wondered if she should bow as well, and decided it couldn't hurt. "I have learned that there are rules to this. An exchange. What would I owe you for teaching me?"

Somerlad grinned. "You're a quick learner, and you get right to the point. I like it." He walked a circle around her, grandly proclaiming, "You are the talk of the Court. A girl arrives from the human world, but she's part Fae. Everyone is fascinated by you. They all want to know what's going to happen next." He draped an arm across her shoulder and held his hand out before them, as if showing her a magnificent view. "Wouldn't it be grand if you attended the Winter Solstice at my side? Just imagine how jealous my friends would be."

She glanced at her mother, who rolled her eyes in exasperation but otherwise seemed unconcerned. She took that to mean the bargain was fair enough. "Umm, I suppose I could. How do the Fae celebrate the solstice?" she asked.

"Oh, the same way we celebrate anything. With drinking, feasting, dancing, carnal delights…"

Noticing her discomfort, her mother spoke up. "You *do not* have to do anything that makes you uncomfortable. It is forbidden in our society to force anyone, human or Fae, to partake in sexual acts against their will."

"Of course!" he agreed quickly. "I forget how prudish humans are, and you've lived among them your whole life. If revelries of the flesh do not interest you, you need not attend such parties."

"And that's it? You just want me to be your companion for the evening?" she asked skeptically.

He shrugged nonchalantly. "That is all."

Mackenna glanced once more at her mother, who nodded. "Very well. I will do it if you teach me how to control my magic."

"Excellent!" He straightened up and extended a hand. "Let's begin then, shall we?"

"Right now?" she asked.

"Why not?"

Somerlad led her through the labyrinthine hallways and out of the enormous tree. As they walked, he told her more about the Fae. "The Winter Solstice is a celebration of Queen Titania as much as it is of earth's renewal."

"That man, the one who stood beside her last night. With the antlers. Is he the king?" she asked.

"Indeed. That was King Cernunnos."

"But the queen was the only one with a throne. Does he not have any power then?" she asked.

"Oh, he does, but only in summer," Somerlad explained. "They take turns, you see. Titania is the Winter Queen. She rules from the Autumn Equinox to the Spring. Then she hands over the rule to her husband, the Summer King, who rules from the Spring Equinox to Autumn. Thus, the Court is kept in balance, just as nature is balanced between life and death, light and dark."

"So… where exactly are we going?" Mackenna asked as they made their way down the path that wound around the trunk of the enormous tree.

"Based on your little display in the Court last night, I thought it would be best if we trained you far away from everyone else for safety," he said.

Mackenna blushed. She supposed that made sense.

As they made their way into the forest surrounding the Faerie city, he said, "So tell me more about your magic. I can assume from watching what happened that strong emotions trigger the flames?"

She nodded. "Yes. Anger, usually. When I was a kid, it would happen if I threw a tantrum, but it was always something small, no more than sparks or the occasional flame. But then when I got older… well, as I…"

"As you started to blossom into adulthood?" he asked, grinning mischievously.

"Uhh." She knew she was blushing once more. "Mhmm."

"There's no need to be embarrassed, Mackenna," he said. "You'll quickly learn that the Fae aren't shy. Puberty, sex, illness, childbirth, death… all of these are natural parts of life. It's no surprise that your powers became stronger during the springtime of your life."

"Yes, well, as I grew older, I was less prone to tantrums, I suppose you could say, but when I did become angry, it was much more frightening. Any flames near me, like the fire in a hearth, would flare up suddenly, sometimes out of control. And my body would light on fire, often starting with my hair. If I can't get it under control, my clothes burn off. And of course, the fire spreads… I sort of burned down part of my hometown. After my father died."

"And last night. Did you feel anger?" he asked.

She thought about it. "No… not necessarily. I mostly felt… overwhelmed. Afraid."

"So not just anger, but other strong emotions," he mused. "What about passion? Has that ever ignited you?"

"Passion? You mean…"

"During sex, yes," he said nonchalantly.

"I… I honestly don't know," she mumbled. "I haven't… I mean, Foulan and I have kissed, but that's all."

He nodded. "So that's one area where we'll have to experiment further. I wouldn't be surprised, however, if the fires ignite when you are feeling particularly lustful. The same happens to me, after all. Thankfully, Fae lovers are much more durable than human."

"You mean… you mean I could end up hurting Foulan? If we…" she trailed off.

"Potentially, yes," he said. "But that's why I'm going to teach you to control it, so hopefully that won't be an issue. Ahh, we've arrived."

They came to a large natural pool surrounded by stones. There was steam rising from the water, which she was surprised to find was hot to the touch. "I've heard of hot springs, but I've never actually seen —" She turned to Somerlad, only to see him stripping off his clothes. "What are you doing?" She looked away quickly as he dropped his pants.

"Going for a swim, of course," he said. "I figured the best way to prevent you from starting a forest fire is to have you practice while in water. And I don't know about you, but I don't fancy walking back through the snow in sopping wet clothes."

She heard a splash, and when she glanced back, he was submerged up to his waist. Thankfully, the steam and shadows meant that she couldn't see anything beneath the surface. She wished he'd told her, so she could have brought clothes to change into—except that she didn't actually *have* any clothes besides the ones on her back. When they'd escaped Kazumi, they hadn't had time to pack any of their belongings or even tell the innkeeper that they were leaving. What would happen to their horses Dawn and Dusk? Hopefully the innkeeper would care for them or at least sell them to someone kind.

Mackenna stripped off her pants, fur coat, and boots but kept her underclothes on. She waded into the pool, groaning in pleasure at the hot water, and sank down until only her head was exposed to the brisk winter air.

"So, where do we begin?" she asked.

"First, with conjuring the flames. Try to think of things that anger you… unless you'd rather we try passion?" he teased. She splashed some water at him. "Watch it!" he cried. "If my head gets wet, I'll die!"

Mackenna gasped, her hands flying to her mouth. "I—I'm so sorry. I didn't know!"

Somerlad laughed. "Relax, I'm kidding." He disappeared under the water, and she held her breath in fear. The Fae reemerged beside her. Briefly he was bald, until the flames suddenly sprang back up on his scalp. "See? No harm done."

Mackenna exhaled in relief. "That's not funny. And the answer would be no. Foulan has my heart."

He sighed mournfully, a hand clutched to his chest. "You wound me, Mackenna. I suppose that's only fair. Foulan is honestly more my type."

"Oh, I'm sorry. I shouldn't have assumed…"

"Relax, Mackenna. I'm not easily offended. You'll find that the Fae are very… fluid in our sexuality. Honestly, some of the other Fae I've slept with, I couldn't even tell you what gender they were. But I do personally prefer strapping young men. It's the beards," he stroked his own smooth face contemplatively. "Jealousy, I suppose. I've tried and tried, but just can't grow my own. I suppose because the only hair I shall ever have is flames."

She wondered about the hair on other parts of his body and quickly diverted her thoughts away. "Right, so what should I do?"

"The first step is to be able to summon it at will. From there, we can work on cutting it off and then on controlling it. So, I want you to try to summon it now."

After a few minutes of nothing happening, she sighed. "I— I'm not sure it will work, honestly," she confessed. "You see, after a particularly large… outburst like last night, I tend to become exhausted. It's like the kindling for the fire has all burned away, and often it won't come back for a few days or even weeks."

He nodded. "That makes sense considering that your magic is tied to your emotional state. But I want you to try nonetheless. If anger is the strongest fuel for you, then I want you to become angry. Think of other times that you've lost control when angry. Think of what happened to cause it and how you felt."

She thought back to the day her father died. She remembered watching the blade sink into his back, the blood spilling out. She remembered the overwhelming rage, and as she did, sparks burst from her skin, but it wasn't enough. She thought about the injustice she'd seen Foulan and the other Wanderers face. Her fists clenched as she ruminated on the unfairness of it all, that they would be treated so horribly after all they had lost. She felt her body grow warmer, the cool air no longer bothering her. Still, she needed more. She thought about last night, about the bounty hunter attacking her and Foulan. When they finally thought they had found safety and shelter in the city of Icedell. When they had started to let their guard down, and that bastard—who had stalked them across a continent—destroyed their peace once more. She remembered the star-shaped blade sinking into Myst's fur, hearing the wolf's cries, and her labored breathing. How worried she'd been that she was going to lose such a loving, loyal companion.

The flames sizzled across her skin and hair. They were not as strong as they had been the night before but were present nonetheless. Perhaps having exhausted her reserves was a good thing. Normally when the fire came, it overwhelmed her reason, burning away any rational thought. But as she gazed at the flames licking across her skin, she found that she could still think clearly.

Over the next few hours, she managed to summon the flames three times, sinking under the water afterwards to dispel them. By the final time, she had become so drained and exhausted that all they did was sputter briefly before extinguishing on their own.

"I think that's good for today," Somerlad said, climbing out of the pool. By now she was too tired to care that he was naked, and she struggled just to pull her clothes on, her muscles quickly becoming stiff from the cold air once she left the hot water. "We'll do it again tomorrow."

"Tomorrow?" she groaned. "I don't think I'll have anything left in me. I feel like I could sleep for a week."

He nodded. "All the more reason to meet tomorrow, and every day, to continue training. Just like training your body, your magic requires you to build up endurance. Think of it this way. Until now you've been able to sprint for a short while before exhausting. I want you to be able to run for miles."

As drained as she was, she saw the logic in it. They trudged back through the snow to the tree, Mackenna's wet underclothes chafing and making her shiver. She focused on putting one foot in front of the other, sighing in relief when they finally entered the warm palace.

When she returned to her mother's rooms, she found that both Foulan and Skári were gone. "They've been put to work," her mother explained. "There is much to be done for the Winter Solstice celebration, and I couldn't think of a good reason for them not to assist. I hope you don't mind."

It wasn't about whether or not she minded. How was Foulan doing with his sudden forced servitude?

"I understand," Shaelyn said, as if reading her thoughts. "It can be difficult for many humans at first. For their pride. But I assure you, they will be treated with… well, not respect, at least decency. Nobody would dare lift a hand to harm them. They won't even be worked beyond their means. But labor will be expected of them as long as they reside here, regardless of who's claimed them."

"I've need of some more clothes," Mackenna informed her mother as she stripped out of her clothing, happy to get out of her wet undergarments. "I suppose Foulan does too. All we have is what we came in."

Shaelyn nodded. "Yes, of course. I'll arrange to get some made for the both of you. Until then, I'm sure you can fit into some of my own garments." Shaelyn went to the wardrobe and opened it, pulling out a warm velvet robe. Mackenna wrapped herself in it gratefully, tying the belt around it to keep it closed.

Mackenna collapsed onto the lounge beside Myst, stroking her fur. She felt a very slight rumbling, and glanced at Myst's face to see her growling… at Shaelyn. "Oh, Myst, that's rude. She's helping us."

Shaelyn smiled at them. "Yes, well, I think I startled her earlier, trying to read her thoughts."

"Read her thoughts?" Mackenna asked in surprise.

Shaelyn nodded. "My affinity is with animals. I can look into their eyes and understand their thoughts. I can also command them, though I prefer not to take away an animal's free will unless absolutely necessary."

"You mean you can speak to her?"

"It's not speaking, exactly," said Shaelyn. "Not like we do, anyway. Animals don't use language to communicate. It's more that I can feel what they feel, see what they see, that sort of thing. For instance, the thoughts and memories of a canine tend to be just as much smell as sight. But it does require a certain prodding into their minds. Smaller animals don't even notice usually, but the more intelligent they are, the more likely they are to understand that what is happening is unnatural and thus to resist it. And your companion is very intelligent. Even though she can't speak our language, I suspect that she understands much of what we say."

"How is it that *we* speak the same language?" Mackenna asked, realizing how odd it was that she could understand all of the Fae she'd met. "I mean, you lived amongst humans, with father. But while I was traveling with Foulan, I heard all sorts of languages. I never knew so many existed. I'm surprised that the Fae all speak the language of my homeland."

"You have your father's curiosity… and his cleverness," her mother said, and Mackenna blushed with pride. "We don't actually all speak the same language. Some Fae don't even speak at all so much as project their thoughts. And we do have our own language, separate from any human one. But the magic of this place removes such barriers, so that any humans who come here can immediately communicate with us."

"Such thoughtful slavery," came a voice at the door. Foulan stood there, holding a tray of food. There was a hardness to his eyes and a frown at his lips. "I've brought you dinner, Mackenna." He set it down on the table beside her. Myst immediately perked up, nudging her nose under Foulan's hand. "Yes, yes, I didn't forget about you. Here you are, girl."

He set a bone in front of the wolf, who immediately started tearing chunks of meat off of it.

"How are they treating you?" Mackenna asked as she too ate.

"Well enough, I suppose," he said. "They have me working in the kitchens. Skári is doing what he does best and catching fish from the lake. How was your training?"

"Good," she replied simply, suddenly feeling awkward. "We trained in the hot springs, so that I wouldn't catch anything on fire here at the palace." Mackenna didn't elaborate. Even though nothing had happened between her and Somerlad, and she didn't have the least bit of interest in him, she was still wary of what Foulan might think. He had enough stress at the moment; she wasn't going to add to it.

Shaelyn cleared her throat. "I'm just going to go see about getting some clothes for you two. I'll be a while." With that, she left them alone.

"Are you sure you're okay?" Mackenna asked him.

He nodded, taking a deep breath. "I'm... infuriated. I feel like an animal caught in a snare. But I'm also happy for you." He sat down beside her.

She leaned against him, her head on his shoulder. Suddenly, their silence was interrupted by a loud grumble. Mackenna realized it came from Foulan's stomach.

"Have they not fed you?" Mackenna asked, sitting up.

He looked away from her. "I... wasn't hungry." His stomach growled again, betraying the lie.

"What's the matter? What are you hiding from me?" She leaned around to get a look at his face. He was blushing, his lips pursed.

"It's just… the stories say that… that you shouldn't eat anything they give you. The Fair Folk. If you do, you'll be trapped forever in Faerie land." He ran a shaky hand through his hair. "You are one of them, so I'm sure you're safe, but if I eat their food as a human, will they have even more control over me?"

"Foulan! You can't starve yourself! And besides, Skári was a servant here before, remember? Once he served his time, they let him leave. Here, eat some of this," she commanded, gesturing to the food. There was more than enough of it. He continued frowning, eyeing it warily. "Look at me," she said, taking his face in her hands. "I promise you: this is not permanent. Once I have learned to control my magic, we will leave here. I won't let them keep you. I'll tear this place apart if I have to to protect you."

He grinned in embarrassment. "I'm supposed to be the one protecting you."

"We protect each other," Mackenna said, and she leaned forward and kissed him on the lips. They were soft and warm beneath her own, and his stubble tickled her lips. His arms quickly wrapped around her, pulling her closer, until she was in his lap. His tongue ran along her lips, asking for entry, and she opened her mouth, surprised by the strange feeling of it gliding across her own.

Another loud grumble sounded, and they broke apart, both glancing down at his stomach. "You need to eat."

"This is all the sustenance I need," he replied, moving in for another kiss.

She pulled back. "Liar!" Mackenna hit him gently on the arm. "Now eat some food."

He gazed up at her from under his dark lashes, and the glint in his eyes sent a thrill through her. "Feed me?"

Mackenna's heart skipped a beat at the seductive look he gave her. She took a grape and brought it to his parted lips. His tongue darted out, catching it between his teeth. She had never thought watching someone eat could be so… sensual. She fed him by hand, relishing the gentle brush of his lips and tongue against her fingers. An idea struck her, and she held a slice of apple between her teeth, lowering her face to his. He took it slowly, his lips lingering on hers.

She was so warm. No, not just warm. Hot. Her face and lips and… the area between her legs. They all felt hot, like she was feverish. She pulled back from his kisses, Somerlad's warning ringing through her head. What if she got too hot? What if she lit on fire, burning Foulan? What if the flames spread so quickly that she burned his whole body, killing him? Mackenna stood up, facing away from him.

"What's wrong?" he asked.

"Nothing, I'm just… I'm exhausted." It wasn't a lie. She was drained. "I think… I think I just need to rest. I'm sorry…"

"Don't be." He took her hand, kissing the back of it gently. "We don't have to be in any hurry. We can go as slow as you want. And if you're tired, then you should sleep."

She nodded, relieved that he didn't push her. Mackenna lay down beside Myst, her head in Foulan's lap. He stroked her hair gently until she fell asleep.

Foulan

A week later, Foulan and Skári were returning to Shaelyn's rooms after a long day of work when they came across the mercenary scrubbing the floors. Thankfully with their separate job duties, Foulan rarely saw them, and usually only from a distance. Every time he did, though, he had to resist the urge to attack them. Besides stalking and terrorizing them for months, the bounty hunter had nearly killed Myst—would have if not for the Fae's magic. As if sensing his anger, they lifted their head, eyes narrowing at him.

Skári's hand rested heavy on his shoulder. "Calm yourself, young man. They can't harm you, but neither can you lay a finger on them. Not while they belong to the queen." Foulan realized his fists had been clenched, and he forced himself to relax them.

Skári led him away, not dropping his hand until they'd turned a corner.

"How have you been doing?" the sailor asked. "Being out at the lake most days, I don't get to check in on you much. How have the other slaves been treating you?"

Foulan grimaced at the term. He hated being called a slave, hated that such a thing was even allowed. But he didn't voice his opinions besides to Mackenna. Instead, he tried to avoid attention as much as possible, not wanting to get caught up in the Faes' scheming and machinations. "Well enough, I suppose. Nobody is hostile to me, if that's what you mean. But they certainly aren't friendly, either."

Skári nodded. "I was afraid that would be the case. After all, unlike the rest of them, you aren't owned by Titania. You haven't had your name stripped from you until you can earn it back."

"Neither have you, though, and they all seem friendly enough," Foulan said.

"But I did, before," Skári replied. "In fact, most of them, except for a few new faces, know me. Though they didn't recognize me at first."

"Wait, you've been here before?" He paused in thought. "You told me stories about a fisherman who visited the Fae lands. Was that you?"

Skári's weathered face crinkled in a grin. "I suppose you could say that, in a sense. I came to the Fae lands, oh, a hundred years ago or so? Like many, I had heard tales of how the Fae could grant me my heart's desire. I was a young dumb lad who cared only for shallow things. My heart's desire was fame. You see, I'd grown up in an orphanage, a poor lad with little hope. My greatest joy was when the fair came to town and I watched the plays. I wanted to be a playwright and a poet.

"Well, I wrote a play. A silly thing. But I took it to a theater. They laughed me away. What would a poor orphan know about fine art? So I kept trying. And the same kept happening. And then I heard the story. About the Fae island, and how, if I made it here, they'd grant me my heart's desire. I journeyed here, nearly dying in the process, and made my request.

"Fifty years of servitude. And what's more, I would barely age while I was here, no more than year or two for each decade of my life. I gladly accepted. What did I have to lose? I would keep my youth. I had no friends or family to speak of except a few other poor orphans I'd grown up with. I had no job or money or prospects."

"In one of the stories, you said the man aged suddenly when he returned to the human world," Foulan remembered. "Is that what happened to you?"

Skári shook his head. "No, the Fae were true to their word, in their own twisted way. After serving my time, I was given my name back and left the island. I was still young. Still hopeful. But a rather bitter irony awaited me. You see, someone had found my play in those fifty years. A director of a theater. They'd put it on, and it was a renowned success. Soon, it became the most popular play in the Realms of Etylania. But as the playwright, Skári, had disappeared, he was assumed dead. I had posthumously become famous."

"What did you do?" Foulan asked.

The old sailor laughed. "What could I do? I certainly couldn't claim to be the playwright, a young man in his twenties, when the author would have easily been in his seventies, if he was still alive at all. When people heard my name, they assumed I had been named after him!"

"Was it just coincidence?" Foulan asked. "Or did the Fae really make you famous?"

"Oh, I don't doubt they had a hand in it. In the time that I served here, I learned how their magic works. It is chaotic. It follows no rules that a human can fathom, except that it is always very literal.

"Well, I found myself once more a penniless, homeless urchin. Nobody in the town of Icedell remembered the young man fifty years prior who'd passed through, intent on seeking the Fae. So I settled down there, took on the trade of a fisherman. After a few years, some other hapless fool came through, having heard the tale of the island. I immediately set about dissuading him. I didn't want to tell my own story and prove that the Fae did indeed uphold their end of the bargain, even if they twisted it. I couldn't risk encouraging him. So I made up the story of the fisherman.

"Over the years it became more embellished as I told it to other adventurers. I made it more tragic with each telling. But it did its job. I managed to turn most of them away from their fool's errand. Those I couldn't, well... I've seen a few here, having made a bargain. The others I can only assumed perished in the attempt."

"Then you've dedicated your life to thwarting the Fae's slavery of humans," Foulan realized.

"Yes, well, let's just keep that between us, shall we?" Skári suggested. "No need to have the queen upset with me."

Mackenna

Thankfully, Shaelyn was able to secure them all some clothing to fit a human shape. Many of the Fae weren't remotely human, and most didn't wear any clothing at all. Those that did wore styles like Mackenna had never seen, often sheer and strangely cut, some made from leaves and bark, others more gems and jewels than cloth. However, the Fae kept basic human clothing in wool and leather specifically for their servants.

Shaelyn even found Mackenna an outfit for swimming in. It covered just the necessities from her shoulders to thighs and was made of shimmering scales that clung to her own skin tightly. A mermaid's shed scales, her mother informed her. It made Mackenna uncomfortable knowing that she was wearing the skin of another living creature that was swimming somewhere nearby at that very moment. But the clothing was lightweight in the water and dried almost as soon as she emerged, so she couldn't complain.

She trained daily with Somerlad. She left at the same time that Foulan and Skári did to go to work, and often returned just before them. It was difficult to tell night from day with the sun never rising. The only difference she could tell was that the sky was slightly lighter at some points than others, but that could easily have been attributed to the ribbons of light that snaked across it.

Somerlad was an excellent trainer. He was patient with her, but still pushed her to her limits. After two weeks, she could summon the fire at will if she closed her eyes and concentrated with all her might. Controlling it, much less extinguishing it, proved to be an entirely different matter. Thankfully, she couldn't hurt Somerlad with it, and the water they trained in prevented it from spreading to the forest around them.

Nevertheless, Mackenna felt distance growing between her and Foulan. It was not that she didn't want him to kiss her and touch her, but whenever he did, she began to worry. What if she lost control? What if, in her ardor, she summoned the flames, engulfing him? She only knew how to bring them forth, not how to hold them back. If he was caught in them, he would likely die before she could put them out.

Yet, she didn't want to confess this, either. He would say he trusted her. That he knew she wouldn't hurt him. And while he might trust her, Mackenna didn't trust herself. So instead, she made excuses.

After another fortnight in the Fae lands, the night of the Winter Solstice arrived. After their training, Somerlad returned to her rooms with her. He had brought her a dress when he'd met her that morning, saying that he was offering it freely, without any trade needed. He claimed he wanted her to be the center of attention at the midwinter fête, thus making him the center of attention as well.

She put on the gown with her mother's assistance. It was richer than anything she had ever worn, and quite honestly, she wasn't exactly sure how to even wear it. It was made from layer upon layer of a silky sheer fabric that faded between purple, pink, and white. The flowing material had flowers and twigs sewn into it that cascaded down the skirt. It came with long sleeves that flared out at her elbows and flowed behind her as she moved.

It was the top of the dress that made her the most nervous. Unlike the skirt, it was only a single layer of fabric, her skin showing through beneath it. The only thing covering her breasts was a vine of flowers extending from her waist to her left shoulder, strategically hiding her nipples and little else.

Mackenna knew that the Fae did not have rules for propriety or modesty. Nevertheless, she felt uncomfortably exposed in the gown. "You look beautiful," her mother reassured her, kissing Mackenna on the forehead.

"That's not really what I was worried about," she replied.

Shaelyn nodded. "I understand. But when in the Faerie lands, you should do as the Fae do. I told myself similar when I traveled to the human lands. Now, I have something else to give you that will go perfectly with your gown." Her mother moved to a cabinet, removing a necklace from it. It was surprisingly simple, especially compared to the gown. From a silver chain hung a small pink crystal intricately wrapped in wire. It hung gently between her breasts.

"Thank you. It's gorgeous," Mackenna whispered.

"It's more than just jewelry," Shaelyn replied. "It has magical properties. I made it just for you. As long as you wear it, you don't have to worry about pregnancies. It should last about a year before the color fades from the crystal, meaning that it needs to be recharged." Mackenna's whole body flushed in embarrassment. Before she could stammer out a reply, her mother waved her hand. "Please, I see the way you and Foulan look at each other. It's clear that you are in love, and I would never stand in the way of such love. But you are too young yet to be having children."

"I'm not sure I would have needed it anyway," she responded bitterly. "I am afraid to even touch him."

"Why?" Shaelyn asked.

Mackenna shrugged, gesturing to herself. "What if I hurt him? What if I killed him with my fire? I can't risk it. I would rather never touch him than risk hurting him."

"Have you spoken with him about this?"

Mackenna shook her head. "I know he will tell me I am worrying too much and that he trusts me. But the fear is just too awful."

Shaelyn placed a hand on Mackenna's cheek comfortingly. "You *will* learn to control your magic with time. But until you do, you will just have to be creative if you wish to be close to him. You know, you are free to use the springs as you wish. You do not need to be with Somerlad to visit them."

Mackenna frowned at her mother in confusion for a moment before the meaning of her words dawned. Despite the embarrassment she felt from speaking of such things with her mother, her heart suddenly felt lighter. Why had she never thought of that herself?

Mackenna threw her arms around her mother, hugging her tightly. "You are a genius! Thank you."

Shaelyn smiled, then held her at arm's length. "Careful, you will crush your flowers. Now, go have fun at the fête."

"You're not coming?" Mackenna asked.

Shaelyn shook her head. "I generally avoid such festivities. I am something of a pariah among my people. While they can't forbid me to go, I would not exactly be welcome."

Mackenna made a note to ask her mother more about that later. Why would simply getting pregnant with a human man really be so bad that her mother would be ostracized for it? But that was a conversation for another time.

Foulan

Foulan stood amongst the frolicking Fae creatures, waiting to see if anyone needed him. He had been told to attend to the party, refilling wine glasses, bringing more food, and assisting where needed. While the formal clothing they had given him was simple, a black doublet and pants that both sported matching gold trim, the fabric was the highest quality he'd ever worn.

There was so much going on in the ballroom that it was almost impossible to move at all, so he had planted himself firmly near a table of food with his pitcher of wine. A group of Fae danced together in a line, while behind them a dwarf did backflips to the applause of his friends. Merfolk splashed in a fountain, singing a haunting tune. A tiny pixie stole a crown of flowers off of an orc and flitted away. A satyr jumped on the food table and kicked treats everywhere as he played a flute. And many embraced amorously as they danced, sometimes in groups of three or four, uncaring of the crowd around them. On three separate occasions, he was invited to join them in a private room, but politely declined.

He'd just finished refilling the glass of a woman whose lower half was a snake when he spied Mackenna. He nearly dropped the jug of wine. She was… breathtaking. Her dress flowed around her like waves as she walked, each layer hinting at skin beneath without quite showing it. Well, except for across her stomach and chest, where plenty of skin was revealed, barely covered by flowers and vines. Her back, however, was completely bare, and his fingers itched to run across her smooth skin. Here, surrounded by her people, wearing their clothing, she truly looked more Fae than human. He wasn't sure how he'd never seen it before, the sharp edges of her face, her sparkling hazel eyes that seemed to shift between brown and green, the ever so slight point to her ears, and the long, graceful limbs that he had once thought made her look gangly.

He was not the only one who noticed her beauty. She was surrounded by Fae of every type, the center of their focus. They flirted and danced with her, many running hands over her skin and hair, as if she was a pet. It seemed many of them were curious about a half-human Fae who had grown up outside the Faelands. He couldn't have gotten close to her even if he'd wanted to.

The festivities lasted for hours. He couldn't fathom how the Fae never seemed to grow tired. He was exhausted simply being surrounded by this many other beings, all flirting and gossiping and scheming. He longed to escape the tree to the surrounding woods, to be enveloped in silence and solitude.

"Longing for home?" a voice asked behind him.

He looked up to find a masculine-appearing Fae before him. He had grey skin, white hair, and short horns. Small wings protruded from between his shoulders. They most resembled those of a bat, though they were so paper thin Foulan could nearly see through them.

"A drink, fair one?" he asked. He'd been learning the names for the different types of Fae, but he didn't recognize this one. He'd also learned not to address them as lady or sir, for gender seemed to be nonexistent or unimportant for many of them. At least when he had forgotten, they did not seem particularly offended.

Foulan refilled the Fae's glass, who gazed at him sadly. "I too long for that world, though I have never been there."

"I'm sorry..." he offered uncertainly.

The Fae shrugged. "That is the sacrifice that we had to make, to have peace from humans. You hunted us, slaughtered us. Those who stayed behind, who refused to leave their homes, I wonder if any of them are still alive."

"Some are," Foulan said, "though I believe most are in hiding. I've traveled through many countries, and all of them have stories of someone meeting the Fae. Most do not end... happily. For the humans."

The Fae took a drink, grinning. "I imagine those about a Fae and human falling in love must end most tragically of all."

"Why do you say that?" Foulan asked.

"How could it ever end happily? We do not have marriage. Your human concept of, what is it called... fidelity? Is strange to us. And besides, a human lifespan is so fleeting and... insignificant."

He bit back a retort, his hands clenching around the pitcher. He had been treated well enough, considering he was essentially a slave. None had abused him in any way, or even worked him beyond his means. In fact, he'd hardly interacted with the Fae much, besides to take an order. But what rankled at him the most was how they clearly viewed humans as lesser creatures and thus did not even recognize their careless cruelty as such.

"I pity you for loving her," the Fae continued. "Now that she has found her own kind, she will quickly forget you. Even now she has been spirited away by her mentor, who is intent on making her his lover."

Foulan felt himself go cold. "What did you say?" he whispered.

"Ahh yes, in this crowd I suppose you did not notice. But I certainly couldn't miss the smell of a particularly potent aphrodisiac in her drink," he said, lowering his voice to a conspiratorial whisper. "To make her more willing."

Foulan tried to move past him, but the Fae caught his arm, the man's grip so tight he nearly yanked Foulan back.

"Where are you going, human?" he asked, laughter in his voice. "You aren't thinking of abandoning your work, are you?"

Foulan glared at him, no longer bothering to hide his anger. "You know, I thought the reason none of you had tried to harm me was because it would simply be too much effort to spare me even that small of a thought. But now I see it's not just humans. You lot care only about yourselves, each one of you. Even your fellow Fae are unworthy of any shred of compassion unless it benefits you. Am I wrong?"

The smile had not left his face. If the Fae was offended, he did not show it. "'Tis true. We are fickle creatures that care only for the pursuit of pleasure. What else is there?"

"Which way did they go?" Foulan hissed. The ballroom had a dozen exits, all leading to different halls that twisted through the enormous tree.

"Now, that information will cost you," the Fae said.

Foulan felt his patience wearing thin. He didn't have time for such bargains. "I have nothing to give you."

"Not true at all. You came with one possession besides the clothing on your back. Your boat."

The boat? Why would he want that? Foulan couldn't read him, nor did he wish to waste time trying to find out. He didn't bother to tell the Fae that the boat wasn't even his. "Fine," he said. "It's yours. Which direction?"

The Fae pointed a sharp fingernail to an archway, then let him go. Foulan spun on his heel, pushing his way through the crowd. He didn't care that he bumped into numerous Fae, nor did he apologize. All that mattered was getting Mackenna away from that scheming bastard.

Foulan burst into the hall, but they were nowhere to be seen. Hearing voices to his left, he followed them, his throat tight. He found Mackenna and Somerlad in an alcove, amongst a group of Fae who were naked and intertwined in various stages of lovemaking. Somerlad had his arm around Mackenna, his hand on her hip with a familiarity that made Foulan's blood boil.

"I told you I wasn't interested in such things," Mackenna's voice was tight, her irritation apparent.

"If you would just have a few drinks and relax, I promise you'll enjoy yourself. You can't tell me you don't find any of them attractive?" Somerlad replied. A Fae woman reached out, taking Mackenna's hand and attempting to pull her forward.

"Hey!" Foulan yelled, grabbing the woman's arm and thrusting it away. He turned on Somerlad. "I think it's pretty clear she said no."

Somerlad's smile dropped. "I don't recall inviting you, human."

"I don't really give two shits if you did," Foulan snapped. "Let's get out of here, Mackenna." He realized that she was staring at him with wide eyes. She shook herself slightly, as if trying to wake from a trance, and nodded.

Somerlad stepped forward, glaring at him. "Maybe she doesn't want to leave."

Foulan didn't need any more coaxing. He curled his hand into a fist and punched the Fae man in the face. Somerlad crumpled to the floor, clutching his nose. The other Fae in the hall froze, watching the scene in a mix of horror and fascination.

"That's for drugging her," Foulan said.

"Wait, drugging? What are you talking about?" Mackenna asked, glancing between them.

"It's not… like that," the Fae hissed, blood dripping down his face. "Just an aphrodisiac. Many of us have had some tonight. It's just to… increase the excitement. It's completely harmless."

Mackenna stared at him in shock. "You gave something to me without my consent? How dare you!" She took a few deep breaths, closing her eyes. When she opened them and spoke once more, her words were hard. "You are lucky you are immune to my fire."

Mackenna turned and stormed away, and Foulan followed. He ignored Somerlad's curses and threats to have Foulan punished. At that point, he didn't care what they did to him, just that she was okay.

"Mackenna…" he said.

She kept walking. "I can't… I need some fresh air."

He nodded, silently following her through the labyrinthine hallways. They quickly found a door that emerged to the outside, but instead of stopping, she continued to walk, following the twisting paths down the trunk of the tree. It wasn't until they had touched the earth that she finally stopped, and he placed a hand gently on her shoulder.

"Please, look at me. Are you okay?" he asked. She turned, wrapping her arms around him tightly. He held her, expecting her to begin crying or yelling. Instead, she simply clung to him, as if afraid to let him go. "I am so sorry that bastard—"

"Forget him," she said. "He had no right, and I feel betrayed and angry… but there is something else that I'm feeling much more strongly right now." He stayed quiet, unsure what she was getting at. "I saw you at the fête. And I couldn't stop staring at you. You look so handsome in that uniform." She gazed up at him. "The urge to run over and kiss you was overwhelming. And when you showed up to rescue me," she grinned. "Well, I'd never felt so, so happy and…" Mackenna licked her bottom lip.

"And what?" Foulan asked, breath hitching.

Mackenna pulled him towards her, her lips crashing against his. She wound her hands in his hair, pressing her body tight to him. He kissed her back without thought, his fingers trailing across her bare back, and he felt her shiver in his arms, though he wasn't entirely certain it was from the cold.

She pulled away to catch her breath. "Needless to say," she gasped, "that aphrodisiac worked, just not in the way he had intended. All night, all I've been able to think about is you. Whenever I could spy a glance at you, I did. All I wanted was to take your hand and leave so we could be alone."

Her voice was thick with passion, and hearing her tell him that she wanted him, feeling her pressed against him, made his body respond. He knew she could feel it, but instead of scaring her away, it only made her press tighter against him.

But this was wrong. "Mackenna… I can't… we can't. I'm sorry." He pulled away from her, and he could see the hurt on her face. "He gave you a drug. If we… if I made love to you now, I'd be no better than that asshole."

She was shaking her head before he'd even finished speaking. "No, it's not… I'm not drunk or anything, Foulan. I am perfectly in control of my faculties. It's like he said. It's only enhanced excitement, excitement that I already feel whenever you're near."

He frowned. He didn't want to admit the hurt he'd been feeling the past fortnight, but he could no longer ignore it. "I'm not so sure. Since we've come here… you've been distant. And I understand. There's a lot going on, and you're busy learning, and everything is new and overwhelming. But I've still felt as if you… were pushing me away." He tried to hold back the tears that pressed at his eyes, his voice growing tight.

"I'm so sorry," she whispered, taking his face in her hands. "And I should have talked to you instead of putting distance between us. But I was afraid."

"Of what?" he asked.

"Myself!" Mackenna threw her hands up in the air as if it should be obvious. "When I lose control, people get hurt or worse. And while it is usually brought on by rage, other strong emotions can trigger it, too. Like fear. Or… passion." She took a deep breath. "I was afraid for us to get too close because I was afraid I would hurt you." Tears ran down her cheeks. "And if I did, I could never live with myself. You are… everything to me, Foulan. I love you."

The words hung between them in the night air. He had never before been so aware of the pounding of his own heart. For a moment he was too stunned with happiness to speak, but when he saw the uncertainty flash across her face, it broke the spell. "I love you too!" he blurted urgently. "I have loved you for so long."

Her face broke into a wide grin. While he had been entranced by her ethereal Fae beauty hours before, now he was captivated by her equally human beauty. The freckles on her cheeks, the tears clinging to her lashes, the little gap between her front teeth, a faint scar beside her lip. He loved every inch of her, Fae and human alike.

"Then, you've learned to control your magic enough for us to…?" he trailed off.

She bit her lip. "Not exactly. I'm still working on that. But tonight, Shaelyn gave me two gifts. A necklace to prevent fertility," she gestured to a crystal that she wore on a chain, "and a solution. And honestly, I can't believe I didn't think of it sooner." She took his hand in hers, a naughty grin on her face. "Follow me. I'll show you."

He let her lead him through the town at the base of the tree. It was quiet tonight, with almost everyone inside the great tree attending the fête. They had no light, but the aurora above them shone bright enough to illuminate their path. They left the town and entered the forest, following a well-worn trail through the snow. Finally, they emerged in a clearing, and Foulan was surprised that the air was warmer, the snow melted around the pool before them. Steam rose from it, and he realized the water was warm, almost hot, to the touch.

"This is where I've been going to train," she said. "The water prevents me from catching anything on fire." She smiled at him shyly. "So, care to join me for a swim?"

"And you're absolutely sure this is what you want?" he asked.

Mackenna nodded. "More than anything. But… I'll need your help with the dress."

It looked delicate enough that he could rip it off of her, but he supposed then she wouldn't have anything to return to the tree in. Foulan helped her undress, untying the sleeves and untwisting the vines on her shoulder that kept the flowers in place across her breasts. They fell to the forest floor, and he unbuttoned her skirt next, the gossamer fabric floating down gently to form a puddle around her feet. She stood before him naked, her fair skin practically glowing in the dim light, and he found himself breathless as he stared at her.

She wrapped her arms around herself, shivering. "It's pretty cold out here once you're starkers," she joked between chattering teeth, before hopping over to the spring and sinking into it with a sigh. "Ahh, much better." He stepped forward to join her. "Umm, aren't you forgetting something? You don't want to walk back in soaking wet clothes. Trust me."

He stripped off his boots, breeches, and shirt as quickly as he could, jumping in beside her before the cold air could even hit his skin. Foulan waded towards her, but once he was close enough to touch her, he felt himself suddenly overcome with shyness. "Hi," he stammered awkwardly.

Mackenna smiled, her face flushed from the heat. "Hi," she repeated.

"Umm… I've never actually… I mean…"

"Me neither," she confessed. "So, I guess we'll learn together."

She closed the distance between them, her naked body pressed against his own. Their lips met, their kisses gentle at first, but soon becoming more urgent. He ran his hands across her arms, back, legs, stomach, breasts. He wanted to touch every bit of her skin, to memorize the feel of her, and her hands wandered in turn. Soon his lips followed suit, tracing kisses down her neck, across her collarbone, to her small pert breasts. She gasped as he kissed each one, moaned as his hand caressed her between her thighs. He judged what to do by the sounds she made, noticing that she especially seemed to enjoy when he touched a particular spot. Her hands touched him as well, finding his desire for her and stroking it.

With each touch, his need for her became more urgent, and he could feel that hers did too. They floated to the edge of the pool, where it was shallower, and he sank down, pulling her on top of him. Her breasts were exposed to the cold air in the shallow water, but she didn't seem to care anymore. It took a few tries, but then their bodies aligned, and she sheathed herself around him.

She paused, her breath hitching. He froze. Had he done something wrong? "Is… is everything okay?" he asked.

She nodded. "Yes. It's just… a little uncomfortable."

His heart sank. He was hurting her. "We can stop."

She shook her head. "No. I just needed a moment to get used to it." She leaned forward, her lips meeting his, her breasts brushing against his chest. Each little movement she made drove him crazy, and soon they found a rhythm. The noises she made, each little gasp and moan and sigh, were like music that was building up to a crescendo. He let her take control, touching and kissing wherever she asked, trying to hold back his own desire so that she could reach hers.

He felt it when she did, saw it in the look on her face. Her hair ignited, but not with a roaring fire like he'd seen before. Instead, the flames were soft, gentle, flickering and dancing around her face, but spreading no further. Her whole body felt hot to the touch, but not enough to burn. His own desire peaked right after hers, and for a long time they held each other, though she was careful to keep her head away from his.

As her breathing returned to normal, the flames slowly extinguished. Once they did, she curled into his arms, her head on his chest. "I love you," she told him again.

"I love you, too." He gazed up at the night sky above them, the ribbons of lights shifting between green and purple and blue against a blanket of twinkling stars. After a while, his eyes grew heavy with fatigue. "We should return."

"But I don't want to go back," she whined.

He smiled. "Yeah, but if you stay in here all night, your skin will get all pruney. And besides, these rocks aren't the most comfortable bed."

"I'm comfortable."

"That's because you're laying on me."

They finally climbed out of the water, redressing quickly in the freezing air. At least the warmth of the springs had kept their clothes from stiffening. He could tell that she was still cold, and no wonder, seeing how thin her dress was. He gave her his doublet as well, ignoring her complaints that he would catch ill in just his undershirt. They walked back to the great tree arm in arm.

Mackenna

After Foulan had left to work the next morning, Mackenna was eating breakfast with her mother when she heard a tap on the wall outside their room. She pulled back the curtain, shocked to see Somerlad standing there as if nothing had changed. His nose had healed overnight, no evidence remaining of Foulan's damage. "You're not even dressed in your bathing clothes yet," he noted.

Mackenna scowled at him. "You seriously think I'm going to keep training with you after what you did last night?"

He looked surprised. "But of course. It was only an aphrodisiac. I don't see what all the fuss is about."

She wished the great tree had real doors so she could slam it in his face. Instead, she dropped the curtain and turned away. He followed her into her mother's sitting room unfazed. Mackenna contemplated breaking his nose again. "Get. Out."

"But why?" he asked, seeming genuinely confused. "You aren't done training."

"You betrayed my trust!" she shouted. "I told you that I wasn't interested in your orgies and you brought me to one anyway! What's more, you drugged me!"

"You had control of yourself," he argued. "And I had planned that party just for you. I chose Fae that looked the most human. I thought at least one of them… Well, I suppose none of them were your type."

Shaelyn's hand rested on her shoulder as her mother stepped up behind her. Mackenna took a few deep breaths, trying not to let the rage overtake her. She certainly didn't want to catch any of her mother's possessions on fire. "It's no use trying to explain it to him," her mother commented. "Most Fae don't have the same sense of morality or decency that people do. Honestly, I didn't either until I lived amongst humans."

"Well, even if you don't understand that it was wrong, understand this: You pissed me off, and we are no longer friends!" Mackenna yelled at Somerlad. "Now get out."

"I see," he said sadly. "Is there no way I can change your mind?"

"Somerlad, tell me, did Queen Titania put you up to this?" her mother asked.

He shrugged. "She made me a deal."

"What exactly did that deal entail?" Mackenna hissed.

"To find you a suitable mate among the Fae. I thought the fête was the best place to start," he replied.

Before Mackenna could question him further, her mother sighed. "I was afraid of this."

"Afraid of what?" Mackenna asked her.

"Titania accepted your existence far too easily and did nothing to punish me. I knew she must have ulterior motives. It makes sense for her to want you to mate with a fellow Fae."

"Why? Whatever for?" Mackenna asked.

"Because we're dying, Mackenna. As a species. We live incredibly long lives compared to humans; some of the eldest among us have seen nearly seven centuries. But we do die eventually. And unfortunately, no more Fae are being born." She folded her hands, a sad smile on her face. "That is why she hates me so much. Not only did I not return or report back, not only did I marry a human, but I got pregnant. Queen Titania and King Cernunnos have tried to conceive for so long, and a few times they did succeed, but the child was always stillborn. I did not even consider the possibility that I could get pregnant by your father. It came as quite a shock to me when it happened. Thankfully, the queen took me at my word when I said you had died."

"But what does that have to do with me?" Mackenna asked.

"I believe the queen and king may have come to the same conclusion I did. After I became pregnant so easily with a human, I wondered if the reason we are sterile has something to do with the island. Or perhaps the fact that we only mate with other Fae. A thousand years ago, when we lived amongst humans, we had no problems making more Fae. Perhaps mixing our blood with humans is necessary for our survival.

"When the queen saw that you had lived after all, I believe she too started to suspect the same thing. The next logical step would be to see if you could get pregnant with a Fae and give birth to a healthy baby."

Mackenna paced, trying to calm the fire building up in her. "So she just wants me as some… some brood mare? I am just an experiment for her?"

"What is the problem, though, really?" Somerlad asked. "So you have a baby, give it to a human servant to raise, and go about your business."

"You're not helping," Shaelyn told him.

"And she didn't once think to ask my opinion?" Mackenna continued. "Or my consent? How dare she!" The flames finally broke free, igniting her hair and across her arms. Before she could begin to panic, however, the fire lifted from her, gathering up in a ball in the middle of the room and burning out. They both turned and looked at Somerlad, whose hand was raised in the air. He shrugged.

"At least he's good for something," Shaelyn noted.

Mackenna sank back into the chair, her head in her hands. "Even if I did get pregnant, how would that change anything? How would it help the queen any?"

Shaelyn took a deep breath. "It would mean what I've suspected, and feared, for quite some time. That the Fae need to return to the human world."

"Why did the Fae even leave in the first place?" Mackenna asked.

"War. We'd lived peacefully alongside humans as far back as we can remember. But with our longer lifespans, we produce offspring much less often, when we were able to have any at all. Humans, with their shorter lifespans, reproduce much more frequently; one day, we found that we were outnumbered, a hundred humans for every one Fae. Some humans worshipped the Fae as gods, but others… others feared and hated us. And not without reason. Many Fae took advantage of humans, ruling over them as tyrants.

"Soon, the tensions grew so high that the humans began attacking the Fae. Our queen at the time, Maeve, met with the human rulers, intent on resolving the fighting between us. The humans claimed that as long as they were so weak against the Fae, they would hate and fear us, but if they knew that they had some way to protect themselves, then it would make the world more balanced. So Maeve agreed to a bargain. She would grant the humans a way to protect themselves against the Fae, but in turn, she asked that humans allow the Fae Court to determine punishment for Fae transgressions. A human was only to defend their lives against a Fae; any other issues were to be brought before the Court.

"The humans brought forth a blade, and Maeve performed a spell to make all Fae weak to it. But Fae magic is not always so straightforward. The humans had intended for the Fae to be weak to any weapon made by man. Instead, the Fae became weak to what the blade was forged from: iron. For a time, there was peace between us. But human lives are much shorter than Fae, and though the treaty was written down, the humans eventually forgot it. They went back on their bargain. Many of them decided that Fae were creatures of evil, to be hunted and exterminated. They did so ruthlessly and without cause, killing any of us they came across.

"Maeve, fearing for the lives of all Fae, fled here, to the top of the world. From an ocean of ice, she created an island just for us, fortified on all sides by sharp mountains and magic. She breathed life into the island, so that we could live here comfortably. And she sent a call to all Fae to welcome them. Many of us fled here. Many others did not make it, cut down by human armies as they tried to cross the continents. Others chose to stay in hiding amongst the humans, refusing to leave their homes.

"In creating the island, however, Maeve used all of her magic, expending every last bit of her energy, and perished. She was buried in the center of the island, and the great tree grew from her corpse. And for a time, all seemed fine; but as the centuries passed, our numbers grew smaller, fewer and fewer children being born as the older generations died. You are the first child born of Fae in over a hundred years."

"I am sorry," Mackenna whispered. "I'm sorry that your… our people are dying. But I am not ready to be a mother, and even if I was, I love Foulan."

Her mother took her hands. "Nor would I let anyone force this on you. You are a free woman. You can make your own choices. And besides, one or two children by you would not fix our problems. We must return to living amongst humans. We must try to make amends, though many of them believe us little more than legends by now. But too many Fae are afraid of change. I have tried telling them that humans do not even use iron weapons anymore; everything now is made of steel, which can still hurt us, but is not lethal like raw iron. But my status here means that most disregard me."

"Why do you stay? No one is keeping you. She does not have your name," Mackenna said.

"No. She tried to take it, but it returned to me soon enough. Such magic does not work for long on our own kind." Shaelyn's eyes were full of sadness as she tucked a strand of Mackenna's hair behind her ear. "The truth is, leaving you and your father broke my heart. I wanted to stay away to protect you both. But without either of you, I felt I had nothing left to live for. I have been little more than a ghost these past two decades, existing but not living. And then I saw you in the Court, saw your face and knew you to be my own, and it was like all of the color suddenly returned to the world. I only regret that I could not see your father again."

Tears spilled quietly down Shaelyn's cheeks, and Mackenna held her close. "He missed you," she said. Were the words too cruel? Should she lie and say he'd moved on? Should she pretend that they had been fine without her? Shaelyn would see through the lie, and anyway, she felt that she had to put into words the unspoken truth that hung between them, so that perhaps they could both finally heal. "When he spoke of you, it was always with such love in his voice. I think he was heartbroken as well that you did not return, but I also think he understood why. He lied to me, but he did it in the hopes of sparing me more pain had I grown up believing that you'd abandoned me." Her mother shuddered with silent sobs. "I wish things had turned out differently. I wish that I had grown up knowing you both."

"I do too," Shaelyn whispered. "Mackenna, I am so, so sorry."

Mackenna's shoulder grew wet with tears, but she continued to hold her mother, comforting her. "I forgive you," she said. "As much as the regret may eat at us, we can't change the past. But at least we have each other now."

The sound of someone clearing their throat interrupted the moment. They both glared at Somerlad, who continued to stand their awkwardly. "So, do you really not intend to train anymore?"

Mackenna sighed, stepping away from her mother and pinching the bridge of her nose. "It will take much for me to forgive you, Somerlad."

He nodded, lips pursed as he thought. "You are the most interesting thing to happen around here for decades. I would hate to no longer have you call me friend. Where might I at least begin?"

"You can begin by not seeking revenge for the broken nose that Foulan gave you last night," Shaelyn said. "Have you already reported it?"

He winced, touching it gingerly, though it appeared perfect once more. "That would be a no. My pride as a Fae and a man has kept my tongue in check."

"And if the queen ever makes such schemes involving me or my friends again, you will warn me," Mackenna said.

"Oh? A double agent working against the queen? How very… spicy. I like it." He grinned. "Very well. With this, you would forgive me and we would return to your training?"

Mackenna pursed her lips but nodded slowly. "Yes, though I can't say I trust you."

He pressed a hand to his chest, grinning. "My dear, you should never trust a Fae, most especially one in Queen Titania's court."

Chambers

Chambers cursed under their breath as they entered the room, seeing the filthy state it was in. There was food and clothing strewn about everywhere, wine and other fluids staining the furniture. Another mess left by a debauched revelry for them to clean up.

They set to work stripping the bedding to take to the laundry along with the clothing, then cleaned up the food. At first, they had thought the Fae were just slobbish, throwing their trash on the ground for the human servants to clean up after them. But they had started to realize that it wasn't exactly malicious so much as a complete lack of understanding regarding responsibility and self-control. Even their concept of possessions was so fluid that Chambers could make no sense of it. One time they had returned the wrong clothing to a room, not realizing their mistake until later. The Fae there simply shrugged, not caring what he wore. Another time, they had cleaned the cobwebs from a Fae's room, only to be shrieked at by the spider creature in residence for destroying her precious artwork. The Fae also seemed to have no sense of currency, trading in either possessions, favors, or bets.

After the first week, Chambers gave up trying to understand these creatures. They just needed to know enough to do their job and somehow, someday escape this godsforsaken island. When the queen had enslaved them, she had even stolen their name, ripping it right out of their head. They would try to think of it, and it would be on the tip of their tongue, the edge of their thoughts, but always slip away before they could grasp it. At least the bitch hadn't taken anything else, like their memories or personality. Chambers wasn't sure if the queen could take more if she wished it, but they didn't want to take their chances by pissing off any Fae.

Even so, their orders rarely came from the Fae themselves, but rather from the senior-ranking human slaves who had been around the longest and whose job it was now to simply oversee the others. The slaves' jobs seemed to be based on seniority as much as skill, with the newest slaves always starting out cleaning.

Of course, those bastards that had come with the witch didn't have any trouble getting cushy jobs, nor did they have their names stolen. Apparently being owned by their friend instead of the queen spared them such humiliation. Chambers saw Foulan every so often working in the kitchen or serving food to the Fae, and they considered getting him alone so they could skewer him with a butcher's knife out of frustration and bitterness, but he was always surrounded, and besides, that was likely to get Chambers executed.

So Chambers did their job, annoying as it was, and at least managed to take some pleasure in it. They had always been one for cleanliness, both of their person and their surroundings, and found that scrubbing floors and cleaning up after the Fae helped ease some of their frustration. At night, all of the queen's slaves slept on cots in one large room. The Fae had no sense of privacy or modesty themselves, so they didn't seem to understand the human need for such things. Many of the humans had been here for years, even decades, and had formed friendships, romances, and family units. More than once they tried to make Chambers feel welcome, including them in conversation, inviting them to eat, asking how they was doing. Chambers ignored them all. They had no need for friends here because they didn't plan on staying long.

They thought of escape often, contemplating different avenues. The Fae didn't really keep tabs on the humans. There were no locks in the palace; most rooms didn't even have doors. When they weren't working, they were free to come and go as they pleased. Many of the other slaves had hobbies outside of their work, which they could leave the tree palace to partake in. The Fae seemed to simply take for granted that they wouldn't try to escape.

And honestly, where could they even escape to? They were on an island in the middle of an icy ocean. They could try to hide in the wilderness of the island but would likely be found quickly. The only true avenue of escape was by boat, and Chambers had no idea if the boat they had come in on was still waiting in that cave.

Chambers finished the rooms they'd been cleaning, moving on to their final ones for the day. However, upon arrival, they were surprised to find it neat and tidy. Not every suite was cleaned every day, only if a Fae requested it. So, why had a Fae requested this one to be cleaned?

A Fae emerged from a bedroom, smiling at them as he reclined in a lounge chair. "Ahh, you've arrived."

"What was it you needed?" Chambers asked. "Does one of the bedrooms need cleaning?"

He waved his hand. "I requested you specifically for companionship, not drudgery. Please, won't you sit?"

Great. Another one that was probably going to get touchy and try to seduce them. They found it annoying more than anything. No one had attempted to force themselves on Chambers, though that didn't exactly mean they were left alone. Often a Fae would try to seduce them or invite them to bed, but when Chambers turned them down, the Fae seemed unfazed. Some were more persistent than others, but they eventually gave up when Chambers said no.

They sat in a chair across from the Fae, raising an eyebrow. "How may I be of service?"

"Do you know what sort of Fae I am?" he asked.

Chambers examined the Fae man, trying to remember all the types they had learned about. The man was human shaped, at least mostly, with a slim body and skin that was almost grey. He had small bat-like wings. While they had seen some Fae with enormous curved horns like a ram's, his were shorter, only a hand's length or so, and protruded upwards. His hair was so light as to be nearly white, and his eyes were a brilliant, almost glowing blue. "A succubus?" Chambers guessed.

"Very close; we do have a lot in common," he replied. "But no, I am what is known as a leanan sídhe, though some refer to us as muses. Some humans even get us confused with vampyrs, but I would never drink blood. Disgusting."

"Is there a purpose to this conversation?" Chambers asked. Was he attempting to frighten them? Chambers knew that the Fae could not hurt them, not without incurring the wrath of the queen.

He smiled. "Ahh, that's what I was looking for. That spark of… action. Defiance. I am wasting your time, you must be thinking. You have work to do. Escapes to plot." Their heart raced. How could he possibly know? "You see," he continued, "my kind are dependent on humans, to a degree. Unlike vampyrs, who require human blood to survive, we *can* live without them. But such life is so dreadfully… dull."

"And you were hoping I would entertain you?"

"You already are, with your plots and ambitions," he said. "My kind are drawn to ambition. We made ourselves but humble servants to those humans who aspired to more, whether they were artists or monarchs, inventors or revolutionaries. We would serve them, giving them inspiration, bringing them uncanny success and luck."

"And the price?" Chambers asked. There was always a price.

"Of course, such success as we would bring could not come for free. But when humans fulfill their dreams, they give off a light, an energy, that sustains us, nay, that invigorates us. It is like a drug. We do not seek the fame for ourselves, for we can feel its joy through them. Unfortunately, with time, some humans were known to go mad or fall ill, perhaps even die, if we stayed with them too long. If they wished us to leave them, all they had to do was introduce us to another human with even greater ambitions, and we would go happily."

"Well, I appreciate the lesson, but I have work to get back to." Chambers began to rise, but he grabbed their shoulder, pushing them back down.

"I was born on this island," the Fae said. "I grew up hearing the stories of my kind, how through them kingdoms would rise and fall, actors and painters become famous, inventors create wonderful new gadgets. But I have never experienced such things for myself. There is no ambition here. The other Fae are all so… content. They have all of their desires met, so there is no need for them to strive for more. And the humans are no better. After they've been here for a time, knowing that their world is changing, aging, passing them by, they too grow complacent. The only ambitions they have are to become the personal slave of a loving Fae or to rise in the ranks and have easier work." He snorted. "I have tried to feed on them, to aid them, but it is useless. I am starving! Starving for life. For motivation. For desire."

"What does this have to do with me?" Chambers hissed in annoyance, trying not to reach out and punch the Fae for touching them.

"You. I felt your spark the moment you arrived, and I've only felt it grow since. I am drawn to it like a moth to a flame. You long for freedom. You long for the thrill of the hunt. You long… for revenge. Against the queen for stealing your name. Against the half-breed witch who dragged you into this mess. I can sense all of it rolling off of you." He seemed to sense their fear as well, for he said, "Ahh, no need to worry; only my kind can sense such things. There are only three of us in the Fae lands. The other two live for what little ambitions they can harvest amongst the Court; I assure you, they haven't noticed you. But I have."

"And what exactly do you want?" Chambers asked.

"To help you. And in so doing, to help myself. I long to live among the humans, to serve one who aspires to greatness. But I could not simply leave and enter the human world. I know so little of its rules. How would I even find one such as I seek and get close enough to them to make a deal? But you could assist me, in return for helping you escape."

"And you'll suck me dry of energy and leave me for dead somewhere, no doubt," Chambers sniffed. "I wasn't born yesterday. I don't make deals that will end in my death."

He shook his head. "I would only feed a little from you, just a hint of your joy. And besides, with my help, you are guaranteed to succeed. You would not have to worry about being caught. And in the process, I can help you get your delicious revenge."

Chambers didn't want to show that their interest was piqued. Any good bounty hunter knew better than to reveal such things. They rolled their eyes. "How would you even do that?"

"We would kidnap her, the halfling witch. The queen has designs for her, to get her pregnant, to seek a solution to our dying species. Stealing the half breed would thwart the queen. And the human boy, he is in love with her. Think of how his poor heart would be broken to know she was spirited away, that she may be lost to him forever. And you could turn her in to the human authorities as you had intended, punishing her for making your life miserable while no doubt making a tidy profit."

Chambers sat back in the chair, eyeing him with a cool expression. In one swoop they could not only fulfill their contract but also get revenge on the three people they hated most. "And all I have to do is give you some of my life essence? How do I know you won't just take it all and kill me?"

"It takes many, many years to drain a human to that point," he said. "We take only a tiny bit at a time. I would only travel with you long enough to become established amongst the humans. The first one I see that piques my interest, I'm gone from your life."

Chambers shook their head. There was too much wiggle room in this contract. "I need something more certain. A definite cutoff point. You have six months from our escape. You swear you will not take enough energy to do me any physical or mental harm, and if you haven't found what you're looking for in that six months, too bad. You're on your own."

He smiled, his eyes almost glowing. "Oh, I do love a shrewd negotiator. I haven't felt this excited in… ever! It's a deal." They held their hand out for the Fae to shake, but he rolled his eyes, grabbing Chambers's chin and kissing them full on the lips before they could stop him. The Fae pulled away after a moment, and Chambers noticed a light shimmering around both their bodies. It faded momentarily.

"Seriously?" they asked in annoyance.

"A deal can only be sealed by your own lips," he replied with a shrug. Chambers remembered that Queen Titania had done much the same.

"Fine. So when do we get out of here?"

"Patience," he chided. "The waters are still too frozen to cross, even with the luck I'd bring you. As soon as the season changes to spring, we kidnap the girl and spirit her away."

"But that could be three or four months from now!"

"And?" he asked in confusion. "'Tis but a moment. You blink and the seasons change."

"Maybe for you. But I'm human," Chambers answered.

He smiled. "As long as you live here amongst the Fae, your aging is slowed dramatically. After all, we want to get the most out of our slaves. So don't worry about your youth wasting away while you're here." The Fae looked thoughtful for a moment. "I tasted something in our kiss, when our bond was forged. You keep a secret, though I cannot surmise the exact nature of it."

Chambers considered the Fae before them. He would help them to escape this island and get their revenge. They had already entered into the contract, so there seemed little point in keeping their ability a secret from him. Chambers pulled out the handheld mirror they kept on their person, glancing between it and the Fae before them. They studied him intently, then their reflection in the mirror, attempting to Change to match the Fae's features.

It was more difficult than any disguise they had ever attempted before. They were able to get the skin and hair right, even the strange facial features. But the horns became little more than nubs, and the wings were out of the question. A headache forming, they dropped the disguise. "Little more than a parlor trick, I'm afraid."

Nonetheless, the Fae man watched them in fascination, a smile spreading across his face. "Oh my. This is going to be fun indeed."

About the Author

Mandy Burkhead is a speculative fiction author living in Chattanooga, Tennessee, with her husband, dog, and cats. She has a BA in English with a creative writing emphasis and an MLIS with a focus on YA literature and programming. She and her husband self-published their debut dark fantasy novel in August 2017 titled *The Black Lily*. She has had three short stories published in anthologies: "The Lady Defiance" in the steampunk anthology *Gears, Ghouls, and Gauges*; "The Cursed Isle" in the horror anthology *The Monsters We Forgot*; and "My Lady Bathory" in *Tainted Love: Women in Horror Anthology*. She also has two published poems. In addition to horror, she enjoys writing fantasy, steampunk, and historical fiction. To pay the bills, she works as a freelance copy editor. Her hobbies include gardening, reading, playing video games, making costumes, and cosplaying. You can find her on Facebook, Instagram, and Twitter @burkshelf and visit her website at www.burkshelf.com.

www.ingramcontent.com/pod-product-compliance
Lightning Source LLC
Chambersburg PA
CBHW021725110726
47902CB00005B/1352